P9-CBE-665

"WHO WOULDN'T LIKE TO TALK TO THE DEAD? WHO HASN'T FELT THE CHILL OF FEAR IN A DARK CELLAR? . . . SUSPENSE THAT CAN MAKE EVEN THE HEART OF A CONFIRMED SKEPTIC BEAT A LITTLE FASTER."
—*The New York Times Book Review*

"A WITCH'S BREW IN THE TRADITION OF SHIRLEY JACKSON . . . Ms. Hawkes is a true mistress of the macabre."
—*Dallas Morning News*

"A MODERN GHOST STORY . . . SPOOKY, SHIVERY, VIVID . . . ENTERTAINING TERROR."   —*Louisville Courier-Journal*

"A THINKING PERSON'S GHOST STORY!"
—*The Boston Herald*

"BEAUTIFUL AND HORRIFYING!"
—*Roanoke Times & World News*

"A GREAT GHOST STORY AND MORE . . . will continue to haunt you for a long time . . . I admire *Julian's House* as literature . . . I urge you to read it."   —Annie Dillard

(For more stunning reviews, please turn page . . .)

JULIAN'S HOUSE

JUDITH HAWKES

A SIGNET BOOK

SIGNET
Published by the Penguin Group
Penguin Books USA Inc., 375 Hudson Street,
New York, New York 10014, U.S.A.
Penguin Books Ltd, 27 Wrights Lane,
London W8 5TZ, England
Penguin Books Australia Ltd, Ringwood,
Victoria, Australia
Penguin Books Canada Ltd, 2801 John Street,
Markham, Ontario, Canada L3R 1B4
Penguin Books (N.Z.) Ltd, 182-190 Wairau Road,
Auckland 10, New Zealand

Penguin Books Ltd, Registered Offices:
Harmondsworth, Middlesex, England

Published by Signet, an imprint of New American Library,
a division of Penguin Books USA Inc. This is an authorized reprint
of a hardcover edition published by Ticknor & Fields.

First Signet Printing, February, 1991
10 9 8 7 6 5 4 3 2 1

 REGISTERED TRADEMARK—MARCA REGISTRADA

PRINTED IN THE UNITED STATES OF AMERICA

Calligraphy by Stella Easland and Robert Overholtzer
Book design by Anne Chalmers
Drawings on pages x and xi by Mary Reilly

PUBLISHER'S NOTE
This is a work of fiction. Names, characters, places, and incidents either are
the product of the author's imagination or are used fictitiously, and any
resemblance to actual persons, living or dead, events, or locales is entirely
coincidental.

FOR KELLY

What if you slept? And what if, in your sleep, you dreamed? And what if, in your dream, you went to heaven and there plucked a strange and beautiful flower? And what if, when you awoke, you had the flower in your hand?

Ah, what then?

—Samuel Taylor Coleridge

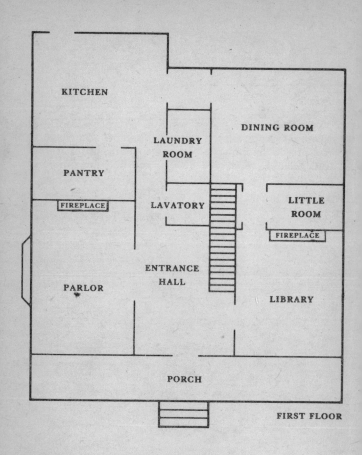

KITCHEN

LAUNDRY ROOM

DINING ROOM

PANTRY

FIREPLACE

LAVATORY

LITTLE ROOM

FIREPLACE

PARLOR

ENTRANCE HALL

LIBRARY

PORCH

FIRST FLOOR

SAMUEL GILFOY HOUSE
23 LILAC STREET
SKIPTON, MASSACHUSETTS

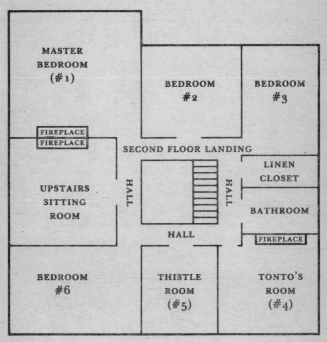

MASTER
BEDROOM
(#1)

BEDROOM
#2

BEDROOM
#3

FIREPLACE
FIREPLACE

SECOND FLOOR LANDING

LINEN
CLOSET

UPSTAIRS
SITTING
ROOM

HALL

HALL

BATHROOM

HALL

FIREPLACE

BEDROOM
#6

THISTLE
ROOM
(#5)

TONTO'S
ROOM
(#4)

SECOND FLOOR

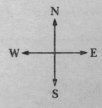

N

W ←——→ E

S

June 1983

At first the new voices are inseparable from the old. Rising, they join the constant murmur that fills the house day and night, all the voices that have sounded within these walls since they were built, saturating them with words.

Then gradually they begin to dominate, these eager new voices and the racket that accompanies them—scrape and bump of footsteps sending the echoes scurrying and raising dust in the air. Gradually they grow louder, clearer, until they drown out all the others.

Or almost all. Far above, in one high room, the flapping of a ragged window shade causes a patch of light to gather and scatter continuously on the opposite wall. Repeated again and again, ceaseless whispering of the old house to itself, this slow swell and burst of light. Then comes the banging of a door down below: some current of air, precipitated up stairwells and along corridors, rushes from the bottom of the house to the top, claps the shade taut against the open window like a sail in a stiff wind. The hush that follows is like listening.

Downstairs in the dim entrance hall there's a ceiling fixture but no bulb. The old man goes first, walking with a shuffle. Slowly he leads the way to the parlor; there he throws back the curtains in a gesture almost theatrical and sunlight floods the room, turning all the grays to gold. Behind his back the two of them look at each other. It is their plan to wait until they have been through the whole house and then talk it over between them; but

xiii

the young man, seeing the light splashed over the faded silks of the chairs, cannot hold back.

"You understood our letter, Mr. Gilfoy? We want to use the house for experimental purposes."

The old man in his black overcoat looks at the young one, seeing only an intent face, hands that fold and refold a piece of paper—evidently the directions, jotted down during their phone conversation, for finding the house. The young woman stands a little behind her husband; like him she is wearing blue jeans. They do not look like scientists, either of them. She glances around the room, but the old man sees that she is listening. It is for her benefit that he now exaggerates his New England twang.

"Psy-chi-cal re-search," he says. "Now that's a mighty fancy name for seeing spooks."

They are smiling. The young man's is perfunctory, hiding annoyance, but hers is real; he can almost warm his hands.

"Well, until we observe, of course, we won't really know"—the husband is speaking now—"what category the phenomena fall into, or even if—"

But the old man stops him. "I've heard the stories. They say the place is haunted. Well, maybe it is. A place as old as this, it's bound to have memories. My grandfather built this house. I was born here, grew up here, never saw a ghost, not one. But now they say it's haunted, and who wants to rent a haunted house—who but spook hunters? If you want it, you're welcome."

The young woman is looking at him; he feels she pities him, and why? The grave young face makes him want to weep. But the dust is everywhere—on the chairs, the curtains, behind his eyes. Somewhere, long ago, did someone else look at him like that? He cannot remember, and he fumbles in the pockets of his overcoat for the lease.

PART 1

DAVID

Former Tenants of the Gilfoy House

NAME	DATES OF OCCUPANCY	AS OF JUNE 1983
Iris Babcock Joanne Wells	April–August 1934	both deceased
DuBois family	June–July 1935	?
Murray family	November 1940– March 1941	daughter, Christine Frey, living in Masonville
Rose Pindar	March 1–24, 1944	still living in Skipton
Thomas and Barbara Kirk	July–September 1948	?
Professor Willis Sterling Miranda Sterling	April 1951– March 1952	living in Wellesley
Rogers family	May–June 1956	living in Tulsa
Nicholas and Karen Abbey Nick Jr. (15) Debbie (14) Mike (12) Susan (9)	June–August 1964	living in Northampton
Richard and Avis Gardner Stephen (8)	March 1–10, 1975	living in Boston

⇻ *1* ⇺

THE TAPE RECORDER really spooked the kid. He couldn't take his eyes off the microphone, as if it were a snake coiled to strike. David had to prod him.

"Come on, Bobby. Just tell me what happened. Forget about the machine."

The kid's eyes flicked to his face, then back to the mike. He chewed his lip; at last words came. "Yes sir. I was, uh, I was cutting across the backyard one morning— you know, taking a short cut, and whap! This brick comes flying down and almost brains me. Misses me by about this much."

David estimated the distance between the small outstretched hands. "By about a foot. Okay. What happened then?"

"Well, I look up. And there he is, looking out the top floor window!"

"There who is?"

"The tramp! He died there, in the house. He busted in one night and climbed up to the attic and hung himself. Now his ghost's there, trying to kill kids and make them ghosts too." A secret little smile twitched his mouth, involuntary delight in his own terror. He swallowed. "So he won't be alone."

"You're sure you saw someone, Bobby?"

"Yes sir!"

"What did he look like?"

"He was—his face was kinda green, you know? Like he was sick or something. And he was holding on to the windowsill, and his hands—they were hooks!"

"And then?"

"I ran," the kid said.

*   *   *

Deposition number 3. Robert Campbell, age eleven. Sitting by himself in the parlor Saturday morning, scribbling in his notebook with the house rising roomy and quiet around him, David thought Bobby's story was his favorite. He was getting quite a collection. Old Mrs. Hopkins, next door, remembered seeing lights in the house when it was untenanted. Jonathan Masters, age ten, had looked through the kitchen window and seen something he could only describe as "a man made of newspaper." But Bobby—Bobby was an artist.

Trying to kill kids and make them ghosts too. So he won't be alone.

David stopped the tape and leaned back, stretching until something, his spine or the flimsy chair under him, cracked in protest. The house was full of creaks and pops, like any old house; he didn't think there was anything supernatural about those. Just the wood talking, ancient boards remembering the weather, years the place had stood empty and felt the seasons in its bones—winters without a fire in the hearth or even so much as a human breath to fog the window pane, hot summers when the doors swelled and stuck. But it was a spacious, comfortable old house; somehow he felt welcome here. His own haunted house. Well, not quite his own: rented from Mr. Gilfoy for three precious months of scientific observation, investigation, and documentation. The summer ahead filled his vision with the same golden bulk it had possessed in his childhood: full of possibilities.

His own haunted house. His first solo. And he was ready—more than ready. They had assisted on half a dozen cases already, he and Sally, fetched and carried for more experienced researchers; they knew the ropes by now. And after nearly three years in psychical research, he needed this—to be out in the field, away from the laboratory with its mountains of computer printouts. Right now he needed to see a ghost.

Like a promise the white curtains stirred at the window. It felt good to be here. Not that he hadn't learned plenty in the lab; he knew he was lucky to be working for a private research facility, and under a guy like Jack Pennybacker, one of the big names in the field. And he knew the lab work was essential—the methodical experiments with index cards and electronic coinflippers, designed to prove the existence of psychic phenomena by statistics. Statistics were the latest thing, the ticket to respectability. But the scientific establishment still tended to look down its nose at parapsychology, to dismiss the whole field as a confederation of the wacky and the gullible.

The science of things that cannot possibly happen, but do. David was used to the looks on people's faces when he admitted that his job involved tracking an elusive force called "psi"—the common denominator in such phenomena as ESP, psychokinesis, reincarnation, haunting, and the like. Psi was the culprit when nature's laws turned themselves inside out: when people foresaw the future, or made a bell ring by looking at it, or communicated with the dead. But most of the time, stalking psi wasn't as wild as it sounded. Most of the time the lab experiments were so rigid, so dry, so capital-S Scientific, that while everyone outside the field considered you the lunatic fringe, you were suffocating from the sterility and the routine. When something like a haunted house came along, you were likely to jump at it like a starving man at a steak.

The front door slammed. Sally was back. She came in with an armload of paper bags, dumping them on the table next to the tape recorder; one fell over and half the contents spilled out. He saw electrical tape, a spool of solder, batteries. He steadied the remaining bags.

"What's this other stuff?"

"Groceries. I got some of that bread you like. It must be almost time for lunch."

She sat across from him in one of the spindly chairs, dark hair in a loose braid over one shoulder, eyes light in her tanned face. She was sweating a little, a sheen in the hollow of her throat, and he realized it was hot out. Here in the parlor it was still cool, sunlight flickering in the leaves outside the bay window. Later in the day it would fill the room, spreading a gold-dust lacquer across the floor and bleaching the colors of upholstery already faded from years of such afternoons. Sally looked at David, at the tape recorder. "Any luck this morning?"

He leafed through his notebook. "I was just listening to yesterday's batch. Talked to Mrs. Hopkins again a little while ago, but I didn't get it on tape. She says there really was a tramp who died falling out of a tree in the yard, something like that. Back in the early fifties. She's a chatty old bird."

"She thinks you're cute," Sally said.

"Oh, it's mutual."

She pulled one of the bags toward her and delved into it. "Jack sent us something in the mail. Do you want to open it?"

"Be my guest."

She found the envelope and tore it open. A newspaper clipping was enclosed. Sally glanced at it and passed it to him.

"OWNER SUES TENANT FOR SAYING HOUSE IS HAUNTED. How subtle of Jack. Is this his way of telling us to be discreet?"

"You can't blame him," she said. "If we got sued, the lab would have to pay any damages. He has to spend too much time fund-raising as it is."

David tossed the clipping aside. It irritated him a little. It was Jack's way of saying they were kids on a lark, and not to get carried away. And that wasn't fair. Just because hauntings happened outside the laboratory, just because they couldn't be controlled in every detail, didn't mean they were worthless as evidence of psi. It was simply that in a haunting things were less predictable. The phenomena were spontaneous, somehow generated by their physical surroundings: a haunting was psi in its natural habitat, and under such conditions its behavior could be spectacular. Sometimes the furniture went flying. You might see shadowy figures, hear disembodied voices or footsteps. When that happened there was an exhilarating sense of being face to face with a mystery, tampering with nature's secrets like a modern-day sorcerer, wielding electronics in place of spells and charms. You might, if you were fortunate, catch spontaneous psi in the act—get something on tape or film that defied explanation by any natural law. And that was what made it all worthwhile.

"Jack's jealous," he said. "He'd love to have this haunting to play with."

Sally was peering into one of the grocery bags. "Well, so far there's been nothing to prove it *is* a haunting."

But it is. And it's mine. Again the sense of welcome

touched him. Idly he hit the play button on the tape recorder.

". . . his face was kinda green, you know?" The kid's voice, a hushed treble. "Like he was—"

Sally was grimacing. He clicked the machine off.

"Did I hear the word lunch mentioned earlier?"

"We ought to go exploring this afternoon," she said. "We've been here almost three days and we've hardly been out of the house. I want to see the neighborhood."

"Don't you want to see the green face?"

"No," Sally said.

"Monday, Tuesday, Wednesday—you're right. Tonight will be our third night. Greenie is shy."

She was looking at him and he raised his hands in surrender. "All right. Lunch. Then the neighborhood."

Nearly four thousand people live in this little New England town. The valleys of western Massachusetts harbor many such places, much alike—Main Street with its dozen shopfronts and unenforced parking signs, at one end a green square where a few park benches surround a block of stone listing the names of local war dead. The town hall, post office, library, Congregational church face onto the square; beyond them the town spreads out, streets wide and shady, the houses drawing back from them like shy children, white under the linden trees. After supper in the summers people sit outside on their porches until darkness falls. The long summer twilights smell of honeysuckle; trees cast shadows that slowly sink into the darkening grass; a neighbor's cat appears through a hole in the hedge—"Ho, Ginger!"—and vanishes under the steps. The dusk carries sounds: down the street, at the bottom of the hill, children cry, "Not it!" Crickets creak gently on the lawn, and slowly night settles in.

Their exploration of the neighborhood ended in the Episcopal churchyard at the top of the hill, where tall dapple-barked sycamores lifted a translucent canopy against the sun.

"I feel like I'm floating in lime juice," David said. "Isn't the light bizarre?"

Sally walked slowly along the rows of graves, her head bent, reading the moss-grown names. He watched her moving among the stones: now she hesitated, now she walked on in the clear green light. He lifted his head. Above, the high branches made a spidery framework for the bright trembling of the leaves. The color dazzled him and he let his gaze sink slowly into the vaulted churchyard like some object sinking into deep water, sinking down the deepness of the air to the green-growing shadows at the bottom where the headstones stood in rows. And there was Sally walking among them, bending her head to read an inscription, then moving on.

She sat at a table in a testing booth. It was his first week at the lab; he and two other researchers watched her through a two-way mirror. She sat writing a series of numbers on a sheet of paper. It didn't look like much. Not unless you knew, as he did, that she was reading the numbers from the mind of someone in a similar testing booth two floors above. After each number she paused, frowning a little, lips parted; then the pencil moved again.

He had fallen in love with that waiting look. It had come as a complete shock, later, to learn that she hated being telepathic, that it made her feel like a freak. He imagined her universe as infinitely richer than his own, the sixth sense like a color subtly changing all others. Standing there in the green churchyard he felt again everything he had felt seeing her that first time: excitement, awe, the raw envy that had become, since their marriage, an almost proprietary pride in her gift; most of all the ache to possess her, as if by doing so he could gain access as well to the extra dimension she inhabited.

She had stopped in front of one of the stones and he went to join her, threading his way through the markers that rose out of the deep grass. The weathered block of granite in front of her was unornamented, only a name and date carved on the face.

"Samuel Collins Gilfoy," he read aloud. "1808–1861."

She was reading the one beside it. "Here's Dorothea, Beloved Wife of Samuel Collins Gilfoy. I wonder if all the Gilfoys are buried here."

David glanced along the row. "Well, here's another one. Sacred to the memory of Lieutenant Samuel Collins Gilfoy, Junior, born 1843, died July 2, 1863 at Gettysburg, in the service of his country. *Sacred to the memory of* must mean he's actually buried on the battlefield." He moved to the next stone. "Mary Dove Gilfoy, Beloved Daughter, etcetera. 1842–1859. Wonder what happened to her—she was only seventeen when she died."

"Help me out, David. I want to make a chart." Sally had taken out a pencil and was making notes on a scrap of paper, moving down the row in the opposite direction. She bent to read the inscription at the base of a stern marble angel with one arm outstretched. "Reverend Joshua Gabriel Gilfoy, Rector of this Parish from 1866 to 1907. *He that doeth the Will of God abideth forever.*"

David walked over to look. "Born 1840, died 1926. Not quite forever—but nice try, Joshua." He was being funny for Sally, but she had gone on. The light trembled as a breeze shook the leaves high overhead; coins of sun and shadow slid over the angel's sculptured curls. Meeting its unfriendly gaze he heard Sally say, "Here's Sophia, Beloved Wife of Joshua. Born 1855, died 1885 mourned by her husband and eight children. Eight children by the time she was thirty!" And then a beat of silence, and then, "Here's Joshua's second wife."

He went to see. She stood in front of the stone next to Sophia's, adding the name and dates to her impromptu family tree. He read the inscription aloud.

"Virginia Blake Gilfoy, Wife and Companion of Joshua G. Gilfoy. Born 1880, died 1931. *My presence shall go with thee, and I will give thee rest.*" The cool light brightened to gold for an instant as the leaves parted overhead. David glanced back at the angel. "You know, Reverend Joshua must have been kind of a goat. He was forty years old when this girl was born."

Sally was already at the next stone, and he took a look. *Lily, 1883–1940, Cherished Daughter of Joshua and Sophia Gilfoy.* "You know," he said, "we seem to be into the third generation here. Shouldn't we be coming across our Mr. Gilfoy's parents pretty soon?"

"Presumably Reverend Mr. Gilfoy was his grandfather," Sally said, walking down the row, "so one of these guys, Gabriel or Prentiss, must be his father. But neither one seems to have a wife."

"Well, there must be some folks missing. I mean, Sophia's stone says she had eight children, and only three of them are accounted for here, as far as I can see. So—" He was walking backward as he talked, and his first impression was that someone had kicked his feet out from under him, his second that the earth had violently upended and slammed into his shoulders from behind. At the last instant his invisible assailant added a kick in the head. Briefly he saw stars. Then they faded, and he was lying on his back in the grass, looking up at the leaves. Sally was bending over him, her face worried.

"Are you okay?"

He resisted the urge to play for sympathy. "I guess so. What happened?"

"I think you tripped."

He sat up; the stars came back. This time he noticed their colors. Violet and orange predominated. They went away again. The churchyard came back. Sally was holding on to his arm.

"Take it easy. You hit your head."

"I did? I guess I did." His left temple hurt. He touched it carefully.

"There's no blood," she said. "But it's going to be quite a bruise. Are you still dizzy?"

"I'm fine." Her solicitude was making him feel about ten years old. I tripped. Great. He got to his feet: no more stars. "They didn't tell me the place was booby-trapped," he said.

Sally was brushing grass and leaves off his back. "Maybe you should sit down for a while."

"Look, I'm okay." He felt like enough of a jerk without her fussing over him. He shrugged her hands off and turned to look at the stone he had hit his head on. There it was: weathered and cracked, a crude death's-head etched above the inscription, the stone itself at a rakish angle as if the sleeper beneath had tossed and turned in restless dreams. He bent and read:

> *As you are, I once was.*
> *As I am, you shall be.*

His laugh was involuntary, more shock than amusement. The stone was bare of name or date or anything else that might identify the occupant of the grave, just the cold mocking message above which the skull grinned like a jack-o'-lantern. The etched eye sockets met and held his gaze. His head gave a throb of pain and he turned to

Sally, wanting to make a joke, something to dispel the faint unscientific prickling along his spine, but she had gone on to the end of the row.

"If there are any more Gilfoys, they ought to be here," she said as he joined her. "But there's only someone named . . . good Lord. Ripley Waters. Is that a joke?"

"In an Episcopal churchyard?" David said. He looked up at the leaves.

⇛ 2 ⇚

WHAT MAKES HAUNTING UNIQUE in the realm of psychical research is the fact that it centers on a specific place. Other types of psychic phenomena seem to be more or less portable, but a haunting is always linked to a house, or a room in a house, or even a corner of a room. The idea is that the physical environment has been imprinted with an image or event that continues to echo there long after it is finished in time. But as for understanding why this should happen or the mechanics behind the process, psychical research hangs fire at just about the same point it did in 1888 when Edmund Gurney, one of its founders, summed up haunting as "an image impressed, we cannot guess how, on we cannot guess what."

Any student of architecture will be quick to point out that the town of Skipton contains better examples of the Victorian style than the old Gilfoy house on Lilac Street. Dr. Bristowe's house, at the corner of Main and Tanglewood, is truer to the period with its towers and bays, rose windows and fanlights, widow's walk and carved balustrades, the lavender shingles that cover the roof like a dragon's glittering hide. The Gilfoy house was built too early, before the century had finished twisting itself into the tortuous intricacy for which it is justly famous; and Samuel Collins Gilfoy, its builder, was by all reports a simple man who wanted nothing more than the wide-porched, steep-gabled dwelling that stands today. Certainly he would not have countenanced any of the architectural conceits that distinguish the finest examples of the Victorian school—the spirals, brackets, quoins, spindles, false fronts, floral patterns, hearts, garlands,

12

gargoyles, sunbursts, and other embellishments designed
to turn houses into wedding cakes. Nothing of the kind is
to be found at the Gilfoy house; at the most there might
be a garden ornament half hidden in the disreputable
backyard, but this is an addition of a later period, and
seems to have come as close to the house as it dares.

But in spite of its failings as an architectural model, the
Gilfoy house has, in the way it keeps to itself under
shady lindens beyond a latticed gate, an atmosphere more
deeply, subtly Victorian than anything created by a turret
or a roof of colored shingles. Inside the gate, so overgrown with honeysuckle that it no longer swings freely
but seems to protest against being opened, the yard slopes
ever so slightly down to the house and you may find your
pace quickening in spite of yourself as you approach. The
broad flagstones leading the way are cracked now and
worn with the pressure of feet going back and forth
across them; grass springs up in the cracks and the once-
sharp edges are soft with moss. Inside the gate a silence
falls. Leaves stir and are still. At the foot of the porch
steps the silence deepens, wrapped around with the fragrance of the shallow pink roses that twine the uprights
and shadow the wide boards with their leaves. And yet it
is more than a silence, as the leaves stir and again are
still: it is a silence of breath held, of a sob stifled in a
pillow, the silence that follows the blow of a fist upon a
table. In the moving leaves this silence seems to murmur
in its sleep—of too many closed doors, keys turning
smoothly in well-oiled locks, glances exchanged without
words. There in the light that flickers among tiers of leaves
the silence seems to reach out and draw everything else
into it: the shabby white frame walls of the house, windows mottled with dust and scattered light, the shade of
the trees, the sloping walk and gate overgrown with vines.

Perhaps it is not the silence itself but the murmur
behind it that lures the neighborhood children even while
it warns them away. Amy Campbell remembers the time
she went with her big brother Bobby and his two friends
to peek in one of the windows. She remembers how the
shadow of the house fell like a chill on the bright hot
Saturday morning, and how she turned and ran back to
the gate, leaving the boys to dare each other closer. As
dusk falls even the boldest of them will not pass that gate

without running, head ducked and eyes averted; and even the slightest rustle of a squirrel on a branch is enough to set the heart jumping. As dusk falls the lilacs that grow inside the gate stand out for a while, pale against the darkening sky; and in this short space of time, while the lilacs are lit, the house seems to rouse itself from dreams—to await some sound, the creak of an unwilling hinge or the sudden hollow echo of a footstep on the porch. The leaves are still; not a breath of movement in the roses, in the grass; too early yet for fireflies. The moment hangs suspended, a summer dusk, a waiting silence, until at last the lilacs fade into the imperceptibly deepening dusk, leaving only a sweetness on the air.

And so the house is haunted. It isn't quiet. The townspeople rather enjoy its reputation, acquired over the years through a series of tenants who have come and gone. But now it seemed that this same reputation, circulating out of town, was what had brought the newest tenants—a young childless couple—to Skipton. Roberta Hopkins told Mary Buck that young David Curtiss had told her that a haunted house was exactly what they wanted. Someone who had lived in Skipton years ago had mentioned it to them. Exactly what they wanted. They had gotten in touch with Sam Gilfoy at once.

After that, said Leonie Saunders, who ran the grocery store and had talked to the young man with the bruise on his temple when he came in for the coffee his wife had forgotten to buy—after that, Leonie told her husband Mitch, the story got even odder. Because they were scientists, it seemed, and it was some kind of fancy research they were doing at the old Gilfoy house; and the young man asked if she, Leonie, had ever had any unusual experiences in connection with the place. But she couldn't oblige him there.

"No sir," she said in her flat, frugal New England voice as she handed him his change and stood with one hand resting on the jar of instant coffee, forgetting to bag it while she considered the haunted house so seriously that David, in spite of her wearing a faded print dress and being old enough to be his mother, found her beautiful. "No, can't say as I have."

* * *

It was partly David's enthusiasm for his project that had led him into the conversation, partly his delight in the small-town atmosphere that had made Mrs. Saunders recognize him immediately as "the new folks at the Gilfoy house" and partly a calculated desire for information. Chris Claiborne, the friend who had told them about the house in the first place, had been vague: his family had moved away from Skipton when he was twelve and his memories, in bright childhood colors, contained few details. Already David, keeping Jack's newspaper article on lawsuits a little guiltily in mind, had begun sounding the neighborhood people on their experiences of the house, taping the interviews whenever possible.

People liked to talk. He heard the tramp story in any number of versions. The tramp was a stranger, just passing through; he was a local man fallen on hard times, overfond of the bottle; he was a lunatic escaped from an asylum; a murderer broken out of prison; a long-lost relative of Sam Gilfoy's, destitute and seeking shelter. He had gone to sleep on the porch of the empty house and frozen to death during the night; he had broken into the house and hanged himself from a beam in the attic; he had fallen from a tree where he had climbed to escape a vicious neighborhood dog. There were no hard facts, but David was not looking for hard facts just yet. He was collecting the folk mythology that surrounds every reputedly haunted house, a bird's nest of exaggeration and superstition into which some strands of truth might be woven.

Sally's part of the task was to gather the stories of people who had actually lived in the house. Somehow she had gotten old Mr. Gilfoy to send her the names of the previous tenants. She had obtained their forwarding addresses from the local post office and mailed them the standard questionnaire used in haunting investigations. Background material was also her department—historical information on the house and its original owners. She had paid another visit to the church up the hill and completed her Gilfoy family tree from the parish records, discovering that their landlord was the youngest son of the Reverend Joshua Gilfoy. The local library was next on her list.

For the moment it was all they could do. Since their arrival (and it had been almost a week now) the place had been absolutely quiet. They had been over it from top to bottom a dozen times—from dusty attic to dim cellar and all the echoing rooms in between, at various hours of the day and night—but the only footsteps, the only voices were their own, and for ghostly music they had to make do with the muted bell of the ice cream truck at the bottom of the hill on the long warm afternoons.

David made a floor plan. It was standard procedure in haunting investigations, but aside from that he enjoyed the process of measuring the rooms, reducing the scale, transferring the three-dimensional house to a series of neat lines and letters on paper. The front door opened into a high-ceilinged entrance hall from which doors led to various rooms on the first floor and steep stairs ascended to the second. On the first floor, across from the parlor with its bay window and sun-mottled chairs, was a library crammed with books, most of them leather-bound; at the back of the house, the kitchen was inhabited by an immense black iron stove that Sally christened Jezebel, and a dining room looked out onto the neglected backyard. The house was let furnished and the furniture was old: wing chairs stuffed to bursting, fringed lamps on rickety tables, in the dining room a sideboard like a baroque tomb. On the wall above it a painted portrait gazed down. "The Rev. Joshua," Sally guessed, and on closer inspection the subject did prove to be wearing a clerical collar. He was badly in need of cleaning.

Connecting the library and dining room was a small room that had clearly served as an office for the mistress of the house. Here the practical business of the household had been conducted: accounts, inventories, the dismissal of unsatisfactory servants—a narrow room housing only a secretary desk with pigeonholes and dozens of drawers, and a spindle-back chair. On the wall was a framed black paper silhouette of a woman's head. The single window looked across a few yards of grass to a high hedge and trees rising beyond it in the vacant lot on the east side of the house. On the outside of one pane a child's grimy handprint was visible. They called it the little room, with the stress on *little*.

On the second floor the stair banister took a left turn and continued, forming an open landing that overlooked the entrance hall below. Turning left again the railing became a wall, forming an inside corridor that ran in a square to connect the second-floor rooms. There were six bedrooms, a bathroom, a linen closet, and a room furnished as a sitting room. David assigned numbers to the bedrooms, and in some cases names as well. The large bedroom above the kitchen, at the back of the house, was designated the master bedroom.

Sally, entering first, stopped and sniffed tentatively; he watched her. "What is it?" he said.

"Something's burning." And she was past him half running, on her way down to the kitchen. Left alone he sniffed but could smell nothing. The room seemed, if anything, a little chilly, its west window shaded from the afternoon sun by a big linden just outside. A massive bed and desk were the only furniture. He disliked them, finding something brutal in the dark, heavy wood. The mantel above the fireplace was carved with a design of interlocking circles; he traced it absent-mindedly with one finger. Sally returned, shaking her head.

"I can't find it, whatever it is. The smell isn't anywhere but here."

David inhaled. "I can't smell anything. What's it like—something electrical?"

"No. Like a wood fire."

He was looking at her and she shrugged.

"Never mind," she said.

A small bedroom at the front of the house, its window framed by the climbing roses on the porch roof, was immediately dubbed the Thistle Room because of the pattern of its wallpaper. The only other room to earn a name was next door to the Thistle Room at the southeast corner of the house; on the strength of a large picture of an Indian brave on a spotted horse hanging over the bed, it was called Tonto's Room. The remaining bedrooms were known only by their numbers, clockwise beginning with the master. The third and top floor housed the attic, dusty and cluttered with cartons, trunks, furniture broken or cast off by previous tenants. The cellar was dry and cool, inhabited by nothing more malevolent than an elderly boiler.

For the first few days they were too busy to mind the quiet. The local people, imagining (if they thought about it at all) floors being swept and beds aired, windows being washed and brass polished, would have been amazed to see them on their hands and knees with screwdrivers and wire cutters and electrical tape, outfitting the venerable rooms with electronic detectors for sound, light, heat, and cold. Vibration pickups were attached to the frame of the house to register possible earth tremors. There were tape recorders and cameras and self-recording thermometers, tangles of wire in the narrow halls, a loudspeaker mounted on the second-floor railing overlooking the entrance hall. Beside the speaker was a numbered panel set with lights, each number corresponding to a room on David's floor plan.

The equipment, which was expensive, belonged to the lab. Its purpose was to monitor the house for changes in the physical environment that might indicate the presence of psi. Both of them had set it up before, in other reputedly haunted houses. The only difference was that the people living in those houses had been intimidated and annoyed by all the electronic paraphernalia: one man had told them it was worse than the ghost. Even in this house with no one but themselves to please, they made things as unobtrusive as possible, tucking wires under carpets and behind chairs. David couldn't help noticing how well they worked together. The tensions in their year-old marriage had miraculously eased, as if pooling their energies on a project outside themselves had been exactly what was needed. Since coming to the house he had been aware of erotic dreams almost every night, images too vague to recall in detail but staying with him by day, obscurely coloring his waking thoughts. Their third night they had tried, for the first time in months, to make love. It had been a farce, of course; he should have known better. The dreams persisted, but he was careful to keep them in their place.

At last their preparations were finished. The equipment had been checked and adjusted and rechecked. Every time he went upstairs David surveyed the neat panel of lights with satisfaction. He was ready, more than ready—but nothing happened; the sun spread slowly like a spilled liquid across the floors in late afternoon, and in the library the crowned walnut grandfather clock, dusted and reset by Sally, ticked the uneventful seconds away. It was the perfect time to start work on a talk Jack had asked him to prepare for the lab's fall seminar series, open to the interested public. The title of the talk was "Theory versus Practice in Haunting Investigation," and it was supposed to be thought-provoking, witty, and not too technical. He had been flattered when Jack had asked him; it was an honor, after all—but just now he was feeling extremely technical and not witty at all.

It wasn't that the lull in the house was unusual. Hauntings were perverse. Lie in wait and nothing happened; turn your back and all hell might break loose. And when it did, in a typical case, there were a dozen people running around, getting in each other's way—the owners of the house, their relatives and nosy neighbors, the harassed researchers, sometimes even the local police and clergy. Here, in this ideal spot, they would be spared at least that particuar nuisance. But it seemed to David, as time went by, that he would almost be grateful for a little more nuisance and a little less peace.

⇛ 3 ⇚

QUESTIONNAIRE FOR FORMER TENANTS
OF THE SAMUEL GILFOY HOUSE

1. Name: **KAREN ABBEY**

2. Current address: **315 SHADY GROVE NORTHAMPTON, MASS**

3. Place of birth: **CLEVELAND, OHIO**

4. Age: **54.**

5. Are you: Single ___ Married **X**

   Widowed ___ Divorced ___

   No. of children **4**

6. Religious affiliation: **PRESBYTERIAN (LUKEWARM)**

7. Highest degree earned: **B.A.**

8. When did you live in the Samuel Gilfoy house at 23 Lilac Street, Skipton, MA?

   JUNE – AUGUST 1964

9. Were you aware before moving into the house that it is locally considered to be haunted?

   Yes ___ No **X**

10. Did you have any unusual experiences in connection with your tenancy in the house?

    Yes **X** No ___ (If no, please skip to Item 20.)

20

11. Were these experiences limited to a specific time frame? Yes **X** No ___

12. If yes, please specify: Morning ___ Evening ___ Afternoon ___ Night **X**

13. Were these experiences localized in a specific room or rooms?
Yes **X** No ___ (If yes, please mark the floorplan provided.)

14. Did the experiences involve:
    X Seeing   ___ Tasting
    X Hearing   ___ The sensation of
    ___ Smelling   touching   or
                                  being touched

15. In connection with the experiences, were objects___ Moved
    ___ Lost
    ___ Broken
    X Undisturbed

16. Did you feel the presence of a ghost in the
? ? house? Yes **X** No **X** (If no, please skip to
' , Item 20.)

17. Please use the following list to circle words that most closely match your impression of the personality of the ghost:
    Male   Sad
    Female   Friendly
    Old   Hostile   **? ?**
    Young   Playful   **' ,**
    Happy   Dangerous

18. Did you actually see an apparition (visible or partly visible figure)? Yes ___ No **X** (If no, please skip to Item 20.)

19. From the following list of activities circle those in which the apparition was engaged:

    Crying   Playing an instrument
    Dancing   Reading
    Eating   Searching for something

Floating	Sewing
Musing	Wandering aimlessly
Pacing	Other _____

20. Have you ever had an experience that could be
described as psychic? Yes ____ No X
(If yes, please describe.) _____

_____

Please use the following pages to describe your experiences in the Gilfoy house in your own words.

My husband and I and our four children moved into the Gilfoy house in June of 1964. We had been looking for a place in a small town in that area and it seemed ideal. We rented the house from Mr. Gilfoy with an option to buy after six months. I remember he was very firm about not wanting to sell outright, although he wouldn't really say why. Of course, we soon found out why!

I remember we got there very late in the day. It was almost dark. Both my husband and I thought we saw a light in one of the upstairs windows, but when we went inside all the rooms were dark. We didn't think much about it at the time, what with getting everybody fed and settled down for the night. The kids were absolutely wild (they'd never had so much space) and even our dog Kris, who usually did nothing but sleep, was running all over the place. Around eleven o'clock things finally settled down, and my husband and I got to bed around midnight. He went right to sleep, but I was lying awake thinking about all the things I had to do in the morning, when all of a sudden somebody started trying to take the house apart with a sledgehammer.

At least that's what it sounded like. My husband sat straight up in bed and started swearing. We both thought it was the kids, of course. By the time he got out of bed and down the hall to the boys' rooms, the noises had stopped. The boys blamed the girls, and the girls laid countercharges, and my husband bawled everyone out and we all went to bed very disgruntled—especially the dog, who was hiding under a chest of drawers and alternately whining and growling. I must stress that this was very unusual behavior for Kris, who customarily displayed about as much verve as an end table. We just thought he was worked up over the move.

The first few weeks we lived in the house were a nightmare. The racket didn't happen every night, and it wasn't always as loud as that first night; sometimes it was more like a knocking sound. But it happened at least three or four nights a week, and my husband was reaching the boiling point. He <u>knew</u> it was the kids, but they wouldn't admit it—or rather each pair of children (we have two girls and two boys) insisted it was the other pair. Finally we talked to our family doctor. He said that someone was having adjustment problems and advised us to ignore the noises and they would eventually stop.

Sometime in the middle of all this (I'm sorry I can't be more specific about dates, but at the time I didn't realize it would be important) our youngest child, Susan (9), woke me up one night to tell me that Tinkerbell was in her room. Naturally I told her she was dreaming and to go back to bed. She went and got her older sister, Debbie (14), who came back with her and woke me again. Debbie said there was a funny light in Susan's room. To quiet them down, I got up and went to look.

As the girls said, there was a light. It was about the size of a flashlight beam, very bright at the center. It really was a lot like Tinkerbell, the way you see her done in stage productions (we had recently taken the kids to one). I thought something in the room must be reflecting the moonlight, or something like that, so the girls and I checked around for dangling bracelets and such, but didn't find any.

At this point I went and woke my husband. He thought I was crazy, but he came and took a look. By this time the boys were up too, and we all sat around watching our mysterious visitor for about half an hour until it disappeared.

After that night, Susan used to see the light in her room fairly often, sometimes several times a week, and there were a couple of occasions when people thought they saw it in other rooms. I'm embarrassed to tell you that we continued to call it Tinkerbell. Maybe that's the reason it never seemed scary to any of us, least of all Susan. She used to have her cousin Sharon come out from Boston for the weekend in the hope that Tink would put on a show.

Another thing we liked about Tink was that the knocking or pounding noises never happened on the nights she came to visit. But they were still going on. The children swore they weren't doing it, but my husband was convinced that one or more of them was the culprit. He suspected the boys most strongly, because they slept at the back of the house (I should mention that the racket always seemed to come from there). I've marked your floor plan (I made kind of a mess!) showing where everyone slept, so you can see (I hope) that my husband and I had the front bedroom next door to the bathroom, the girls the other two front bedooms, and the boys the two smaller bedrooms in the back. The big corner bedroom at the back, over the kitchen, we were planning to make into a game room for the kids.

One night Debbie came and woke us up and said that she could hear knocking sounds, not loud but fairly steady, coming from the game room, which was straight down the hall from her room. Instead of turning on lights and storming around the way he usually did, my husband got a flashlight and sneaked down the hall to the boys' rooms, expecting to find them empty. Instead he found both boys sitting in the dark in Mike's room, next door to the game room, listening to the noises and looking scared stiff. That left Susan, but I went to check on her and she was fast asleep. My husband announced that he was going to open the game room door and see exactly what was making the racket, but the kids were all worked up into a fright and they begged him not to, and Debbie started to cry. By this time the noises had stopped anyway.

At this point we decided that something had to be done. During the scene in Mike's room the kids had confessed that some of the neighborhood children had told them the house was haunted by the ghost of a maniac who had jumped off the roof. My husband laughed that off and said that when he caught whoever was making those noises they were going to wish they had jumped off the roof. The next night he started sleeping in the game room.

For several nights nothing happened—no noises, no Tinkerbell, nothing. My husband was pretty smug. He finally decided that the ghost had been scared off and he could return to his own bed. Too soon! I don't remember whether it was that same night or the night after, but the pounding started up again as if whatever-it-was had taken a good rest and felt full of beans, ready to take the house apart. It woke us all up. My husband was truly fed up by now, and we all lined up in the hall outside the game room to watch him be a hero. We had every light in the place burning and he had the fireplace poker from downstairs—I tell you it was impossible, hearing that racket, not to believe there was someone or something in there.

So there we all were. The kids and I were standing in the hall about halfway between the game room and Debbie's room. My husband stopped outside the game room door and yelled, "Hey!" Then he kicked it open. The pounding stopped right away and there wasn't a sound in that pitch-dark room. Then—cold.

A cold wind came out of that room like no wind I've ever felt in my life. This was late July, remember, and as hot as any other July. My husband dropped the poker and jumped back. The rest of us felt that cold blast all the way back where we were standing. I'm afraid we lost our nerve completely. We ran for it, and my husband ran after us and we all piled into Debbie's room and slammed the door. My husband was swearing, Kris was backed into a corner barking his head off, the younger children were crying, and the older children were screaming at the dog to shut up. I have to admit the dog's behavior scared me almost as much as the cold. He was usually such a marshmallow, but right then I was afraid to go near him. Finally he calmed down—it must have been after about five minutes—so we opened the door and things seemed peaceful. When we went out into the hall, the cold was gone.

We didn't know what to make of it, but it wasn't something we wanted to live with. Besides the stories from the neighborhood kids, when I mentioned the noises to Mrs. Hopkins next door, she told me that the house had been haunted for years. I even got an anonymous letter warning us not to live there! We finally decided that it would be better to find another place before school started in September, so we looked again and found something we liked in Northampton. You can be sure we asked a lot of questions before we moved in! Mr. Gilfoy was very nice about letting us out of our lease, although he didn't mention anything about haunting and neither did we. I wanted to, but my husband wouldn't let me.

I should add two things: one, that we put Kris in a kennel for the remainder of our stay in the house (for his peace of mind and ours) and two, that we heard the noises several more times between "that night" and the day we moved out, but we left them strictly alone. Once was enough!

I hope this report isn't too much of a mess and that your investigation is a success. If you find out anything I'd love to hear about it. The house is so beautiful that it seems a crime for it to be spoiled that way. Oh, I almost forgot—on items 16 and 17 of your questionnaire it looks a little as if I lost my mind. But in fact the light and the pounding noises had a kind of <u>presence</u>, although I wouldn't call it <u>personality</u> the way I would in thinking of a ghost. The light seemed friendly and gentle, not exactly playful, and the noises hostile and dangerous.

You should be hearing from at least some of my children before long. I am enclosing a statement from my husband, in addition to the floor plan and questionnaire. Good luck!

Sincerely,

Karen Abbey

The personal account was typed messily onto their form. The husband's statement, written in ink on a sheet of yellow legal-size paper, said simply:

I have read my wife's statement and consider it accurate in all respects. I wish to add only that neither of us is a ready believer in the supernatural. I might add that I served in the Marine Corps during the Korean War, and that nothing I experienced in combat ever unnerved me half as much as the blast of cold air coming out of that room.

Nicholas F. Abbey

"Well," Sally said. "There's at least one haunted area. Happy now?"

"No. It's chilly in there, but nothing to scare a marine."

"The cold goes with the noises," she said slowly.

"And the noises are not cooperating."

Sally was sitting on the rug in front of the parlor fireplace, examining the floor plan marked by Mrs. Abbey. David watched her a moment.

"I'm wondering if we should call in a professional medium to get things going. Jack said he knew a couple of reliable ones in the Boston area."

She looked up from the diagram, frowning a little, shaking her head.

"Just to get things going, Sal. We're wasting time."

"Don't be so impatient."

"What if we've been had? Maybe the house isn't producing phenomena anymore."

She smiled a little. "Give it a chance."

"I call ten days a chance."

"Eight days."

"All right, eight days. The point is, it didn't lie this low for the Abbeys."

"Maybe it's gotten lazy."

David let his breath out suddenly. "Then let's wake it up. A medium—"

"No. I really think you're wrong."

"But Sally, why?"

She put down the floor plan and moved to kneel in front of him where he sat in one of the striped chairs, resting her hands on his knees. "I don't know. I just think—let's wait a little longer."

"And then?"

"And then let's wait a little longer."

He looked at her, thinking that it must be the intensity of her face, like a focused light, that gave it beauty: that serious preoccupied look like a prophet's. Her smile, when it came, was dazzling; she had somehow never learned an automatic social smile. He leaned forward and rested his chin on top of her head. "It'll probably be the most peaceful summer of our lives."

⇶ 4 ⇷

Dear Dr. Curtiss,

Enclosed are the forms you sent and my personal recollections of living in the Samuel Gilfoy house in Skipton. I must insist that under no circumstances will I allow my name to be attached to this statement if made public in any way. I appreciate your cooperation in this matter.

My father (now deceased) and I were in residence in the house for nearly a year, from 1 April 1951 to 26 March 1952. During that time we were aware of a number of disturbances, most of which took place at night, specifically percussive sounds of varying loudness and the erratic behavior of lighting fixtures and other household objects.

My father and I, as educated people, were amused to learn that the local people regarded the house as haunted. It was quite plain to us that the so-called "spirit raps" and "ghostly footsteps" were supplied by a family of squirrels infesting the attic, and that there were similar natural explanations for the other peculiarities of the house. In spite of this, however, we found the almost constant disturbances both wearisome and annoying.

One such incident concerned a wineglass that was broken one night at the table. No one was touching the glass. Its bowl was shattered while the stem remained upright. Someone must have thrown a pebble through the open window, and I am sure you

29

will understand me when I say that the children
in the neighborhood were a particularly mischievous
group and openly hostile to us. I believe they really
preferred the house empty so they could continue
to entertain themselves with ghoulish stories. They
certainly resented our presence there. One of their
favorite pranks was to pretend that we ourselves
were ghosts and to run screaming at the sight of
us. I ignored such rude behavior, of course, but my
father, who was a shy and somewhat oversensitive
person, was confused and hurt by it.

Miss Miranda Sterling's letter went on, but David had
had enough. When Sally had finished it he said, "Just
give me the highlights."

"Well, the maid stole her bedside clock and wouldn't
admit it. The heat didn't work in the master bedroom.
The frying pan (I like this) used to spin around on the
stove. The local exterminator was a crook because he
said he got rid of the squirrels but they kept on making a
racket at night. The neighbors had a noisy dog that
howled all the time."

"The place seems to have a bad effect on dogs," David
said.

"Mrs. Hopkins has cats now," Sally said. "We should
check to confirm that she had a dog when the Sterlings
were living here." She pushed the hair off her forehead.
"Oh, I'm forgetting the most interesting thing. Remember Mrs. Abbey said she got an anonymous letter warning her that the place was haunted? Well, so did the
Sterlings."

While she had been reading the letter David had become almost supine in his chair; now he sat up. "Damn,
Sally! You know what that means? It's proof that there
was psi activity in the house before the tramp ever came
along. The Sterlings were here in fifty-one and the beginning of fifty-two. Mrs. Hopkins said the tramp was here
in the early fifties. Okay, if he died in 1950 he could have
caused the Sterlings' haunting. But prior to the Sterlings,
the last tenants were here in the thirties and forties.
Whatever was haunting them, it wasn't the tramp."

"You're assuming the letter was written by one of

those previous tenants," she said. "It could have been just a local busybody. Remember, we haven't talked to those early tenants. We have no proof that any haunting existed prior to the Sterlings."

He stood up and started to pace. "But suppose we did. Suppose we could prove—well, at least that the tramp's death took place after the Sterlings moved out. That would eliminate him as a haunting agent." He turned at the window and came back in her direction. "We've got to get some facts on him. This is important."

"I don't see why it's so important." She was folding Sterling's letter.

"You're not listening! If the psi activity was here before the tramp, then it isn't the tramp who's doing the haunting."

"I understand that. But what difference does it make? I know it's an interesting point, but it's not *the* point. We're here to get documented evidence that the haunting actually exists, not to come up with the identity of the ghost."

David sat down again with a sigh, then started to grin. "Oh, come on. Don't you want to know who the green face at the window belongs to?"

Reports from other former tenants were coming in. Completed forms were returned by Mr. and Mrs. Rogers in Oklahoma and Susan Abbey in San Francisco. Mrs. Rogers was an ardent believer in the spirit world. She filled two handwritten pages with heartfelt ramblings about the unhappy spirit inhabiting the house. Specifically, she mentioned a sound she described as "fluttering." Her husband's statement was more matter-of-fact; he mentioned the knocking sounds, which he called "tapping," and the sensation of cold in the master bedroom, although he had plainly never experienced it in the spectacular sense that the Abbey family had. He also mentioned hearing, on several occasions when it could have had no basis in reality, the distinct sound of a clock being wound with a key. Susan Abbey's statement confirmed the appearance of the light known as Tinkerbell, the banging or knocking sounds, and the cold blast of air. She added that she and her sister, alone in the house one afternoon, had heard "some weird murmuring." The inflection had been that of someone asking a question over and over, although they had not been able to make out any specific words.

The reports held an encouraging degree of consistency on several points, but on the whole the picture was hampered by percentages. Too few tenants had responded. The Murray and DuBois families had not been located, nor had Thomas Kirk, whose forwarding address from the 1948 archives of the Skipton post office was apparently no longer valid, since Sally's letter to him had been returned marked ADDRESSEE UNKNOWN. The two old ladies whose lease had lasted four months in 1934 were dead. Mrs. Rose Pindar, the only tenant on the list still living in Skipton, had not returned David's phone calls. And Mrs. Gardner, whose stay in the house for ten days in 1975 was the shortest on record, returned a terse note saying she did not wish to discuss it.

"What's with these people?" David said one night when he had been going through the file on the tenants. "Don't they realize they're being offered the chance to add their two cents' worth to the total sum of scientific knowledge? They ought to be begging to talk to us."

They were in the parlor where they usually sat after supper. The curtains were open, and against the deepening dusk the room with its lights and colors was reflected in the panes of the bay window. Sally was reading a book she had taken from the library across the hall, and now she looked up.

"What people?"

"Pindar. Gardner. They're a couple of clams."

"Maybe they just can't be bothered," she said.

"Pindar, maybe. But this letter from Gardner smacks of hostility. Like she was so freaked out by whatever happened that she hates us for reminding her of it." He went to sit beside her on the rug in front of the fireplace, her favorite spot, thrusting the letter between her and the book. *I do not wish to discuss anything about that house, now or in the future. Please do not attempt further contact with me on this or any subject.* It was hard not to read emotion into the hurried, jagged handwriting.

"Pretty strong reaction for some raps and a little cold air," he said. "She might have experienced something really juicy."

Sally glanced sideways at him. "Like what? The green face?"

He pushed her off balance. He had learned to avoid such playful physical contact after the first few awkward months of their marriage, realizing that it was unfair of him to initiate anything that resembled a prelude to lovemaking. But now the gesture came easily, spontaneously, and even his surprise at himself was somehow soothed away by a half conscious sense of light and calm underlying the house as if it were a vessel rocked on a gentle sea. Sally defended herself; they scuffled and her book went flying.

"Look out—" She broke away and retrieved it, examining the binding for damage. He took it from her and looked it over, somebody's memoirs bound in faded red cloth, gilt letters dull on the spine.

"No harm done." As he handed it back to her something fluttered from the pages: a pressed linden leaf, golden, heart-shaped, veins darkly etched. Falling, it caught the lamplight. They both reached out but it eluded them, catching invisible currents of air and circling once, twice, before coming to rest softly on the floor, like a kiss of greeting.

➺ 5 ⋘

EARLY IN THEIR SECOND WEEK the temperature went up, and it began to get buggy. Some of the windows in the house, most notably the one in their bedroom at the top of the stairs, lacked screens and they spent a night or two enduring mosquito torture before David remembered seeing some screens in the attic. They went up together to bring them down. Better late than never. He found himself scratching a bite on his arm as they climbed the narrow stairs.

It was a gem of an attic. Slanting eaves were magnificently cobwebbed, the cobwebs themselves spangled with light from the fan-shaped windows in the front and back gables. The junk was intriguing: a football lying in a baby's cradle, a tarnished ship's barometer announcing perpetual rain. There was a quart jar filled with buttons, a boomerang, a pair of woven panniers, a bird's nest, a Quaker Oats carton stuffed with Christmas wrapping, along with the customary conglomeration of bedsprings and broken lamps. The screens were over in one corner. Most of them were in sad shape, but four were intact—enough, David thought, to take care of the problem.

Sally was poking around in a pile of junk on the other side of the room. He stacked the screens at the top of the stairs and wandered over to the window overlooking the backyard—the same, he recalled, that had featured the green face in Bobby Campbell's deposition. Close to the dirty glass he peered through a mesh of leaves at the yard below, imagining a small figure crossing the grass.

Now if I were the green face I'd chuck a brick, he thought. Assuming I had a green hand to chuck it with.

He tried to open the window but the catch was rusted shut. So much for flying bricks. Turning away from the window he caught sight of his own reflection in a dusty mirror that was propped against a stack of boxes nearby. Between himself and his image the afternoon sun cast a band of light filled with dust motes that spun slowly and endlessly in the air. He could scarcely see himself. He squinted at the mirror, printed WASH ME in the dust on its surface, and stood back to see the effect. Contained in the boundaries of the letters his reflection became slivers of bright color in the gray plane, entirely separate from anything recognizable as himself. He leaned forward, liking the flash of colors, mysterious and festive. At the peak of the W he met an eye, blue. But it was his own, and he transferred his interest to the pile of boxes behind the mirror. On the top was a shoebox filled with old postcards. The Cathedral at Rouen. *Thanks so much for your second letter, and the picture. It is fine! Delighted father is better.* The Battery, Charleston, S.C. *We went out in the boat today. It's hot. We leave for New York Thursday.* The Library of Congress, Washington, D.C. *Received your letter. Will answer soon.* The next line was indecipherable. He was puzzling over it when he heard the music.

Hesitant at first, a rusty note or two and then silence, deeper than the silence had been before, a hush in which the spinning of the sunlit dust was almost audible. Then another note, and another, dropping into the slanting stream of afternoon light, music faint and tinny and a little cracked in tone but music all the same, a song wistful and faded, bringing with it a rush of sweetness and loss. Suspended in it was the summer, green-laced with leaves, festooned with shadowy roses; a curtain blowing softly at a window. The melody had a catch in it like the indrawn breath before a sob. It filled the attic from eaves to floor, sifting down with the dust in the radiant air. Sally was sitting back on her heels, listening, a small wooden box open in her hands.

He could not have said when it stopped, so like an echo was it to begin with and so it seemed to linger, reluctant to be gone. The notes came more and more slowly; just when they seemed to have stopped for good there was one more, and then at last David came awake to the silence that had fallen again. He put down the box of postcards and went to Sally.

She said nothing, handing him the box when he knelt beside her. It was maybe four inches by six, a dark wood coated with dust except where her fingers had left marks. He examined the works inside. It was the type of music box that begins to play when opened: the raising of the lid released a spring and set a small flywheel in motion. He touched the prickly brass cylinder curiously.

"I didn't get the tune, did you?"

"Stephen Foster. 'Jeanie with the Light Brown Hair.' "

"Ah." He had located the key on the underside of the box, and now he started to wind it.

Sally said, "Don't."

The sharp word made him look at her, and looking he saw what he had missed before—that she was upset, controlling herself with an effort. For an instant he thought it was something he had done, and then he understood: the music—no, not the music, the box itself—had affected her. It was straight out of the textbooks, a phenomenon called psychometry or object reading, in which incidents in the history of an object, apparently encoded in its physical structure, are communicated through touch. Hold a bracelet and see a golden field, figures in the distance. A pair of glasses—sunlight on rippling water, a sensation of turning, spinning. As if each object were a book, its history written in atoms. The familiar mixture of envy and awe flooded him.

"What—?" he said. She shook her head, lips tight. Whatever it was, she didn't want to talk about it. But what was it? Curiosity gnawed him. He ran his fingers over the surface of the box, as if by doing so he could detect its secrets for himself, but all it offered him was dust. The wood beneath was a rich golden brown streaked with black; he wiped it clean on his shirt.

"What kind of wood is it?" Sally said.

"Rosewood, something like that." It was an effort to hold back his questions, his almost painful need to know what the box had communicated to her. *Incidents in the history of an object.* She reached out and he relinquished it, seeing its beauty in her hand more than in his own: the simple unornamented lid, the wood's flowing grain. Her head was bent over it and he thought at first she was examining it for some flaw; then something caught the light, something bright falling—a tear falling on the lid of the box, darkening the wood where it fell. She said something under her breath and turned her head away. He touched her arm.

"Sal—"

She shook her head but his hand closed on her arm, drawing her to him. He took the box away from her and set it on the floor. She gave way then and let him hold her. "What is it?" he said.

"I don't know." The sobs were making her almost incoherent. "I don't know." He rocked her gently as they knelt there on the dusty attic floor, the stream of light from the window retreating from them little by little in the fading of the afternoon.

"June 11. Still nothing to record in the way of actual phenomena, but this afternoon Sally had what may have been a psychometric experience. We found an old music box in the attic which affected her with a feeling of overwhelming sadness when she held it in her hands. The feeling diminished when she put the box down. From the initials J.G. TO V.B.G. carved on the inside of the lid, we deduce that the box was a gift from our landlord's father, the Reverend Joshua Gilfoy, to his second wife, Virginia Blake Gilfoy. She died in 1931.

"Although as a rule Sally more or less automatically blocks influences of this kind, she admitted to being distracted by the music, which began as soon as she opened the box. She had no clear perception of any actual incident, only the aforementioned feeling of great sadness."

The clock in the library across the hall struck the half hour as David turned off the tape recorder. Eleven-thirty. Sally was upstairs asleep; she had been depressed all evening. He had a vague sense of guilt as he took the cassette out of the machine, a half knowledge that she would not want this afternoon's incident included in their report on the house. But it had happened, after all—and it might be relevant. He quelled his guilt as he put the tape in a mailer. Tomorrow it would go to the lab, where it would be copied and filed away, the copy sent to the ASPR, the American Society for Psychical Research in New York. It was an attempt, one of many, to placate the skeptics—a way of ensuring that events were recorded in the order in which they happened, not rearranged later to support the investigators' conclusions. The tenants' statements had received the same treatment. He frowned, thinking of having to omit Miss Sterling's name from her statement, and picked up one of the reference books lying open beside the tape recorder. He had been rereading the sections on psychometry.

It is a postulated property of matter that it carries with it permanently, as a sort of influence or aura, a complete history of itself. Psychometry is the clairvoyant faculty enabling certain mediums, in a normal state, to perceive incidents in those histories. . . .

Visions are usually full-size and encompass the medium who, to see eveything properly, must turn and look around. They occur in light or darkness, and with the eyes open or closed. They come best when the mind is quiescent, but the visions themselves may create in the medium the strongest excitement and emotion. . . . To obtain relief from distressing perceptions the medium will suddenly drop the article. They cease immediately, but the disquiet may persist for a long time.

The text was an old one from the twenties, before the era of statistics, when psychical research was in its fuzzy and trusting infancy. But he had turned to it in reaction to pages of recent experiments demonstrating evidence of psychometry by the use of index cards in sealed plastic bags. Now as his eyes flicked over the words he was seeing Sally's face, closed and unhappy. "The medium" —he knew she would rebel at that term applied to her. She had a distaste, a horror of it; she said it conjured up black cats and crystal balls; she was worse than the most untutored skeptic about it. "Psychic" and "sensitive" were not so bad, though she would not willingly answer to them either. When David, first meeting her, carried away by her performance in the telepathy experiment, had referred to her as psychic, she had amazed him by saying coldly, "I'm not psychic. I have a certain telepathic ability. One person in twenty has it—maybe more." He could not fathom her reluctance then—couldn't now. He would have given anything to possess her gift. Even as a kid, hearing the word "clairvoyant" and being told it meant "clear-seeing," he had been shot through with chills of excitement—had been a sucker for the simplest hoaxes and party games, so badly did he want to believe. The Tarot had fascinated him, and books about medieval magic filled with references to all the paraphernalia of the art: rings and amulets and garlands, incense, inscriptions, diagrams, prayers and hymns. He was enthralled by the ceremony, the ritual; it seemed to him to make perfect sense, this oblique approach to an aspect of life that would not allow itself to be confronted directly. Later, when he began to study the whole question in earnest, it was with the same fascination that he read about experiments with light-tight boxes and white noise. The symbols on the cards used in telepathy runs—the circle, square, star, cross, and wavy lines—filled him with the same fever as had once the Ace of pentacles, the Knight of Wands. It was still a kind of magic to him, capricious as is the best magic, but nonetheless true.

Meeting Sally, he had been able to accord an intellectual understanding, nothing more, to her sense of being at the mercy of something she could not comprehend or control. She had come to parapsychology, he knew, in search of some rational explanation for her frightening ability to perceive other people's thoughts. ESP. Extrasensory perception. She hated talking about it, and he could only faintly grasp that she felt helpless in the face of it, violated somehow. When she consented to talk at all, she talked in a jumbled way about "pressure," about "it." He could grasp what she meant by "it," he thought— the tantalizing, seemingly limitless power that revealed itself only in momentary flashes, in the monotonous lab experiments as much as in the flamboyance of the occult. But he could not grasp her fear of it. Fool's courage, maybe, but he felt that if he could somehow have acquired her gift, he would gladly have paid any price for it.

The clock struck midnight. A dog began to howl somewhere outside. He yawned and rubbed his eyes until patterns danced on the inside of the lids.

Whose mutt is that, anyhow? Mrs. Hopkins has cats. Must be the people behind us.

Something clicked then: Miss Sterling's letter. *A noisy dog.* Suddenly wide awake, he got up from his chair and went out into the front hall, but by the time he got there the noise had stopped. He stood for a minute listening. Quiet now, not a sound. He put the tape in the pocket of his jacket, where he would remember to mail it in the morning.

Up the steep stairs softly. They were using the bedroom at the top of the stairs, next door to the master. He turned out the hall light and touched a switch to activate the electrical system that would monitor the house while they slept. *From ghosties and ghoulies and long-leggedy beasties, and things that go bump in the night, good Lord deliver us.* The door to their room was ajar; he went in and undressed in the dark. Not a sound in the house, only the faint creak of bedsprings as he lay down next to Sally.

And I am not a ghost. Am I?

He wasn't sleepy. Against the moonlit window he could see her outline, silver-edged; she lay with her back to him. He reached for her and then withdrew his hand, surprised at himself. Why wake her? He was hopeless as a lover—they both knew that by now. What was the good of proving it again?

He turned on his back and settled his head on the pillow. The first few times they had slept together he had been able to manage something, enough anyway to convince himself (as badly as he wanted to be convinced) that he was cured, magically and at last, of the impotence that had plagued his sexual experiences till then. He had outgrown it, or else it had simply been a matter of finding the right woman. But those few successes had apparently been a fluke, a statistical oddity that evened itself out soon enough. The majority of their attempts ended in mutual frustration, and by now they had all but abandoned the pretense of a sexual side to their marriage. His inadequacy baffled and mortified him; it seemed to have been visited on him like a Biblical affliction, beyond justice or reason. A psychologist would doubtless paint a different picture. But the idea of getting professional help made him cringe, although he supposed he should make the effort, for Sally's sake at least. Still, when he had mentioned his deficiency as a kind of bad joke, she had said it didn't matter. And whether she had meant it or not, he wanted to believe her: it was so much simpler to treat the subject as closed. And so it was. Until recently, since they had been living in the house, when he found himself wanting her again, both physically and in some less direct way that had never been satisfied even in their rare successful couplings. He wondered whether, if he had been telepathic, they could have achieved some sort of magical mind-merger, like advanced beings in a sci-fi movie. But he knew from dozens of lab sessions that he possessed not a shred of such ability.

The pillow was like a rock. Squeezing softness from it he called on common sense. There were other interests in life, after all. He had his work. It was profoundly exciting; it was important. *The meeting place of religion, philosophy, and science*—that description of parapsy chology still gave him a kick. It was uncharted territory where he could really make his mark, do something big. A field that stimulated him intellectually, filled him with a constant sense of wonder and the occasional dose of humility. Whether you wanted to call it the space-time continuum or the transcendent All, most of the time he could convince himself that such a vision of the cosmos was enough to render the physical joining of two paltry beings a trivial matter—at best a clumsy mimicry of true union. But then in the midst of his reasoning the bottom dropped out of everything and he wondered why he should have been denied this supreme human act of creation and consolation—felt himself isolated, flawed, mocked by the harmony he longed for. He turned suddenly toward Sally beside him, pressing his face blindly against her back. She was warm; the rhythm of her breathing altered as she woke. Then she turned over with a sigh, asleep again almost at once. There was not a sound in the house.

➤➤➤ 6 ◄◄◄

RAIN SUITED THE OLD HOUSE—rain rattling on the high gables, tapping at the windows, fringing the edge of the porch roof in a self-renewing curtain of glimmering drops. Rain rushing down the rusty old gutters and spurting off in waterfalls to form puddles in the yard; the heart-shaped linden leaves hanging glossy and heavy or blowing off the trees and across the yard to collect in sodden heaps against the latticework under the porch. Everywhere inside there was the sound of rain falling: up in the attic, under the eaves, a loud drumming; in the Thistle Room a muffled patter of drops on the bedraggled roses outside the window. In the sitting room upstairs, where curved pieces of Victorian furniture faced one another in silence across the dingy carpet, there was a fitful tap-tap like the classic ghostly hand on the pane as gusts of wind rose in the west; while in the dark places of the house, the closet under the stairs and the cave of the library, the sound sank to a hollow and distant rushing like an underground river. In the parlor the fireplace damper had been left open and a small ashy puddle was forming on the hearth. In the kitchen, where they sat eating breakfast, the rain was no more than a soughing in the unmown grass, coming in to them through the back door that stood open to the warm, wet breeze. It was the first rain since they had come to the house. The unkempt garden soaked it up; the dusty tangle of vines and leaves covering the fence between their backyard and Mrs. Hopkins's bloomed a lush green. Rain suited the old house, but it did not suit David. This Saturday morning nothing did.

"I'm fed up."

Sally glanced at him and he said, "Nothing's happening." The calendar hung on the wall above the kitchen table: he tapped it with his knife. "Look at that. Two weeks. And nothing—not a goddamn thing. Sally, look—we've got to get a medium in here."

The knife had left a buttery spot on the day's date. She looked at it. "All right," she said.

"All right? You mean it's okay with you?"

"It's okay with me."

He looked hard at her, but she was drinking her coffee. Less than a week ago she had been dead set against the idea: what had happened to change her mind? That business with the music box, but that was all—wasn't it? He was seized with a sudden doubt of his own perceptions. Was the house really as quiet as he thought? Some mornings when he came into the parlor it seemed that the chairs had shifted, or the curtains were open when he thought he remembered closing them. But if such things had actually happened, the instruments would have recorded them. It was more inside his own head that the shifts and changes seemed to take place, out of reach of the instruments. So much of haunting appears to be an elusive kind of collaboration between the house in question and the subliminal levels of consciousness of the people in it, and this can be dismissed as imagination or accepted as a meeting of psychic atmospheres. The house may generate a signal or an image, discernible on no instrument but reverberating in the deep places of the mind . . . He sat watching Sally. Maybe the house was getting to her: maybe she needed an ally, someone to take the pressure off. Maybe—but she looked at him now, meeting his eyes squarely.

"You're right," she said. "It's getting boring."

He waited an hour—it was Saturday morning, after all—before calling Jack Pennybacker at the lab in Maryland. He would be there, of course; he was there every day, even Christmas, even New Year's. It was his life, and among the researchers and assistants there was a common suspicion that, if indeed human personality does survive biological death, Jack's face with its short beard would continue to appear over shoulders and around doorways at the lab forever. David, listening to the phone ring, imagined the clinical rooms where people compared sheets of numbers or tried to influence the fall of mechanically thrown dice, the sensory deprivation chambers and the comfortable offices where mediums in trance answered word-association tests while a galvanometer registered their responses. There was a computer called Nostradamus. There were files labeled Xenoglossy, Sheep-Goat, Telesthesia, and one labeled Apparitions.

"David! How's it going? Any luck yet?"

"None, and that's why I'm calling. We want to get a medium in here."

He heard Jack laugh. "Dave, if Sally Beckett can't raise some action in that house, nobody can." The use of her maiden name told him that Jack was thinking of Sally not as a friend, someone he had eaten lunch with, argued with, lent money to, but as a case history in the annals of psychical research, a historical figure like Basil Shackleton or Lenore Piper.

"Well, you know it isn't exactly her line."

"Yeah, I know, I know. Okay, I'll give you some names. Got a pencil?"

An hour later he went upstairs to look for Sally. He finally found her in the attic. She had been rescuing boxes from a leak in the roof; now an ancient teapot sat on the floor, catching the water. The rain was still falling, not so hard now, patter on the roof punctuated by a steady musical dripping into the tarnished pot. He peered dubiously up at the eaves. "Does our lease cover this kind of thing?"

She shifted the last carton and glanced at him, dusting off her hands. "It's only that one spot."

"Still, it could have been a mess if you hadn't caught it. How the hell did you know it was leaking?"

She avoided his eyes. "It's an old house."

It was an old house. Therefore, the roof might leak. Was it simple deductive logic or more than that? He recalled his thoughts at breakfast. Was she tuned into the house somehow—aware, in spite of herself, of every nook and cranny in the place? Or was he making too much out of it? He went over to look at the salvaged boxes.

"What *is* all this stuff?"

She shook her head. "It's like an antique shop up here. Look at this."

It was a fragile little writing desk that had been hidden by the stacks of boxes. She had cleared it off and now it stood vulnerable and startled, like a deer caught in the glare of headlights.

"Pretty. Anything interesting in it?" He was already pulling at the handle of the single shallow drawer; it opened a few inches and then stuck. He saw a few hairpins, the ruled lines of a printed sales receipt. "Roofing materials," he said, examining it. "I think that's called irony." It was dated 1928. He fiddled with the drawer some more, trying to coax it the rest of the way out.

"And what's that?" Sally was pointing at something on the floor by the desk: the small metal figure of a crouching dog. He bent and picked it up. An old-fashioned inkwell. He hefted it. It was heavy, probably solid brass except for the black crusty well around which the dog's muscular body was flexed. The square base fit neatly into his palm.

"This is nice," he said. "Let's take it downstairs."

She made a face.

"What's the matter? It's man's best friend."

"I don't like it," she said. "It's ugly."

"It's not ugly. It's nice. We'll put it in the library; it'll be perfect." He ran a finger along the dog's bony spine.

Sally shrugged. "Did you get hold of Jack?"

"He sent you his love."

"And?"

"And I called the medium. I called two, but one was about to go on a Caribbean cruise. The other one is coming."

"When?"

"Tomorrow."

She turned to the desk, ran her fingers along the edge. "That's so soon," she said.

"Why wait?"

No answer. David took her by the shoulder. "Well?"

"You're right," she said.

"Say it with feeling."

She smiled and his hand tightened. "Will you promise not to short-sheet her bed?"

"I can't promise that."

His arms went around her seemingly of their own accord. The sound of the rain came close, and the gray light; he felt the roof and floor and walls around them like a larger embrace. The house held them.

⋙ 7 ⋘

"ANYONE WHO WALKS in his sleep is a medium," says A. Campbell Holms in his book *The Facts of Psychic Science*, published in 1925. He goes on to give other characteristics in his sweeping way: mediums are more often female than male; they are customarily nervous and emotional; frequently they have inherited their gift. As a rule this gift is in one of two modes: mental or physical. Mental mediumship includes clairvoyance, object reading (psychometry), healing, trance communication, and the like. In trance the medium may be either unconscious or fully awake and aware; in either case she is a passive vessel for the workings of psi. In physical mediumship objects rise and float through the air; glowing shapes may appear; there are voices, raps, and lights. While this latter type is the more spectacular, it is also more commonly exposed as fraud—it seems that mediums are rarely averse to trickery when their real talents fail them. And failure comes often even to genuine mediums, for theirs is a gift which, like everything else in the psychic realm, follows its own divine caprice.

Psychologists dismiss all mediums as cases of fragmented personality. The spirit control (to believers, the spirit of a deceased person who speaks through the medium in trance from the "other side" and generally acts as her sponsor in that world) is seen as a secondary personality, a symptom of schizophrenia. Messages from the spirit domain, on the other hand, hail a good medium as "a lighted doorway between two worlds . . . a beacon light or a star, visible to all." Through her, the departed may hope to communicate, in a limited way, with their loved ones still

48

on earth—to send those greetings and reassurances that seem, because of the unknown perils of their passage, to arrive all too often in incomprehensible form.

It is somewhere between these two extreme views that psychical research has taken its position. For scientific purposes, a good medium is a person with a high sensitivity to psi, who acts in its presence as a kind of lens that focuses and refracts. As such she is in great demand, but at the same time she must be suspiciously observed for any attempt at deception. Few mediums, nervous and emotional or otherwise, have the desire or the patience to put up with tiring and often boring experiments during which they are watched like criminals; and the unfortunate result is that no more than a handful have ever bothered to cooperate in the effort to gather scientific evidence about psi.

The medium's name was Rosanna Paine. She was a short, slight black woman, her hair braided with bright-colored African beads that swung and clicked softly with each movement of her head. Despite her exotic appearance she seemed down-to-earth, her eyes and smile direct; and David thought that Sally, shaking hands with her, seemed relieved. He led the way to the parlor, talking. Had she had any trouble with his directions? (She had driven from Boston.) He talked, hearing himself: the town, the weather (it was fine again), the lilacs . . . At the door to the parlor the medium stopped and stood motionless for a moment before stepping over the threshold. Then she followed him inside. Sally came last.

"Well," David said, "we're glad you're here." He indicated chairs; they all sat. Rosanna leaned back, crossing her legs. She wore small gold rings in her ears, loose stylish clothing; she seemed elegant and sophisticated. David was a little intimidated as well as pleased. Jack had recommended her very highly, and he found himself suddenly anxious about measuring up professionally to the other people she must have worked with. She produced cigarettes from her bag and lit one, glancing around for an ashtray. There was one on the mantel; he got up to pass it to her and then took his seat again.

"Okay. As I told you on the phone, the house has a

reputation for being haunted. Obviously I can't give you any details at this point. But we've been here two weeks and so far there's nothing doing. We're starting to wonder if the place is still psychically active, and we'd like to see what a sitting might turn up. How's that with you?"

The medium inhaled smoke. "Fine. I guess I should fill you in on myself. I'm a mental medium, trained but not professional—in other words I don't read palms for a living. I'm a theater set designer. I have a control named Andy, who usually takes charge when I'm in trance. As a rule I go into deep trance and am unaware of anything that goes on during the sitting. The trance usually lasts fifteen to twenty minutes. That's about it, I guess. Anything else you need to know?"

David considered, then shook his head. "I don't think so. Jack Pennybacker said you were one of the best, and absolutely reliable. That's good enough for me."

"Good old Jack. He had Andy and me performing like a couple of dancing bears." She smiled wryly; he found himself thinking that she was sexy.

"Does anybody want coffee?" Sally said.

It seemed they all did. They went out to the kitchen and Sally put water on to boil while David got out cups.

"It's instant, I'm afraid. We're complete savages."

"That's fine," Rosanna said.

They sat around the kitchen table. To avoid the subject of the haunting (a medium should be told nothing of a house or its history), David talked about Jack Pennybacker. His best Pennybacker story was one about a fraudulent medium, but he avoided it out of delicacy and settled instead for the one about the time the computer went on the fritz. Rosanna was a good listener, laughing at the right lines and asking questions; Sally, who had heard the story a hundred times and had in fact been present when it happened, listened with a smile. When the story was finished, and the coffee, David tipped his chair back. There was a pause. Rosanna nodded at the ancient stove.

"That's quite an art object you've got there." It filled almost one whole wall of the kitchen, resembling most of all some satanic instrument of torture with its crenelations and embellishments of black iron, its levers and valves.

Sally said, "That's Jezebel. She's not as bad as she looks." She was trying, David could see, to be friendly, to push past her ingrained distaste for mediums in general and make this particular woman feel welcome. She had worked with mediums before, of course, at the lab, but he knew they made her edgy: she felt some sinister connection with them, as if her gift could have led her down the path they had taken. He could sense her discomfort whenever Rosanna mentioned Andy, the spirit who spoke through her during trance. Sometimes such spirit controls claimed to have been Egyptian priests or historical figures; one medium had boasted Rudolph Valentino as his control.

Rosanna was fingering the handle of her empty cup. "When do you want to have the sitting?"

"Whenever you're ready," David said.

She smiled a little. "I'm ready."

"Now?"

"Sure."

"Great," he said. They got up from the table with a scraping of chairs. David found himself with butterflies and tried to hide them. He didn't want to seem too eager in front of Rosanna. But her casual confidence affected him with a feverish, almost exalted excitement, the same thing he had felt watching Sally that first time at the lab—seeing her mark numbers on a sheet of paper as precisely and matter-of-factly as if she were reading them from a blackboard rather than from the mind of another person. He had heard the same awe in Jack's voice as he looked over her results, saying in an undertone, "She's good. She's *good.*"

". . . best in a room where we can shut out as much outside light as possible," Rosanna was saying.

"The parlor's out, then; those curtains are lace," Sally said.

"What about the library?" David said. "It's dark as a dungeon in there." The tenants' reports suggested that the haunting centered in the master bedroom, but he did not want to hold the initial sitting in there. It was too much like playing his high card; having brought the medium in, he wanted to proceed slowly, cautiously, to make sure the situation did not get out of hand. It seemed best to let her try her luck in a neutral area first.

It was dark in the library and, when they had closed the heavy curtains, even darker. Rosanna turned on the lamp on the reading table.

"It doesn't have to be pitch black—I don't plan to produce any spooky hands or anything. It's just that outside light is a distraction."

In the light of the single lamp the library was, in David's opinion, an overwhelmingly appropriate spot for the summoning of spirits. The book-covered walls rose into shadow; the corners of the room seemed immeasurably far away. The drawn curtains, dark green, fell in voluminous folds to the floor. The furniture caught the lamplight and returned it in somber gleams: ornate grandfather clock, chairs upholstered in dull leather, the reading table with its powerful lion's paws. Next to the lamp on the table was the crouching-dog inkwell David had brought down from the attic. He had polished it the night before; the tense curve of the dog's body glowed.

"Cheery little place," the medium said.

David recalled his reading: *the tracing of the ceremonial circle, with its inscriptions and divine names; the triangle two feet outside this for rebellious spirits; the double seal and pentagram of Solomon to be worn by the operator together with the seal of the spirit to be summoned* . . . Things have changed since the days of the old magicians. Now they sat in three comfortable chairs, pushed into a circle around the table. Rosanna sat with hands loosely clasped in her lap and eyes closed. David watched her with curiosity. Sally had brought in the tape recorder; now she switched it on, positioned the mike, and sat back: with the single creak of her chair all sound ceased and they were silent, waiting.

Waiting . . . The tall clock sounded, as clocks are wont to do in such stillnesses, appallingly loud. The tape recorder made no noise at all: twice Sally looked to make sure it was running. David, watching the medium, was nonetheless vividly aware of the gleam and swing of the pendulum in the clock cabinet, the muted birdcalls outside in the yard, a trembling thread of daylight between the drawn curtains across the room. Rosanna sat nearest the lamp. Her closed eyes and the colored beads in her hair gave her motionless face the semblance of an exquisite African mask.

Gradually the silence rose around them to engulf even the clock's ticking and the outside sounds; the silence took the shape of table and lamp, chairs and books, became mahogany and leather and brass and brocade, shadows and edges and angles, joined the invisible flowing of the air. Inside the silence and part of it was the slow rise and fall of Rosanna's breathing, like a beating pulse at the center. David could not take his eyes off her. In his experience, even mediums with ineffectual everyday personalities usually took on a certain presence, the appearance at least of power, for the duration of the sitting. But this was something more compelling than he had yet seen, as if the small woman sitting opposite him was an instrument for the gathering and focusing of an immense energy, impalpable but very near. The thought brushed him that so must the priestesses and sibyls of ancient times have seemed—infinitely deep, caves of the earth and sky. He felt the presence of unlimited possibilities, some of them dangerous.

As he watched, the circle of light in which she sat seemed to quiver. He blinked and leaned forward, trying to decide if he had imagined it; a soft moaning had begun in her throat and her head jerked slightly. The moaning gave way almost immediately to a faint whispering during which her lips scarcely moved. She seemed calmer; the restless movements of her head had subsided quickly, but the whispering went on, an uncanny sound just at the threshold of hearing. Again David had the sense of confronting something immeasurable—of venturing into an alien element. Excitement twisted in him; he realized he was getting an erection. Sometimes it happened in these situations. All at once she spoke.

"There's someone—it's a young man."

David's glance met Sally's quickly and returned to Rosanna. Her breath was coming in gasps, her voice hoarse. "He wants—he wants—" She stopped as if listening. There was a longish pause.

David, hardly daring, said, "What does he want?"

The labored breathing went on, as if she hadn't heard him, and then at last: "He says he's lost—the lost one."

Excitement rose up David's spine. He glanced at Sally, but she was adjusting something on the tape recorder. He tried to keep his voice calm. "Where does he want to go?"

The answer came quickly this time. "Home."

"Where is home?"

"Home."

It was a flicker of annoyance he had to suppress now. He had been present at other sittings where things went round and round like this for an hour. Whoever, or whatever, it was that communicated through mediums in trance seemed somehow incapable of giving a straight answer to a direct question.

He tried again. "Why can't he go home?"

"Lost—he's lost."

(Round and round we go.) "How was he lost?"

For a moment he thought he had scored a hit. Her breathing changed; her eyelids fluttered. Then, leaning forward, watching her intently, he found himself all at once looking into her surprised open eyes. She blinked several times, as if she were having trouble focusing, and gave him an inquiring look. She was no longer in trance.

"What . . ." he said. She frowned a little, started to speak, and then the sound of a shuddering indrawn breath silenced them both. They looked at Sally. David's confusion exploded into astonishment.

She was in trance. There could be no doubt: he had seen dozens of people in mediumistic trance, and all the signs were there—the closed eyes, the rough breathing, the movements like a nightmare-dreamer's. He felt a prickling on his scalp. As they watched, her lips moved, as if she were reading to herself, but no sound came. He jumped when Rosanna touched his arm.

"Has she ever been in trance before?" She spoke close to his ear. He shook his head.

"Then we'd better get her out of it."

For an instant, no more, he felt a protest rising in

him—a need to question Sally, or whatever was controlling her: to find out what it wanted. But almost at once he realized that there was danger. He knew she kept up a constant barrier against intrusions of this kind, a mental filter that allowed her to function more or less like other people. Yet this thing had overcome her resistance. He thought, staring at her, of the energy he had felt beneath the surface of Rosanna's trance a few minutes before, and his throat went dry. He had nodded almost as soon as Rosanna had spoken.

She moved to Sally's chair and reached out to grasp her neck from behind, bending close. He saw her fingers tighten. "Sally," she said. The tone was one of sharp command.

There was a moment, one tick of the clock, and then Sally came out of it like a drowning victim bursting to the surface of deep water—sobbing for breath, eyes wide, face bathed in sweat. Rosanna steadied her. "It's okay," she said, as if she were reassuring a child. "It's all right."

David took her hands: they were like ice.

"What in God's name—" Sally's voice broke on the last word and she swallowed and took a deep breath.

"Take it easy," Rosanna said. "You went into trance. It's over now."

Sally stared, the color leaving her face. Her eyes went from Rosanna to David and then around the room with its lamplit shadows. "That's impossible," she said. "I've been in sittings before, and I never—that's impossible." She was shaking all over; even her voice shook. David, wanting to hold her, was afraid of undermining what little poise she had left. He knew she would not want that to happen in front of the medium. He let go of her hands to reach over and stop the tape.

"Let's talk this over," he said, pretending calm. "Maybe we can figure out what happened." He went around the room opening curtains, letting in daylight, then busied himself with the tape recorder, rewinding the tape. When he looked up at last Sally had gotten herself under control. Rosanna had moved away to light a cigarette.

"Okay," he said. "Rosanna, you said that usually you have no memory of what goes on while you're in trance. Was it any different this time?"

"No. I remember starting to go into trance. I always

remember that part. But that's all. The next thing I knew, you were looking at me—very expectantly. Was I saying something important?"

"I thought you were about to. In a minute we'll play the tape. Sally? What about you? Do you remember—going off?"

"No." She was rigid with control, painful to watch. "I remember concentrating on what Rosanna was saying. Then nothing, until"—a breath before she went on—"until I saw the churchyard."

"The churchyard?"

"The one up on the hill."

"Where the Gilfoys are buried? You saw it?"

"Yes."

"And?"

"And nothing. That was all."

"That was all?"

She smiled crookedly. "Sorry." There was a pause, which grew.

"Maybe we could hear that tape now," Rosanna said.

David set the machine in motion.

"About two-ten," Sally said. He ran the tape ahead and then set it to play. They listened. There was the rhythm of Rosanna's breathing, pervasive and hypnotic, and then her voice saying loudly, "There's someone—it's a young man." The sensitive recording needles jumped into the red. "He wants—he wants—" The words broke off and the breathing resumed, a syrupy sound.

David's voice then: "What does he want?"

The breathing went on; David counted the breaths—in, then out. The distorted sound gave a nightmare quality like a surrealist film. He fancied he could hear behind it the creak of a chair or a floorboard, the clock, a faint hiss like air moving. He looked at the faces of the two women opposite him. Rosanna was intent on the tape, hearing the exchange for the first time. Sally, he could see, was forcing herself to concentrate.

"He says he's lost—the lost one." The sound on the tape dropped all at once to normal; he remembered Sally adjusting it. Rosanna was leaning forward now.

His own voice on the tape: "Where does he want to go?"

"Home."

Question, answer, pause, question, pause—and then he heard himself say, "What?" and there was another pause, and then a deep indrawn breath like someone seized without warning in the dark. Sally's face and neck flushed red. "Turn it off," she said. "Please." He reached forward and snapped the machine into muteness.

"Okay," Rosanna said, before the moment had a chance to lengthen. "A lost young man who wants to go home. Does that tell you anything?"

"Well—" David said.

"Wait a minute," Sally said. "Wait a minute. We're acting like amateurs, David. If you've got a hypothesis, for Pete's sake don't tell it to Rosanna. Strictly speaking she shouldn't even have listened to the playback." She looked at them. Her painful blush had subsided for the most part, but there were patches of red still in her cheeks.

"She's right," Rosanna said before he could answer. "You shouldn't discuss it in front of me. Even if it didn't influence the next sitting, we'd never know for sure. I don't think the playback matters, because if I'd been in a waking trance I'd have heard it all anyway. But I shouldn't have asked about the young man—I guess I got a little carried away. The less I know, the better."

David nodded. He knew that, of course; Sally going into trance must have shaken him up more than he realized. He turned to Rosanna.

"On the phone we talked in terms of a couple of days. If it turns out to be longer, can you stay?"

"Maybe. Let's play it by ear." She smiled. "I'd love to be able to send Jack a real big bill."

"What about trying another sitting now?"

"No," the medium said, and he was aware at once that the refusal was for Sally's sake as much as her own. Sally was not ready to face another sitting yet; in her fragile condition there was no telling what might happen. He was so stimulated by the sitting, so eager to make progress on it, that he was being blind to the most obvious facts. He felt a sudden gratitude to Rosanna. "What I'd really like to do right now," she was saying, "is take a nap. These things wear me out."

"I'll take you upstairs," Sally said.

*   *   *

Left to himself, David paced. He wasn't thinking, really, just following a flow of disjointed images: Sally's face with her lips moving in trance, Rosanna's eyes opening suddenly, wide and dark, meeting his. The success of the sitting, even though he was not thinking of it in such specific terms, was what kept him on his feet, moving around the room. He was too agitated to sit still. He paced. Even with the curtains open, the library was not a bright room. The lindens were thickest at this corner of the yard and, by this time of day, the sun was on the other side of the house. He heard Sally come down the stairs; then she was in the doorway.

"I put her in the Thistle Room," she said. "It was the one she wanted."

"Great. Maybe she'll get some action in there."

She busied herself with the tape recorder and he watched, seeing the tension in the bent line of her head and back as she switched the machine off and unplugged it, coiling the cord neatly. He knew she was shocked and humiliated by what had happened—knew she didn't want to talk about it. But they had to. The trance, her vision of the churchyard—what did it mean? He opened his mouth and at the same moment, as if she read his intention and wanted to block it, she said, "What was it you were going to say before—about the young man who's lost?"

Against her determination his resolve slackened. She wouldn't look at him; then she did, full on, face defiant. "Remember? You were about to say something in front of Rosanna?"

"Well," he said. He couldn't force her. "Remember that marker in the churchyard for the guy who was killed at Gettysburg? I forget his name."

"Samuel, I think."

"Samuel. Safe bet—most of them are named Samuel. But he died young. Okay?"

"Okay." She was frowning slightly, not sure where he was heading.

"All right. Listen." The feeling of success was breaking through now, becoming real, a delayed reaction. He was sure he had hit on something. He pushed his hands into his pockets and started to pace. "The young man in the sitting is lost; he wants to go home. Remember Samuel's marker? It was *in memory of*. He isn't really buried there."

"Oh," she said. "I see what you're getting at, but—"

"I know, I'm jumping to conclusions. But it makes sense. He's young. He dies violently, in a strange place. Maybe he was buried in an unmarked grave on the battlefield, maybe he wasn't buried at all. Anyway, it's a crisis situation. And in a crisis situation it's perfectly common for a manifestation to occur a long distance from the scene of death—"

"But crisis phenomena are usually apparitions," Sally said. "And if you discount the green face, which I'm afraid I do, we don't have any reports of apparitions here—just lights and raps and cold drafts. Besides, isn't a crisis apparition usually a one-shot deal—doesn't it appear at the moment of crisis, and that's that? This house has a history of recurrent phenomena."

"Well, but once he got back here, wouldn't the psychic energy of the place be enough to keep him going?" She said nothing and he said, "Well?"

"I don't know. I think it's too soon to hypothesize. It'll only confuse things."

She was right, of course. It was much too soon. But he was already too attached to his hypothesis to let it go so quickly. "Look," he said. "It fits. When I asked how he was lost, the question obviously caused a lot of agitation—enough to break Rosanna's trance. Then you went into trance and saw the churchyard. The whole family is buried there—except for him. The lost one." He spread his hands in triumph.

Sally was twisting the cord of the tape recorder. "There are other Gilfoys missing from the churchyard too. And what about the tramp? He'd have a perfect right to call himself the lost one."

"That damn tramp! I forgot to ask Jack to have him checked out. But anyway, our guy, the lost one, is young."

"The tramp could have been a young man," she said. "Tramps aren't born old."

"Okay, all right." He glanced at the tall clock in the corner. "I'll call Jack tonight."

* * *

To the Victorians, who invented psychical research, the cause of haunting seemed obvious. Spirits of the dead were known to linger in certain places, unable to rest on account of some suffering or injustice experienced there in life or at the moment of death. A number of Victorian ghosts were understandably irate about not receiving a proper burial, and these in some cases announced their presence by an appropriate odor. Apparitions walked the halls or entered rooms through locked doors, intent on their unfinished business. If a ghost had a legitimate complaint and could interest someone among the living in putting matters right, there was a good chance the haunting would stop. Ghosts were reasonable in those days, and plentiful. There was something about the Victorian psyche that scattered them across the landscape like daffodils in spring.

Today, however, most of the theories about haunting repudiate this idea of a conscious ghost. The disturbances are considered to be simply a residue, the echo of emotions or events long past, amplified and prolonged in some way by their physical setting. Frederick Myers called them "mere dream-fancies of the dead," and G.N.M. Tyrrell "idea patterns loosely connected." C. D. Broad finds that the best haunting cases resemble "an aimless mechanical repetition of the dreams or waking fancies of a person brooding over certain incidents and scenes in his past life." Bozzano wonders if all physical objects, a spoon as well as a house, may become invested to some extent with the matrix of events in which they are embedded: to him psychometry is "the haunting of small objects."

Were the Victorians wrong, then? Not entirely, for even today a certain amount of evidence exists on the side of active and conscious haunting, and there are cases for which the echo theory is simply inadequate. Michael Grosso suggests that a particularly traumatic death may be responsible for cases of this kind. "It is conceivable that a delay in the process of the ordinary personality's extinction might occur in some circumstances—for instance, where violent emotions predominate at the time of death." The trauma may fragment the personality, reducing it to a compulsive reenactment of certain moments or events in the past; or perhaps there is merely a

need for the bewildered consciousness, unexpectedly released from its body, to cling to familiar surroundings.
The British mystic Evelyn Underhill compares the clamor
of such transient souls to the crying of gulls at the shores of
the sea and adds, "There is a sameness to all edge-places."

When Rosanna woke up two hours later they gave her a
floor plan and sent her on a tour of the house. It was
strictly against protocol for them to accompany her: even as
professionals they could not be certain of guarding against
unconscious body movements that might betray something
of their knowledge of the house. And so she went alone. Her
copy of the floor plan, once she had marked the areas she
perceived as haunted, would be compared with the ex-
tenants' floor plans for possibly significant correlation.

David and Sally stood out in the street, leaning on the
front gate. It was just nightfall; they could follow Rosanna's
progress as the windows brightened and darkened beyond
the trees. David couldn't check his imagination—he could
almost hear her footsteps as she moved alone through the
silent rooms. For the first time since they had come to
the house he experienced a trace of the uncanny sensation traditionally associated with haunting. He looked
across the yard past the lilacs that hung like lamps in the
twilight. Was the place suddenly awake? A spill of light
from an upstairs window frosted the top of the hedge
between the house and Mrs. Hopkins's next door. The
upstairs sitting room. He pictured the medium there,
moving to the fireplace, to the window. Of all the rooms
in the house, this was the one that best captured what he
thought of (with no pun intended) as the spirit of the
house. The brown velvet seat of the low sofa was worn
through in spots; the pattern of the carpet (some sort of
large white flowers—surely not cabbages—on a pale green
ground) had faded almost to invisibility. Yet there was
something poignant in the shabbiness, the past made
present in a host of little things—a cracked china figure
of a seated child, the fringed curtains, the globe of the
table lamp painted with roses. The whole atmosphere
forbade intrusion. Not surprising, he thought, that it had
kept its essence through a series of tenants.

He glanced at Sally beside him. Already it was too
dark to see her face clearly. Since the sitting she had

been quieter than usual. He knew she was upset, but what could he do? By blundering in, insisting on discussing it, he could only make it worse for her. He was afraid of disturbing the equilibrium they had found in the past few weeks, that had come seemingly from out of nowhere and could as easily return there. Yet he felt he must say something. Her hand lay on the gate; he took it.

"Sally."

"What?" Her voice was so subdued that he felt like an ogre. Speech deserted him; he stood holding her hand. "There's Rosanna," she said then, and looking up he saw the medium standing in the lit doorway of the house, beckoning them in.

She had marked four rooms as haunted, but she explained that the term was relative.

"All old houses have a kind of hum, like a low-grade current—I don't know how else to describe it. If I took that into account, I'd have to mark every room. What I did instead was mark the areas where it seems stronger in relation to the rest of the house—you know what I mean . . .?"

David nodded, looking at the floor plan, remembering the suspicion that had crossed his mind a couple of days before—that the house had been getting on Sally's nerves. *A kind of hum, like a low-grade current.* Downstairs Rosanna had marked the parlor and the little room as haunted, upstairs the sitting room and master bedroom. He noticed that she had not marked the Thistle Room.

"Incidentally," the medium was saying, "did you have a fire recently in that corner bedroom in the back? There's a smoky smell in there."

He glanced at Sally, recalling that she had mentioned a smell of burning undetectable to him. She was examining the floor plan and did not look up. "That may be paranormal," he said to Rosanna. "I'm glad you mentioned it."

"Where do you want to hold the next sitting?" she said.

David considered. "I think the sitting room upstairs." He still did not want to use the master bedroom, not just yet. He was saving it, a treat to look forward to. "Is that okay with you?"

"Sure." She smiled. "It looks comfortable."

He smiled back. He was disappointed that she had not marked the Thistle Room, where the mysterious light known as Tinkerbell had appeared; but the disappointment was minor compared to his general sense of pleasure and excitement. He had not realized how much he had been dreading the possibility that the house was no longer haunted. Rosanna's assurance that it was, along with the afternoon's successful sitting, filled him with buoyancy. He floated at high tide. At last things were going to happen.

➽ 8 ⧸⧸

OR WERE THEY? The following morning after breakfast, when they had gathered in the upstairs sitting room and closed the curtains to block out the sunlight as much as possible, they sat waiting. And waiting. There was time to notice how incongruous the tape recorder looked on the ornate low table where they had placed it, gleams of metal and plastic against the dull sheen of old wood once lovingly cared for. There was time to notice the tremendous racket the birds were making outside, calling and answering, one inanely repeating a refrain that sounded like "Birdy, birdy" in the tree just outside the window. To David the noise evoked bright summer mornings from his childhood, off with a bike and a baseball glove. There was time to remember the color of the bike (blue) and the pleasant feel of supple leather against his palm. He looked over at Rosanna. She sat motionless, hands in her lap, eyes closed. Beyond her Sally sat tense and watchful. Waiting.

Without stirring he let his eyes flick to his watch. They had been like this for nearly fifteen minutes, and there was still no change in Rosanna's breathing, nothing to indicate that she was falling into trance. Nor was there any of what he had felt yesterday as an intensification of the atmosphere, a transformation of her essence from everyday personality into a device used by some power outside herself; in fact, the absence of any such transformation was so complete that he wondered if he had imagined it. Today she was simply someone who had helped to dry the breakfast dishes. He tried to surrender himself to the atmosphere of the room, as she must be doing, but his mind slid along the surfaces. He couldn't

64

concentrate—it might as well have been a dentist's waiting room. Each of his senses clamored comically for attention: he was thirsty, his ankle itched, he thought he could smell lilacs, he could hear his watch ticking; his eyes skimmed colors and textures, followed an invading beam of sunlight that flickered at the carpet's edge . . . He caught himself just drifting into sleep and looked at his watch again. Twenty-five minutes.

A few seconds later Rosanna opened her eyes and shrugged. "I give up," she said. "I'm not getting a thing."

The three of them exchanged looks.

"No problem," David said. He hoped his frustration didn't show; he didn't want to undermine her self-confidence. Over and over again in laboratory situations it had been shown that increased emotional tension caused a sharp decline in psi effects. "We can try again this afternoon, if you're game."

"Sure."

Sally switched off the tape recorder.

"Funny," Rosanna said. She frowned, then shrugged it off. "By the way, I have another room to add to my list of haunted areas. The one I'm sleeping in."

David and Sally both looked at her, then at each other. The Thistle Room.

"Something happened last night?"

"Nothing specific," the medium said. "Just—company."

David was unsure of the etiquette here. Was she expected to work while she was sleeping? "Would you like to change rooms?" he said.

"Not at all." She seemed surprised by the suggestion. "Whatever it is, it's nothing bad."

They separated until lunchtime: Sally off to the local library, David to do a little work on his lecture, Rosanna outside to the bedraggled garden in the northeast corner of the backyard. At lunch, over sandwiches in the kitchen, she reported her findings. There were rose bushes, too long neglected to be producing much in the way of flowers; and buried under a thick growth of ivy there was a sundial, its face black with grime, the pointer broken off.

David remembered something. "Were there any bricks?"

"Bricks? There's a sort of brick walk, just a little circle around the sundial."

"Any loose ones?"

Rosanna raised her eyebrows. "I didn't really look."

"One of the neighborhood kids claims somebody threw a brick at him from an attic window," he explained. "The house isn't brick. But if there are bricks on the property—"

"Probably what gave him the idea," Sally said. "He's got imagination, that kid. Isn't he the one who saw the green face?"

"Green face?" Rosanna's eyebrows were up again.

"Didn't we tell you about that?" David finished his sandwich and reached for the coffee. "It comes and goes. You'll get used to it."

They sat around the table drinking coffee; Rosanna lit a cigarette. David was ready to begin the afternoon sitting, but Rosanna appeared to be in no hurry and he did not want to seem to be pressuring her. She and Sally were talking about a mutual acquaintance at the lab whom he knew only slightly, and the conversation did not arouse his interest. At last he got up and began to clear the dishes off the table and pile them in the sink. Sally glanced at him, but Rosanna went on with her cigarette, watching the curl of the smoke in silence. Finally she looked across the table at Sally, then over at David, then down at the table.

"I'm not sure how to put this," she said. David's first thought was that she had sensed his disappointment this morning and was going to use it as an excuse to back out. Mediums were so damnably touchy—the least little thing— but she was saying something and he listened, standing by the sink.

"I've been thinking about this morning's sitting, and it just doesn't make sense. That room is active. There's a lot there. But it couldn't get through—something was blocking it." She looked up at Sally and hesitated. Then: "I think it was you."

In the pause that followed, David heard the faucet drip, fat bead of water landing in a brimming cup with an obscene sound. He reached over and wrenched the handle.

"I don't mean you're doing it on purpose," Rosanna said. "But probably because of what happened yesterday—"

"You're probably right," Sally said. Her voice was expressionless; her face, turned toward Rosanna, was only partly visible to David. "I'll be glad to sit out, if you think it'll help."

"It might," Rosanna said. She made a movement as if to reach across the table to Sally, but didn't, and looked at David instead. He felt urged to say something, make some move, some decisive gesture. Afraid of hurting Sally, he was at the same time certain that Rosanna was right. But Sally might be relieved to be excluded from the sittings, and even if she wasn't, they could hardly ask the medium to stay here wasting time. He heard his voice in the air almost before he was aware of speaking.

"We can give it a try," he said.

"My name is Andy."

David's hands tightened on the arms of his chair. The voice came from Rosanna's lips, but as in the first sitting it sounded huskier than her normal speaking voice. Was the inflection slightly different? He wasn't sure. The stillness that filled the sitting room was as oppressive as the rising temperature; the creak of his chair seemed deafening as he shifted his weight.

"Can you help us?" he said.

A pause, then: "I'll try."

David glanced at the tape recorder to make sure it was picking up their voices, watched the needles jump reassuringly as he said, "We want to know the identity of the young man who calls himself the lost one."

A long wait this time. Rosanna's breathing, slow and audible until now, began to quicken. The tempo became uneven. He watched her lips part and close again; once her eyelids trembled and he was afraid she was coming out of trance, but her eyes did not actually open. He wondered if he had asked too much of Andy, began casting around for a way to rephrase the question. But before he found it, the answer came.

"The young man you are thinking of is no longer here. He is at peace. He has forgotten his life on this side."

This was a puzzle. "You mean he isn't lost anymore?"

"He is with loved ones."

David tried a different tack. "Was his death a violent one? Does the memory distress him?"

"He has forgotten all that now. He is with loved ones."

"I see." He resisted the urge to swear. The problem

was that you couldn't ask a spirit control what in hell it meant. Reasonable explanations were not something spirits excelled at. Under pressure they tended to proffer reams of nonsense, or else depart in a huff. But how could a spirit be lost and homeless one day and at peace with his loved ones the next? The nonsense of it intrigued him. "Can I communicate with him? Will he talk to me?"

A lengthy silence: the answer was apparently no. "Andy?" David said. More silence. He wondered if he had committed some faux pas by afterlife standards; there was no way of knowing. He gave up and brought Rosanna out of trance the way he had seen her bring Sally, by holding the back of her neck and speaking her name. When she opened her eyes he said, "We've got a mystery here."

She looked surprised. "What happened? I was in trance, wasn't I? I remember going off—"

"We'll play the tape back," he said. "You'll see what I mean."

He called Sally in and they listened to the tape. There was no sound distortion as there had been in the library and in consequence the entire playback seemed less eerie. To David the difference between Rosanna's normal voice and her Andy voice was less pronounced on tape than it had seemed during the sitting. No one spoke during the playback. When it was over he said, "Well, does everybody agree there's something funny going on?" He looked at Sally. She was frowning.

Rosanna said, "I made contact with this young man yesterday. You mean to tell me he's all straightened out by today?"

"I didn't say it," David pointed out. "Andy did."

"Well, it doesn't make sense."

"Is Andy pulling our leg?"

She shook her head. "He doesn't do things like that."

"Well—" David broke off and shrugged. "I'm stumped, then. Where do we go from here?"

No one seemed to know. At last Rosanna went off to take her post-sitting nap. When she had gone Sally closed the sitting room door and turned to face him.

"You know, she shouldn't be listening to these playbacks. It's completely contrary to procedure."

"Well, but it's true that if she'd been in waking trance

she would have heard it anyway." It wasn't much of a defense and he knew it. He needed to get a grip on himself, be more professional about this. "You're right," he said. "Next time we'll kick her out."

They played the tape again, but it offered no inspiration. David started to pace.

"What's with this guy? Yesterday he was the lost one. Today he's blissfully happy. Is he some kind of post-mortem schizophrenic, or did we really manage to contact him yesterday just before he caught the last train to paradise? Why should he kick up enough fuss to send nine different sets of people packing, over a period of fifty years, and then suddenly decide—between yesterday and today—to forget the whole thing?"

She had no suggestions.

"Okay," he said. "If he's lost again tomorrow we'll know he's a crackpot."

"Maybe Andy's the crackpot," she said.

"Rosanna says not."

"Is that reliable?"

He looked at her sitting on the sofa. The sun was low and the room swam with light. She sat with one arm along the back of the sofa, absently stroking the worn fabric; strands of her hair glinted in the light. "Don't you like her?" he said.

Sally blinked. "What's that got to do with it?"

"Nothing, I guess. But Jack says she's absolutely trustworthy. *Do* you like her?"

"Of course I do."

But he wasn't sure. There was a wariness in her attitude toward Rosanna, more than just Sally's usual reserve or her distaste for mediums in general. He wasn't sure what had made her agree to the idea of bringing in a medium at all. And then that business at lunch, about her blocking Rosanna's trance—that hadn't helped.

What was she doing while we were shut up in here together without her? What was she feeling?

Was she jealous? For a moment he wondered. But that was crazy. He did think Rosanna was sexy—the psychic gift always acted as a kind of theoretical aphrodisiac with him, if the psychic in question happened to be young and female—but thoughts were a long way from actions in his case, as Sally of all people knew best. It had never seemed to bother her before. And he couldn't believe it did now. More likely it was just a general sense of being left out. Not surprising that she wanted to exclude Rosanna from the playbacks, probably less for proper procedure than as a way of evening the score. He leaned forward to remove the tape from the machine; the movement brought him close to her and he reached out and touched her hand. She smiled, but her eyes glanced off his and he wished, for perhaps the millionth time since he had known her, that he could read her mind.

⇶ 9 ⇷

THEY SPENT THE EVENING downstairs in the parlor. Rosanna had explored the library and come up with some surprises: several books on demonology, a medical text entitled *Anatomy of the Cat,* and a small book of excruciatingly bad poetry bound in mottled green leather. She insisted on reading some of it aloud, with much expression:

> "When May bedecks the naked trees
> With tassels and embroideries . . ."

David, laughing more at her dramatic delivery than the words themselves, was thinking how lucky it was that she was so agreeable, when she could just as easily have been moody and theatrical, spouting a lot of nonsense about the Beyond. Sally could not put up with that—nor, for long, could he. Professional psychics were, after all, notoriously shady characters, even when their powers were genuine: people had had their pockets picked in sittings with one well-known medium. But Rosanna was a different breed. She was friendly but not too friendly, she had a sense of humor; and best of all, she had made real coffee for them this morning. He liked the clicking of beads in her hair when she threw back her head to laugh, the classic combination of white teeth and dark skin. He liked her professionalism, the easy confidence she brought to the sittings. But the sittings were the problem. It was not her fault, but the sittings were going nowhere. She had finished the poem; she and Sally were marveling at it. He came to a decision.

"Rosanna. How would you feel about another sitting, late tonight?"

"How late?"

"Say around midnight."

"Okay with me," the medium said.

He got up from his chair, stretched. "I think it's about time we tried the master bedroom," he said.

It was nearly twenty past twelve when they finally got underway: David was having trouble with his equipment. The overhead light in the master bedroom did not work. Neither did the desk lamp; he commandeered one from another room. Then there were wiring problems. He had trouble finding enough active outlets for the lamp, the tape recorder, and the other equipment he planned to keep in operation during the sitting—instruments such as the self-recording thermometer which ran constantly in this room in a so-far vain effort to capture a paranormal drop in temperature. Rosanna and Sally helped him set things up. The chill in the room, although the thermometer as usual refused to register it, was apparent to all of them; and by the time everything was ready their hands were numb. David glanced at the thermometer's revolving drum for the tenth time.

"Damndest thing."

The two women were shivering. He blew on his hands.

"Look, this is silly. There's no point in freezing when we've got a working fireplace right here. I'm going to make a fire."

Rosanna shrugged. "Why not? It already smells like one."

He wondered if Sally smelled it too; he did not. But if she did she said nothing. He remembered a woodpile by the back steps, and they all went down for logs. By the time they had brought up half a dozen, twisted a newspaper into spills and started the first flames going, it seemed warmer, whether from their exertions or the fire's actual heat it was impossible to say. David stood back, pleased, holding out his hands to the beginning blaze. Around him the shadows danced. "That's more like it."

He had brought chairs in earlier. Now they set up the tape recorder and Sally left the room, closing the door behind her. He and Rosanna sat down.

The silence was slow to settle in. The burning logs

popped and shot showers of sparks that fell with a tiny crepitating sound on the hearthstone, and there was a muffled twittering somewhere; he thought with chagrin that the fire was probably smoking out a family of birds with a nest in the chimney. Still, if that were the only disaster he would be lucky. The whole house might be smoked out as well; it had not occurred to him that the chimney might be blocked. But it seemed to be drawing all right. The twittering died away at last; the logs sub-sided to a faint hissing, and he sat looking across at Rosanna and the firelight moving on her face. She was relaxed in her chair, breathing rhythmically, the indrawn breaths all but inaudible and the exhalations a series of deep sighs. There was not a sound from outside the room—he wondered briefly what Sally was doing—and inside only Rosanna's breathing and the soft crackling of the flames. He no longer felt the cold. He checked the tape recorder and settled back in his chair to wait.

The darkness outside the window made this sitting different from the earlier ones, in which he had been very much aware of the maneuverings of sunlight through the curtains. The fire too made a difference. The lamp on the desk had a 40-watt bulb, and the fire did more or less as it pleased in the room, flinging shadows around like veils, imaging itself brightly in places both traditional and unexpected: the brass doorknob, the lampstand, the bed's polished headboard, the clear plastic window of the tape recorder and the metal rim of the thermometer's spinning drum. The floorboards in front of the hearthstone were a clear flickering gold. He found himself remembering a fragment from an anthropology book: *Firelight does not dispel darkness. It just shows things in the darkness while the darkness is still there.*

As if answering his thought, the bulb of the lamp blew out at that instant with a flash and a soft pop, making him jump. By an effort of will he kept himself from swearing aloud. He looked at Rosanna: her breathing had begun to alter, signifying the beginning of trance. The ruddy light sketched her face dramatically now; the lamp had been giving more illumination than he thought. He reached over and tried screwing the bulb more tightly into its socket, burning his fingers in the process; it was still hot, but unquestionably dead.

Now what? He had forgotten a flashlight—a stupid oversight, since the presence of psi often resulted in power failures or at least erratic behavior on the part of electrical equipment. By bending close to the tape recorder he managed to ascertain that it was still running. That made it seem probable that the bulb's failure was simply an unlucky coincidence. Still, he would have liked to have the lamp on. There was something highly unscientific about firelight; his jumping pulse told him that. During daylight, or in some other room, it would hardly have mattered, but now suddenly all the stories about this particular room came crowding into his head. He was considering bringing Rosanna out of trance and starting over when she began to mutter and move her head. Too late now.

The guttural whispering went on for nearly a minute. Andy did not announce his presence as was customary, and finally David decided to take the initiative. "Andy?" he said.

The whispering stopped. There was silence: he waited, wondering. Then a voice—not Rosanna's, nor did it sound like Andy's—said, "Week after week . . . week after week . . ."

It was a woman's voice, high pitched and complaining. David kept quiet, scarcely breathing. Was this some moment from the past, reverberating continuously in this room and accessible to those, like Rosanna, with the ability to perceive it? Did he believe that? He thought he did. The voice went on: "Can't you stop? Can't you just . . . stop?" But where was Andy? And the lost one? Reverberating moments were all very well, but this room was his high card, the one he was counting on . . .

"It doesn't," said whatever was using Rosanna's vocal cords—a departed spirit or a mindless psychophysical residue embedded in the structure of the house or, as the psychologists said, a part of Rosanna's subconscious acting the role—"It doesn't, it isn't, it doesn't, it isn't—" and then the communication was broken off suddenly, brutally, as if someone had slammed a door. Rosanna made a choking noise; her lips twisted but no sound came. David could see her eyes moving back and forth under their lids. She seemed to be trying desperately to speak; her lips struggled to shape words but still none came, only uneven gasps like a fugitive's breathing. In the firelight her face had a golden sheen of sweat. The trance was like Sally's had been, that first afternoon in the library—something frightening about it, as if she were being forcibly subdued. He leaned forward, watching her apprehensively. Should he wake her? But she was experienced, after all, not like Sally; and he did not want to drive away whatever it was that had taken such urgent possession of her. He watched her, uncertainty paralyzing him. The door of the room opened suddenly and Sally stood there, silhouetted against the bright-lit hallway outside. She started to speak; he held up a hand to silence her. Then all at once something screamed, half with Rosanna's voice and half with its own.

"No!"

The sound tearing through the still house.

"No!"

jerking him to his feet. He felt a chill go over him and sweat break out on top of it, turning to ice on his skin. At the same moment he imagined the recording index jumping into the red, and wondered at his two selves: the physical man and the intellectual one, shuddering with animal terror and worrying about the quality of his tape recording. And still another, separate from those two and speculating about them.

"Lost—"

The word coalesced the three Davids into one. He bent over the medium. "Samuel?" he said. "Samuel?"

Tears ran from under her closed lids, sliding down her cheeks in tracks that glistened in the firelight. He bent closer, trying to hear what she was saying, but it was the same word over and over—"Lost."

Then Sally was beside him. "We've got to stop this, David."

"Okay, okay. But she said herself she doesn't feel anything when she's in trance—"

"She said she doesn't *remember* anything."

"Well, it's the same thing. I mean—"

"It is not." She was staring at Rosanna and he saw her swallow. "What happened to the lights?" she said.

"The bulb blew."

Rosanna took a long sobbing breath and Sally said, "David—"

Defeated, he leaned close to the medium and clasped the back of her neck. It was clammy. "Rosanna."

But it was the other one who answered him.

"No," it said, and then screamed, "No!" Rosanna's body wrenched forward so violently that her flung tears struck his face. He almost lost his balance; his hand slipped from her neck. She twisted sideways and then back; the chair rocked on its legs. A sound, half shriek and half sob, jerked from her, then she sagged forward limply and David caught her to keep her from hitting the floor, his eyes meeting Sally's in something like panic. "Now what?" he said, holding his voice even.

She shook her head mutely. In the theatrical light her eyes looked enormous: he knew she was imagining herself in Rosanna's place. The medium's body, inert now, hung in his arms. He was concentrating on easing her back into the chair when it seemed to him that Sally slammed the door hard—a loud bang that startled him into almost losing his grip on Rosanna. "What the hell!" he said. But Sally was right there beside him—and the door, when he twisted around to look, was still open to the hall. Their eyes met just as it came again, a hollow boom that seemed to emanate from the walls around them. *The raps go with the cold.* Beneath the panic a spark of exultation stirred. His high card was an ace.

"David—" Sally was staring at Rosanna. He looked down and saw a trickle of blood running from the medium's nose.

"Christ," he said. He looked wildly around for something to staunch the blood. No third bang had followed the first two, but the anticipation of it stretched the air taut.

"We've got to get her out of here," Sally said through clenched teeth. He found his own clenched too; belatedly he realized that the room was viciously cold. His stomach felt queasy.

He said: "I've got to stay here and observe—"

Her voice jumped registers. "Just get her out into the hall."

He lifted Rosanna from the chair and turned toward

the door. In spite of her smallness he had trouble holding her, his muscles watery and loose. The door seemed far away. Then behind him the fire snapped and rippled like a curtain of hot wind—jerking his head around he saw one of the logs upend and crash across the hearthstone, bursting flame. Sally, white-faced, grabbed the poker and thrust it back; cascades of sparks flew. He was between the bed and the door; he dumped Rosanna unceremoniously on the dusty mattress and ran to Sally. The fire was roaring, flames reaching the carving beneath the mantelpiece, searing the wood: he snatched the poker out of her hand and began to beat at the logs in a frenzy, sending sparks everywhere. Chunks of burning wood scattered and fell into the deep ash left by the newspaper. He kicked the ashes, smothering flames, backing the fire into a corner like an animal at bay, using his feet and the poker to bury the logs in ash. Hissing, the fire began to die: impossible not to hear malevolence in that sound. He looked down at his blackened sneakers, then at Sally. She looked back. Was it over? There was a hot lump of tension still in his chest and he could not stop shaking. Around them the house was full of heavy silence. They stood in the path of light from the open door, watching the pale ashes drift noiselessly in the darkness. The room was unmercifully cold. Then, somewhere nearby, a dog howled. David jumped to the window, flung it open and bellowed, "Shut up!" The heat in his chest dissipated; he felt better almost immediately. The howling stopped. He leaned on the sill, feeling the tension leave him as the cold air of the room flowed past him into the summer night.

It was over. Turning back into the room he surveyed the scene. The fireplace was a mess. Sally was standing by the tape recorder; he was about to ask her if it was still running when a sound from the bed made him jump and start shaking all over again—he had completely forgotten Rosanna. Sally turned too. The medium's eyes opened as they reached her and he saw them go from him to Sally; then she sat up slowly. Her nose had stopped bleeding, but her mouth and chin were blood-streaked. She looked around the darkened room, shivering.

"It's cold. What happened?"

David let his breath out. "Were you aware of anything . . . unusual?"

"No." She licked her lips, grimaced, touched her face. Her hand came away sticky; she examined it. Then she looked at them again. "I gather there was something."

"Well," he said. He looked at Sally and tried to smile. She tried in answer—then sat down so abruptly on the edge of the bed that he could tell her knees had given way. "You might say so," he said.

⋙ 10 ⋘

By the next morning, when they had slept late and breakfasted later, sitting around the kitchen table finishing bacon and eggs and a second pot of Rosanna's coffee, the night's scare had diminished to the level of an adventure—one with enough spice to keep them discussing it. To David, there in the daylight among pots and pans and the smells of bacon and good coffee, the important thing was that they had finally achieved some results. The raps were on tape; the self-recording thermometer had registered a drop to 41 degrees Fahrenheit between 12:40 and 12:48. Downstairs in the library—and this was possibly related, just as possibly coincidental—the brass crouching-dog inkwell had fallen off the table. His high card had paid off indeed. His own dose of panic during the sitting seemed a small price to pay, although the recollection made him uncomfortable and he promised himself privately to keep his head next time.

Rosanna's attitude, interested and completely unafraid, pleased him immensely. She wanted to hear all the details. It disturbed her not at all that an unknown entity had moved her body, spoken with her vocal cords, even used her tears.

"It's happened before," she said. "Well, not to this extent—the nosebleed was something new. But in effect it happens every time Andy takes control during a sitting. It's just a question of degree."

"Telergy," David said. He was delighted to find her so matter-of-fact; he hoped it was as reassuring to Sally as it was to him. Sally had been badly shaken—seeing herself, he knew, in Rosanna's place. She hadn't said much and he didn't think she had slept much. "It's a term coined by

79

Myers in one of his books to mean the operation of the brain's motor centers by an outside mind."

Rosanna was nodding. "And you say this outside mind just butted in?"

"Seemed that way. There was some sort of low-frequency gibberish and then there he was."

"The lost one."

"Yeah. He seemed to bypass Andy completely. Like he was so anxious to communicate that he couldn't be bothered to use the proper channels." David leaned back in his chair, remembering. "You know, I think we've got hold of some kind of nut job. I mean, is he lost or is he at peace? He can't seem to make up his mind." He glanced questioningly at Sally.

"He didn't seem at peace to me," she said.

Her heartfelt tone made him smile. All's well that ends well. "I meant to ask you," he said. "What made you show up when you did?"

She looked blank. "Didn't you call me?"

"No."

"I thought—I guess I heard Rosanna scream."

He was fairly sure that she had appeared before Rosanna had screamed. But he was not absolutely certain, and there was no point making a fuss about it. He let it go for now.

After breakfast he went up to look at the master bedroom, taking along a broom, a dustpan, and a garbage bag. When he opened the door the cold was scarcely noticeable, something you might dismiss as a morning chill, unless you knew better. Not much remained of the previous night's hullabaloo—streaks of soot and ash on the floor, a bloodstain on the ancient mattress. Shades of Victorian wedding nights. He grinned and began to sweep the ashes into the fireplace; then knelt on the hearth-stone and used the dustpan as a shovel to fill the garbage bag. Ashes floated around him. He coughed, wondering what had made the fire flare up like that. That had been the moment when he had felt the situation beyond his control. Paranormal? At the time he hadn't doubted that the sudden burst of flame was caused by the same force that had taken possession of Rosanna, but today the connection seemed less clear. He leaned into the fire-place, trying to look up the chimney. Was it possible something had fallen into the fire, an old bird's nest, for instance?

He could see nothing at first, then a possible glint of daylight far above. The cramped position was making him dizzy. Light and dark swam together; the chill seeped over his skin. Blackened bricks surrounded him.

All at once, right next to his ear, a voice whispered something unintelligible.

He jumped and lost his balance, bumping the left side of his head on the edge of a brick, sitting down hard on the hearthstone. The fireplace loomed before him, blackly beckoning, like the mouth of a tunnel. He stared into it, rubbing his head, shivering a little, his eyes light and empty. His temple stung. He could not remember where he was or what he had been doing.

"David?"

Sally was coming down the hall. Memory flooded back into him. What was he doing just sitting here? He was supposed to be cleaning up last night's mess. He shook himself, picked up the dustpan and scooped ashes. She stopped in the door of the room and he looked up. She was staring at him.

"What have you done to yourself?" she said.

"What?"

"It's soot, I guess. You look like a chimney sweep."

He looked down: his knees were black, his hands, probably his face too. "Christ," he said.

She was laughing. "They're supposed to be good luck," she said.

He brandished the dustpan. "I'm a scientist. We don't believe in luck."

In the early afternoon the three of them went out to mail the tape from the sitting. Sally had transcribed it and David had written an accompanying report, which they both initialed. The dispassionate language of the report bore little resemblance to the actual sitting. David had described the raps as "loud percussive noises emanating from no clear direction" and the lost one's violent possession of Rosanna as "an apparent instance of Myers's concept of telergy." The light bulb's failure, the flareup of the fire, and Rosanna's nosebleed were mentioned as "possibly paranormal in nature." It all sounded respectably stuffy. But David, who had read hundreds of such reports and was well aware of the volumes contained between the lines, could not help feeling that the neat brown package containing tape and report was infinitely precious; and he carried it carefully as they went out the front gate and turned right, up the hill.

Across the street a group of kids turned to stare. One of them waved and David waved back.

"Bobby, scryer of green faces," he said to Rosanna. "Nice kid."

"They're all nice kids," Sally said. "Every time we come out of the house, they're so glad to see us alive."

"Well, after all. Remember how you felt about haunted houses when you were a kid?"

"There was one on my block," Rosanna said.

"There was one on everybody's block."

The overhanging lindens let down a filigree of light onto the sidewalk. The houses on Lilac Street were old, set far apart, for the most part behind hedges or picket fences. A bicycle lay on its side in one yard; in another a small girl clutching a kitten watched them pass without acknowledging David's wave.

Near the top of the hill the mailbox waited. David dropped his package in and stepped back, satisfied. Rosanna was looking beyond him to the crest of the hill.

"Pretty church. Have you been inside?"

"Only the churchyard."

"Oh." The medium turned to Sally. "This is the one you saw in trance?"

Sally's nod was curt.

"Let's see if the church is open," David said.

They went toward it, passing the churchyard deep in green shadow. Sally slowed, then stopped.

"Wait a minute. Weren't they . . . ?" She was looking at the trees in the churchyard and frowning. "I thought they were elms."

"Elms?" David looked up at them. His knowledge of trees fell into two categories: Christmas trees and other trees. "Well, aren't they?"

She put one hand on top of her head as if to anchor it, like a hat in a wind. "No. They aren't. I must be nuts. They're sycamores."

Rosanna said, "There aren't many elms in New England now. Most of them died from Dutch elm disease."

"That's right," Sally said. "I knew that. Then why did I think—?"

"Anybody can get mixed up."

"But they're completely different. The leaves, the bark, the shape of the whole tree . . ." Her voice trailed off and then came back. "I could swear . . ."

David was looking ahead at the church door. "Come on," he said. "It's open."

Inside it was light and quiet, rows of empty wooden pews stretching down to the altar rail. The windows, tall and narrow and delicately curved at the top, were paned with clear glass that let in the sun; the white-painted walls caught and contained the light, and the whole small place seemed suspended in a breathless brightness. There were fragments of color here and there: the red and gold marker hanging from the open Bible on the lectern stirred slowly in the breeze from the open door, and as David moved down the aisle gleams of light ran along the backs of the pews.

"Very New England," he said, deliberately resisting the spell. Rosanna opened the door to a pew and sat down. He hoped she wasn't going to start praying: religion embarrassed him. He looked around for Sally, but she had gone back outside.

"Yeah—puritanical." It seemed he need not have worried about Rosanna. As he watched she bounced up and down slightly on the wooden seat and made a face. "No cushions."

He entered the pew and sat down at her side. He had expected to find a minister or official of some sort, but except for the two of them the place seemed deserted. The lack of supervision charmed him, evidence that they were in a small town.

"Did you ever have a religious phase?" Rosanna said, as if answering his unvoiced feeling of a minute before.

"No. It was always a bore to me. We went to church, but it was always just a waste of Sunday morning." He leaned back. She was right; the pew was uncomfortable. "Did you?"

"Did I! When I was twelve my parents sent me to church camp. I fell in love with one of the counselors."

"That's not religion," he said, smiling.

"Sure it was. I worshiped her. Her name was Janet and she had long red hair and freckles. Of course it was against the rules for me to be in love with her, so I had to be in love with Jesus instead."

"And were you?"

"Nope. I pretended I was. But it was Janet all the time."

"How long did it last?" he said.

"She went back to college at the end of the summer. I wrote to her but she never wrote back. I got a card from her at Christmas, though. She was a nice girl."

"And the next summer? You met a lifeguard and forgot all about her?"

"I never really forgot her." She was looking straight ahead as she spoke, the memory so vividly imprinted on her face that for an instant he felt the ache of the unanswered letter, the bittersweet Christmas card. He had a sudden unaccountable urge to kiss her. His arm was already resting along the back of the pew behind her; it was a simple matter to lean forward and intercept her mouth as she turned to say something. She didn't resist, but after a moment he felt her lips smile under his. Then they were apart. He was unsure whether she had freed herself or he had let her go; she was still smiling and he felt himself smile back. Nonetheless he wasn't quite sure what to say. It seemed like a good time to go outside.

"Let's see what Sally's up to." He slid out of the pew and held the door open for her. Following her out of the church he found himself sweating, his hands shaking a little, thoughts in a spin.

What the hell came over me? Of course she's attractive. But what a stupid, unprofessional thing to do. I must be out of my mind.

Possible scenarios, all horrifying, occurred to him. She could have gotten angry, just when they were starting to get some action in the house. Worse, she could have responded, presenting him with a problem he had neither the desire nor the ability to solve. The more he thought about it, the more insane the impulse seemed to him. He felt less shame, less guilt—suppose Sally had walked in right at that moment?—than simple shock. What had come over him? It was almost as if the recent nights of shadowy erotic dreams had been quietly rearranging his subconscious, moving all the furniture around so that he had suddenly stumbled up against something unexpected in the dark. He wiped his palms on his jeans as he stepped out into the sunshine. No harm done, he supposed. But he'd better watch his step.

Rosanna stood in front of the church gazing up at the steeple, shading her eyes with one hand. The street was empty.

"Where's Sally?" he said, and she nodded toward the churchyard. Looking over the iron fence he saw Sally walking along a row of gravestones. She did not seem to be reading the inscriptions, nor even to be fully aware of her surroundings; her movements, and the glimpse he had of her face as she reached the end of the row and turned, were intensely preoccupied. He started to open the gate. Behind him Rosanna said, "Wait a minute."

"What for?"

"Let her find what she's looking for."

He glanced back at her. "How do you know she's looking for something?"

"Hunch." She was watching Sally closely now. He looked at her and then at Sally, who had stopped and was standing still. In the green dappled shade her motionless figure flickered like one of the shadows. As he watched, gripping the bars of the gate, she moved forward and then knelt suddenly, plunging both hands into the lush grass. Rosanna was beside him then.

"Come on," she said. "Let's see what she's got."

He opened the gate—not thinking, just obeying—and they went in, threading their way among the rows of graves until they reached her. She looked up.

"There's something here—another stone, I think. It's fallen over."

David knelt beside her and looked: the edge of a stone protruded a few inches from the ground where her hands held back the grass. "Sure enough," he said. "How'd you find it?"

"I—" She reddened. "I'm not sure."

The three of them looked at one another. Sally seemed almost apologetic. Excitement washed through David.

"Let's see what it says."

They had to dig. Grass and soil had almost completely

covered the fallen marker, although from the angle at which it lay David conjectured that none of it could be more than a few inches underground. Still, the tangle of grass roots was stubborn and in a few minutes they had made little progress. Their hands were filthy and one of Rosanna's knuckles was bleeding from a scrape on the edge of the stone. David slapped his pockets and came up with keys, which he used to saw the tougher roots. "Australopithecus," he said. "Tool-using Man." Even so, it took several minutes more to clear one end; then at last they could see letters, carved on the face of the stone and filled now with soil. David scraped frantically with the keys. Then:

"I'll be damned. I'll be damned."

Worn, cracked, filthy but legible nonetheless after wind and rain and time and the creeping tenacious roots of grass, the letters spelled out a name: *Julian Gilfoy*. And underneath: *1885–1906*.

"Excuse me. Excuse me!"

Tall and thin, gray-haired, white shirt, black trousers, suspenders. The man could not, David decided, be anyone else but a New England sexton, and understandably an irate one. He rose to his feet and thought better of offering a dirty hand.

"Good afternoon. I'm David Curtiss. I can assure you we're really not grave robbers . . ." His smile did not win any response, so he went on quickly: "The fact is, we seem to have discovered a lost grave."

"What's that you say?" The sexton came closer, peering down at the stone. "A lost grave?"

"The stone was half buried," Sally said. "My husband tripped over it." She ignored David's look.

"Julian Gilfoy," Rosanna said helpfully to the sexton, who was bending closer to the stone. "There seem to be a lot of Gilfoys buried here. Are they a prominent family in Skipton?"

"Used to be," the man said. "Used to be." For a moment he seemed to drift; then he straightened suddenly. "But see here. I can't have you folks digging around like this in the churchyard. First thing you know—"

"We understand perfectly," David said. "The least we

can do is help you set this stone back in place. I suppose you wouldn't happen to have a spade?"

"Spade?" The sexton looked blank for a moment. "Yes, I—a spade. I'll get it."

He went off toward the back of the church building.

"That wasn't too terrific a line about grave robbing," Rosanna said to David. "With your current address, we'll be lucky if we don't get stoned, or whatever it is they do nowadays to witches."

"Don't worry. The green face will protect us."

They were half consciously abstaining from talking about the grave before the sexton returned, aware that they could hardly continue such a conversation in his presence. But among the three of them, David standing, Sally and Rosanna still on their knees beside the stone, there was a tautness of expectation stretched almost to the snapping point. Rosanna pulled up a long blade of grass, put it between her thumbs and blew—an eerie and mournful screech that made the other two jump.

"Sorry," she said, and threw it away.

"Let's behave ourselves," David said. "Here he comes."

With the spade things went faster, but not much. The sexton seemed determined to give the whole procedure respectability by his participation, and he insisted on doing the digging himself. It was a slow, deliberate process. David stood and chewed his lip and counted to a hundred and eighty and watched the sun shimmering on the rose-colored shingles of the steeple. Here beneath the sycamores it was cool and pleasant. In order to fill the silence that contained only the scrape of the spade against stone and the soft fall of earth, he said, "Hot out today. It's nice here in the shade."

The sexton paused in his task, sitting back on his heels to look up and around him at the trees, and David cursed himself mentally.

"Yep. These trees are real beauties. Helped plant 'em myself, forty-fifty years ago."

"Did you really?" Rosanna said. There was something wicked in her politeness.

"Sure did. They weren't much taller than I was then. That was a long time ago. Now they're near as big as the elms were."

As the elms were. It seemed to David that the shiver

passing through him was an outward thing, something that shook the whole churchyard like a wind in the leaves, silencing the birds and stilling the movement of sunbeams on the grass.

"What elms?" he said, looking only at the sexton.

"It was all elms in this churchyard fifty years ago," the old man said. "They died in two-three months, every last one of them. I saw them die. It was the Dutch elm that got 'em—got all the elms in town. There's not a one left." He began to dig again. David looked at Sally; Rosanna was looking at her too. She reached out and put her hand on Sally's wrist, and at the touch Sally's lips tightened but she did not look up, keeping her eyes fixed on the sexton bent over his spade. David saw her swallow.

The digging was finished. David was allowed to assist in heaving the marker upright; Rosanna and Sally packed soil behind to brace it. Then they all stood and looked. Clumps of moist earth and roots still clung to the face of the stone. Below the name and date were several lines, worn shallow and almost illegible. Sally dropped to her knees again, brushing away crumbs of soil from the inscription, following the carved lines with her fingers. Hesitantly she began to read aloud, her hand moving across the stone as if she were blind.

"The night . . . is . . . dark . . . and I . . . am far from home . . . Lead Thou . . . me on."

The words dropped solemnly into the lime-colored air, seeming to float on the stillness for a moment after she had stopped speaking. Then they were gone, and high overhead the leaves rustled in a light wind.

"The lost one," Rosanna said. "My God." She held out her arm to David. "Look. Goose bumps."

"Me too," he said.

The sexton stood holding his spade, looking from one to the other. Sally had not moved, and when David touched her shoulder she flinched as if he had struck her.

⇛ *11* ⇚

IT WAS WITH DIFFICULTY that David restrained himself on the walk home down the hill. He wanted to shout, run, do handsprings (he did not know how to do handsprings) —offer some physical expression of his jubilation. Because the magic, the impossible had happened. It was Sally's trance vision of the churchyard that had shown her the elms, trees that had existed in Julian Gilfoy's lifetime but had died and been cut down long before she was born. And in the churchyard, the way she had been drawn to the grave itself like a magnet, not knowing why, until the inscription identified Julian as the young man who called himself the lost one. It was a clear violation of the laws of everyday reality as set forth in Broad's Basic Limiting Principle Number Four. *After the death of the body, the personal consciousness associated with it throughout life either ceases to exist or ceases to be able to manifest its existence to the living* . . . Following Sally and Rosanna into the house, he closed the front door behind him and let out an Indian war whoop that made them turn and stare. He could feel the stark idiocy of the grin on his face. "Have we got any champagne?" he said.

They had to make do with coffee. David was too keyed up to sit with the other two at the kitchen table; he paced instead. Sally's shock seemed to have worn off and they all talked at once.

"There's just one thing I don't get," David said. "Why did Andy give us a bum steer? He said the lost one was happy, that he'd forgotten his life on this side. And it seems pretty clear, from what happened last night and this afternoon, that Andy was wrong."

89

Rosanna frowned. "That's not possible. You must have misunderstood him."

"I understood him all right. It's just that his information was wrong."

"I can settle this," Sally said. She put her cup down and went out. They heard her go upstairs. When she returned she was carrying the notebook that contained transcriptions of the sitting tapes. "It's all in here," she said.

There was silence as she turned the pages.

"Okay, here it is. David says: *We want to know the identity of the young man who calls himself the lost one.* And Andy says: *The young man you are thinking of is no longer here. He is at peace. He has forgotten his life on this side.*"

"There—see?" David felt vindicated. "He was wrong. Andy was wrong."

"I can't believe that." Rosanna seemed upset.

Sally was reading the transcription over to herself; suddenly she said, "Wait. I don't think he was wrong, David. I think you just didn't understand him."

"What's to understand? He said—"

"No, listen. He says, *The young man you are thinking of.* You were already convinced that Samuel, the boy who died at Gettysburg, was the lost one—you had a whole theory about crisis apparitions. Andy was reading your thought and telling you it was wrong."

"Let me see." He took the notebook from her and scanned the page. "You know, you could be right. You could be."

"That has to be it," Rosanna said.

David was aggrieved. It was bad enough that his colleagues were always telling him not to jump to conclusions. Now here was some tight-assed spirit getting on his case too. "Well, hell," he said. "It's awfully obscure."

"Maybe to you." Rosanna was annoyed, and showed it. He found it impossible to believe that less than two hours ago he had been kissing her.

"But look," Sally was saying, "this is all beside the point." They both looked at her and she gestured with her coffee cup. "We have no evidence that Julian, whoever he was, is actively haunting this house any more than Samuel was. He could be happy and at peace too. The lost one might just be an echo, a residue he left behind."

"Echo?" David couldn't believe she meant it. "You're saying an *echo* showed you that trance vision of the elms, then led you straight to the buried stone?"

"Who said anyone led me to the stone? Maybe I was just looking for what you tripped over the last time we were there."

It was not what she had said at first, in the churchyard, and it sounded to him like a rationalization invented after the fact. But he knew that dogged look; he would get nowhere by arguing with her. He tacked instead. "Well, what about last night? You can't tell me he wasn't actively trying to communicate last night." He still had the notebook in his hand; he turned the pages, read the transcription over and then looked up in frustration. "It doesn't come through here. But he was there. I felt him." He heard himself in disgust. *I felt him.* How unscientific could you get? He focused on Sally: "What about you? You said you heard me call you, but I didn't. Who did?"

He saw by her eyes that it shook her, but she answered him steadily enough. "I don't know. I'm not saying there's nothing here. I'm just saying it isn't necessarily conscious. It could be just a mindless loop going around."

David closed the notebook, put it on the table. "Okay. I guess the next step is to try another sitting. Maybe we can get a better fix on exactly what's going on." He risked a look at Rosanna. "Besides, it'll give me a chance to apologize to Andy."

Her smile was wry, but it was a smile.

It is hard to dispute the fact that there is a general poverty of communication between the dead and the living. But if you believe, as spiritualists do, that after death the personality continues to exist in spirit form, then it is only natural to wonder why we do not hear more from the dead—and why, when we do, their remarks so rarely make sense.

It seems obvious that the lack of a physical body is at the core of the problem. The spirit, in order to get a message to the living, must make use of the physical apparatus of a medium in trance; and the awkwardness of operating another person's brain or vocal cords must be exponentially greater than that of trying to drive an unfamiliar car. To confuse things further, the medium's own thoughts and perceptions invariably become mixed with the substance of the message, and the final product may be hopelessly garbled.

But the real snag in communication between the dead and the living must be more than this mechanical problem, this lack of hands and voices. For, if anything, it is personality—that bundle of wishes, dreams, impressions, and memories—that survives, but personality stripped and altered, adrift in a place in which the perceptions of the five senses no longer have meaning. How can we possibly talk together? Our language, says Lawrence LeShan, is designed to describe relationships of specific objects and events, not the "interplay of shifting patterns" characteristic of the metaphysical universe. For the dead, all emphases have shifted. Is it surprising, then, that they seem to attach importance to details that seem trifling to us, or dismiss the issues we consider vital? The only wonder is that they should bother talking to us at all.

It was the damnable part of this business, David thought, and also undeniably part of its charm, that just when you thought you were getting somewhere, suddenly you weren't. It was a Lewis Carroll universe, enough to make you give up and go into banking, or else into some more dependable kind of exploration—deep-sea diving, for instance. At least the ocean didn't dry up when your back was turned.

They had gone into a sitting as soon as they could load a tape into the machine. They had all been thrown into a state of expectancy by the finding of Julian Gilfoy's grave; there was a sense that they were being helped along, consciously or otherwise handed the pieces necessary to complete the puzzle. And then Andy, on whom they were depending to make contact with Julian, flatly refused to communicate.

It was the last thing in the world they had anticipated, and yet the minutes ticked by, maliciously distinct on

David's watch, and the tape reels went around, recording nothing but the ticking stillness in the master bedroom. A bird called in the yard and was answered by one in the tree outside the window. David crossed his legs, rubbed his hands together against the chill in the room, glanced at the blackened opening of the fireplace. His exhilaration was fading, giving way to annoyance at Rosanna. Was she still angry because he had doubted Andy? It was ridiculous; he had said he was sorry. As he sat watching her face, all at once she opened her eyes.

"I'm not doing this on purpose, you know."

There was a qualm in his belly; then he felt himself turning red. He wanted to deny that he had been thinking any such thing; but a suspicion, not pleasant, that she knew exactly what he had been thinking kept him quiet. He made an awkward movement with his head that might have been an apology.

After forty minutes they gave up. David was miserably aware that in letting himself blame Rosanna for the sitting's failure he had committed one of the cardinal sins of psychical research. In a laboratory science involving primarily human participants, one of the crucial unknown factors is the relationship between experimenter and subject. It is impossible to gauge how great a part is played by this nebulous variable in psychical research, but one sequence has proved itself over and over: an experimenter's boredom or impatience is always matched by a drop in the subject's psi results. Up till now it had been an abstraction for David, an interesting technical point to discuss over lunch with other researchers. He had never found it difficult to be pleasant to the various subjects who came and went at the lab. The haunting cases in which he had assisted in the past had always been too much of a novelty in themselves for the actual results to make much difference to him; and there had always been other, more experienced researchers present whom he watched and copied, who sat through the most boring and frustrating sessions with equanimity.

But I'm experienced.

Or at least I damn well ought to be.

It hurt to think he was behaving unprofessionally. Was Rosanna comparing him to other parapsychologists she had worked with, dismissing him as an incompetent idiot? She hadn't been conscious for his panic during last night's sitting, but there was the pass he had made that afternoon in the church, and now this . . . She had gone out into the hall, leaving him to gather up the equipment, and he heard Sally asking her how the sitting had gone.

"It didn't."

Her tone was flat. Shifting his grip on the tape recorder he wondered if he had botched things completely.

≫ *12* ≪

BY SUPPERTIME, at least part of the excitement had come back. They sat around the kitchen table talking over the events in the churchyard.

"It's a hell of a thing to put on somebody's tombstone, isn't it?" David crumpled his napkin. "*The night is dark . . . What was the rest of it?"

". . . *and I am far from home. Lead Thou me on,*" Rosanna said. "Not so strange, actually. It's a verse from a hymn, 'Lead, Kindly Light.' " She hummed a phrase, then broke off. "We used to sing it at church camp."

"Well," he said, "it's a hell of an epitaph for poor old Julian."

"Do you have any idea who he was?" Rosanna said.

"None." Sally started to clear the table. "Except that he must be one of the sons of the preacher—the Reverend Joshua. The one whose picture is in the dining room."

David tipped his chair onto its back legs and rocked slowly. "His dates are 1885 to 1906. That makes him twenty-one. So we know that about him too." Coffee was perking on the stove. Rosanna retrieved it and poured three cups; David took his, watching steam curl off the surface. "And we know he's lost, or thinks he is. But we don't know how he died, or anything else about him. And even when we get through to him"—he thought the *when* was a nice touch, a vote of confidence for Andy— "even then, I doubt he's going to be very specific. You know how they are."

After supper David went upstairs to do some thinking. The room he and Sally were using as a bedroom looked out over the backyard, and the window stood open to the evening. Down under the trees it was already dark, but over to the left he could still make out bits of the white picket fence that separated their yard from Mrs. Hopkins's next door. Only a few feet here and there along its length were free from the honeysuckle that buried the rest, but Mrs. Hopkins had religiously painted these bare spots. Downstairs in the kitchen the light was still on; the window cast an amber ghost of itself on the grass, a light-shadow that would brighten as night fell.

He opened Sally's notebook and began to read the transcripts of the sittings over again. For a time the rattle of turning pages and the bump of bugs against the newly installed screen were the only sounds, while the circle of lamplight sharpened and defined itself in the darkening room. He read the words over until he knew them by heart. Questions crowded him. Last night—what made the fire go crazy? And that smoky smell in the master bedroom: both Sally and Rosanna mentioned it. Is it connected with the fire's weird behavior? And how about Rosanna's nosebleed? And what made Sally show up at the door, thinking she'd heard me call? And today—how'd she find that stone?

One thing was clear enough, had been making itself increasingly clear over the past couple of days. It was Sally, as much as Rosanna, around whom the paranormal events in this case seemed to center. Sally who had gone into trance and seen the churchyard as Julian Gilfoy must have known it, Sally who had been summoned to the master bedroom only seconds before the lost one took possession of Rosanna, Sally who had discovered the grave.

The night is dark and I am far from home.

The night *was* dark. He moved closer to the circle of light. *Says he's lost . . . the lost one.* The lost one. Who was Julian Gilfoy? How did he die? Something in the master bedroom. The lost one. What happened? And what's happening now? An echo, a tag-end of emotional distress left behind and picked up by Rosanna, by Sally, the way infrared film picks up the heat of an object no longer present?

I don't believe that.

He shut the notebook, rested chin on hands. The sitting last night: Sally in the doorway, Rosanna's voice cut off in the middle of a word, as if someone had taken her by the throat. An unconscious echo, mindlessly repeating itself? No. He had felt consciousness, felt confronted by personality. A young man, a little younger than himself. Here in this house, alive once, like himself, warm and breathing: and now? *Says he's lost . . . the lost one.* Rosanna screaming, tears and blood on her face. What happened? What does it mean? His eyes met his reflection's in the half open window; he turned slowly and looked into the darkness around him.

I'll find out, Julian Gilfoy. Damned if I won't. There must be some way to help you.

The night is dark. Somewhere a dog started barking. He jumped up and went to the window but the sound seemed to come from below, almost as if it were downstairs, inside the house. His throat suddenly dry, he went to the door of the room and stood listening. Silence now. *The night is dark.* It was dark, all right, and darker downstairs in the front hall. Where the hell was Sally? And Rosanna? Then he heard it: a single short bark, deep and menacing. It came from downstairs.

This time the sound galvanized him. He started down the stairs quickly, heart racing; and then somehow in the dark, in the rush, he missed his footing. The stairs were steep, worn glass-smooth by feet hurrying up and down over the years; his sneakers were old and practically treadless. He felt himself stumble, felt the banister under his hand jerk away like a shying horse; his shoulder hit the opposite wall hard, knocking the breath out of him. He flailed for balance but couldn't find it—weirdly he saw silhouetted above him at a mad angle the second-floor railing, shadowy bars backlit by the open bedroom door. Then he was spinning, plunging, feeling the stairs slither and buck under his feet, the wild rush of momentum and fear—and behind it, even as he fell, his nerves buzzing with the sense of something waiting there below him in the darkness.

The newel post saved him. His outflung hand struck it and gripped: the impetus of his fall slung him all the way around it and deposited him in a sitting position against the outside of the staircase, pouring with sweat and feeling utterly drunk. Around him the house was silent; he could hear only his own gasping breath. When he could move, he picked himself up painfully and wiped the sweat out of his eyes.

Where the hell is everybody?

And the barking—was it really inside the house?

His heart was pounding in a very unprofessional way. The front hall was dark. The closed doors to the parlor and library were rectangles of blackness; he couldn't make himself cross the empty space between them to the light switch beside the front door. It was hard to dismiss what he had heard, hard not to believe in a dog, a big one, somewhere in the dark rooms around him. Normally he wasn't afraid of dogs. But this situation wasn't exactly normal.

Where the hell are Sally and Rosanna?

There was light coming from the kitchen and he went toward it, legs still wobbly. His shoulder hurt. So did his hand. The kitchen was deserted, supper dishes washed and piled in the drainer, a fly smacking the window pane.

Didn't they hear the dog? Where are they?

Opening the back door into summer night seeded with the chirping of crickets. They were not outside. He let the screen swing shut and left the kitchen, rubbing his shoulder. Back to the front hall.

Don't think about the dog. Not yet. Just find them. They must be upstairs. Go upstairs and find them.

His mind talking soothingly to his body like an adult to a nervous child. Talking calmly on, while his eyes saw, and his mind recorded what they had seen, and still tried not to acknowledge it.

The library door now stood open.

A tingle starting at the base of his neck, spreading outward. The door had been closed a few moments before—hadn't it? All at once he wasn't sure. "Sally?" he said. "Rosanna?" The silence came back in answer.

He bolted up the stairs suddenly, ran down the dim hallway to the Thistle Room and threw open the door without knocking, seeing darkness inside. Fumbling for the light switch inside the door, clicking the room into brightness. It was empty. A shirt, bright blue, hung over the back of the rocking chair. Paperback book facedown on the bed.

Where

He made himself take a deep breath, forcing down the

panic that had risen inside him. Made himself turn out the light. Close the door. Start on a methodical search of the second floor, checking the rooms one after another, as quickly as he could without running. He would not let himself run. One room, then the next, then the next. Chairs met him, and tall mahogany beds, his own sweating face in the mirrors and the mournful gaze of the Indian brave on the wall of Tonto's Room. With every empty room he tightened the hatches on his thought processes a little more.

Don't think.

Just find them.

At the door of the master bedroom he braced himself for the chill, but it seemed less noticeable than usual. He was backing out when the smell reached him.

A smell faintly smoky and aromatic, like a wood fire. He swallowed, looked at the empty hearth, and sniffed cautiously. He was not imagining it.

Must be left over from last night.

But it wasn't there this morning.

Don't think. Just find them.

The logical thing, of course, would be simply to shout for them. But some impulse, involuntary and unscientific, warned him not to call attention to himself. He was vulnerable. He was alone.

Down the stairs again, making sure of every step, gripping the banister. At the bottom he came to a stop, not knowing what to do next, unable to take his eyes off the open library door.

This is crazy

Where the hell are they

Don't leave me alone here

In that instant the weight of the house dropped on him with a suddenness that snuffed out thought, immobilizing him where he stood. Reason vanished; panic welled up, irresistible. He wanted to cry out and could not—to run, but the gray walls and doors seemed immeasurably far away, without substance, only the angle of the staircase clear and jutting up savagely into nothing.

He was lost in a void, a landscape of threatening shadowforms

He was in a wasteland, everything around him veiled and altered

He was dead and it had happened without warning and now he was alone and would be alone always

He was trapped forever in this gray restless place where something unthinkable awaited him, biding its time

Alone

Lost

Lost

The sound of the telephone came then, like a burst of white light. He saw the front door, ran to it, flung it open to the outside.

On the porch someone stirred. A voice said, "David?"

He leaned in the doorway, supporting himself more on the frame than on legs that were shaking too much to hold him. "I didn't know where you were," he said. They sat on the porch steps, faces turned toward him. Behind him in the house the phone was still ringing. He couldn't move. Rosanna stood up.

"I'll get it." She went past him into the house. Behind him the light in the front hall came on. He moved unsteadily into the darkness.

"Sally?"

"Hi."

He sat beside her. Light from the doorway fell on her back; her face was in shadow. She seemed subdued.

"What were you doing out here?"

"Nothing. Just talking."

Sitting here with her, his experience just now seemed impossible, unreal. His body, sweating and shaking, said otherwise. But he found himself uncertain of what had actually happened. The barking he had heard—had it really come from inside the house? More likely it had been outside, somewhere close by. The library door might have been open all along; he hadn't really looked that carefully the first time. It began to seem as if he had managed to scare himself royally, nothing more. In retrospect his behavior appeared amateurish and shameful; now he felt shakily grateful that there had been no one around to witness it.

Beside him Sally was very quiet. He put his hand on her knee; she jumped. "Hey," he said. "Are you okay?"

"Yes." Her hand, icy, caught his and held it hard. They sat not speaking. He wondered what she wasn't telling him. Well, what wasn't he telling her? He squeezed her hand. Inside the house he could hear Rosanna still talking on the phone. There was a pause; then she was behind them in the doorway.

"Bad news." They both looked at her and she said, "I can't stay."

David half rose, letting go of Sally's hand. "What—"

"Complications at home. I've got to get back tomorrow." She came forward and stood with them on the porch; they were all standing now, the light from the doorway on their faces. "I'm sorry," she said. "I really am."

"What about later on?" David said. "Could you come back?"

"It's a possibility. If you want me to."

"Of course we do," he said automatically. He looked at Sally but she said nothing. They all stood there a moment longer; a car went by in the street. Then Rosanna turned back into the house.

"I'd better pack."

PART II

COLIN

⋙ 13 ⋘

"IF YOU'RE INTERESTED in the past, maybe I can help."

It was a bad beginning, but he was always bad with strangers. Usually he left them alone. Not many strangers came into the Skipton Public Library, and the few who did tended to treat him as a kind of talking card catalog or nursemaid to the cantankerous copying machine, nothing more. With Skipton people, of course, it was different: they had known him from childhood, their own and then their children's, but in a way they too seemed to think of him in terms of overdue books and lowered voices. Not that he minded. He was proud of his library, the small white frame building sheltered by its splendid red maple—ridiculously proud, he supposed, for his emotion encompassed even the bicycle rack out front and the black letters painted on the door. He was proud of the cross-referenced card catalog, the quiet shelves of books, the scarred reading tables polished to a shine—for he did all the work himself, except for mopping the floors. Earl Fitch came every Friday morning at six to do that.

Above all he was proud of his own private project, the town history on which he spent hours of research and honest love. If he did not look up when Carrie Nelson laid the two overdue volumes of *War and Peace* on the desk, it was not from gallantry as Carrie supposed, but because he was discovering that Olympus Avenue had originally been Burr Avenue, named in honor of Aaron Burr and formally changed at an emergency meeting of the Town Council in 1805. At such moments his existence, his equilibrium, was complete. He was a fool to risk it by speaking to a stranger.

But the young woman had been in several times over the past fortnight; he had noticed her over in the History and Genealogy section. Seeing her out of the corner of his eye he had almost taken her for a teenage boy in her dungarees and faded plaid shirt, dark hair braided and hanging down her back. But boys do not move like that, the way he remembered his mother moving, more than half a century since, slender and smiling in a white dress that swept the grass as she came toward him across the lawn. Nor do boys have such faces. Yesterday she had come up to the desk and asked him about old newspapers.

"Well, I have the *New York Times* complete on microfilm." There was that pride of his again. The microfilm machine was new, less than a year old, and regarded by most Skipton people with deep suspicion. But he had badgered them into it, those old skinflints on the Town Council: told them no self-respecting library would be without one. And he loved gadgets. So far it had been scarcely touched, but people would come around. He had a little joke with Carrie that it had been paid for entirely with her accumulated fines.

"Actually I meant local newspapers. Did Skipton ever have one of its own?"

"Not a local paper, no. What you want is the *Masonville Echo*. It covers the news from all the small towns in this area, and it's been in more or less continuous circulation since the late 1880s. I have it on microfilm as well."

She had chosen the beginning of 1906 and spent most of the afternoon over it; now today she was back again, taking up where she had left off. But she seemed dissatisfied, looking up from the screen to stare into space, and it was during one of these intervals that he went over and spoke to her. Her gaze seemed to cross tremendous distances before it rested on him: he felt the skin shrink a little on his bones at the impact. Her eyes were green. She did not smile—yet he liked her face. But he was always bad with strangers, and he found himself repeating nervously, before she could answer, "If you're interested, that is."

She hesitated a moment. Then: "What I'm looking for is some information on the Gilfoy family."

"The Gilfoys, yes, let me see." Hearing himself stumble over words, wondering what possible connection she could have with the Gilfoys. Sam didn't even live here anymore, just held on to his property and showed up from time to time, looking grimmer and grayer. But hadn't Earl Fitch told him, just yesterday, that the place had been rented again? "I believe—well, there may be, that is, there's a little information here, but I think most of the family papers must be still in the house on Lilac Street. I believe it's recently been rented, but if you like I can give you the address of the owner, Mr. Samuel Gilfoy of Boston. He—"

She smiled suddenly. "Mr. Gilfoy is my landlord."

"Your—" The smile, clear and warm, distracted him.

"My husband and I are renting the Lilac Street house."

Looking at her he thought that Sam Gilfoy had no conscience, none at all. Of course it was all superstition, what they said about the house; still it had a reputation. It wasn't a good place to live. Sooner or later she was bound to hear the stories. He had a sudden wish to defend her—he could not have said from what, exactly: the house, or the well-meaning busybodies who would tell her it was haunted, or possibly it was something less concrete that he would have liked to spare her, sorrow or worry or old age. And all this in response to a young woman's smile! No one had ever laughed at him for having such preposterous feelings, because in spite of the fact that he was an old man he had never expressed them to anyone, and he did not do so now. He said, "Oh."

"What I'm looking for is information on the Reverend Joshua Gilfoy and his immediate family," she said. "Contemporary sources."

"Reverend Gilfoy, yes. He was one of Skipton's great men." He had grown up hearing the praises of the Reverend Joshua Gilfoy—scholar, orator, man of God. It was the last phrase that had caught his imagination: as a boy he had pictured Reverend Gilfoy talking with God like Moses on the mountain. A child's fantasy; still there had been an Old Testament quality about the man, even looking back. A fine man. Maybe Sam had commissioned this young woman to write his biography. "I'll see what I can find for you," he said.

People would have called them both shy, difficult to know, and perhaps this is what drew them together, along with their common interest in the past: as if they stood together at one end of a shadowy tunnel shot with shafts of light, narrowing their eyes to see the far end, too absorbed to be self-conscious. Whatever it was, they were friends almost at once. People smiled to see how completely young Mrs. Curtiss had captivated old Mr. Robinson ("Please call me Colin," he said). She sat at the microfilm machine, turning the advance knob or adjusting the focus, while now and again he brought her a book, some reference he had found, a slip of paper sticking out at the place, and once a real prize—a roll of microfilm from the *New York Times*. Sometimes she pushed her chair back and he sat on the edge of the table and they talked, the sun from the tall windows suspending them in brightness. It might have been a trick of the light that made a boy's figure of the old man with his white flyaway hair and quick gestures as he sat talking. But it was his real self sitting there, too happy to guess at what was happening to him, in the great wash of light under which his years were almost invisible, like the pale envelope of flesh in an X ray.

New York Times, August 26, 1904

SAYS PREACHER ORDERED MURDER

Residents of Skipton, Mass. aren't talking this week, at least not to outsiders. This reporter met a stone wall of silence in attempting to learn exactly what transpired in this little town of two thousand Sunday last.

That was the day on which Winslow Flagg, prominent community member and landowner, was shot to death at a church picnic supper following the evening service at the First Episcopal Church in Skipton. His assailant remains unidentified. Witnesses to the shooting, when questioned, respond either with silence or with the laconic suggestion that Flagg was accidentally struck by a hunter's stray bullet.

The back lawn of the church, where picnic suppers are customarily held after Sunday evening services in the summer months, is adjacent to a tract of woods owned by Mrs. Julia Hilbert, an elderly widow who stated that she does permit hunting on her property. However, Miss Letitia Flagg, a daughter of the victim who was present at the picnic, rejects the stray bullet theory. She failed to spot the assailant, but told this reporter there is no doubt in her mind that Flagg was killed by a fellow parishioner.

"The preacher told them to do it," she said. "He said it was God's will."

The Episcopal minister, Reverend Joshua G. Gilfoy, denied ordering his congregation to kill Flagg. He said the text of his evening sermon was Job 18:5—"Yea, the light of the wicked shall be put out, and the spark of his fire shall not shine"—and that he had spoken extemporaneously on that theme. He did not recall his exact words. A church member said that the sermon contained no statement to warrant Miss Flagg's accusation.

A Skipton citizen who asked not to be identified said that Flagg's business and social practices were a scandal in the community. "He had no morals," our informant said.

In spite of his flaws Flagg was a powerful figure in Skipton, holding a place on the Town Council and regularly attending the prestigious First Episcopal Church.

County Sheriff B. E. Wells is proceeding with an investigation of the shooting. But Skiptonians aren't talking.

The next item was waiting on the table when she looked up from the microfilm screen: a small book bound in dark blue leather with an elaborate rose embossed on the cover. Below the rose was the title, *Memories of a New England Girlhood,* by Mrs. Fannie Shippers. There was a marker at page 88.

Every Sunday, of course, we went to church, wearing our very best clothes. Papa always wore his beaver hat, which had been brushed to a beautiful sheen by no less a personage than Mama, who would trust none of the servants with such an important task. If it were fine we walked; otherwise we drove in the carriage, and there was always a great deal of fuss over who was to be allowed to sit next to Papa, even though it was only a short drive.

The First Episcopal Church was at the top of Lilac Street. It was not large but very pretty, a white wooden building with a small steeple. We went in, Papa and Mama first, then Diana and Louisa and I, followed by Roger and Donald. We had to genuflect before entering the family pew. A graceful genuflection was considered by my sisters and myself to be so important (for after all, the young men watching us were of the best families in town) that I remember we used to practice at home, genuflecting to our own images in the mirror, until one day Aunt Annie caught us at it and said it was blasphemous.

The minister was the Reverend Joshua Gilfoy, very noble and severe, with beautiful silver hair. All the ladies adored him and the gentlemen respected him; his sermons alternated between righteous thunder and tender forgiveness in a way that was quite irresistible, and Louisa once confessed to me that when she said her prayers she always imagined God as looking like Reverend Gilfoy—more blasphemy! He was not quite perfect, however; for he was completely tone-deaf, and used to roar out the hymns in a monotone. His wife was dead, for which everyone pitied him very much, and he had a large family of handsome boys and plain girls. Some years later, after I had married and moved to Boston, I heard that he had remarried—a woman much younger than he, in fact, the same age as one of his daughters.

She looked up; he could never tell how she knew he was there. It was a little disconcerting sometimes. "The second wife," she said.

"Second wife?"

"She was our Mr. Gilfoy's mother. David and I had just assumed that he was a grandson of the Reverend Joshua. But we checked the parish register at the church and there he was, Joshua's youngest son." Her pencil tapped a list of names in her notebook and he bent to look.

"Gabriel, Mary, Douglas, Prentiss, Rebecca, Clara, Lily, Julian, Samuel. It was the era of large families, wasn't it?"

"All but Samuel are children by the first wife, Sophia Nye. She died giving birth to Julian, or at least their birth and death dates coincide in the register. Sometimes the bare facts are pretty bare. That's why all this"—she laid her hand on the old book—"is so marvelous. You've been a tremendous help."

As a young man he had been known for his fiery blushes. But the blood didn't move so quickly to his face now, and that was a mercy. "I'm glad," he said. But her attention was back on the notebook page with its list of names.

"These people—the sons and daughters. Do you know anything about any of them?"

He scanned the names again. Gilfoy . . . the name like a stone thrown into a pond, sending ripples far back into the past . . . "I think one of the girls was—you know, slow. I'm not sure which one, but I remember . . . what was it? Once she came into Buck's, you know, the general store, where I was clerking for the summer, and pulled a lot of bolts of cloth off the counter onto the floor. Then someone came and got her, one of her sisters, I suppose. She was a grown woman, but very small and slight. Then there was something about a dog, Reverend Gilfoy's, I think, refusing to leave his grave—one of those stories." He frowned, trying to remember more clearly, then gave it up. "It was a long time ago."

That afternoon he met David, who came by the library to collect Sally. By the time she had finished showing him the references they had collected, the three of them had the place to themselves; and Colin let them persuade him to put a note on the door and accompany them to Kimball's for iced tea. It had been years since he had tasted Kimball's iced tea. But there was no Proustian flood of awakened memories—only the flavor, bitter behind the sugar from brewing too long, and familiar as yesterday. He sat between David and Sally at the counter. They both talked at once; finally David prevailed.

"What about this Flagg guy? Did Gilfoy really incite his congregation to kill him?"

David was tall, had light curly hair, smiled a lot, dressed like Sally in old jeans and sneakers. He gave an impression of slenderness until you noticed the muscles in his arms. He sat loosely on the revolving stool. Every so often he pushed off from the counter with one hand, rotated a quarter turn and stopped himself neatly with the other. Colin stirred his tea, set the long spoon on the counter.

"That's just journalistic flap. Reverend Gilfoy was known for his oratory, but I doubt he could have convinced a man to commit murder who wasn't already planning it. No, it was just coincidence, although possibly the murderer may have read encouragement into his words."

David leaned on the counter, turning his glass between his hands. "The murderer—who was he? Sounds like everyone knew, even if they weren't telling."

The teenager behind the counter, one of the Fortenberry youngsters, had looked up at the word "murderer," and Colin pitched his voice lower.

"Apparently it wasn't that simple. There were any number of people with reason to hate Flagg. One of them must have been pushed too far. But no one was ever charged with the crime. In fact, I believe the coroner's jury returned a verdict of accidental death. People really preferred to think of it as an act of God."

"Why would God want to kill Winslow Flagg?" David executed a quarter rotation. "I liked the phrase 'no morals.' But what did he actually do?"

"Well, for one thing he was hungry for other people's land. He had a big family, and every time a son or daughter would marry, Flagg would present the new couple with a parcel of land adjoining his own. It was like a feudal demesne. But of course it was the neighboring farmers who suffered. They might not want to sell their land, but they didn't have a choice. Somehow, if Mr. Flagg wanted your land, he always managed to get it in the end. Farmers who held out found that their credit was no longer good at the general store, their loan applications were turned down at the bank, their mortgages called. There was no escaping his sphere of influence. And yet I doubt he ever did anything strictly illegal." His throat was dry from so much talking and he sipped his tea. "But there were plenty of other ways he flouted the social code. Women were very drawn to him; he was a powerful, vital man and apparently very handsome. My mother said once that there was an aura of danger about him that women loved—in that stuffy, socially correct era it was like a breath of mountain air. Just to have him bow to them on the street was an event. And inevitably some of them must have succumbed to his charm, although there was never an actual scandal, only rumors now and then. But you can imagine that once he was gone, the community breathed easier."

"Struck down by the will of God," David said. "As made known by the Reverend Joshua."

"I'm sure that connection didn't exist. Reverend Gilfoy was a man of unquestionable moral integrity. He never would have condoned murder."

They all sat quietly for a moment. In David's empty glass the melting ice cubes shifted position with a clink that was answered by the ringing of the cash register at the other end of the counter as someone (Carl Jackson, Colin saw, glancing up) bought something and left. He took out his watch and checked it: time to be getting back.

"An outraged husband or a disgruntled landowner," David said. "Well, as a former student of anthropology I can tell you that loss of honor and property are the two most popular reasons for committing murder in the history of the human race. So that doesn't narrow it down much."

"What happened to his family, Colin, after he was killed?" Sally said. "Did they move away?"

"No, they're still around. They live on a farm about twenty miles north of town, come in occasionally for supplies and whatnot. They keep mostly to themselves."

David drained his glass with a rattle of ice cubes and set it down on the counter. "Can't say as I blame them."

Colin found himself wondering again, when they had left Kimball's and stood talking on the sidewalk, exactly what their interest was in the Gilfoy family. A biography of Reverend Gilfoy still seemed the most likely explanation, but they hadn't really said, and he hadn't asked. Of course, it was none of his business—still, it was irresponsible of Sam to let them have that house. People passed as they stood there together: familiar faces, Tim Buck Jr. on his way to Kermie's for his nightly spree, Jack Townsend leaving the post office, Mrs. Morrison with her new baby. He had known them all from childhood. They were nice people, all of them. But sooner or later one of them, or someone just as nice, would tell Sally or David about the house. It might be done with a laugh, as if the whole thing were a joke; it might be done out of concern—but it would be done. "Well, you know what they say about that house. You don't? You mean to say no one's told you?"

They were saying goodbye now, starting off down the sidewalk, turning back to wave. He raised his hand in answer. It was absurd how much he minded seeing them go. He watched them down the sidewalk, suddenly aware as if for the first time that he was an old man, and solitary.

He had been a frail little boy with light, almost white hair and an expression of comical dignity; or at least so it appeared in an old photograph showing him standing at the gate of the house where he had been born and where he still lived. The years between then and now had seemed to pass very quickly. His family and close friends were all dead. He had a dog, cooked for himself, looked after the yard on Sundays (he had stopped attending church when his mother died in '47); but his real existence was the library: mending a dogeared book, explaining the card catalog to a class of youngsters from the grammar school, making up a weekly packet of novels for bedridden Mrs. McClintock, or pursuing his own researches—prying some obscure fact from its niche in the past, emerging from the dusty files like a miner, clutching his nugget of truth. It had been a long time since he had spent an afternoon like this one, in the company of friends. Yet he seldom felt lonely, so woven was his life with the life of the town over the years—nothing grandiose (though he had lived here in wartime and depression) but merely the small coin of every day: marriages and births, record snowfalls and days when the mercury topped 100, Dr. Bristowe's giant oak split in two by lightning. He could remember seeing Judge Saunders's horse and buggy parked on Main Street next to Chandler Jackson's model-T, remember when the elms died, when the highway north of town had been virgin forest.

And always the people, familiar faces aging, people growing up and growing old and dying. Sometimes it was the young who died: Luke Fortenberry, the farrier, kicked in the head by a horse, Peter Halsey killed in Vietnam, Amanda Cunningham dying slowly of cancer. But some people seemed to go on forever: year after year he saw them in the post office or buying birdseed at Buck's, a little grayer, a little more bent. The pace was imperceptible, like the movement of hands on a clock. You meant to watch, to see it happen; then something distracted you and you forgot, and next thing you knew . . . It took something like this, meeting new people, to wake him up, make him marvel at how much time had passed. And he was one of the old ones by now, no point in fooling himself. Seventy-eight—or was it seventy-nine? He counted backward guiltily: seventy-nine. He didn't feel that old!

He got tired of course, quicker than he used to; sometimes at the end of the day his back ached. But his eyes
and ears were still sharp enough, and his mind. He could
recall clear as yesterday the names and faces of his boy-
hood friends, the words to half the hymns in the Episcopal hymnbook, his first time out hunting with his father
and the crunch of their boots in the new-fallen snow.

⇛ 14 ⇚

BY THE NEXT AFTERNOON Colin had come to a decision. It would be best, he thought, if he were to tell them himself about the house. Then he could ensure that it was done sensibly rather than for dramatic effect. And if later on they heard some of the more unpleasant stories—well, at least they would have been forewarned.

So he had decided. But then he forgot. Maybe he had congratulated himself too soon on the sharpness of his mind, although he preferred to blame the copy machine. In any case he was too late.

The temperamental, antiquated machine had broken down again, as it often did in the afternoons—something to do with overheating, he thought. Whatever the reason, the paper had knitted itself into the inner workings of the machine and had to be extracted in the form of confetti. He was doing this, and Sally was helping him, when David's voice behind them said, "Will the patient live?"

They turned; he stood there smiling. He seemed excited. Sally stood up quickly.

"Is everything okay?"

"Everything's fine." He was holding an envelope; now he offered it to her. "This just came in the mail."

She took it and glanced at it, then back at David. The envelope had already been opened and she took the letter out, unfolded it, and looked at it. Looked up at David again. He was smiling. It occurred to Colin then that he was being nosy, and he turned back to the copy machine, hearing Sally say, "This is the same thing Karen Abbey and Miss Sterling got."

"Yup."

"It's got to be someone here in town."

"Local postmark," David said.

Colin removed the last scrap of paper, closed the machine and switched it on. A few lights blinked; an encouraging whir came from within.

"All fixed?" Sally said.

"I think so. I need to try it out."

"Allow me." David took the sheet of paper out of Sally's hand and laid it facedown on the glass, pressing the print button. More whirring, a blinding flash, and the copy slid neatly into the tray next to Colin. It was face up, a series of words printed in capital letters on a plain sheet of paper.

THE HOUSE IS BAD. MOVE OUT.

It was then he remembered his intention to tell them himself. He looked at them but they didn't seem surprised.

"We seem to have an anonymous well-wisher in town," David said.

"But that's ridiculous," he heard himself saying. "There's nothing wrong with that house. Just some children's stories. Some people in town like to believe them. But you two—you're too sensible to pay any attention to that sort of thing."

"Oh, Colin," Sally said. "That sort of thing, as you call it, is our whole reason for renting the house."

He must have looked as dumbfounded as he felt, because she said gently, "We're trying to find out if it's really haunted—and if so, how."

They knew, then; they'd known all along. He tried to rearrange his thinking to accommodate this new fact. "How do you mean, how?"

"There are different kinds of manifestations. Poltergeist phenomena, for instance—dishes flying through the air, blankets pulled off beds—with no apparent cause. Sometimes there's a natural explanation, sometimes not. Then there are other kinds. Sounds, sights, even smells. The manifestations can be random—or what seems random to us—or they can follow a fairly obvious pattern. That's where the family history comes in. It seems that sometimes something that happened in the past can continue to cause a disturbance."

"A ghost, you mean?"

"A disturbance," Sally said.

"What kind of thing in the past? Like a curse?"

She smiled a little. "More likely a violent emotional occurrence, like a violent death. Sometimes—we don't know why, although there are theories—there are reverberations, sensations that last for years, that can be felt by complete strangers that know nothing about what happened in the place. That's usually what we mean when we say a house is haunted."

Colin stirred the pile of confetti on the floor with one foot. "Well, you know, supposedly there was a tramp—"

"David and I think the tramp is a red herring. We're having him researched, but we have reports of haunting incidents that predate him. We think it's more likely a member of the family."

"One of the Gilfoys?"

"Probably."

The fragment that had been drifting at the edge of his brain for several days, since she had showed him the list of Reverend Gilfoy's children, came into focus all at once. "Then that would be—what was his name? Julius?"

"Julian?" David's interruption was so sharp that Colin blinked, momentarily rattled. Then he got hold of the memory again.

"Julian. He fell, didn't he?"

"Fell where?" Sally seemed as agitated as David. "How do you know? Why didn't you tell me?"

"I really only just remembered it," he said. "I didn't realize—I didn't understand exactly what you were looking for."

She smiled then. "I know. I was trying to be discreet. It's not supposed to be ethical to make a big point of someone's house being haunted."

"But does Sam know why you rented the house?"

"Yes, he does," David said. "But we aren't sure he realizes what it entails. Not that it'll do him or his property any harm. Anything we find out will be reported in a scientific publication for a very select reading public. And it'll probably be so boring that only a handful of them will read it. Now—tell us everything you know about Julian's death."

"Let me think a minute." How much did he really

remember? A young man falling to his death. Julian Gilfoy . . . the name echoing in his mother's voice. His mother talking in low tones to a friend while Colin lay on the floor reading a book, knowing he was not supposed to be listening . . . "I'm almost positive there was something about a quarrel. Julian and his father."

"The Reverend Joshua."

"Yes. There was an argument, and Julian rushed out in a fury, and the stairs—they're very steep, aren't they? You should ask Sam to have them carpeted."

"But what about Julian?"

"I guess he broke his neck."

They were quiet a minute; then she said, "What were they fighting about?"

"Sally, I don't know. I must have been a small child when he died; my memory is that I overheard my mother repeating the story to someone many years later. It was no more than a rumor, really. I have a general impression that Julian was no good, always in some kind of trouble. To a man like Reverend Gilfoy, such a son would have been a great disappointment. I'm sure there was friction between them."

"The family black sheep." Sally picked up the photocopy of the letter and folded it. "That makes sense, I guess."

"Yup," David said.

"It does?" Colin said.

For a long moment he wondered if either of them had heard him; then David looked at him and grinned. "It's a long story. How would you like to come to supper at a haunted house?"

≫ 15 ≪

"INCREDIBLE," HE SAID. "Amazing." He leaned back in his chair and gazed at the age-darkened portrait over the sideboard (they were using the dining room in his honor). "But you know, in an old house like this, there must have been any number of deaths—invalids, old people. Why should Julian be the only ghost?"

They both started to answer at once; Sally gave way to David. He sat forward, elbows on the table while he talked. "The key, Colin, is the violence of the death, not the death itself. As you say, any number of people may have died in their beds. But Julian died suddenly, violently, in the middle of a high-key emotional situation. Whatever normally happens to the personality when someone dies, it seems that violent death messes up that process somehow. Say that usually the spirit goes on to a happy hunting ground, or is absorbed into a transcendent oversoul, or whatever you like. Well, the theory is that when someone dies violently, this customary sequence is disrupted. The personality undergoes a sort of trauma, gets trapped into some kind of loop, a repetition of the violent emotional circumstances surrounding the death. That's what causes the type of disturbance known as haunting."

Colin had put his fork down; now he picked it up but found he wasn't hungry. "But isn't there some way to help the—personality—get free? Exorcism, or something like that?"

Sally said, "David is oversimplifying a little, Colin. Most of the time, what appears to be present in a haunting isn't a whole personality. It's just a collection of emotional fragments held together somehow by the physical environment. We don't know why the house and the fragments interact, or how. But you'll be better off thinking of a haunted house more as a kind of echo chamber than as a place where lost souls are trapped forever. As for this house, the first step is to prove that it's haunted, and we haven't even done that yet."

"Well, everyone says . . ." He heard himself with disbelief. Did he actually credit those stories? He honestly didn't know. He couldn't help wondering why else Sam had such trouble keeping tenants here. Words printed anonymously on a sheet of paper: *The house is bad.*

Sally was saying, "Yes, everybody says it's haunted. But proving it is tricky—actually trying to make a connection between the death and the haunting, two events that may be widely separated in time. And often the link between them is pretty ambiguous. You hardly ever get a recognizable phantom stalking the halls. More often it's like what we've had reported here—inexplicable lights or noises, or just people feeling creepy. It's hard to prove that this kind of thing is caused by a death that may have happened, in some cases, hundreds of years ago."

Colin was still looking at the portrait of Joshua Gilfoy. The tarnished brass chandelier that hung crookedly over the table had two bulbs out, and in the poor illumination it was easy to imagine that the painted image was looking back.

"I don't think Reverend Gilfoy would have liked the idea of his house being haunted," he said, and David smiled.

"Certainly not by an unregenerate son."

After dinner David showed him over the house. He thought he remembered being there before—not with Sam, he and Sam had never been friends; but running some errand, maybe, delivering something from Buck's Hardware & General, where he had worked summers as a boy. A mere wisp, the memory; nothing to catch hold of. Standing in the front hall with David he seemed to feel it brush against him lightly. Then it was gone.

"You see that loudspeaker." David was pointing to the

railing of the second-floor gallery overlooking the front hall. "It's the central hook-up for detection instruments all over the house—cameras, tape recorders, vibration pickups, and so on. For instance, as Sally mentioned, we've had reports of unusual lights and noises occurring in this house. Now, if that happens, we'll know exactly when and where, and we'll have a permanent record proving that it actually happened. Not just someone's imagination getting out of hand."

"And has it happened?" Colin said.

David's expression was wry. "Not yet."

He led the way upstairs and Colin, following, was again aware of some memory that turned in its sleep. He wanted to stand still and let it wake, but David was talking and he did not want to seem inattentive.

"This indicator panel lets us know the specific room from which the central buzzer is being activated. You see each of these lights is labeled . . . Now I'll show you what would happen if I were, say, an unsuspecting ghost making my midnight rounds. First we'll activate the up-stairs system." He clicked a switch. "Okay, we're in business. When you hear the buzzer and see the light flashing, you can shut it off with this switch. Wait here."

He went off down the hall, turning a corner. Colin watched him go. The vague sense of familiarity he felt with the house tantalized him: as soon as he concentrated on it, it fled. He gave up and began to study the panel of lights in front of him, reading the labels without compre-hension: B1, B2, SR, DP, DR, K.—K meant kitchen, he supposed; DR was dining room—the sudden buzz, though not exactly ear-splitting, was loud enough to make him jump. He fumbled at the panel, saw the light marked SR flashing, clicked the switch. Silence followed: a suspen-sion in which he felt, with shame, his heart pounding.

David appeared at the end of the corridor, beckoning, insubstantial in the dim light, a convincing phantom. Then, as Sally called something from downstairs, he stepped forward into the light and shouted back. "What?"

"I said what's going on up there?"

"Just us ghosts."

"That's what I thought." Her voice retreated toward

the kitchen. Colin followed David. The corridor turned left; halfway down its second leg a door stood open. They went in and David switched on the light. It was a kind of sitting room, comfortable looking and, he realized after a moment, very old-fashioned. David was bending over a small metal box placed discreetly behind the door. Colin joined him, admiring the mysterious dials and needles.

"What's this?"

"A capacitance meter. Every physical object possesses electrical capacitance, and this meter was set to register the amount of electricity present in this room before I came in. When I came in, I added my own electricity to the room's—which caused the meter to overload and set off the buzzer."

Colin nodded mutely. David went across the room.

"Now look at this."

A half-developed photograph protruded from a Polaroid camera on a tripod in one corner of the room. David pulled the picture free and handed it to him; he took it and watched in fascination as the image finished forming. It showed David entering the room.

"A genuine spook if I ever saw one." David pointed to the bottom border of the photograph, where there was a number series: 20:52:21. "The camera is equipped with a timer that registers the exact time of the disturbance."

Colin looked at the numbers again. "Twenty?"

"Computerese for eight p.m."

Now he was embarrassed. "I should have known that." He examined the photograph. "Has anyone ever really taken a picture of a ghost?"

"Not to anyone else's satisfaction. This equipment is mostly to gather information, not to provide any kind of conclusive proof. In other words, if the capacitance changes and the picture doesn't show anything, then we can assume that the change was caused by something that doesn't register on photographic film—something physical but not in the visible spectrum, or the others we can measure, ultraviolet and infrared. The camera is filtered to respond to all of those. It's also equipped with a light-sensitive photocell that will trigger it even if the light-object possesses no electrical capacitance."

"But if people have seen lights here," Colin said, "they must be in the visible spectrum. So sooner or later you'll get a picture."

"Not necessarily. The lights might be hallucinations—some kind of interaction between the psychic atmosphere of the house and the subliminal perceptions of the people in it. But a camera has no subliminal perceptions. Neither does a capacitance meter. So if either instrument picks up the lights, then the hallucination hypothesis can be ruled out. Same thing with the tape recorders. We might imagine a sound. But they don't register anything that isn't really there."

"I see." Colin looked at the photograph again. "May I keep this?"

"Compliments of the house." David bent over the meter to reset the dials. Colin looked around the room. Two chairs upholstered in needlepoint, a low sofa, fringed curtains, and a marble fireplace. Beside the sofa was a small table, on the table a lamp . . . There was something about the lamp. It was old-fashioned, a double globe hand-painted with delicate roses . . . It was heavier than it looked. His arms had ached from carrying it. All the way from Buck's Hardware & General, down Main Street and turn on Tanglewood, up Tanglewood to Lilac and halfway up the hill. But he had offered to take it upstairs, he remembered (it was all coming back now, with a rush that dizzied him), because it was heavy and he had not wanted to let her carry it. He had followed her up the stairs. He had seen her before, of course, but always passing in the street or in church, never without her hat and veil and gloves. And she had never smiled at him like that, the way she had smiled opening the door, so that he felt his heart beating against the package as he followed her up the steep stairs. Her back was as narrow as a girl's. As they turned down the upstairs corridor someone called out to her from one of the rooms: an old man's voice, querulous and shaky, and she stopped at the door. He did not hear what she said, only the sound of her voice full of calm light like her smile, the fullness of a quiet sea. It seemed to him as he stood there, arms aching with his burden, that if he strained he would hear something beyond that lulling sound, something mythic and faintly perilous (for he read too much, everyone said so; never had his nose out of a book), a singing over the waters or some such thing. But before he could hear it she came out, closing the door behind her, and took him down the hall to the sitting room where they unpacked the lamp together. He used his pocketknife to cut the string. They knelt on the floor, lifting it out of the box; for a moment, an instant, their hands touched. "But it's so heavy!" she said, and he said it wasn't, standing up to set it on the table, his arm muscles trembling with fatigue. He had carried it all the way from Buck's. She was still kneeling and she looked up at him. There was gray in her smooth brown hair; it shocked him to see it. But she must have been over thirty, he thought, standing beside the table exactly where he had stood then, looking down at the spot, the exact place where she had knelt so many years ago—she must have been nearer forty . . .

"Colin?" David was in the doorway, looking quizzical.

"Oh—sorry."

They went back down the hall to the landing, stopping at the indicator panel to admire the neatly wired board like two boys ogling the controls of a model train.

"It's a wonderful system," Colin said at last. "But isn't it impossible to live here without constantly setting it off?"

"Actually it works out okay." David touched the board protectively as if even this implied criticism was too much. "We can monitor individual rooms or floors, which lets us keep tabs on suspicious areas without making the whole place off limits. We only turn the whole business on at night, which works out well because psi activity seems to prefer the night shift, as a rule. Of course we have to remember a few things—the first night the system was operative we forgot to stop the clock in the library from striking. We went to bed about eleven-thirty and at twelve the buzzer went off. We thought we'd hit pay dirt."

Colin shook his head in admiration. "I hadn't realized it was all so scientific."

"Most people don't. To most of the world it's still a matter of Ouija boards and crystal gazing."

"But this is very sophisticated."

"Yes, we've got some good equipment. Sally and I work for a private research laboratory that supplies it all."

"It's a brand-new science, isn't it?"

David smiled. "Older than quantum mechanics. Ever heard of the Morton ghost?"

"I don't think so."

"It's the best-documented ghost in the history of ghost documenting. Seen by more than fifty people on dozens of different occasions. It was the subject of what may possibly have been the first scientific experiment in the history of psychical research, in 1885. The experimenter was a woman, a Miss R. C. Morton."

"And the experiment?"

"She tied a piece of string across the stairs." David laughed at Colin's expression. "Simple and conclusive, the ideal experiment. The ghost used to go up and down the stairs. She wanted to determine whether its substance was material or immaterial—"

"I see," Colin said. "And the string didn't break?"

"The string didn't break."

Colin said, "It seems—I don't know—such a strange profession for a young couple. How did you get interested in it? How did Sally?"

Without answering David took him into a room across the hall, at the top of the stairs. There were books piled on the table under the lamp, one dresser drawer half pulled out—it was their bedroom, he realized. David was rummaging through a pile of magazines on the windowsill. He pulled one out and searched the contents, found a page, handed it to Colin.

"Read."

He read. The magazine was a scientific journal; the article described an experiment. There were cards, five of them, each printed with a different symbol. There was an agent *(A)*, a percipient *(P)*, something else called PRN, a dispositional factor, an occurrent factor—the terms left him completely in the dark. He read on. Every ten seconds, *A* looked at one of the cards in one room, while at the same moment, in another room, *P* wrote down on a sheet of paper the symbol printed on the card that *A* had turned up. This process was repeated forty times in a series of ten sessions. That was the experiment. A chart followed, showing the number of times P had guessed correctly. It seemed impossible that P could be such a good guesser. But it seemed that more than guessing was involved. Half a page of equations, like no equations he had ever seen before, followed the chart. The article concluded: "The probability of such results being achieved by chance is ten million to one."

Colin looked up. "I'm not sure I understand. In fact, I'm sure I don't."

David pointed to the page. "The percipient in this experiment"—his finger found one of the printed P's in the text and tapped it—

"Yes?"

"That's Sally."

Colin felt his mouth open. A looked at a card in one room— in another room P wrote down the symbol that A saw. "But that's mind reading," he said. "At least—isn't it?"

"Telepathy. Yes."

"Sally can do that?"

"She sure can."

Colin shook his head slowly. It made sense, now that he thought about it—occasions when she answered some remark before he voiced it, times she seemed to sense his presence without looking up. Admittedly that happened sometimes with other people too . . . He glanced quickly at David. "And you—are you . . . ?"

David's turn to shake his head. "Your thoughts are safe with me."

Sally was calling them from the foot of the stairs. "Are you two going to stay up there all night?" They came out into the hall and looked over the railing at her. She opened her hands expressively. "I've made coffee. Real coffee."

"You're getting the VIP treatment," David said, and Colin vaguely smiled.

The coffee was in the parlor, where windows stood open in the bay. A night breeze filled the thin curtains, then suddenly left them limp. The lamplight was welcoming and he found himself entering eagerly, settling into one of the striped chairs with a deep contentment.

"What I don't understand," he said, "is how you came to choose this house. How did you know it was supposed to be haunted?"

"We met someone at a party—a man who'd grown up here in town. Of course, you hear haunted house stories all the time, especially at parties, but it never hurts to check them out. And the prospect of being able to *rent* a haunted house is a psychic investigator's dream. To have it all to yourself . . ."

"It's always awkward when people have a house they think is haunted and they ask you to come in and investigate," Sally said. "They get annoyed if you don't find something right away. Or they get annoyed if you do. They don't like the paraphernalia; they resent your presence; they touch things they shouldn't touch—it's their house, after all, but—"

"But it's a damned nuisance having them around," David said. "And sometimes you find yourself opening emotional cans of worms that belong more to psychology than parapsychology. Poltergeist cases especially—Mother spanks Johnny and the refrigerator falls over. Then we come in from outside and point out a connection between the two events. people don't like it."

"I had no idea it was so complicated," Colin said.

"Oh, it's that."

They were all silent for a minute. The wind stirred the white curtains. Colin, watching the movement, said, "Has anyone ever seen the ghost in this house?"

"Not that we know of. But that doesn't mean anything. First of all, most people are reluctant to admit seeing an apparition. They know they're going to be laughed at. Second, an apparition isn't essential to a haunting. The kinds of things we've had reported here— for instance, the pounding noises we experienced—are just as legitimate as a whole platoon of apparitions, provided we can make a case for their being of paranormal origin."

"But where does Julian come in?"

"Well, from the sittings, we think he's the one doing the haunting."

Colin was confused. "But doesn't that make him a ghost?"

"Oh, yes. But not an apparition. Not all ghosts are visible. Some materialize completely: the Morton ghost was greeted by a friendly dog that only realized its mistake when it got up close. Some are more or less transparent—that's your classic ghost—and some are just sounds or smells or unaccountable emotional experiences."

"And Julian is the last."

"Well, we think he's responsible. We have no conclusive evidence—yet."

"But the sittings?"

"The sittings," David said, "don't prove anything. At least they don't cut any scientific ice. A lot of people, even in our field, would say we were just messing around. We brought Rosanna in as a kind of catalyst, to try and stir things up. Now, the phrase 'the lost one' compared with Julian's epitaph is an interesting correlation, but what does it mean? Even assuming it means haunting, there are subsets involved. We're faced with the two hypotheses Sally and I presented to you earlier. First, that what we contacted during the sitting may have been just a psychic echo of Julian endlessly repeating itself in the house, with no more true consciousness than a TV someone's forgotten to turn off. Second, that we may be confronting an actual personality who has survived bodily death—someone who's trying to communicate with us as best he can without a voice, or a hand to tap us on the shoulder with."

In spite of himself Colin could not suppress a shiver at the thought of this ghostly hand. "But surely there's some way of determining which it is?"

"Well, not yet," David said. "It seems significant that when I asked how Julian was lost, Sally went into trance and saw the churchyard with elms growing in it, the way it must have looked when he was buried there. As if he were responding to my question. That looks like consciousness, but it's not that simple. For instance, there's something called telesthesia. It's a postulated process by which one person can perceive the general contents of another's mind—different from telepathy in that no conscious thought is being consciously sent or received. Now, it's within the realm of possibility that Sally perceived the contents of, say, Mrs. Hopkins's mind, and learned about the elms from her—without knowing she was getting it, or without Mrs. Hopkins even knowing she was sending it."

Sally made an impatient movement. Colin said, "What's that called again?"

"Telesthesia."

"And isn't it paranormal?"

"Sure. But here you're getting into a question of degree. A lot of people who accept ESP as a proven fact will still balk at the idea of a personality surviving bodily death. Just consider—"

"David," Sally said. "You're lecturing."

He stopped and grinned, reddening a little. "Oh. Yeah."

⇒ *16* ⇐

HE HAD FORGOTTEN how pleasant it was to have the streets to himself late at night—forgotten how they became long silent arcades of leaf and shadow lit by the diminishing white globes of street lamps; how back behind the hedges and picket fences the darkened houses offered here and there a yellow square of window, a child's voice sleepily protesting bedtime, a burst of laughter, a scratchy record spinning round and round. *Stars fell on Alabama—last night—oh last night.* All the old songs were popular again, alive again in the sidewalk warmth that rolled like surf against the cooling night air as he walked, the sound of the cicadas loud and louder and then falling away in a long pulsing ebb until he could hear his own footsteps in the stillness. How long since he had heard that sound, walking home so late with just himself and the street lamps floating in the leaves? Not since Grif died, his last real friend—not since the war. Those evenings sitting past midnight on the porch at Grif's, arguing about Balzac, Tolstoy, Dickens, books their passion. Grif on the steps, himself on the porch railing, their shirtsleeves rolled up, a couple of beers . . . After a couple of beers Grif would start to talk about some girl. Of course Grif always had some girl on his mind; he was young, nearly ten years Colin's junior. There was always some girl. Was it Betsy the waitress that week, or Anne the schoolteacher, or Christine, who had just moved into town? There wasn't much difference, at least not to him (presumably Grif could distinguish between them, although at times Colin wondered), and on those nights it all came to the same thing anyway. "Tell me honestly, Collie . . ." and Grif would be off: what she said, what he said, was

132

there anything to beat that? And he, Colin, sat rolling
the cool bottle slowly between his palms, not listening
really (although Grif was his best friend), thinking not of
girls but of women, not individuals but a species apart,
keepers of the sacred flame or some such thing. The
image cheapened in its articulating: otherwise he possessed it deeply and clearly. Held up against most of the
women he knew (and there weren't many; he was horri-
bly shy) it fit not at all. Then there would be the porch at
night, Grif coming out through the lighted screen door
with two more beers—"Tell me honestly, Collie"—and
honestly he didn't know. Not about Christine or Betsy or
Anne or Donna (who had left her husband), but only
about women in books, or—even less substantial—a
moment, an instant, a smile like light on a calm sea.

And until tonight he had forgotten not the smile, but
the woman who smiled: had thought he dreamed it, or
read it in a book.

Of course he was an innocent about women. He knew
it and so did Grif, who talked to him about them simply
out of habit, or friendship, because they both loved books.
And all the time Grif talked he sat listening like someone
hearing a language foreign yet vaguely familiar, understanding a word here and there, somtimes a whole phrase
together, but continually losing the thread so that as the
fragments emerged he was unable to connect them one to
another. For only now and then did it match up with
what he felt: only once in a long while did he see in Anne
or Betsy, suddenly illumined, the dark fleeting silhouette
of a woman. It was his own fault of course, for burying
himself in books. Because real women were not like
Desdemona or Guinevere or Anna Karenina—not even
like Becky Sharp. They were simply Christine Murray,
who cried when Grif did not like her new hairdo, or
Betsy Squires, whose conversation consisted mainly of a
giggle, three notes in an ascending scale. But then in the
midst of them there would be someone like Leonie Saunders, a tall flat cotton-print figure like a child's rag doll,
handing a heavy bag of groceries across the counter, the
cords standing out in her arms—and he, poor book-
bemused Colin, would see behind her an image, a shadow,
Rebecca at the well. It happened without warning: a
hesitation, a turn of the head, or a door opening and a

smile—and some knot in his chest, unfelt till then, would loosen. Because sometimes the image faded, sometimes he doubted himself, his dreams and his books. But then Mary Barnes, coming out of Buck's, stopped and bent her head over the rose seedlings she was carrying, or Sally Curtiss turned the pages of an old book with competent, gentle hands.

The present came down in front of him slowly, like the curtain at the end of a play. Trees and silence and the street stretching ahead, empty beneath its lamps. He took a breath: almost home. Here was the old Stratton place, the same pickets he had passed every day on his way to school, bad luck if you did not touch every single one. He touched them now lightly, whimsically, an old man whose slight figure in the shadows might have been that of a boy playing a mysterious game.

And then his gate, and the house where he had lived alone since his mother's death—alone except for Locky, his wire-haired terrier, rising now from the front step, stretching, wagging a greeting. They went inside together, old man and old dog; Colin fed him and then sat down at the kitchen table to look at his mail. It was all junk except for a gardening catalog he had sent for; he looked through pages of seedlings and weed killers, a miracle tool that performed six functions . . . His eyes went past the page to the square of darkness beyond the window screen. *The night is dark and I am far from home.* Was it possible for a young man's spirit to go on existing in an old house, trapped there while the century moved from the horse and buggy into space travel? The catalog slipped off his lap and fell unnoticed to the floor while he sat unmoving, staring at the dark screen as if he could see beyond it. And indeed against the blackness faces came close, changing like wind-stirred water; figures moved and drifted, fading and brightening on the tide. *Ginny? Ginny? Who's there? I thought I heard* . . . the trembling, complaining voice calling out as they passed the room. She went to the door while Colin waited in the hall, the heavy package in his arms, and the murmur of her answer soothed him as it must have soothed the old man within. He was sixteen years old, a shy boy who loved to read, liked to fish in the pond on old Mr. Wallace's property. With the money he was making at Buck's in the summers he wanted to buy a bicycle. When he finished high school he wanted to go to the state university. And he wanted to learn to fly a plane. He wanted all these things, and others without name or form, so badly that sometimes at night he got out of bed and stood at the window, feeling the cool air on his skin while his blood traced the hot web of veins beneath. In the enormous darkness of the sky the stars too beat with a liquid, living pulse.

Something cold in the palm of his hand—Locky's nose, and the shallow bright brown eyes looking at him. "Hello, old boy." He glanced at the clock on the kitchen wall: late, past midnight. putting out the light, hearing the dog's nails click on the floorboards as he went into the next room, Colin stood a moment in the dark. There was nothing here to banish the past: not the walls around him or the familiar shadows of furniture, his footsteps in the hall or the creak of his bedroom door, nothing to summon him gently to the present, so that when he turned on the lamp, he drew back startled at the sight of the face in the mirror, furrowed and sunken and white-haired, so unlike his own.

February 12, 1906

A number of citizens had a narrow escape on Skipton's Main Street yesterday afternoon when a dairyman's wagon filled with milk cans collided with a horse and buggy. The dairyman, R. R. Hodges, was driving his team north on Olympus when the runaway began. The horses reached Main Street at a full gallop, turned down Main and ran along the sidewalk, scattering pedestrians and urged on by the shouts of mischievous schoolboys. A horse and buggy belonging to Judge Lionel Saunders was hitched in front of Kimball's Apothecary, and the runaway team collided with this vehicle. Remarkably, no one was hurt.

They looked, Colin thought, like two kids reading a forbidden book, heads together over the microfilm viewer. And he was a third, standing behind them, reading over Sally's shoulder. David turned the advance knob and another page of the *Masonville Echo* slid into view.

"You know," Colin said, "there must be an easier way."

Sally turned around to face him. "You'd think so, wouldn't you? It ought to be the simplest thing in the world to find out the exact date of someone's death. But our luck has been terrible. The year was on Julian's gravestone. But the date of burial wasn't entered in the parish records. So we asked the county board of health for a copy of the death certificate. But they had a fire in 1924, and most of those records were destroyed." She sat back, rubbing her eyes. "I've got a headache. This thing is tough to read."

Colin was following his own thoughts. "That's funny, isn't it—that it isn't in the parish records? I mean, he *is* buried there."

"Understandable," David said. "His father was the minister there at the time. It would have been his job to enter the burial date. Maybe he just wasn't up to it." He looked at his watch and switched the viewer off. "It's past noon. Let's get something to eat and then have another go."

They had sandwiches in Colin's office, a small back room looking out on a playground. The window stood open to the sun and heat and the racket of children's voices. Colin said, "I don't quite understand why you need the exact date of Julian's death."

"It's not the exact date we need, it's the facts we can get from the newspaper account of the accident. Details." David took a huge bite of his sandwich. "The date would be a help in just knowing where to look."

Colin sighed. "There should be an index for that paper. But I've talked to Marian Bowen at the Masonville Library about it and she says she can't afford to pay someone to compile one. It's not an easy job."

"Never mind. We'll find it. Only three hundred and twenty-two days to go."

After lunch they went back to work; at least David did. Sally took one look at the tall pile of microfilm boxes and said she had had enough for the day.

"Tomorrow we should work in shifts. It doesn't take both of us."

"You're right." David picked up the top box. "What are you going to do now?"

"Buy groceries. We're out of everything."

It was a summer weekday afternoon, sunny and drowsy; the library was almost empty. There was Delia Phillips mulling over one of the trays in the card catalog, and Warren Wade reading the Boston papers in the corner, and around two o'clock Mrs. Dalton came in and paid the 35-cent fine she had been owing since Christmas. Sun stretched the bright silhouettes of the windows longer and longer on the floor, and when one of them reached

Delia's feet she looked up a little startled as if someone had touched her intimately. But the sun-fashioned windows ignored her, draping themselves over tables and chairs and creeping over the floor and up the walls and shelves of books. Warren Wade blinked in the brightness and lifted the newspaper higher to shut it out, and Delia felt another warm touch on her ankle and didn't step back out of the way this time but stood reading the card marked "Hastings, Battle of" and feeling the warmth slide up her calf, and David Curtiss, leaning back from the microfilm machine to stretch, put his head into the light and felt his hair on fire like a god's.

Colin saw him tip his chair against the light and hang there a moment suspended with his hair blazing and his arms flung out. Now he stretched as if his bones would crack, let the chair tilt slowly forward, carrying him out of the path of the light, until all four legs rested on the floor. He switched off the microfilm machine, stood up, and crossed the floor to Colin's desk. "I'm calling it a day."

"How far did you get?"

"About halfway into March."

"And nothing yet?"

"Nothing."

"I think I'll just leave the film in the machine," Colin said. "You're coming in tomorrow morning?"

"You bet."

The windows had finished growing by this time; they lay spread out over floor and furniture and walls so that the whole place was windows and windows, long rectangles of cross-barred light, glowing, dusty, the color of apricots; the real windows themselves were pale and linear in comparison, sitting primly in the walls instead of splashed and spilling over the broken surfaces of the room. The color of the light-windows deepened and softened while Colin sat on at his desk, taking notes for his town history; slowly the color began to fade from apricot to a sad medieval gold, and then to rose and violet. He looked up when he could no longer see the page he was reading: Warren was gone, Delia was gone, leaving a drawer half out of the card catalog.

He went to slide it in and stood letting the stillness and the wistful light settle over him; through the open win-

dows came the smell of evening, heavy trees stirring in
the warm fading summer air. It might have been the air
that made him feel like an old man, all his summers run
together, colors bleeding into one another, violet and gold
and shadow-green, and with them the faces, those of his
childhood and those of his old age, so that just this
morning he had almost put out a hand to a brown-haired
boy bent over a book, almost said "William," when
William had been dead ten years, had not been a brown-
haired boy for fifty.

Most summer evenings he opened the library for an
hour or two after supper, but tonight he was tired, thinking about going to bed early. Shelves and tables and
chairs were all in shadow. There were only a few gleams
of light remaining; one caught the curved hood of the
microfilm machine. He walked over to it, admiring it,
touching the knobs and switches: clicked one and the
image sprang brightly into view—*The Masonville Echo,
March 17, 1906.* A hunting accident, a new town ordi-
nance concerning the keeping of pigs in certain of
Masonville's residential areas, a pie-baking contest spon-
sored by the First Episcopal Church in Skipton: he smiled
as he glanced over the front page. It was late and he was
tired, but the old typefaces had a charm to them and the
advance knob turned easily in his fingers as he went on
reading. Some of the names were as familiar to him as his
own—Bristowe and Saunders and Hopkins, the old Skipton
families. Miss Rebecca Gilfoy had won a blue ribbon for
her apple pie. Timothy Campbell, twelve, had qualified
for entry in the Regional Spelling Championship (his last
opponent had gone down on the word "feasible"). Behind the fuzzy headlines and crooked columns of type
they seemed, Rebecca and Timothy, Judge Saunders and
Captain Hopkins and the others, to follow a round of
church picnics and county fairs, lighthearted accidents
(Mr. Sutton drove his buggy into the river) and minor
scandals (there was something questionable about one of
the young-lady schoolteachers in Helmingham) and near
disasters (no one was in the Huxtable barn when it collapsed); people gathered in smiling talkative groups,
dressed the way he remembered them from his childhood, the men stiff and dark and wearing hats, the women

in their long high-collared dresses, standing and moving against an oblique brightness.

A heavy snow had fallen on March 19, causing property damage in two counties. Colin, reading about collapsed roofs and burst pipes and frozen geese, let his glance slide down the page and felt the breath stop in his mouth. TRAGEDY IN SKIPTON said the headline near the bottom, and the old-fashioned letters, slightly out of kilter with one another, seemed to beat once, twice with a hard pulse under his gaze. Then slowly, without realizing it, he sank down in the chair in front of the viewing screen, put his chin in his hands, and read.

The home of one of Skipton's most prominent citizens, the Reverend Joshua Gilfoy, was the scene of a tragic accident last evening when Julian Gilfoy, the minister's youngest son, fell down a steep flight of stairs to his death. No one witnessed the fall, although several members of the family including two of the youth's sisters, Miss Mary and Miss Clara Gilfoy, and his stepmother, Mrs. Virginia Gilfoy, rushed to the scene immediately upon hearing the noise of the fall. They discovered the young man lying at the foot of the stairs. Dr. E. C. Bristowe was sent for and pronounced him dead of a brain haemorrhage caused by a fractured skull.

Young Gilfoy, twenty, was a student at Harvard College in the tradition of his family. Since last May he had been on a leave of absence from his studies for reasons of health, his father said. Dr. Bristowe said it was possible that dizziness had caused the fatal fall.

The *Echo* extends its deepest sympathies to the Gilfoy family in this tragic loss.

It seemed to him that he had been sitting bent over the shining page for a long time: there was a sharp pain between his shoulder blades. Outside the windows it had gotten dark, and the only illumination in the room came from the glowing screen. By its light he found his desk and felt the shape of the telephone under his hand.

For some reason it was hard to gather his thoughts. Their number would be too new to be listed in the directory. He dialed Information and asked for the number of David Curtiss, two *s*'s, on Lilac Street in Skipton. The operator offered to connect him and he thanked her, the words floating outside his head in the dark room, small and far away against the sounds within—a crash and then doors opening, running footsteps and voices suddenly rising . . . Against the darkness she opened a door and smiled; there was gray in the light brown of her hair. The smile went into him like an arrow, exactly as the books had always promised, straight into his heart in spite of the heavy box marked BUCK'S HARDWARE & GENERAL: FRAGILE GOODS that he held against his chest. He was sixteen years old. Her eyes were blue. The faint distant ringing against his ear stopped; there was a click and a voice said clearly, "Hello?" The old man gazed steadily at the face in the blackness before him.

"David? It's Colin. I think I've found what you're looking for."

⇛ 18 ⇚

IT WAS PROBABLY no more than fifteen minutes before they arrived, so it seemed impossible that in such a short interval he could have forgotten they were coming. But he had. Another sign of old age, no doubt. He was sitting there by himself in the dark and the voices and footsteps outside startled him: he jumped to his feet like a sentry caught sleeping. The door opened.

"Colin?"

"Here I am."

"Why the blackout?"

"Well . . . if the lights are on, it means I'm open for business. I just thought . . ." He heard himself talking, making a reason for his reluctance to banish the darkness and all it contained.

The lit screen of the viewer drew them. He heard David stumble against something, probably a chair, and curse. Then they were standing in front of the glow from the machine, two dark shapes side by side and motionless. He joined them, watching the white light's reflection on their downturned faces. David looked up.

"Bravo, Colin, this is it! What's the date—March twentieth."

"It says 'last evening.' That would make it the nineteenth."

"The nineteenth, then. It's interesting, this bit about poor health. Was Julian an invalid?"

"Not that I know of. I suspect that may be a polite fiction to cover the fact of his not being at college. He may have been suspended or expelled."

"Maybe he'd ruined his health with wild living," David

142

said. Sally had said nothing all this time; she stood looking down at the page, and now he touched her arm.
"Hello?"

She looked up. "I was just trying to visualize it. If
there was a quarrel—which room was Joshua's, do you
suppose?"

"Well, my guess would be—"

"The corner room," Colin said. "Above the kitchen."

There was a silence; the two white-lit faces burned in
front of him. Then David said, "You sound very sure
about that."

"I am sure. I mean, pretty sure. You see, I remember
his being in that room once when I was in the house . . .
I guess I should have told you."

"When was this?"

"Oh, a very long time ago. I only remembered it when
you had me over for supper the other night."

"And you saw him in that room?"

"No, I only heard him. I was carrying something
upstairs—it was a delivery; I used to work at Buck's as a
delivery boy . . ." It all sounded so trivial that he was
ashamed at having mentioned it, but they were waiting
for him to go on. "Anyway, I was carrying it upstairs,
and when we went past the door of that corner room, he
called out."

"What did he say?"

"Just who was it; that was all, I think. He must have
been bedridden by then; he was an invalid for some years
before he died."

David's face, illuminated from below by the white light,
had the grotesque look of a sideshow magician, all peaks
and shadows. "He called out—and then?"

"Well, she went to the door and spoke to him. I didn't
hear what she said."

"She?"

"Mrs. Gilfoy." Colin was surprised by his own reluctance to talk about her.

"Joshua's second wife," Sally said. "Julian's stepmother."

David was following his own train of thought. "So that
was demonstrably Joshua's room. The room that now
generates a lot of psi activity—the cold, the raps, that

very active sitting with Rosanna. That story about the quarrel between Julian and Joshua has got to be true! And it took place in that room. They argue, Julian rushes out, starts down the stairs and falls. Now, if we knew what they were fighting about—"

"David . . ."

David's grin was demonic in the weird light. "I guess we've made enough progress for one night."

Colin ended up accepting their invitation to come back to the house for coffee. Halfway to Lilac Street he remembered that he hadn't had supper, but it didn't matter and in any case there was no chance to mention it; David talked nonstop, gesturing in the dark as they walked.

"Obviously the fact that their quarrel wasn't mentioned in the newspaper doesn't mean a thing. It's hardly the kind of thing you'd tell a reporter. But how the hell are we going to substantiate a rumor of an argument that took place seventy-plus years ago?"

No one had any suggestions. They turned up the hill. It was not late; there were still children out playing and from the porches the sound of voices reached them. A screen banged; someone called, "Jackie—Jackie—" A car passed, headlights sweeping the street ahead, freezing a cat gold-eyed in the glare. A small figure darted past them. "Hi, Mr. Robinson!" "Hello, hello there," Colin said—and the quick light steps continued on.

At the gate they stopped. David pushed it open: a squeak of hinges and then silence. The house rose in darkness beyond, walls melting into the shadow-shapes of trees, and they all stood still, looking at the lit windows. So it had stood over the years and would go on standing, whether they or others stopped at the gate: the glimmering, beckoning light beyond the leaves knew no difference. Or did it? Who can encompass the fullness of an old house—the moments collected there like colored layers of sediment in which are embedded a glance, a quarrel, the soft closing of a door? The mere scope of it is too vast to consider. Try, and the mind stutters; images overlap without sense or sequence, infinite. Nonetheless it is all here.

Inside it was quiet as they entered the parlor and saw the lamplight pooled in the seats of chairs. They had been having coffee, Colin saw, when he called: there were the cups, one on the arm of a chair, another on the rug. David collected them absently. Retrieving the one from the floor he stopped on one knee and remained motionless with a cup in either hand, staring at the air.

"March. March. Wasn't there something—Sally, where's that list of tenants?"

"Upstairs. I'll get it." She left the room.

Colin watched her go, then looked at David who, still half kneeling, resembled a slightly crazed religious visionary. "Does something special happen in March?" he asked.

David gestured; cups jittered in saucers. "Maybe." He got up and set the dishes, forgotten, on the mantelpiece. "Maybe." He started to pace.

Sally came back with a notebook in her hand, turning the pages quickly. "Here. Here." The three of them bent over it. *Former Tenants of the Gilfoy House,* Colin read. Sally's finger moved down the list.

"Here we go. Murray: in, November; out, March. Pindar: in and out, March. Sterling: in, April; out the following March; Gardner: in and out, March. Four out of nine, and one of them Sterling the skeptic—"

"Plus Gardner and Pindar, whose stays were the shortest on record. Did you notice that? Pindar arrives March first, 1944 and moves out three weeks later. The Gardners arrive March first, 1975 and stay exactly ten days. Is it just coincidence that neither of them will talk to us?"

"And nobody stayed all the way through a March," Sally said. "Look. Every other month is covered."

"So we can at least postulate that psi activity increases in March—"

"And our lease only runs through August," Sally said. "So it's going to be a little hard to stick around and prove it."

"Does all this mean," Colin said cautiously, "that the house is *more* haunted in March?"

They both looked at him. Sally said, "Well, it's possible."

"Because of Julian having died in March?"

"It's one hypothesis," David said. "A very attractive one."

Colin was looking at the list. "Murray," he said. "Murray. I wonder."

"So do we. We couldn't locate them."

"If it's the people I'm thinking of—"

"You know them, Colin?"

"I suppose it's a common name. But I knew someone many years ago—a Christine Murray. She lives in Masonville now, I think." He glanced up to find them both staring at him.

"Could you find out?" David said. "Could you ask her if she ever lived here?"

"I suppose I could call her. I haven't seen her in years."

"Colin, it's very important. We need to know what goes on here in March, and we haven't had any luck talking to the people who've lived here in March, except for one who blames everything on the plumbing or the squirrels in the attic. If we could just get one good clear statement, it would be tremendously helpful, don't you see? If you could call your friend, set up an interview—"

"David." Sally put her hand on his arm. "Would you mind, Colin? If you feel funny about it . . ."

She looked worried, and he hated to see her look like that. "Of course I wouldn't mind," he said.

"Fantastic!" David remembered the coffee cups and gathered them up. "I'm going to make some coffee. Listen, if she'll talk to us . . . you have no idea . . ." His voice went on, down the hall to the kitchen, then the sound of running water covered the words. Sally sat down on the rug; Colin took a chair nearby.

"It's very exciting," he said.

"Yes."

"You look sad, Sally."

"I'm just thinking about those people."

"You mean Julian?"

"All of them."

He felt that strange sensation in his chest, like something unfolding. "You know, it's funny about her—Mrs. Gilfoy."

"How do you mean?"

He shifted in his chair. The lamplight had a hazy, tender quality like the light in old photographs. "Oh, just—I had forgotten who she was, but I hadn't ever forgotten her. Now that doesn't make much sense, does it?"

"What was she like, Colin?"

He looked down at her where she sat looking up; the young face seemed to shimmer in the light. He had the sense, not quite sane, that this moment had been superimposed on them from the outside, a gift of the house. "She was like you," he said.

David's footsteps were coming back down the hall and she turned her head away, toward the door. Was she angry? Embarrassed? He scarcely knew what had made him say it. Just a feeling—but here was David, saying, "What we've got right now is a hell of a lot of circumstantial evidence, and that's not enough."

"Enough for what?" Colin said.

"Enough to say we haven't been wasting our time, barking up the wrong tree, on a wild goose chase. Pick your favorite cliché."

"But if Julian died in March, and a lot of people moved out in March, doesn't that prove—"

"Four out of nine," Sally said. "And it's entirely possible that there's no relation between the events. Even if there's a haunting—which we haven't proved—and even if Julian is responsible—which we haven't proved—there's still a lot of room for doubt. For instance, there's no evidence to support the view that ghosts are aware of time in the same way we are. 'March' is a pretty arbitrary label."

"But I thought it was always on the anniversary of the murder, you know, that whoever it was walked around carrying her head in her arms . . ."

David was grinning. "Well, like all folk mythology, that may hold some truth. The fact is, we don't know. In this case, psi activity may actually increase in March. Or maybe the pipes always freeze in March. The only way we're going to find out is either to stay till March ourselves, which isn't really feasible, or else talk to someone who moved out in March and is willing to tell us why. Now, if your friend Murray—"

"A friend of a friend, really," Colin said absently, preoccupied with the astonishing void spreading through him at the thought that they would be going; of course, they simply wanted to complete their research and then they would move on . . .

"Well, whosever friend she is—if she'll talk to us, then we may get somewhere."

⟫⟫⟫ *19* ⟪⟪⟪

CHRISTINE, HE RECALLED, had married Johnny Frey from Masonville. He vaguely remembered being angry at her for that, thinking her heartless, so soon after Grif's death. But it had been wartime, after all; everybody was a little crazy. He had been out of the fighting himself, too old to enlist, and his mother's sole support (she was bedridden by then). His contribution to the war had been to serve as an air raid warden here in Skipton, and his sense of Christine's betrayal had been complicated by a festering sense of his own. Now Johnny was dead too; he had seen it in the *Echo* a few years back. But Christine was still listed in the Skipton-Masonville-Helmingham phone book—*Frey, Mrs. John G.*

It was awkward. When he called her, at first she didn't remember him (and why should she, Grif's shy bookish friend who had blushed, likely as not, every time she spoke to him) and when at last she did, her tone changed from cool to embarrassingly warm. It was with some difficulty that he managed to bring the conversation around to the point of the call. Had she ever lived in the old Gilfoy house in Skipton, the one on Lilac Street? She had? Well, he had some young friends who were very curious about the house, very anxious to ask her about it. Could he bring them to see her? Four o'clock. Fine. They would be there at four.

The house was big and square, attended by plaster lions and blue hydrangeas. They parked the car, passed between the lions and climbed the steps to the house with its brass knocker in the shape of a dolphin. There they waited a moment, looking at one another, before David lifted the knocker and let it fall.

He hadn't seen Christine since the forties, half a lifetime, and it was not surprising that he did not recognize the woman who answered the door. The soft gray of her hair framed the soft pink of her face; she was an attractive older woman, a stranger. But she was inviting them inside, and he must say something.

"Christine, these are the young people I told you about, who are interested in the Gilfoy house. Sally and David Curtiss. Christine Frey."

They were shaking hands; he had done it; his part was finished. He looked around the room at the plump chairs, filmy curtains, thick carpet underfoot, a Pekinese that appeared silently from nowhere and stared at him with bulging eyes. He tried to picture Grif with his angles and sharp edges surrounded by all this softness, and could not. Instead he listened to what they were saying.

"When Colin called, of course, I was so surprised" —she had her head on one side, looking up at David— "but of course it was a delight to hear from him. We've been out of touch for years, but since my dear husband died I've found such comfort in my old friends . . ."

David's nod conveyed sympathetic interest. Colin knew him well enough by now to see the driving eagerness behind the charm. He stood easily, suntanned and curly-haired, but with a focus, a purpose that kept the room's softness at bay. It did not dare close in. Sally had bent to pat the dog; now she straightened and met Colin's eyes. He felt rather than saw her smile.

"What we'd like to do," David was saying, "is just have you tell us about living in the house, everything you can remember. Then we'll ask you to fill out a printed questionnaire. If you don't mind, I'd like to record our conversation on tape." He patted the knapsack slung over his shoulder; Christine's eyes went to it and then back to his face with its engaging smile.

"Well, I don't see why not . . . though I always sound so awful on those things, not like myself at all. My nephew has one—"

"Everybody sounds terrible on them," David agreed. "But I can promise you that the only people who will ever hear it will be scientists, and they'll be much more interested in what you're saying than how you sound."

"Scientists?" She touched her hair nervously. "Why—"

"I'm afraid," Colin said, "that I didn't really explain—"

"Oh, okay," David said.

Christine seemed to recall all at once that she was the hostess. "Let's sit down. I made some lemonade."

It was on a low table surrounded by a cluster of chairs, a tall pitcher on a lace doily. They sat; there was silence while the lemonade gurgled into thimble-sized glass cups. Colin sipped, feeling the softness of the room close in.

"Well," David said, and it withdrew slightly. "Well, here's our situation. Sally and I got interested in the Gilfoy house because, as you may know, it has a reputation for being haunted. Of course sometimes stories get started and they don't really mean anything, but there have been cases where certain unexplained occurrences have made houses virtually uninhabitable. We're interested in finding out what's going on in such cases—if not explaining it, at least documenting it. Showing that certain things did happen, and what they consisted of."

He paused and Christine said, "Wasn't there a movie . . . ?"

He frowned faintly and Sally looked down at her cup, hiding a smile. "Yes," David was saying. "Well, there are lots of movies. But parapsychology is a very serious science. It might not be as exciting as the Hollywood version, but it's a lot more exact. What will happen with this tape of our conversation is that it will go on file with the other data we've collected about the house. All of it will be analyzed; various hypotheses will be offered; then the whole thing will probably be written up in some scientific journal."

Christine looked pleased at the prospect: she liked the words, Colin thought—"data," "hypotheses." His tiny cup was empty and he put it down carefully on the doily. The lemonade was much too sweet. David had taken the small tape recorder out of his knapsack and was holding it on his knees, pointing the microphone toward Christine. She looked at it nervously.

"Should I begin?" Stage whisper.

David nodded. "Go ahead," he said in his normal voice. "Just tell us about living in the house."

"Well. Well, let me see. It was before the war, that's the Second World War, or before we had gone into it, anyway—the fall of 'forty or 'forty-one, it must have been. My family and I had moved here from Boston. My father had just retired from the rope business."

David was nodding encouragingly, his eyes light and intent on the recording index of the tape machine. Sally sat back in her chair, still holding her empty cup. Colin relaxed. It was a relief not to be expected to say anything. Yet he had helped them; he was glad of that.

Christine had decided that it was the autumn of 1940. "Because my sister got married just before we moved to Skipton and Jerry, that's her oldest boy, was born the next year, just two days after Pearl Harbor. I remember my mother saying, 'What a world we're giving that child' and starting to cry . . ." If David was impatient now he did not show it; his eyes were on the recording index and the lashes never flickered.

Colin sat listening less to the words than to the sound of her voice in the pink and gray afternoon, watching the sunlight struggle through the gauzy curtains to fall exhausted across the backs of the chairs. A process was beginning as he sat there, a slow visceral realization that the woman across from him, wrinkled and gray-haired, was actually the girl he had known in her twenties—actually Christine, with her lithe body and bright yellow hair, who painted her nails red and danced on the coffee table in Grif's living room the last night of his leave, danced in her stockinged feet while the radio played "Wrap Your Troubles in Dreams." She was always touching up her face, always at work with her mirror and her little bag, perfecting her eyes or her mouth or her hair. "Oh, let it alone," Grif would say, "you look all right," his mouth turning down at the corner. And she would make a face at him, watching herself in the tiny mirror. They were amazingly vivid, the young woman and the lanky sardonic soldier, both of them gaudy with the crude glamour of youth and of the era, eager to wrestle life into submission. Watching them he felt confused and shadowy, as if their presence drained him of substance, left him hollow. Everything in him that remembered the past, all the long continuity of his life that had seemed a blessing until now, seemed to make a wrenching movement outward, toward the bright faces that were no longer a trick of his memory but more real than the room around him. Then it was over, as quickly as the rising and sinking of a wave, and the impression faded and he was back in the present again, with a knot in his throat and a prickling in his eyes and the flustered sense that he had been quietly making a fool of himself.

"It was my mother who heard the noises," Christine was saying. "I never heard anything unusual myself. But I did see a strange light sometimes."

When she hesitated David said, "Yes? Could you describe what you saw? Try to remember the circumstances if you can."

She touched her hair and laughed a little. "Well, mercy. It was a long time ago. But let me see . . . I think the first time I saw it was one evening when I had been out. I was coming in the gate and I looked up and saw a light in the window of my room. Naturally I just thought my mother must have turned on the lamp. But when I got upstairs, the room was dark. My parents were both downstairs listening to the radio, so they couldn't have turned out the lamp."

"Which room was yours?"

"The little one in front, right in the center. It had one window."

"And the light was bright enough for you to see it from the gate?"

"Oh, yes."

"Did you ever see it again?"

"Oh, yes. Once I woke up and it was in the room with me. And another time I saw it on the stairs. And once— you know that sitting room on the second floor? Once it was in there. I think that's all."

"Exactly what did it look like?" David said.

"Well, it was almost like—you know the circle of light a flashlight makes when you shine it on something close? Like that. But more vivid—more of a glow."

"Like a lightning bug?"

"Just like a—oh! Do you think that's what it was?" She looked stricken, like a child deprived of belief in Santa Claus.

"Not likely," David said. "Didn't you say this was late autumn? I was just trying to ascertain the quality of the light."

"Oh, I see. And besides, it was steady, this light. It didn't blink on and off the way a lightning bug does. Oh, you gave me a scare!"

His smile was mechanical. "Do you remember the color of the light, Mrs. Frey?"

"Well, it was yellowish. Or maybe bluish green. It was just—oh, *light* colored. You can call me Christine."

"But not an unusual color, Christine?"

"No."

"Did you get any kind of feeling from the light?"

"Feeling?" she said.

"For instance, did it seem dangerous? Or, say, friendly?"

"Well, it—it just seemed like a light. Certainly not dangerous."

"Okay. Now, I'm interested in the noises you say your mother heard. Did she ever describe them to you?"

"Yes. They were scratching noises."

"Scratching noises," David repeated.

"Like something scratching on the wall. They kept her awake. My father never heard them, but he was a very sound sleeper."

"Did she say whether they seemed to come from one particular spot?"

"The wall behind her head. They slept in the bedroom at the top of the stairs."

From his knapsack David produced a floor plan of the house. "Could you show me which wall you mean? Here's the room your parents slept in."

She gazed blankly at the piece of paper. "Oh, I—I never could read maps."

"Oh, this isn't a map." His tone was soothing. "It's just a kind of bird's-eye view of the inside of the house. Here are the stairs, see? Now just imagine you're standing at the top of the stairs . . ."

It took some coaxing, but Christine finally managed to place the scratching sounds as coming from the wall between her parents' room and the master bedroom. "That wasn't so hard, was it?" To Colin's now practiced ear David sounded slightly weary. "Now, approximately how often did your mother hear these sounds, did she tell you?"

"Oh, every night. Or almost every night."

"Over how long a period of time?"

"From the time we moved into the house until we moved out."

"And the noises were the reason you moved out?"

"Oh no. My father thought they were all in her head. We moved out after his accident."

"Accident?"

"He fell down the stairs and hurt his back. Even after he got better, he had trouble negotiating any sort of stairs, so we moved to a house with a bedroom on the first floor. I didn't meet you until after we'd moved, did I, Colin?"

David was sitting stone-silent, staring down at the tape recorder, and Christine's hand went to her mouth. "Oh, I'm sorry! I forgot this was being recorded!"

He looked up quickly and smiled. "What? Oh, it doesn't matter. You said your father fell down the stairs in the house?"

All at once Colin was aware of the inside of his mouth, horrible with the too sweet aftertaste of the lemonade. He looked at Sally but her face was expressionless, watching Christine's.

"That's right. He hurt his back pretty badly."

David sat back, steadying the tape recorder in his lap, moving his shoulders as though they were stiff. "You said he never heard the scratching noises. Did he ever mention hearing any other unusual noises?"

"No, I don't think so."

"Did your family own a pet dog?"

"No. I've always loved dogs, but my father didn't like them." The Pekinese was by her feet and she bent and lifted it to her lap. "But now I have my little Precious, don't I?" she said to the dog. It snorted, wriggled free, and jumped down.

"Christine," David said, "how long before your family moved out of the house did your father have his accident? Do you remember when it happened?"

"Oh yes. Yes I do, because it was just before my sister's birthday. She was living in St. Louis, and we had to call and wish her a happy birthday from the hospital, because Daddy was in traction. It must have been around the middle of March."

David looked at Sally and then at Colin with a dazed, silly face.

"The middle of March," he said. "Thank you, Christine. You've been very helpful. Thank you very much."

⋙ 20 ⋘

FROM THE BEGINNING, talking to them, hearing their theories and hypotheses and seeing their sophisticated instruments, Colin had simply accepted what they were telling him: not only about the old Gilfoy house, but about their complicated science itself. There were such things as haunted houses, it seemed, and the Gilfoy house might be such a place. It was a question not of ghosts and goblins but of facts, their collection and documentation and analysis, all very scientific and rational. This was their truth, and since they were clearly intelligent, serious, civilized people, he had accepted it. Now, aware of his tongue coated with a sugary film and his heartbeat making itself a nuisance, he found himself beginning to believe it, and the difference astonished him.

"Finally," David was saying. They had stopped at a diner for coffee as an antidote to the lemonade, and he sat with his elbows on the table in the booth, one hand clasping the other fist. "Finally we're getting somewhere."

The paper mats on the table were printed with a quiz about soccer. Sally had produced a pencil and was doing hers. "Two people falling down a steep flight of stairs over a period of forty years isn't proof of anything," she said without looking up.

"Two people? I'll bet it's a hell of a lot more than just two people. I fell down the goddamn things myself."

Colin saw the pencil come to a stop. She looked up. "You what? When?"

"I don't remember—wait, yes I do. It was the night Rosanna got the phone call. The night before she left."

A strand of hair had fallen over Sally's forehead; she

157

pushed it back, regarding David steadily. "You didn't tell me."

"I don't tell you every time I crack my elbow on that blasted cabinet door in the bathroom, either, but it happens."

They were, Colin realized, very close to quarreling, and he had no clear idea of how they had reached that point. He stirred his black coffee unnecessarily.

"It seems to me," Sally said carefully, "that you might have mentioned it after we found out how Julian died."

There was a pause; then David said, "Well, I'm mentioning it now." He met her look with a smiling little shrug. "Look, I was embarrassed. Okay? It seems like I've done nothing but trip over my own feet since we moved into the house."

Sally put the pencil down and picked up her cup. "Well still, David, that makes three in eighty years. I don't know what the probability would be on something like that, but—"

He interrupted her. "No, but wait. Out of those eighty years the house has been empty a good part of the time. The actual occupancy must break down to a lot less. And there may be other factors. I think I'll give Jack a call, let him run it through the computer. And let's get hold of the other tenants—find out if it happened to them, and when."

Colin had an idea. "Could there be something about the stairs themselves, some structural flaw, that's causing the accidents? I read a book once—"

"Bravo, Colin. We'll make a psychic investigator of you yet. Of course we'll have to check that factor too." David was creasing his place mat into a series of tiny mountain ranges. "All in all," he smoothed the mat out again, "it was a very interesting afternoon. Some things seem to be falling into place. Excuse the phrase."

"The noises and the light," Sally said.

"I should have asked her about the cold spot in Joshua's room. Actually I'm a little surprised she didn't mention it. Everyone else has."

"She may not have thought it was anything unusual," Sally said. "It was winter, after all. And that room doesn't get much sun."

"This light she saw," Colin said. "Other people have seen it too, haven't they?"

"Yes—in fact, in one family it was known as Tinkerbell. If you want to get formal it's called a spirit light. They're fairly common, though no one's ever been able to catch one. They're sort of standard issue at questionable séances, and they've been unmasked as everything from Christmas tree lights to glowworms. Still, enough of them have gone unexplained to make it an interesting question."

"And how do the noises fit in?"

David had bent the handle of his spoon out of shape; thoughtfully he bent it back. "Well, if you mean do they fit in with the lights, no. Or apparently not. The noises—raps—are again very common, again standard-issue stuff. Nobody knows what causes them, some kind of energy release or something. They can range from a light tapping, or scratching as Christine's mother called it, to a pretty deafening racket. We got some loud ones during our sitting with Rosanna in Joshua's room. Basically, the noises and the light don't seem to be connected, but they are both common haunting phenomena, and the more people we get who have experienced them, the more points for our side."

They all sat silent a minute. The coffee was finished and there were no other customers; the bored waitress leaned over the counter top, reading a magazine. "Now what?" Sally said.

David pinched his lip. "Now I think we need to talk to Mr. Gilfoy."

"Mr. Gilfoy? Why?"

"Because he may be able to confirm this business about the quarrel between Joshua and Julian the night Julian died. And—"

"No," she said.

"No?"

"Look." She faced him squarely across the table. "This is an unpleasant incident involving his father and his brother, not just some people he hardly knew. We've already implied that his childhood home is haunted. Now you want to rub his nose in the family dirt. Leave him out of it."

David was amused. "You're protecting him from me."

"I'm not. I just—"

"Okay," he said. "Okay. I have another idea." He shifted suddenly on the padded bench. "Listen, Colin."

Colin, who had thought himself forgotten, jumped a little. "Yes?"

"That was a gold mine."

"I'm glad I could help."

"Good. Because I have a feeling there's a lot more you can do."

"I can?" he said, feeling Sally look at him and then at David, who was leaning forward now, hands clasped around his empty cup.

"I think so. Joshua had other children besides our Mr. Gilfoy, remember. And some of them may still be around, or their children. It's possible that one of them may know something about the quarrel. You know, some family story that's been handed down. If we could talk to them . . ."

Colin considered. "Well, I know there's no one named Gilfoy still living in Skipton, not since Sam moved to Boston. But it would be easy enough to find out who Reverend Gilfoy's daughters married. Is that what you need to know?"

"It isn't just that. We're outsiders, you know. People have been very nice, but we can't really expect them to open up to us the way—well, Christine would never have talked to us if you hadn't set it up. If you could find out who these people are, then sort of give us an intro, the way you did with her—"

"But suppose I don't know them?"

"Oh, you know everybody." David's smile was persuasive. Embarrassed, Colin looked at Sally but her head was stubbornly bent over the soccer quiz. The waitress brought their check. David was still smiling at him. "Well?"

"All right," Colin said.

As it happened he did know them, at least slightly. He had gone to school with Sarah Nims, daughter of Thomas Nims and Mary Gilfoy; and he knew, as people know one another in small towns, the Waite brothers, Robert and Matthew, sons of Clara Gilfoy and Francis Waite. There had been a Waite daughter named Ann or Anna —he remembered a pretty child in pigtails—but she was dead. So much a morning's research brought him, along with a few other facts: Douglas Gilfoy, the only one of Joshua's sons to marry, had left Skipton in 1908 without a trace, and Rebecca Gilfoy, marrying late, had died during delivery of a stillborn daughter.

"I'm not really clear in my mind," he said to Sally, who was sitting at the other end of the desk making up last month's overdue-book list for him, "what it is these people are supposed to be able to tell us."

She added a name to the list and picked up the next card. "This isn't exactly orthodox procedure. David's looking for some kind of confirmation of the rumor you told us about—that Julian and Joshua had a fight the night Julian died. He's hoping someone will know what they were arguing about."

"I see. Well, that makes sense."

"No, it doesn't." When he looked at her she smiled, and he wondered if he had imagined the words sounding sharp. "We haven't had a single clear paranormal occurrence since we've been in the house, and it's been almost a month. All this corroborative research is a little premature. Yesterday David was up in the attic going through the family papers, which Mr. Gilfoy never gave us permission to do, searching for some magic clue that will explain everything."

"You can't really blame him," Colin said. "He's bored."

"So am I. But you can't push this kind of thing. He's trying to force this connection between the quarrel and the haunting, to show that Joshua cursed Julian, or disowned him or something. Then he can say that we had already obtained this information paranormally, during the 'lost one' sitting—in other words, that Julian told us."

"But didn't he?"

She put down the card she was holding and clasped her hands, staring down at them. "Maybe. But that's stretching it. The sitting was so vague. And before we found Julian's grave, David had made at least as convincing a case for the lost one being Julian's uncle Samuel, who was killed at Gettysburg. In this business it's so easy to start chasing your own tail! You start seeing things that aren't really there, just because they seem to fit the facts. Now, suppose we had a sitting that gave clear evidence of a quarrel, a disinheritance, whatever, or suppose there was some sequence of paranormal activity indicating this traumatic event—that would be time enough to start looking for corroborative evidence of our findings. David is two jumps ahead."

"Well, can't you tell him—"

She shook her head. The brusque movement went through him with a little jolt. Marriage, in his parents' era, was supposed to represent perfect harmony and bliss; and he had continued, out of laziness he supposed, to assign this storybook pattern to all married couples. There had been times when he had been aware of tension between his new young friends. But they had not acknowledged such moments and he had followed their lead. Now Sally's headshake, pushing the pretense aside, confused and obscurely pleased him. He felt giddy, picked up and set down elsewhere like one of Lewis Carroll's chessmen, needing to catch his breath.

"But," he said, "things *have* happened. At least some things. Even if you don't count the sittings, there are the lights and the noises, and the stairs. You've got all that."

"What we've got is hearsay. Okay, we heard some raps. But they could have been caused by Rosanna, not by the house. And we haven't seen any lights, and neither have our cameras. As for those damned stairs—" Unexpectedly she smiled.

"You really don't think the accidents mean anything?"

"I don't know. I guess it's a statistical thing." She took the remaining cards out of the overdue tray and squared them gently with her fingertips. "David called the information in to the computer people at our lab last night. He also called our cooperative ex-tenants, the Rogerses and the Abbeys, and our not-so-cooperatives, Miranda Sterling and the Gardners, to ask if anyone had ever fallen down the stairs while they were living in the house."

"And no one had."

"Oh, yes. Someone had." She smiled again. "Karen Abbey reported that Kris, their golden retriever, was sleeping at the top of the stairs one afternoon and happened to roll over."

"Oh no," Colin said. "Oh well. And that was all?"

"That was all. Except that I think Mrs. Gardner is going to have her number changed so she can have a moment's peace from us. And we have to get someone in with a level and a plumb line to check the stairs."

"Do you think that's the answer—that they're uneven or something?"

"Well, we'll see. Even if they aren't, when you consider the number of people who've lived in the house and the number of times they must have been up and down . . . and they *are* steep . . . and David admits that when he fell it was dark and he wasn't looking where he was going. It did sound uncanny, coming from Christine right after we found out about Julian. But it's too much like *Alfred Hitchcock Presents* for me. I think there'll be an explanation, but not a paranormal one."

➺ 21 ⫷

"OPERATION GRANDCHILDREN" as David called it, was not proving to be much of a success. Sarah Nims, now Sarah Brody, had a vague idea that her mother's brother Julian had been killed in the First World War. David's efforts to explain over the phone that it was Prentiss, not Julian, who had died in the war were hampered by a piping voice in the background that kept insisting, "Watch this, Grandma! Watch this!" Matthew Waite, to whom Colin introduced him the following afternoon, recalled the name but nothing more. He said he would ask his brother—"But it won't do any good. He had a stroke last year and he doesn't remember much." David, frustrated and looking for sympathy from Sally, got sarcasm instead.

"Why don't you just put an ad in the paper? 'Gilfoy Family Secrets Wanted.' "

"What's eating you?"

"Oh, nothing. I just seem to recall that Jack asked us to be discreet."

"I'm being discreet."

"David, this is a small town. If you ask *A* a question, pretty soon *B*—and *C* and *D* and *E*—are going to know about it."

He rubbed his lip. "Sounds like geometry. I always liked geometry."

But she was right, and it was made manifest a day or two later. Colin, looking up from his desk at the library, found himself eye to eye with a towhaired boy of about ten. The child stood without moving, pale eyes so unblinking that Colin was momentarily hypnotized. Then slowly: "What can I do for you, son?"

164

The boy licked his lips and the words emerged in a rush, without inflection. "Miss Ellen says anyone wants to know the truth about the Gilfoys better talk to her."

The truth about the Gilfoys. Colin considered both words and boy. He didn't know the child, but there was a certain look—he thought he could make a good guess. "What's your name, son?"

"James Flagg."

"Come with me, James."

David was seated at one of the reading tables, working his way through the New England telephone directories in search of possible descendants of Douglas Gilfoy. He looked up quizzically as they stopped beside his chair.

"This," Colin said, "is Mr. Curtiss, the gentleman who is interested in the Gilfoys. David, this is James Flagg. He has something to tell you."

Deadpan the boy rolled out his streamer of words again. David cocked an eyebrow at Colin. "The truth, huh? Who's Miss Ellen?"

"My great-aunt," James Flagg said.

David studied the small face. "All right," he said. "Where is she?"

"At home. She's old. She don't go out."

"There is a farm," Colin added.

"Do you know how to get there?" David asked him.

"Not really."

"You can follow the truck," the boy said. "Hurry it up."

David hid a smile. "Okay. Where's the truck?"

"Front of Buck's."

"We'll be there in ten minutes."

The boy nodded, then turned and fled. David watched him go.

"Well, glory be. Coming, Colin?"

"I wouldn't miss it."

"Let's call Sally and tell her to pick us up in the bug."

The truck ("That's it," Colin said) was a battered pickup that had once been white. The back was filled with light-haired children of various sizes; half a dozen pairs of pale blue eyes surveyed them as they pulled up behind. They could not see the driver, but one of the children tapped on the back windshield and at once the truck pulled off. The Volkswagen followed.

Outside town the truck turned north. David, who had been following closely, dropped back a little.

"Those kids are making me jumpy." During the drive through town the children's blank faces had been turned unwaveringly toward the car, swinging like so many compass needles on the turns.

"Which one did you talk to?" Sally wanted to know.

"Hell, don't ask me. I could swear to at least three of them. What's with these people, Colin? Do you know them?"

"I really don't. They keep to themselves."

A quiet minute passed as the three of them watched the truck ahead with its silent cargo. The oldest child could not have been more than fourteen, but the only movement among them was the whipping of their pale hair in the wind.

"I think I'm enjoying this," David said at last. "Summoned to the bedside of a New England matriarch. There ought to be background music."

"And detergent commercials," Sally said.

"Those too."

Ten miles farther on, the truck turned left off the highway onto a narrow gravel road that twisted through pine trees. There were potholes, some of them deep. Inside the Volkswagen the three of them jounced up and down. David gripped the wheel hard.

"I feel like a gin fizz."

The truck had disappeared around a series of turns, but they were not worried about losing it; so far there had been no roads leading off the one they were following. Pine woods flanked the road on both sides. Sally caught David's shoulder suddenly.

"Look out—"

He braked; gravel rattled against the hubcaps. A rabbit flashed across the road in front of them. Colin wondered how on earth she could have seen it in time, but she was saying something.

"Do they own this land, Colin?"

"As far as I know, yes. But it's just a fraction of their former holdings. In the shakedown that followed Flagg's death, almost all his land was parceled out to its original owners. But no one ever really came back. The land has pretty much returned to forest. It seems no one wants the Flaggs for neighbors."

"Can't imagine why not." David drove around another pothole. "You could get up a softball team."

The road went on. A stream appeared, running alongside them for a while, dull under the cloudy sky; they rattled over a bridge and it appeared on the other side of the road; then it disappeared. The trees thinned and they could see the truck; then they lost it again over the crest of a hill.

"They forgot to mention that Aunt Ellen lives in Santa Monica."

"*Miss* Ellen," Sally said.

"We must be almost there," Colin said.

David, who should have been watching the road, was looking at Sally instead. "The truth about the Gilfoys. Do you suppose she's a senile maniac?"

"It would serve you right."

"Darling. Did you remember the tape recorder?"

"Yes."

The truck came in sight up ahead, slowing and turning to the right, off the road. David followed. They went over a bridge, saw the stream below them, deep in a ravine. The bridge ended in a ramshackle gate propped open with a rusty automobile fender. Beyond the gate the ground rose; they saw a large farmhouse and, beyond that, an enormous barn. Both buildings were shabby, needing paint, showing the sag of age and neglect; a disconnected sink lay in front of the house with its legs in the air like a dead cow. Ahead, the truck jounced to a stop amid a welter of old tires and ancient oil drums outside the barn. The children poured out of the back while the door of the cab swung open and a man climbed out: late twenties, fair coloring, a mature version of the children. He watched as the VW pulled up behind the truck. The children had climbed onto a pile of used lumber and sat in a motionless tableau. A yellow dog came out of the barn, tail down.

David was first out of the car, then Sally; Colin, in the backseat, had to fight free from a tangle of shoulder harness blocking his way. By the time he emerged David had reached the man beside the truck and was offering his hand.

"Hi, I'm David Curtiss. This is my wife Sally, our friend Mr. Robinson—"

The other man ignored his hand. "The old lady wants to see you. She's in the house." He spat suddenly, quite close to David's feet, and started across the rutted ground toward the house. After a shocked moment they followed in silence. Colin, walking next to Sally, glanced back: the children and the dog were bringing up the rear. He looked at Sally; she shrugged and made a face, mock alarm. Ahead of them David had already entered the house. Then it was their turn.

Colin's first impression was that the room was crammed with furniture. His second confirmed it, with a refinement. The room was crammed with chairs. There were chairs everywhere—rocking chairs, overstuffed armchairs, spindleback chairs, rush-seat chairs, folding chairs, aluminum lawn chairs. Some of them were clearly antiques and some were junk. The few articles of furniture that were not chairs were tables, all of them piled with junk and bric-a-brac, china ladies and shotgun shells promiscuously mingled. Above the fireplace hung a portrait, exquisitely rendered, of a young girl in a summer dress, gazing out undismayed at the chaos spread below her. The predominant odor in the room was one of wet dog.

A woman stood watching them in an open doorway to the left of the fireplace; her blouse, carelessly buttoned, revealed a dirty slip underneath. After a moment she retreated without speaking. David and Sally and Colin stood in the wilderness of chairs and looked at one another. When the driver of the truck spoke they all jumped a little.

"Here they are, Miss Ellen. Come about the Gilfoys."

A tremor of movement in one corner of the room: there she sat, in a rocking chair. The ornately carved back rose high above her head—a tiny shawl-wrapped woman slowly rocking. She did not answer, and the man began again.

"Miss Ellen—"

The voice, when it came, was small and sharp. "I heard you, Marcus. I heard what you said."

Silence; the chair rocked soundlessly. At last the voice said, "Sit down."

It was not a difficult command to obey. They sat, as in the game of musical chairs, on whatever was nearest. Colin found himself in a massive club chair with slick leather upholstery. There was a patch of something sticky on one of the arms; he avoided it and looked up to find the old woman watching him. How old was she? The eyes in the wrinkled face were sibyl-bright. She rocked, watching. Then:

"You want the truth about the Gilfoys. You should have come to me. You should have come to Miss Ellen Flagg."

David, sitting on a metal folding chair with a peeling red vinyl seat, took a breath. "We'd be very interested in anything you can tell us, anything you remember—"

"I remember, mister. I remember the Gilfoys. I remember them." She fell silent, rocking. They waited. Faint noises came from other parts of the house: the murmur of a television set, water running. David started to speak again but the old woman's voice cut across his suddenly.

"Prentiss Gilfoy was in love with me." Colin watched wrinkled lids lower themselves over the old eyes; the frail body rocked in its chair. "He never spoke because he stammered. But I found the initials, his and mine, cut in a tree." Her eyes opened. "Prentiss Gilfoy—I would have scratched his face!"

Colin swallowed, glancing at Sally. She sat in a straight-backed chair, holding David's knapsack on her lap. It contained the tape recorder, he realized, seeing the gleam of the microphone clipped inside the flap.

"I remember the Gilfoys all right," Miss Ellen said. "Damn them all to hell." The rocker squealed as she leaned forward suddenly. "That old man killed my father," she said. "The dirty praying bastard." The words held a venom dried to dust. She sank back as if empty. They waited.

David shifted in his chair. "The old man," he said.

"Do you mean Reverend Gilfoy?" The shawled head gave a quick birdlike nod. "How did he do that?"

Miss Ellen made a sound; belatedly Colin recognized it as a laugh. "He prayed, mister. That's all. He prayed to God, and God sent a bullet down from heaven into my father's lung. That's what the stupid fools in this town wanted to believe—that it was God's will. Well, it wasn't. It was Joshua Gilfoy's will."

"You're saying Gilfoy arranged the shooting?" David said.

"If you mean did he put the gun in somebody's hand, no. I don't say he did that. I doubt he was man enough for that. But he had his ways. He was the minister, you know. people told him things. He knew who in this town had good cause to hate my father. And he must have taken one of those men and worked on him until the poor fool thought he was heaven's own messenger . . ." Her voice trailed off and David sat forward.

"Miss Ellen, even if that happened, even if somebody could have been manipulated like that, why would Reverend Gilfoy have wanted your father killed?"

The old woman made her laughing sound again. "He hated my father," she said, "because his precious daughter Rebecca was crazy for my father. She couldn't stay away from him. That's the truth, mister. And you won't hear it from anyone but me."

There was a startled pause during which Colin was certain he could hear the tape winding on its reels. He needed to swallow but was afraid of calling attention to himself. Overhead, footsteps sounded, then a heavy thump like a boot being dropped, and another. Toward the back of the house a woman's muffled shriek ended in laughter.

David was on the edge of his seat. "Reverend Gilfoy's daughter was in love with your father?"

Miss Ellen smiled, showing a row of tiny yellow teeth, and Colin felt something very like a chill rise up his spine. "Crazy in love, mister. She was a pretty thing. My father didn't want her. He had more women than he knew what to do with. But he took her. For her father's sake, you might say." The smile faded. "And what did your precious Reverend do? Did he come for my father with a horsewhip, like a man? He did not. He stood up in church on a Sunday morning and preached that it was the Lord's will for my father to die."

David was shaking his head—from astonishment, Colin thought, rather than disbelief—but the old woman misread the movement and her yellow smile came again. "My father was a handsome man. Women flocked to him. He was no saint, mister. But neither was Joshua Gilfoy."

Colin's mind felt like a pool roughly stirred with a sharp stick; gradually the whirling sediment was beginning to settle. Was it true, what she was saying? Or just an old woman's spite? The strangeness of the whole scene struck him all at once—the sibyl-crone in her corner, the three of them hanging on her words, the empty chairs around them like silent listeners—but David was talking and he made himself pay attention.

"What happened to Rebecca after your father was killed?"

The shawled head stirred. "She was sent away, to relatives in Boston. The whole business was kept secret. But I knew. I was her best friend. That's what people thought. Ha! I knew it was my father she came to see. My father . . ." Her eyes clouded and she seemed to lose the thread of what she had been saying. "My father was a handsome man."

"Rebecca was your friend," David said helpfully. "What about Gilfoy's other children? Did you know them well?"

The old woman's lips moved soundlessly for a moment, then: "Rebecca was the old man's favorite. He never cared two pins for the others. The girls were all plain, all but her. The boys were handsome enough." Her mouth twisted. "A fine bunch of men! Gabe never spoke above a whisper, Prentiss had his tongue tied in a knot. Douglas was the only one who knew how to laugh, but even he did as he was told. Gilfoys! Damn them all to hell."

It always seemed to come back to that, Colin thought; but David was closing in on his point. "And the youngest son—Julian?"

Miss Ellen closed her eyes and rocked. "He was just a boy," she said.

"How did he get along with his father? Was there— friction between them?"

"He had a pair of dogs, Julian did." She rocked slowly. Her eyes were still closed, voice sinking to a mumble. "A black retriever and a white dog . . . looked like a wolf. After he died they ran wild, had to be shot . . ." The last words faded to a whisper and David slipped his next question in quickly.

"Miss Ellen, do you remember hearing any stories, any rumors about the night Julian died—about an argument between him and his father, anything like that?"

She opened her eyes. "They tried to keep it from Lily," she said. "But it was no good . . . she knew." Her head nodded forward, eyes closing again. Now that she had delivered her denunciation of Joshua Gilfoy, Colin thought, her ancient mechanism was winding down. David was leaning forward in his chair, desperate to keep her going.

"Lily was one of his sisters, wasn't she? Did she overhear—"

The old eyes opened blearily again; Miss Ellen touched her forehead with a clawlike finger. "She was simple. Something went wrong when she was born. Her whole life she was like a child. She worshiped Julian." Her head sank forward, then lifted. "They tried to tell her he wasn't dead. But she knew."

David drew breath. "Do you think she overheard them arguing?"

Colin saw Sally look quickly at David and then back at Miss Ellen. The chair rocked slowly.

"Maybe," Miss Ellen said.

"Then they *were* arguing?"

"They were always arguing," Miss Ellen said. "Damn them all to—" Her eyes closed.

David gripped his knees. "Miss Ellen, do you have any idea what it was about?"

"What?" the old woman said.

"The argument between Julian and his father. Reverend Gilfoy." He stressed the last two words, clearly hoping they would liven her up, and her eyes opened.

"That filthy murderer." The old eyes rested on David. "He's in hell."

"But . . ."

The eyes closed tiredly. "They're all in hell."

"Miss Ellen . . ."

The rocking had stopped. The shawl-covered head slipped sideways against the carved back of the chair and the old woman began to snore softly.

From his place in the corner Marcus Flagg said, "That's all you're going to get out of her today, mister. She ain't talked that much in a month."

"I see," David said. "Well, thanks for bringing us out here." They all stood up, Sally holding the knapsack carefully.

"Got to give the old lady what she wants," Flagg said. "She's ninety-eight. Wanted to say her piece."

Colin took a last look at the corner where the rocking chair stood. Already it was difficult to connect the frail sleeping body with the furious spirit that had condemned the entire Gilfoy family to eternal damnation. He tried to imagine her as a young girl and found it beyond him. Yet Prentiss Gilfoy had carved her initials in a tree.

As they left the house the children seemed to materialize from nowhere, a tight silent group. But they kept their distance, not responding to David's wave or the double beep from the Volkswagen's horn as it bumped down the rutted drive.

Colin, looking out the rear window, saw that four or five adults had come out onto the porch of the house to watch them leave. "Well," he said as they crossed the bridge and turned onto the road with a crunching of gravel beneath the wheels.

David grinned at him in the rearview mirror.

"All in a day's work, my boy." He turned to Sally: "Do I dare ask if you had the tape running?"

"Yes."

"Good girl."

They drove for nearly a mile in silence, absorbed in their own thoughts, and then all started to talk at once.

"Wasn't she—"

"That was quite—"

"Did you see—"

"That was quite a tidbit about Flagg and Rebecca Gilfoy," David said, winning out.

"If it was true," Sally said.

"Why would she make it up? I believed her. Did you, Colin?"

"I'm not sure," Colin said. "It seems—"

"It sure puts Gilfoy in a different light. Somebody tells him in confession that they hate Flagg, and he manipulates that hatred, maybe even hints at absolution—"

"Oh, David!" Sally sounded outraged. "There's no regular confession in the Episcopal church. And even the idea that someone confided in him was complete conjecture on her part."

"Well, even if he hired somebody to plug Flagg, he still comes off as a creep. She was right—he should have gone after Flagg with a horsewhip." David avoided a pothole just in time.

"And broadcast the truth about Flagg and Rebecca? He couldn't do that. Women's reputations in those days—"

"Oh, baloney," David said. "He should have just—"

She interrupted him. "Colin, who in town owns a pair of dogs like the ones she mentioned belonging to Julian?"

"A black retriever and a white shepherd, wasn't that it? No one, so far as I know. I've never seen them, anyway."

"Well, I have," Sally said.

The car swerved as David turned to look at her; then he brought it back under control. "When?" he said.

"Several times. Always at dusk."

"Where?"

"In the backyard."

"Our backyard?"

"Yes."

"Dammit, Sally!"

"Well," she said, "they could be strays."

"Were they barking?"

"No. They didn't make a sound."

"But you saw them."

"Yes."

The car was going fast; pine woods swept by on either side. "Use the camera next time," David said. "Okay?"

"Okay."

Colin was uneasy in the silence that followed; he searched for some harmless remark to break it. "She certainly is a character," he said at last.

David met his eyes in the rearview mirror. "I think I'm in love."

≫ 22 ≪

BACK AT THE HOUSE, over coffee, they played the tape.
David penciled notes on the back of an envelope. The
quaver of the old woman's voice was more pronounced
on tape than it had seemed in actuality, and Colin found
himself wondering just how ancient he would sound. He
didn't think he wanted to know. When it was over David
started the machine rewinding, then consulted his envelope.

"Okay, I'll tell you—no, you tell me. What's the main
impression you get from this interview?"

While Colin gathered his thoughts Sally said, "My
main impression is that Joshua is in hell."

"Wise guy. But it's true, isn't it? Joshua comes off as a
real skunk."

"Well, naturally. She thinks he was the cause of her
father's death."

"Yes, but wait a minute. Wait a minute." David waved
his envelope. "That doesn't alter certain facts, and listen
to them. He doesn't care about his children, except for
Rebecca. His sons sound as if they were all afraid of him.
And when his favorite daughter is seduced by a man he
hates, he preaches a sermon that—"

"What are you getting at?" Sally said. "You got every
one of those so-called facts from Miss Ellen. You can't
accept her view of the situation as unadulterated fact.
She hates Joshua Gilfoy."

David seemed only slightly deflated. "Okay, maybe
I'm approaching this from the wrong angle. Let's leave
Joshua for a moment and take Julian." Glancing at his
envelope again: "Miss Ellen hates the Gilfoys, but what's
her reaction when we ask her about Julian? She says,

'He was just a boy.' Coming from her, that's tantamount to praise. Add the fact that his retarded sister adores him—"

"And he's a dog lover," Sally said dryly.

"I wasn't going to mention that, but since you brought it up, he's a dog lover. And who do you suppose had the dogs shot after he died? Could it have been our friend Joshua?"

She shrugged and rolled her eyes up to the ceiling. "Why not? There's just as much basis for that assumption as there is for saying that his sermon was responsible for getting Flagg killed."

"Look, it's perfectly possible—even probable—that she's telling the truth about that."

"David." Sally got up and walked halfway across the room, stopped and stood facing them, her hands spread out. "You're making all kinds of wild assumptions that can't possibly be proved! Miss Ellen is obviously hostile to Joshua Gilfoy. Even if she thinks she's telling the truth, how can we trust what she's saying? Even if she *is* telling the truth, how can we ever prove it? And then you go and push her into saying that Julian and Joshua were arguing the night Julian died—"

"Hell, I was just tryng to get her to the point before she nodded out—"

Sally took a deep breath and let her hands fall to her sides. "Okay. But you know perfectly well that anybody listening to that tape would say you put the words in her mouth."

He crumpled the envelope and dropped it on the table, leaned forward and removed the tape from the machine and put it in its box. He placed the box carefully on the table. Then he said, "Look, all I'm saying is that our original picture of the situation may not have been the whole truth. It's possible that Joshua isn't a hundred percent saint. It's possible that Julian isn't a hundred percent sinner. Okay?"

"Fine," Sally said. She came back to her chair and sat down. David leaned back, clasping both hands behind his neck.

"We're starting to get them sorted out, anyway. Prentiss stutters, Gabriel whispers, Douglas laughs. All the girls except Rebecca are homely, and one of them is retarded.

Sounds like a handful for young what'shername—the second wife. Wonder why on earth she married him."

Sally started to laugh. "Look, he must have been considered a catch—pillar of the community, all that stuff. I hate to suggest it, but there may even have been genuine feeling between them."

David made a face. "Maybe. There's that music box."

"Music box?" Colin said.

"We found it in the attic. It has their initials inside, plays a love song. What's the song, Sal?"

"Jeanie with the Light Brown Hair."

"Oh," Colin said. Sally looked at him.

"Oh, what?"

"Well, she was called Ginny. You see? The sound is similar. And she did have brown hair, light brown."

Now David was looking at him too, curious. "I keep forgetting you knew her."

"It was a long time ago," Colin said.

"Want to see the box?" He didn't wait for an answer. "Where is it, Sally? Did we bring it down from the attic?"

"No, it's still up there."

"I'll get it."

In David's absence there was a silence. Sally fiddled with the tape recorder; Colin watched her.

"Sally?"

"What."

"Do you think she was telling the truth—Miss Ellen?"

Her hands stilled. "I don't know. There's no way we'll ever know." When he said nothing she looked up. "But I could understand—and forgive—a man just about anything if his daughter had been used that way. Couldn't you?"

"Well, just . . . what she said about the horsewhip. That I could understand. But—"

She reached across the table suddenly, strong young hands covering his. "We'll just never know. Only Joshua knew. Not Miss Ellen. And certainly not us."

"It doesn't matter," he said. He meant to be reassuring, but he must have done it wrong because her eyes filled with tears. They could hear David coming down the stairs. As he came into the room, the box in his hand, Sally got up quickly and went out. Colin looked after her, then at the box David was thrusting at him. He took it, a small box, the wood rich golden brown streaked with black. He opened the lid and saw the initials: J.G. TO V.B.G. "How does it work?" he said.

"Supposed to play when you open it. Let's see, maybe it's not wound up."

But its initial silence seemed to have been due to some stiffness of the old spring now loosened by the transfer from one hand to another. The music began as soon as David took the box. He set it carefully on the mantelpiece. A shower of notes spilled from it now with all the energy of clockwork; as Colin sat listening the sound seemed to echo in the old-fashioned room, surrounding him so that he was no longer aware of Sally's absence or of David standing nearby. It was not that he lost his sense of where he was, but that the music had shifted his perception of time from the actual world's to its own—a small internal time marked only by the song's unfolding and somehow containing within it, undiminished, all the past. Nothing was lost; it was all here. He had the impression, anyway, of infinite facets superimposed on the room around him, like the mesh of a golden net. Sweetness flooded him.

Mid-note it stopped: the cranky spring again, or it might simply have run down. Colin found himself sad and a little embarrassed; without the music his emotion seemed just an old man's vagary. He searched for his watch. "I ought to be getting back. Thank you for a very interesting afternoon."

"Never a dull moment. We'll see you soon?"

"Of course."

The house was quiet as he went out: no sign of Sally. At the gate he stopped and looked back. The sun had come out momentarily and the house stood among the trees in a net of dappled light. He closed the gate behind him carefully, quietly, like someone afraid of disturbing a sleeper. But the sleeper might have been himself.

Back at the library his out-to-lunch sign had blown down from the door. Two teenage girls were sitting on the steps; he let them in, apologizing, and they disappeared among the shelves. Colin sat down at his desk, pulled the card file of notes for his town history toward him, picked up his pen. The year was 1900. On the surface Skipton was a staid, proper little town. Business was good. An overcoat cost eight dollars, a bottle of sherry seventy cents, shoes under two dollars, a player piano five hundred. Below the surface people quarreled or drank or made doubtful business deals; somehow, secretly, Rebecca Gilfoy managed to meet her lover. He opened a thick volume of minutes from the Town Council meetings of that year and moved his eyes over the yellowed pages, but behind his eyes, his mind constructed over and over again the melody of a song.

It haunted him: no other word for it. He couldn't shake it off. He realized he had always been vaguely familiar with the song without any conscious memory of actually hearing it from beginning to end, or listening to it if he had. But cranking out of the music box, small and tinny and mechanical, it had captured him utterly; he was reminded of some fragile-seeming vine, honeysuckle or morning glory, that imprisons with its delicate tendrils. The melody had a lift to it and then a catch like a sob in the throat, hanging there an instant and then resolving to some cadence, piercingly sweet, in which the ache still echoed. *I dream of Jeanie with the light brown hair . . .* and then what? The sun, breaking through clouds, lit the scarred desk top. The old man sat with his white head in his hands, his elbows propped on the thick volume in front of him; he might have been reading, but he was not. All at once he pushed his chair back, got up and crossed the room, searching along a row of books, pulling one out. Once he had opened it and found his place he stood motionless for several minutes. Once he turned a page. At last he closed the book and carried it across the room to his desk, where he picked up the phone.

The two girls approached the desk, their arms full of books, just as David and Sally came through the door. They all stood waiting while he found the date stamp and ink pad, fumbling them in his hurry, made the entries on the cards and pushed the pile of books back across the desk. The girls thanked him and gathered them up; the taller one, the Waring girl, dropped one on the floor and David picked it up for her. There were blushes and more thanks. The door closed behind the girls. Colin pushed another book across the desk without speaking. David picked it up.

"*The Songs of Stephen Foster*. Are we having a sing-along?"

Sally was looking at him. "Are you all right, Colin? You sounded funny on the phone."

"I'm fine. But I think you'll want to look at page thirty-seven."

"Page thirty-seven coming up." David flipped the pages. "It's our music box song. How nice."

"Read the second verse," Colin said.

David bent over it. Sally was still looking at Colin, her face questioning. He spoke quietly, not wanting to disturb David. "Remember the Fannie Shippers book? Reverend Gilfoy was tone deaf. He used to sing the hymns in a monotone. Sally, Reverend Gilfoy was not a music lover."

There was only time for her to look puzzled before David said, "Holy Pete." The songbook was a piano-vocal score and the lines of text were set into the music, so that he had been reading slowly. Now he was looking up. His face registered astonishment. Sally glanced at him, quickly back at Colin, then down at the page. David traced the printed lines for her with his forefinger, which was shaking.

Sighing like the night wind and sobbing like the rain,
Wailing for the lost one that comes not again.

He took a breath. "Holy bloody Pete."

Sally's eyes went to Colin. "The lost one."

"And the music box," David said. "I will be wholly, utterly, completely damned. This has been staring us in the face all along. J.G. isn't Joshua."

"No," Colin said. "It's Julian."

PART III

SALLY

⇶ 23 ⇷

SHE LIKED SITTING at their bedroom window at twilight. It overlooked the backyard; a table had been pushed up against the sill and she could sit there with a book, though she didn't read. The book was simply to mollify the need to think of herself as a practical person, busy and purposeful, not the type to sit woolgathering at windows. The book was a sop and she knew it, but she could not have sat there without it. It was always a scientific journal of some kind, an article about beta radiation or wave functions which she would read later, after supper or in bed. The open pages held the last of the sky's light when everything else in the room had sunk into shadow.

It was the sound of the cicadas that had first brought her to the window—this strident chorus pouring out of the trees at nightfall, layers of sound overlapping to a crescendo then dying away in a long downward breath like summer's end—an ancient, pagan sadness. Gradually as she sat watching, the lightning bugs became visible, one liquid gleam and then another, each carving its tiny gold track in the dusk and vanishing.

She could not honestly recall when she had first seen the dogs, or from what direction they had appeared. They had come so silently that by the time she noticed them they were already there, chasing each other around the low scruffy bushes that separated the garden from the rest of the yard. Two big dogs, a white shepherd and a black retriever, their game seemingly more dance than chase—a leisurely measure in which they circled one bush and then another until it was impossible to tell which was pursuer and which pursued. They made no sound at all; there was only the chorus of cicadas mounting to its height in the warm dusk and then beginning its long slow fall away. At last the darkness hid them from sight.

Standing in the kitchen making supper, she thought it wasn't fair, really, for David to be annoyed at her. There was no way she could have known they were anything but a couple of neighborhood dogs. But this afternoon she had asked around, and no one had admitted to owning or ever seeing such a pair of dogs. That was enough to convince David that they were apparitions of Julian's dogs. For her part, she wasn't so sure.

Water spilled over the edge of the pot filling in the sink. She shut the faucet off and set the pot on the stove, scratching a match on the black iron surface, turning a knob. Blue flame shot a foot in the air and then subsided. "Oh, Jezebel," she said.

David came into the kitchen, stopping to look over her shoulder. "What are you making?"

"Pasta with tomato sauce."

He made an appreciative noise, stepped back to scan the shelves and began choosing spices, whistling through his teeth. He was in a good mood, pleased at the way things were moving. "Funny Colin wouldn't come to supper," he said.

She glanced at him, then away, choosing words carefully. "I think he's kind of upset."

"Upset? Why?"

"About Ginny," she said.

The spice jars clinked as he set them down. "You're kidding."

"Oh, David."

"Well, aren't you?"

She turned to face him. "No. I think she stood for something to him, some kind of ideal. And now we've messed it up. He doesn't want to think of her as someone who was sleeping with her stepson."

"That's ridiculous," David said. "Why should he care? He hardly knew her. Besides, he's got no business having ideals at his age."

She looked away, hating him, the sensation hot and sick inside her. After a minute she felt his hand on her back.

"Sweetheart, I'm only kidding. I didn't realize. We'll have to make it up to him somehow, that's all. How about supper tomorrow night?"

She picked up an onion from the counter and put it in his hand. "Here. Cut this up."

"You just want to see me cry."

She leaned against the counter and folded her arms, watching him peel the onion. There were times when she would have liked to be able to take him more for granted. Since childhood she had slowly learned to filter out her abnormal awareness of other people's thoughts and emotions, so that what had once been a constant bombardment of outside images had dwindled by now to an occasional intrusion, infrequent and unwelcome, when she was tired or distracted. She had almost learned to treat people as they treated one another—as reflections, extensions, projections of themselves. But not David. He was always present for her with a kind of violence: not his specific thoughts, but his essential substance. She could not help being aware of the very bones of him— the impatient, fastidious, vulnerable bones. He chopped the onion expertly; the pieces remained in neat stacks that he pushed together with the knife. "Ideals aside," he said, "I'd like to check our landlord's date of birth."

"You think he's Julian's child?"

"Don't you?"

Now she picked up a bottle of olive oil and turned it in her hands. "I guess it's possible."

"Not just possible. Probable." He lit a burner on the stove, stepped back until the flame subsided. "Easy, Jez. You can hide an affair, but not a baby. That's what the big fight was about, obviously. Joshua found out. Odds are, our Mr. Gilfoy was born less than nine months after Julian's death."

She said nothing. He poured oil into a skillet, set it on the stove, waited until it heated up and then dropped the pieces of onion in. They crackled faintly as they began to cook and he stirred them with the point of the knife. *"Sighing like the night wind and sobbing like the rain, wailing for the lost one that comes not again,"* he said softly. A cricket piped in the darkness beyond the screen door. Sally felt a warm chill run over her.

"Don't be corny," she said.

"Have we got any garlic?"

She handed him a clove and he began to peel it. "You know," he said, "I keep wondering if Julian fell by accident."

"You mean somebody sneaked up behind and pushed him?"

"Well—Joshua was a dangerous man to have for an enemy. Look what happened to Winslow Flagg."

"Oh, David," she said, and saw him smile at her tone. "That Flagg business is complete hearsay—and Julian was his son."

"Son or not, he was messing around with the old man's wife. That's reason enough—"

"Reason enough for what?" she said. "What are you postulating? That he sneaked up behind Julian and gave him a shove?"

"It's not impossible," David said. "Remember Julian's reputation. He might have been drunk."

"I'm sure he was. It's probably why he fell." This time she heard the sharpness in her voice and made an effort to modulate it. "It's not the point, anyway. We aren't here to find skeletons in the family closet. We're here to find out if the house is haunted. And that means instrument readings of psi activity, and—oh, hell," she said, seeing him trying not to laugh. "You weren't even serious, were you?"

He dropped the garlic in with the onion and stirred it. "No. But it would be a nice twist."

She shook her head. He always had to make a story if he could, something with a beginning and an end, or a twist, even though he knew perfectly well that things didn't happen that way in psychical research. You could comb the official records all the way back to the beginning without finding more than a handful of cases that would do for tales late at night, around the fire. Most were only fragments, thousands of them, tantalizing and never explained, in which someone had seen a child in white or heard a sound of bells or some such thing. Those were the facts—but whatever matrix they belonged to, whatever they signified, was locked in mystery.

After supper David immersed himself in their combined notes on the case so far, the parlor table beside him piled precariously with reference books and back issues of the pale blue *Journal of the American Society for Psychical Research*. He was, she knew, checking details, considering possibilities. To him it was all a gigantic jigsaw puzzle; he chose pieces and tried to join them together, discarded one and chose another, all the while trying to guess the finished pattern. The odd-shaped bits, those that seemed to fit nowhere, intrigued him as much as they annoyed him. And why not? To him it was an intellectual game, a challenge for his wits.

She looked down at the physics periodical open in her lap. She was always promising herself to get back into physics; it was the field she had been trained in and she missed it: the mind-stretching abstractions, the elegant and complex equations with their shining chains of symbols describing concepts beyond the reach of words. Physics was her love. It was not love that had driven her into parapsychology—not love, but the need to confront something that had hung over her like a shadow for as long as she could remember.

Across the room David shifted in his chair and muttered over his notes; she glanced toward him again. Sometimes it was a temptation to blame him for her involvement in parapsychology, but she knew that wasn't fair—knew she had been in deep before they met. She had been a brand new physics Ph.D., hesitating between accepting a teaching job and applying for a research grant, when one of her professors had mentioned a parapsychologist friend of his who needed volunteers for a series of experiments in ESP. It had surprised her then, although by now she knew better, that physicists should have parapsychologist friends. What surprised her even more was finding herself among the volunteers. She had spent her whole life learning to stifle her telepathic ability because it disgusted and frightened her—because as a child she had grasped only that she was different, in some impossible and terrifying way, from everyone around her. Now all at once, fresh out of graduate school and exalted by the power and glory of science, she thought with Marie Curie: *Nothing in life is to be feared. It is only to be understood.* All at once it seemed as if telepathy were just one more domino in a line with electricity and the atom, ready to fall before the force of scientific method—to be written down in equations, harnessed into usefulness and respectability. In this spirit she had volunteered.

There were six volunteers of varying ages, all nervous. Jack Pennybacker kept them busy. There were sessions with Rhine's famous ESP cards, with light panels, with sensory deprivation, with random numbers generated by computer. When the series was over and the other volunteers left, Jack talked her into staying on. "I need you," he said. "You've got it." But what was it? As the second series of experiments progressed she began to lose her enthusiasm. It began to seem that science was not, after all, omnipotent. The equations were not forthcoming. Telepathy was skittish, a will-o'-the-wisp, sometimes there, sometimes not. It registered on no instrument, obeyed no recognizable law; in fact it did nothing—except happen. It was a truism around the lab that the experience of telepathy was more like catching a cold than catching a fish, but more like catching a fish than catching a train. In the waning of her confidence Sally recognized her venture into parapsychology for what it actually was—a desperate need to conquer something that seemed to possess her more than she possessed it: a hoping against impossible odds.

She might have gone back to physics then, if it hadn't been for David—if she hadn't fallen in love with him in a sudden loss of equilibrium that made her feel the aptness of the verb. She had fallen hard enough to hurt. For her their marriage had been a process of learning to hold back, to offer only the light undemanding affection with which he seemed comfortable. To want too much, to give too much, was to come up against the smile and the charm he used like a roadblock. It was not that he was difficult to live with. He was easygoing, a good companion; had a sense of humor, shared the household work, was a better cook than she was. She respected his intelligence, its quickness and boldness. Even his impatience in their work, his tendency to jump to conclusions and fudge the scientific method, was not something she could really condemn. Professionally it frazzled her nerves, but privately she suspected it was what separated the innovators from the cautious plodders. She considered herself one of the latter; they were well matched in that way too.

It might have been a perfect marriage if she had not been in love with him, and she had grown to feel obscurely humiliated by this, as if her need for emotional and physical intimacy was somehow excessive. In the beginning she had assumed that the tense, precarious nature of their sexual encounters would improve with time, but she had been wrong: things had deteriorated to the point where it was easier, less painful to put the whole issue out of her head, as he seemed to do. If it wasn't "fair," at least she had come to understand that under certain conditions such words have no meaning.

Now it almost seemed that the last few weeks had brought a change between them, an indefinable sense of drawing closer together. Was it only that they were working as a team, on the first real project of their own, or was there more to it than that—something in the atmosphere of the house itself?

Define your terms.

It wasn't easy. Physics had trained her to accept the fluidity of time and space, of boundaries and barriers, of identity itself. She understood that light was both wave and particle at once, that an electron was neither in motion nor at rest. But these were abstractions. Reality was the house—four walls and a roof, a place where past and present were so insidiously mingled that she could not always separate the two. Ever since she and David had come here, she had tried to seal herself off from the surrounding environment like a diver or an astronaut, not always with success. She saw, heard, felt things; fragments penetrated the defenses she had set up—yet what she meant by "atmosphere" was far more elusive than these: a subtle emotional static at the very edge of perception, intersecting and modulating the patterns she and David had brought with them to the house.

Across the room he stretched, dropped his notebook, turned toward her. "How about giving me a hand with that stuff in the attic tomorrow? I'm drowning in paper up there."

"We've got no business looking at those papers," she said. "Not without Mr. Gilfoy's permission."

"For Pete's sake, what difference does it make? If we find anything relevant I'll get his permission then. If I ask him before we look, and he says no, then it could get sticky." She said nothing and he said, "Well?"

"Well what?"

"Will you help me?"

"No," she said. "I think it's unethical."

David yawned, stretching until the flimsy chair let out a sharp, almost human squeal. "You cut me to the quick."

The fluidity of time and space, of boundaries and barriers, of identity itself. She was dreaming—dreaming so deeply that the sound of the buzzer came from out of her past and she rolled over, groping for the alarm clock to shut it off. There was no clock. Her hand understood first, then her brain, and the present came like a shock of cold water, leaving her wide awake and breathless.

"David—"

He was awake at once, grabbing his jeans off a chair; she heard his bare feet thud across the floor as she swung herself out of bed to follow him into the hall, catching up the flashlight from the dresser in passing. On the panel outside their room one of the lights was flashing: the one marked D.P. Downstairs parlor. David flicked a switch, silencing the buzzer, and in the sudden hush they heard music.

Music. Faint, all but inaudible, so that you held your breath to listen, scarcely more than a ruffling of the surface of the silence, but unmistakable all the same: there was music. The house was dark around them, a series of geometric forms combined in space, shadowy and dreaming, every line and angle holding the past like a brimming liquid ready to spill over at a touch. And the music came like the falling of luminous drops in the darkness, each one glimmering and gone. David started down the stairs; she followed. A step creaked. She steadied herself, one hand on the banister. It was not that she was afraid. But the darkness and the faint music had a power of their own that bypassed her thinking brain and ran straight along her nerves. In her cotton nightgown she was conscious of every moving current of air. She followed David, holding the flashlight without turning it on.

At the foot of the stairs he stopped and waited for her. They crossed the entrance hall together. The parlor doors were a wide rectangle of dim light; inside the room the curtains cast the filmiest of shadows on the floor. The half-moon, perfect as a paper cut-out, clung to one pane of the bay window. As they stopped in the doorway the song spilled over them, plaintive and tender, like warm tears falling. Slowly they fell, and more slowly; Sally put her hand on David's arm. There was silence.

He was gone from her side then: he was in the room, turning on the lamp. Shadows hardened; colors flooded home. David stood shirtless and barefoot against the dark bay window, looking at the music box on the mantel. The lid was open. Sally bent down behind the door to shut off the running tape recorder. When she looked up again he was still standing immobile.

She said, "Did you close it after you showed it to Colin this afternoon?"

"I think so. But dammit, I don't remember." He pounded his forehead with one fist and turned to face her. "But it was played out! And I know I didn't rewind it."

"You're sure it was played out?"

"Don't you remember? When I played it for Colin—"

"I was upstairs," she said.

"Well, it stopped on its own."

She went across the room and looked at the box without touching it. J.G. TO V.B.G. The grain of the dark wood caught the eye and drew it along. Behind her David said, "Oh, Christ."

"What's the matter?"

"Well, I was just thinking. Even if it stopped, that doesn't mean it was played out. It could have just been stuck. I remember it was stuck when Colin first opened it." He stood beside her, reached out, flicked the box with one finger. It gave out a single note. David groaned and sat down hard in one of the rickety chairs, raking his hands through his hair. Sally stood in front of the box a moment longer, examining the glinting metal cylinder, then looked down at him, putting her hand on his head. He lifted his face to her absurdly contorted, mouth pulled down, eyes and nose screwed tight.

"This does it. I'm going to become a used car salesman."

She started to laugh and he grabbed her wrist, pulling her down on his lap.

"You laugh. Wait till you see me in a bow tie." His hair tickled her cheek. She closed her eyes, holding her breath; his arms tightened around her. "A red bow tie." His body heat flooding through her joined the shining pressure of lamplight on her closed lids to suspend her in a limbo of tremulous delight. From somewhere in limbo his fingers touched her face, turning it to him; they kissed. All around them was silence and amber-colored light in this one corner of the darkened house where they sat embracing. It was brightest where they were, beside the lamp, but even the shadows in the corners and along the walls seemed lit, transparent, theirs indistinguishable among the others. Time seemed to slow, to shift on an axis of which they were the base.

All at once the music box gave out two cracked notes into the stillness, making them jump, and then a third as they sat clutching each other and staring at it. They waited: there was nothing more. They exchanged a look then, beginning to laugh. She scrambled up; he went to the mantelpiece and closed the box with a snap.

"That's enough out of you."

⋙ 24 ⋘

THE MOOD was still with them in the morning, lying over their daily routine exactly the way the mist at this hour lay over the yard outside, transforming the familiar into something that beckoned and bemused. Sally, who didn't believe for a moment that last night's music box performance had been paranormal, was equally resistant to the idea that the house could be influencing their relationship in any way. At least she told herself she did not believe it, recognizing that she did not want to. It was easy enough to imagine echoes of Ginny and Julian surrounding them. But to attribute their new closeness to a love affair finished for three quarters of a century, the house itself the only link, was patently absurd. Out in the backyard, trees emerged from the ground mist like green towers in a white sea.

After breakfast David went upstairs to continue his inspection of the Gilfoy family papers. She puttered around downstairs by herself, feeling like a prig for refusing to help him. Unethical. What a word. If he had accepted her judgment with less good humor she would have felt more comfortable with it. As it was, she argued silently with him—or with herself, she wasn't sure which—for a while and then, uncertain whether she had won or lost, found herself on her way to the attic.

Under the cobwebbed eaves the floor was patterned with sunlight, the dust footprinted here and there from their earlier visits. Across the room David, surrounded by boxes, looked up. His face startled her for a moment; then she realized his nose and mouth were covered by a white paper dust mask.

"You look spooky." She went toward him. The mask changed shape; she guessed he was smiling.

"Did you come to help or to hinder?"

"Both, I guess," she said. "Have you found anything?"

"I have. The Reverend Gilfoy paid his cook four dollars a week. Four lousy bucks! Is that Christian charity? It's a miracle the whole family wasn't poisoned in revenge."

"That was probably the going rate in those days," she said.

"No doubt." He waved to his left. "Mind taking a look in those three trunks? I haven't gotten to them yet. The masks are over there if you want one."

She decided against the mask; the trunks didn't look as dusty as the boxes. Two of them were large, the third smaller. They seemed to contain old books. She chose a volume and looked at the flyleaf: *Shapes That Haunt the Dusk.* Ghost stories. Turning the pages she came upon a scrap of paper covered with spidery handwriting—a recipe for spiced cider. She replaced it carefully, and the book. It began to look like a very long day.

Nearby was the little writing desk she had discovered on her last visit. She turned her attention to it, admiring the slender bowed legs, the top inlaid with a decorative border of pale gold wood. The whole piece was eloquent of a past era when furniture possessed gender; and in this case the gender was distinctly feminine. She tried the drawer. It slid out a few inches and then stopped; she remembered it was jammed. She played with it a little, trying to loosen it.

"Something's stuck in there." David, behind her, had pulled the dust mask down so that it hung around his neck. "You know," he said, "this was probably Ginny's desk. There might be something interesting in it."

Probably Ginny's desk. She didn't ask for the basis of that conclusion. He knelt in front of the desk, braced it with his free hand, and yanked the drawer handle. There was a violence about his efforts that did not bode well for the fragile desk. "Don't break it," she said. "Okay?"

"Trust me." He got to his feet and regarded the desk, hands on hips, then picked it up with a grunt and shook it hard. Things rattled inside; dust flew. Sally sneezed. David set the desk down and leaned on it, out of breath.

"Now. You try it."

She took hold of the handle and pulled. The drawer slid smoothly out. They turned gratified faces to each other, and then together they looked down at the clutter in the drawer. An oblong silver napkin ring engraved with the initials A.M.B., a loose prism from a lamp or chandelier, a few hairpins, a nibless fountain pen, envelopes and papers. David took a handful, glancing through them.

"Listen to this. Dated February 4, 1916. 'Dear Master Gilfoy. Thank you so much for your letter. I am always glad to hear from young readers who enjoy my books. I think you may want to wait a year or two before trying *King of the Buffalo*. *The Story of Frisky* or *Uncle Billy, the Curious Cobbler* would be best for you at your age. Sincerely, Eunice Pickering.' Who's Eunice Pickering?"

"Never heard of her."

"I wonder if I'm old enough for *King of the Buffalo*," David said.

She took the other papers out of his hand and looked at them. A receipt from a roofing company, dated 1928. A card, the postmark blurred, picturing the railroad depot at Provincetown, Cape Cod. The back read: "Thanks for the clippings, which I passed along to Grandfather. How's Tip?" and was illegibly signed. It was addressed to Mrs. Joshua Gilfoy. A program from a musical performance in Boston on June 11, 1912, showed signs of having been folded into a fan. Sally fanned herself thoughtfully. Then David said, "Bingo. Here's what was jamming it."

She looked up. It was a photograph he had in his hand, one corner badly mutilated where it had been caught in the drawer. A formal portrait of a young man, with the warm sepia tone of old photographs and the curious look of innocence belonging to pictures made in the era when photography was still fairly new. She was conscious of putting up barriers between herself and the picture almost at once: of seeing not personality portrayed, but an artistic exercise of darks and lights and angles and planes, for there was no doubt that it was masterfully done. The left side of the face was lit subtly more than the right, which was slightly turned away, so that the soft brown shadows and muted highlights were in perfect balance.

By now she had established enough distance to let her look at the young man himself.

He was not handsome. The features were pleasant but undistinguished, and one eyebrow, drawn down more than the other, gave him a faintly belligerent expression. But there was nonetheless something very attractive about the young face. It was stubborn and solid: a face that might come, with time and familiarity, to seem beautiful. He wore a high white collar closed with a loose white tie, and some sort of dark robe or cloak. His straight dark hair looked very soft.

"Julian," David said.

"Maybe. Or Joshua as a young man, or our landlord Samuel, or maybe even Tip."

"Who?"

She showed him the postcard; he glanced at the message and then back at the photograph. "It's Julian. It's got to be."

"Why?" she said.

"Come on, Sal. It's Ginny's desk."

"Then it could just as easily be Joshua or Samuel. And besides, how do we know for sure it's her desk?" She took the napkin ring out of the drawer and held it up to him. "A.M.B. Those aren't her initials."

"What about that postcard you just showed me?" David said. "It was addressed to her. And this Dear Master Gilfoy letter—look at the date. That's our Samuel, her son."

"And maybe this is his portrait."

David looked at her with curiosity. "Why are you so set on its not being Julian?"

"I don't give a damn who it is." She turned away abruptly. "I'm just saying there are several possibilities—"

"Okay," he said. "Okay."

"Well, you're acting like there's no doubt at all."

"Look," he said, "we can ask Colin. He knew Samuel as a young man."

"Oh, David. Even if it isn't Samuel, that still doesn't mean it's Julian."

"Well, we can get an expert to date it for us. Or we can ask the old lady—Miss Ellen. She knew Julian."

Sally went to the window and stared out at sunlit green

leaves. The mist had burned off by now and the yard was bright and hot and without magic. "Ask her, then."

There was a pause and he said, "I will."

Behind her there were rustling sounds: he was going through the rest of the contents of the drawer. She looked at the leaves, mentally reviewing what he had said, what she had said—realizing that there was no logical reason for what she was feeling, this hot shaking weakness that was like anger or fear. She turned finally and went to stand next to him. He had found two other old photographs, snapshot size, which he had placed on top of the desk next to the portrait, and she examined them in silence.

Three children in old-fashioned swimsuits stood ankle-deep in water, holding hands. The one in the center, a boy, was smiling; the two girls, older and younger, on either side of him were not. In the glassy water their wavering reflections trailed off the bottom edge of the picture. The other photograph showed two smiling young women in wide-brimmed hats and long high-collared dresses, standing arm in arm in front of a stone wall. She pointed to the second picture.

"New York."

"How do you know?"

"Look at the wall. That's Central Park."

"Amazing, Holmes. Simply amazing."

"Elementary, really." She succeeded in matching his tone.

After lunch they set off for the library, taking all three of the photographs. It was mid-July, and hot, but the overhanging linden branches kept Lilac Street in shade. By now they were beginning to know people. Mr. Chalmers, trimming his hedge, nodded to them; Ellen Peyton, her arms filled with groceries, said hello. Bobby, Johnny, and Matt, the neighborhood kids, were out with baseball gloves, Bobby's dog Beanie jumping at their heels. A girl on a bike flew past down the hill, pigtails streaming, and Sally turned to watch her. The bordering trees made the street into a tunnel of dappled light, a splash of brightness at the foot of the hill where Lilac met busier Tanglewood. In that luminous shade the eye was drawn outward from the dwindling figure of the cyclist as if by ripples radiating from a disturbance in a still pond's surface. Sally saw trees and hedges and old white houses, a hopscotch game chalked on the sidewalk, a line of flapping laundry. Ordinary street, ordinary town.

From where she stood, all she could see of the Gilfoy house was a corner of the porch through a gap in the trees, and it looked no different from the other houses—maybe a little shabbier, the yard overgrown. But she knew better. She thought of the other haunted houses she and David had encountered during their training—a stone farmhouse in western Pennsylvania, an apartment in a shabby building in a run-down section of Brooklyn, a middle-class home in a Maryland suburb. Each had its history, its repertoire of phenomena, its frightened, distraught inhabitants. Poltergeists flung eggs and stones; doors unlocked and opened themselves; there were sounds of coughing and the rustling of clothes. Words mysteriously appeared on paper and then the paper itself spontaneously caught fire. A girl in a lavender dress haunted one end of an upstairs corridor. To herself Sally had to admit that it would be a relief when the Gilfoy house started to produce such phenomena, if it ever did. The only clearly paranormal events so far had been associated with Rosanna's sitting in the master bedroom, when the air temperature had dropped to 41 degrees and a pair of loud percussive noises had practically deafened them. But before the medium's arrival, and since her departure, there had been nothing—nothing but a music box probably left open by David. And she couldn't help finding the lull more disquieting than the most spectacular phenomena. They had come, after all, to document evidence of a haunting. According to the reports of the former tenants, there was ample reason to believe that the house's reputation had at least a minimal foundation in fact. But instead of activity they found quiet, instead of events there were shadows—a feeling here, a doubt there; and most insidious of all was this sense that if they were waiting, the house was too. But for what? David had stopped ahead and was looking back at her, his face impatient. She hurried to catch up.

Colin was not at his desk when they arrived at the library. Another minute and he appeared, hands full of crumpled paper: the copy machine was acting up again. His obvious pleasure in seeing them brought back Sally's guilt of the day before. They had harmed him then, whether he realized it or not—destroyed what David would call one of his illusions; and she could not shake off the feeling that this was only the beginning.

But David was showing him the photographs, laying them in a row on the desk: the children, the two women, the young man. Colin studied them for a moment, then picked up the last. "Is this Julian?"

"We were hoping you could tell us," David said.

"I never knew him, you know."

"Of course not. But you can eliminate one possibility, at least. Is it Samuel Gilfoy—the present one?"

Colin glanced at the picture again. Decisively, still looking at it, he said, "No."

"You're sure?"

"There is a resemblance. But Sam I knew. This isn't Sam."

"Could it be Joshua as a young man?" David said.

"I suppose so, although . . ." Colin peered more closely at the photograph. "The quality is awfully good. The gradation of tone, I mean, things like that. Don't forget, photography was still pretty primitive when Joshua was this young. I suppose a real photography buff could give you an approximate date on it with no trouble. Where did you find it?"

"In the attic. What about these other two? Any ideas?"

Colin examined them; a long minute passed. Then: "The children I don't know about. But this," the left-hand figure in the photograph of the two women by the wall, "this is Virginia Gilfoy. Ginny."

"Ah." David leaned over to look.

After a moment Sally looked too. It was hard to tell much about her from the picture. Both women wore enormous wide-brimmed hats, and Ginny's face, unlike her friend's, whose head was thrown back, was in shadow. But in some way its lack of definition—not much more than a smile, a glimmer of eyes—made the other details come clearer: the slenderness, the high collar of the dress emerging from the long coat she wore, the pressure of her hand on her friend's sleeve, a slightly quizzical tilt to her head as if she did not quite trust the camera to function. There was an air of mystery, intensely femi-nine, about the smiling shadow-faced figure in its old-fashioned clothing. Behind her the movement of leaves now long dead made a blurred pattern of light and dark. Sally, looking down at the faded brown image, thought: Before Julian, or after? And then: After. And then, angry at herself, turned away.

People were waiting to check out books. David invited Colin to supper; then they were leaving, out into the afternoon sunshine, David carefully tucking the photo-graphs back into their envelope.

"What next?"

David balanced the envelope on his palms as they walked. He was in a good mood. "Next? I thought I'd ask Mrs. Hopkins to marry me. Would you mind?"

"I thought you were going to show that picture to Ellen Flagg."

"I don't really think we need to, do you? I'm convinced."

"Convinced? Of what?"

"Come on," he said. "I'll admit there was a good chance of its being Samuel. But it's not Joshua. Aside from what Colin said about the technical quality—it just isn't Joshua."

"Your logic is fascinating, David."

"Well, do you think it's Joshua?"

"Probably not. But as I said, that doesn't mean it's Julian."

They walked half a block in silence. Cars passed them in the street. Sally stepped carefully over a caterpillar on the sidewalk. At last David said, "I don't get it. This morning when I talked about showing it to Miss Ellen you got upset. Now you're upset because I'm talking about *not* showing it to her. What do you want me to do?"

Sally did not look at him. She did not know herself why the photograph disturbed her. "I'm not upset," she said. And she thought her voice did sound normal. "It's just that it's irrelevant. Can't you see that? It doesn't matter whose picture it is, Julian's or Joshua's or Wen-dell Willkie's! It doesn't prove anything. It's beside the point. The point is whether or not anything paranormal is going on in that house."

He didn't answer. Was he angry? Or had she hurt him, as she wanted to without really understanding why? She withdrew into herself violently, not wanting to know. They walked the rest of the way home without speaking.

She decided to spend the rest of the afternoon working in the backyard. She had started on it a week or so earlier, simply because its scruffiness had begun to depress her, and already there were signs of improvement. She had borrowed Mrs. Hopkins's gardening clippers and forced a semblance of neatness on the bushes demarcating the garden, while in the garden proper the lank rosebushes had produced a flower or two, as if in gratitude. She had, to David's amusement, cut the grass one afternoon, a bandanna tied around her head, sweating as she pushed the spitting antiquated mower (Mrs. Hopkins's again) back and forth across the yard. But even David had been forced to admit that the place looked better. On several occasions Mrs. Hopkins, cutting her enormous roses in a gardening hat, had come to the overgrown fence between the two yards to offer encouragement or advice, to worry that Sally would get sunstroke, or recall that years ago there had been pansies growing all along the back of the house. On impulse Sally bought a packet of pansy seeds at Buck's and planted them, not knowing if they would bloom.

Today it was too hot for Mrs. Hopkins to be out. Sun shimmered in the grass and weighted the surface of the leaves, a bright unstirring. Sally wiped sweat from her eyes as she worked, wishing she had put on her bandanna. She was trying to clear the sundial in the garden from the ivy that threatened to cover it completely; the tangled stems were tough and bitter-smelling, and in spite of Mrs. Hopkins's clippers it was hard work. But the act of keeping her hands busy did not, as she had hoped, stop her from thinking—and in spite of firm resolutions to the contrary she thought about the photograph of Julian Gilfoy.

Not necessarily Julian. No positive proof it's Julian. Just because it was in Ginny's desk, *if* that's Ginny's desk—that's no proof. Old photographs have a way of drifting around, ending up anywhere. Could be anyone.

The logic was not much help. Whether or not the

photo was of Julian, it had unbalanced all her ideas about him: the image she had half consciously held of a rake, a dandy, a wastrel—some kind of nineteenth-century stage villain. The young face in the photograph had disturbed her with its childlike stubbornness and candor. There was no cunning in it, no polish, and whatever power it possessed was still without focus. Only the potential was there. Looking at it she had felt an unwilling pity for the young life abruptly ended.

Wailing for the lost one that comes not again. The words came unbidden and she shrugged them off, impatient with herself, sentiment masquerading as emotion. She preferred the original story with its picture-book simplicity: the saintly father, the wicked son. The colors and shadows, added little by little, made her uncomfortable. They were a distraction, and she would have liked to dismiss them. If she could. The straight dark hair had looked, even in the photograph, indescribably soft.

With an effort she concentrated on the ivy-shrouded pedestal. Slowly the heat, the snick of the clippers, and the rustle of stems and leaves began to exert their own power, lulling her into mindless concentration on her task. A bird called; a shadow of wings crossed the grass. The face of the dial was encrusted with a layer of grime, from which the stub of the broken pointer protruded like a spar from a sunken ship. She scraped some of the dirt away with the blade of the clippers, then rubbed the dial with one finger and was rewarded with a metallic gleam. Bronze. She bent closer to see what number she had uncovered and was surprised to find the letter C. C? The Roman numeral one hundred—what was that doing on a sundial? One hundred o'clock? Intrigued now, she retreated to the house for steel wool, paper towels, and a pan of soapy water. One hundred o'clock. The water, combining with the dirt on the dial, made mud: brown streaks trickled down the pedestal and dripped into the ivy, but under her scrubbing things were slowly becoming clearer. The C was not a Roman numeral but a letter, part of a word, a string of words across the bottom of the dial face. She kept scrubbing and was at last rewarded with a sentence.

I COUNT ONLY SUNNY HOURS.

The bronze shone dully. Above the words an hourglass

spread a pair of feathered wings. Sally wiped the last of the mud from the dial, and at the same moment felt someone touch her.

It came from behind, a hand on her arm—the unexpectedness making her jump, turn quickly—but there was no one, the yard empty except for her, colors trembling in the heat, no other movement, no sound. But there had been something, *someone*, just in that instant. A hand had grasped her bare arm just above the elbow; she had felt the warm strong pressure of fingers on her skin.

Uncanniness slapped her like a wave. The sundial felt hot now to her touch; she backed away from it and the clippers, falling from her numb grasp, hit the base of the pedestal with a clink scarcely audible against the rushing noise that mounted inside her head as she stood shivering in the July sun. Over everything there was a blazing silence. She was cold, the sun a dazzling mockery, this bright stillness in which she seemed to be alone and yet not. She hunched her shoulders suddenly, hugging herself against the cold, staring at the sundial.

You imagined it. The sun, the heat . . .

But she knew she hadn't. She had felt it as plainly as she felt her own hands gripping her shoulders now. She tightened her fingers as if she could somehow blot out the memory that remained in her nerves: the clasp of fingers, firm but not ungentle . . . A shudder went through her and she shook her head violently.

Gradually the cold left her. A bird called across the hot afternoon; a squirrel ran along a branch. As if on their own her hands slid down her arms and fell to her sides, hanging there limp. She felt drained, as if she had run a marathon, without even the strength left for fear. But hollowness filled her as she glanced toward the white clapboard walls of the house sunk in shade, and then back at the sundial.

Haunted. Just a word, but what did it mean if not this deep still sense that she was being observed somehow, watched not so much by someone at one of the windows as by the house itself, or by some consciousness inhabiting it like a mind inhabiting a body? The touch had been that of a human hand. But it had come from the house. A chill went through her, echo of the cold that had possessed her before. She was vulnerable—if she touched the sundial, and in a hundred other ways. The place was playing with her, using her, channeling memories through her, making them quicken and come alive. She looked toward the house once more, her face set, before retrieving the clippers gingerly from the foot of the sundial. The rest of the afternoon she spent pulling up the weeds that grew luxuriantly along the fence.

≫≫ 25 ≪≪

"LET'S EAT HERE in the kitchen," David said. "That painting of Joshua in the dining room makes me nervous."

"You could always take it down," Colin said.

"I don't know. I favor something more subtle, like turning it to the wall."

Colin seemed comfortable, she thought—glad to be there. If only David would talk about something other than the haunting. Standing at the stove with her back to them she could afford to smile at this last thought: as well wish for the moon. And in all honesty, was it Colin she wanted to shield, or herself? The discoveries of the last two days, this kaleidoscopic shifting of perspectives on events long since over and done, had disturbed her and she didn't really know why. That damned photograph, she caught herself thinking—and pushed the thought away, listening instead to the conversation behind her.

"You don't happen to remember, do you, Colin, if I closed the music box after I showed it to you yesterday?" David's method of setting the table consisted of putting a knife, fork, and spoon in each person's right hand and a paper napkin in his left. Colin, slightly bewildered, sat trying to think.

"I really don't. Why?"

"Well, if I didn't, I didn't. But if I did"—he came to the stove, took two of the plates Sally was filling, set one in front of Colin and sat down holding the other—"if I did . . ."

Sally brought her plate to the table and sat down. David was still holding his at an angle in midair. "That's going to drip," she said, and he put it down absently on the table.

"If I did, then we had a paranormal occurrence here last night."

Colin looked, she thought, impressed enough to gratify even David. He still held his eating utensils in one hand and the half-folded napkin in the other, completely ignoring his food.

"Eat," she said gently, touching his arm. "Go on, David. Don't keep him in suspense."

"Okay. Remember, Colin, it was only paranormal *if* I closed the music box after I showed it to you. And since nobody remembers whether I did or not, it's totally useless as far as real evidence goes. But it makes a good story."

And that, she thought, listening to him tell it, was important to him. As important as the painstaking collection of data, the documenting of evidence, the final report with its list of possible hypotheses at the end, only the third or fourth of which would read: *The disturbances were paranormal in nature and were caused by the ghost of a person or persons known to have formerly occupied the house . . .* She stopped herself: she was being unfair. If he could take it lightly, all the better. One of them had to.

Colin was eating dutifully, his whole attention on David. There was no question that it made a good story. When it was over he sat bemused, fork suspended in air. Then: "Could a ghost really generate that kind of force? Enough to open the box?"

David opened his hands, palms up. "Why not? Poltergeists throw furniture."

"Oh. Of course."

"If it happens again," David said, "we'll catch him."

"How?"

"This afternoon I rigged a little vibration-sensitive platform for the box to sit on. Any tampering with it will trip a switch, which will trigger a camera as well as activate our central buzzer. And for the record, at exactly four-twenty this afternoon I officially noted the box as closed."

Colin was still thinking. "But even if it was just stuck instead of being run down, why should it start playing, just like that, in the middle of the night? Doesn't that qualify as paranormal?"

"Not if there's a possible natural explanation," Sally said. "In order for an event to be paranormal it has to violate some natural law."

"Blip," David said.

"I beg your pardon?" Colin said.

"Basic limiting principles," Sally said. "BLP. Blip. It's David's abbreviation for the way C. D. Broad describes the reality we experience through our senses—the world we function in. The basic limiting principles are things like not being able to see the future, or make tables jump into the air without touching them. When something violates one of the basic limiting principles, it's considered paranormal."

"Oh," Colin said. "Blip. I see. But if the music box was stuck, how did it get unstuck? Nobody touched it."

"That's true," she said. "But it could have been a byproduct of some perfectly natural process, like the house settling. It happens we can count that one out, because we do have a vibration pick-up which would have registered any movement in the frame of the house. Or it could be something as simple as the wood of the box moving as its moisture content changed. A change in the humidity of the air could cause that, but there wouldn't be anything paranormal about it."

"I understand. But isn't it significant that it happened— well, so soon after we found out that Julian is . . . connected . . . with the box?"

"Not really," she said. "For one thing, you have to remember that we have no actual proof he *is* connected."

"No actual proof! What about the phrase 'the lost one'? He used it to identify himself. And it comes from the song."

"Well, that could be coincidence."

"That's a pretty walloping coincidence," Colin said.

"Yes. But normal reality does offer walloping coincidences at times. So it wouldn't necessarily be paranormal. Anyway, even if you accept Julian's connection with the box, the fact that it started to play last night isn't really significant. It's just the first time we've had the box out since we found it. That's all. The chances that David left it open are appreciably greater, statistically, than the chances that it was opened paranormally."

David said, "Colin, you'll find there's one thing parapsychologists love more than apparitions, and that's statistics. Who wants coffee?"

They took it into the parlor. Colin peered at the music box on the mantelpiece from a respectful distance. David saw him.

"Don't worry, the platform isn't activated right now. Nothing in this room is."

"Because we're in here? But what if something were to happen—right here? Now?"

"Well, it would count for something if we all saw it. But it's unlikely anything will happen. Most of the reports we've gotten on this house have put the psi occurrences late at night—after people have gone to bed—and most of them have happened upstairs."

"You mean," Colin said, "that upstairs is more haunted than downstairs?"

"Not just upstairs. Two or three rooms in particular."

"Is that possible?"

"Sure." David leaned on the mantelpiece—his lecturing stance. Sally glanced at Colin but he was listening, rapt. "It's standard procedure in a haunting investigation to pass out floor plans and ask the residents of the house to mark the areas they consider especially 'haunted'—places where they've actually seen an apparition, or just places that make them feel creepy. The next step is to bring in a number of psychically sensitive individuals who go through the house and mark *their* impressions on a set of floor plans. Then you do the same thing with a bunch of skeptics—people who flatly don't believe in ghosts and couldn't if they tried. They mark the places that seem to them to be likely spots for the gullible to start seeing spooks—you know, behind the cellar door and so on. Then you compare them."

"And what do you get?"

"Everything and then some. Sometimes the correlations are remarkable. Or everybody may say something completely different."

"What about in this case?"

David was enjoying himself. "Here we've done very well. We've been especially lucky in having a number of different sets of people to report in . . ."

His voice went on, forming a background for Sally's thoughts. The tenants had reported raps, lights, a rush of cold air. Those were the obvious haunting incidents, the ones that sent people packing. But what about that hand on her arm this afternoon by the sundial? She covered the place with her own fingers now. A clasp of warm fingers on flesh, touch lasting only a moment. The lab had supplied them with cameras, tape recorders, thermometers—but no piece of equipment capable of measuring such a sensation. She had nothing beyond her own nerve endings to say that it had happened at all.

And that was this haunting in a nutshell. Tenuous, subjective, made up of events that were more like insinuations of events. Like the vague dreams of a restless sleeper, erupting now and again into some nightmare that centered on the master bedroom. The tenants' reports had focused on the more spectacular phenomena; either they had not noticed or had not felt comfortable mentioning the gentle shiftings and veerings of reality that cast their own peculiar halo over the house.

Her arm ached; her fingers had unconsciously tightened their grip as she sat thinking. She put her hands in her lap and tried to pay attention to what David was saying.

". . . so basically what we've got here is a diversity of reports with a similarity of impressions."

"And your medium—were her impressions similar?"

"Yes, the correlation was very high. And our most successful sitting with her was in Joshua's room, which all the tenants marked as a haunted area."

Haunted. Sally rubbed her arm, then looked at Colin. "You haven't touched your coffee," she said. "Would you rather have tea?"

It is a curious fact that the outer edge of the retina of the eye is more sensitive to light than the central part, and so can perceive things that disappear if we look straight at them. Perhaps the same can be said for the outer edges of consciousness, the myths and dreams in which strange unities are formed.

This is a dream of meeting, the end of a journey, a lighted shore drawing closer, a door opening on something long sought. The movement is always forward toward its goal; obstacles melt away and happiness lights the heart. Then in an instant the scene is changed: darkness descends, and in place of familiar landmarks there is only a cold desert, where veiled figures stand gray on the horizon, out of reach. All is confusion, danger. Then one of the far-off figures turns and reveals features that resemble, indescribably altered, the longed-for face.

Sally could not remember what she had been dreaming. She only knew that when she woke, her eyes were wet with tears. David's hand was joggling her shoulder.

"I'm awake," she said.

"Come on, then. We've got some action."

She heard the buzzer now: dull, a bee under water. David was already out in the hall and she went after him. This time it was the sitting room light, flashing on and off, on and off. He clicked the buzzer and there was silence. Silence. Not a sound. She could hear his breathing, and her own. Together they started down the hall to the sitting room. It was very dark. She switched on the flashlight and they followed its beam, the floorboards creaking underfoot as floorboards are said to do when a ghost makes its rounds. Down the hall: turn the corner: the sitting room door was closed, as they had left it earlier on their nightly check. David looked at her.

"Ready?"

She nodded.

He grasped the knob and turned it: the door swung inward. The room was dark, the curtained windows paler rectangles. She put out the flashlight. They stood waiting a moment and then David stepped into the room. She followed. Furniture rose vaguely out of the darkness: back of the low sofa, bowl of the lamp silvered with moonlight. It was all very. still. David muttered something about the buzzer malfunctioning. She heard him fumble with the lamp; then it came on. They stood looking at each other and then around them at the room—undisturbed, peaceful. David's watch said 2:37. Sally glanced down at the equipment behind the door, wondering if the door could have been opened and then closed again, but the dials read negative.

Then David said, "Hey. Are we dumb." His carefully casual tone of voice was an inverse ratio betraying the pitch of his excitement. She looked up: he pointed. A photograph protruded from the automatically triggered Polaroid camera in the corner of the room.

There had been plenty of time for it to develop fully. He pulled it free and they both looked at it, expecting literally anything. In fact there was, in the upper left-hand corner of the frame, a whitish blur against the dark background of the room, between the door and the northeast corner. The time registered on the bottom of the photograph was 02:31:46.

David blew his breath out all at once. "That's Tinkerbell," he said.

Sally looked at him quizzically.

"Tinkerbell. Susan Abbey's light." He was a little dazed. "Sally, dammit—look at it! We've got something!"

"It looks that way," she said. The blur appeared to be about the size of a tennis ball. "There may have been more than one," she said. "It's right at the edge of the frame."

"However many there were, they didn't stay long." He looked at her in such honest unscientific amazement that she had to smile. "Wonder what the hell it was?"

"Maybe it'll come back," she said. "Try turning off the light."

He put out the lamp and they stood in the dark. Silence settled down on them; they strained against it and against the darkness, afraid of missing something.

"Did we scare it off?" David's voice just above a whisper.

"Assuming it's the same thing the Abbeys saw—"

"And Christine."

"And Christine," she said. "Assuming that, it wasn't

so shy with them. The Abbeys watched it for half an hour."

The stillness closed around them again. Sally's eyes were becoming used to the dark now: the silvered folds of curtains, the chairs and lamps and sofa taking shape little by little, deeper wells of blackness beneath and beyond. The white marble fireplace was clearly visible, carved in shadow and moonlight. Her glance, alert for the small circle of light that Susan Abbey had named Tinkerbell, moved slowly around the room—walls, corners, door, the still figure of David beside her, fireplace and windows again—four walls surrounding and containing David and herself for a space of time as others had been surrounded and contained, leaving behind a little of themselves without knowing it, shedding anger or tenderness or pleasure or despair to mingle with the substance of the room until it was full to overflowing. Behind the darkness there was a light of afternoons and evenings and mornings, finished by the standards of human perception but still present nonetheless in this room. It was all here. Someone had stood at the window and twisted a fold of the curtain tight and tighter in her hand; someone else, standing by the fireplace, had dropped a glass and a quick stain had spread on the carpet. And still the curtain twisted, still the glass fell and made its dark wet mark. There were voices, subdued and then rising and breaking off—a sound like singing— a sound like whispering—and sounds behind the sounds, and behind the light there was darkness and then more light across which shadows moved in procession, another and another and another—David yawned suddenly, put out his arms and stretched.

"Let's forget it. It's gone, for tonight anyway, don't you think?"

She took a deep breath and nodded. She had been drifting off, falling asleep on her feet: that was all. That was all. Just the same she felt shaky. When he turned on the lamp she moved away, not wanting him to notice. She need not have worried; he was too busy checking and resetting the equipment. While he worked she wandered over to the fireplace and ran her hand along the smooth marble curves. Suddenly she knelt beside it.

"Sally? What is it?"

She looked up. "I don't know—nothing. Just a stain on the carpet."

He was yawning again. "Let's go to bed. I'm finished here." Flourishing the photograph: "Not a bad night's work, even if we didn't get to see Tink for ourselves."

"No," she said, brushing her hand over the carpet, over the faded stain so faint it might have been a shadow, so faint in fact that anyone might miss it who did not know it was there, feeling as she stood up a moment of giddiness, of light and dark infinitely receding, before she followed David from the room.

⋙ 26 ⋘

THE NEXT MORNING, discussing it, they knew two things.

One was that the camera had been triggered. The other was that it had registered something on film. Beyond that they could not be sure. Neither of them had actually seen the light itself and, as David grudgingly admitted, it could have had some natural origin—a lightning bug, for instance. Neither of them had thought to check the room at the time. And there they stuck.

"Okay," David said finally. "You can't deny one point. Which is this. We've been here for weeks and nothing's happened—until we manage to reconstruct some of Julian's story. And then, right away, things begin to happen. The music box. The light. If that's coincidence, it's some coincidence."

"Well, if you take those incidents in context, I admit it looks—"

"Take them in context? How the hell else am I supposed to take them? They happened in context, didn't they?"

"David—"

"Sorry."

But she knew how he felt. There were so many small challenges, so many little hurdles—finding a house with a reputation, getting permission to use it, setting up the equipment, making sure it was functioning properly, gathering data in the face of skepticism, ridicule, hostility, even fear—that it was easy to lose sight of the fact that their final goal was in many ways simply a last frustration. In the end you didn't know what you knew: you couldn't be sure. You had the facts, and you had four or five hypotheses drawn from them, among which you had what you privately believed to be the truth—but you didn't *know*. Once in a while it got to you, even David. He got up from the table and carried the breakfast dishes to the sink, turning on the water with such force that something toppled and fell with a clatter.

She went on sitting at the table. She had tried, lying awake after they returned to bed last night, to reason herself out of the panic following those few moments in the dark sitting room, that interval in which she had seemed to drift in some limbo of the house's devising. She had told herself that she had been half asleep, caught off balance, but the logic rang hollow. Last night wasn't the first time. There had been too many other incidents, too many times when the house had slipped past her guard with an insouciant ease that made her, sitting here now in the kitchen with sunlight lying in golden squares on the floor, go cold as she tallied them up. The music box. The first sitting with Rosanna, when she had gone into trance. The two dogs. The voice calling her name the night of the sitting in the master bedroom—David's, she had thought at the time, but David said not. The hand touching her arm at the sundial. And now last night, with its relentless progression of images pushing through her. She knew how to take care of herself: how to fend off the blizzard of psychic noise sent out by other people; it was a reflex by now, automatic. But here in the house it was different—a more subtle invasion that seemed to come from inside her, an echo from the house itself.

Last night—what had stopped it? David had moved, spoken, offered her a link with the solid world of here and now, of objects and forms. With both feet firmly planted in that safe world, he was impervious to everything that threatened her in this place. As long as she had that anchor . . . The sight of him standing at the sink, polo shirt half untucked and one back pocket of his jeans torn, obliterated all other thoughts at once like the quick wash of surf over sand: a hot weakness in her legs, a surge of physical desire so intense that she experienced it as vertigo. She wanted him, and there was nothing she could do about it; she had learned not to initiate such encounters because then their failure became her fault, something he could hate her for. And she had learned also that she could not afford to be hated by David, even for a little while. It was easier to get a damp cloth and clean the crumbs off the kitchen table with an energy that made it shine.

The next few days were enough to convince them that, for whatever reason, the pattern had changed. After weeks of quiescence the house was beginning to show evidence of paranormal activity. The light (they continued to call it Tinkerbell) appeared two nights out of three: once in the sitting room and once in the Thistle Room. As yet they had not actually seen it, although they had the beginning of a collection of photographs ("Damn thing loves having its picture taken," David said). After its first appearance they had sprayed the sitting room thoroughly with insecticide and kept the windows closed; the air in the room was oppressive, but scientifically controlled.

"My only objection to this thing," David said, "is that it never sticks around for more than a minute or two. What do you suppose the Abbeys did to make it do a full show?"

"You may be looking at the situation backward," Sally pointed out. "The only times they'd be likely to notice it would be the times it was around for a while. Presumably it made a lot of short appearances for them too, but they never knew because they didn't have our instruments."

"So it follows that sooner or later we'll get a longer visit."

"I guess it follows."

"You know," he said, "I'm wondering if it wouldn't be a good idea to get Rosanna back here for a few days."

"No," she said quickly, and then: "That is, I don't think it's necessary. It might even mess things up. Now that we're finally getting some action, why switch the formula? It's obviously working."

He said nothing and she wondered if she had talked too fast, if her panic had showed. Because it was panic, nothing less, that was evoked by the thought of seeing Rosanna again.

"You're right," he said. "Why switch the formula?" He got up from his chair, stretched. "I guess I'll do something about supper."

She heard him go down the hall to the kitchen; presently there was a noise of pots and pans. The clock on the mantel next to the music box said half past seven. They had bought a bottle of wine that afternoon and drunk it sitting in the parlor, watching the light lengthen and trying not to get depressed. There was always a sense of anticlimax when the routine settled in: one of the lab's most experienced researchers had once admitted to Sally the longing, buried beneath years of scientific training, to encounter a real rip-roaring spook. For herself she wasn't sure, but she thought she could answer for David.

She finished the wine that was left in her glass. From the open windows in the bay the evening air came softly in, filling the lacy curtains. "Damn," she whispered, more like a prayer or an endearment than a curse, and put her face in her hands. Whatever it was, the wine or the summer air or the mention of Rosanna's name, she felt tears very close.

Damn this house.

That night before Rosanna left: that stupid, stupid night.

David was yelling at her from the kitchen. "Have we got any cooking sherry? I can't find it."

"Second shelf. Toward the back."

"I don't see—oh, here it is." He started to whistle; pans clattered. She found herself thinking of Rosanna again. She had tried not to, with some success, since the medium's departure. Not that she disliked Rosanna as a person. But mediums in general made her uncomfortable; she had only consented to bringing one into this case because the house had begun to get on her nerves. Nothing had actually happened during that first fortnight, but she had been oppressed by a constant sense that something was about to; and all at once the passive waiting had become too much for her. The medium had seemed like a way of forcing the issue, taking control. Instead there had been the fiasco of the first "lost one" sitting, when she herself had gone into trance, and from that moment she had felt the medium's interest focused on her in a way that added pressure rather than diminishing it—pressure that culminated in their conversation on the porch the night before Rosanna had returned to Boston.

When did you first realize about yourself?

The encounter had not been something she sought. She would have avoided it if possible, just as now she would have chosen not to recall it. Picking up her empty cup, turning it in her hands.

When did you first realize

She pushed the memory away but it pushed back. A summer evening like this one, warm with the smell of grass and the last lilacs, loud with cicadas.

When did you

Bulking so large now in her head that her thoughts, trying to escape, bumped up against it regardless. A summer evening after supper. Sitting by herself out on the porch steps, the door opening behind her, then a step on the hollow boards and Rosanna sitting down beside her without speaking. The cicadas momentarily silent, beginning to sing again. Lit end of Rosanna's cigarette glowing red, smoke invisibly rising, part of the dusk.

We sat there while it got darker. The lightning bugs started up. She leaned back against one of the porch uprights.

"When did you first realize about yourself?"

"Realize what?"

She thought that was funny. "That you were psychic."

"That's a broad term."

"Oh relax, will you? This isn't a scientific seminar. I'm asking you a simple question."

What did I say? Something about Jack, about those first experiments.

"Telepathy?"

"Yes."

"And before that?"

"I don't remember."

Putting out her cigarette. "You don't like to talk about it, do you?"

"No."

Silence: lightning bugs flickering in the trees like strands of blinking Christmas tree bulbs.

"I was about ten when Andy died." Her tone comfortable; she could have been passing along her favorite recipe. "Yeah, I knew Andy on this side. We grew up together; our moms were best friends. We even had the same birthday—he was a year older." Quiet a moment.

"You know, some people say children who die grow up on the other side. Maybe they do. But Andy was the damndest kid, and that's how I still feel him—the damndest kid." Smile in her voice. "Blue eyes and this crazy white-blond hair and a chipped front tooth. One of those kids who could do anything with his hands, pitch a perfect curve ball or fix a busted watch. The damndest kid."

Interested in spite of myself. "How did he die?"

"Drowned. Swimming in a lake with a bunch of friends. The water was muddy; he hit his head diving. By the time they found him it was way too late." Loose board creaking as she changed position. "About six months later I got pneumonia. I was in the hospital for a few weeks. When I got home I used to lie on the living room sofa wrapped up in a quilt, watching TV. One afternoon I was lying there and all at once I heard Andy say, 'Zulu hurt her hand.' Zulu was Andy's mother—it was a nickname, short for Susan Louise, a real joke because she was the whitest chick you ever saw, even blonder than he was. My mother came into the room and I said it to her just like that: 'Zulu hurt her hand.'

"She gave me a funny look—thought I'd been having a dream. But that night Zulu called and said she'd been at the hospital all afternoon. She'd caught two fingers in the car door. My mother asked me how I knew. I said Andy told me."

"Uh-oh."

"Yeah. Well, my mother's first reaction was to whale me. My dad stopped her. Rational man. Thought I should see a doctor. Well, of course, as soon as I let on to our old GP that I'd heard Andy talking to me, he decided I should see a shrink. That's when I got lucky. Dr. Baxter, the shrink, was quite a guy. He knew enough about psychic phenomena to recognize a case of clairvoyance when he saw one, and he was a bit of a mystic as well. He talked to me, encouraged me to train my gift, gave me books to read. The more I read about mysticism, the more it made sense to me—that our concepts of time and space are artificial, that there are no objects, only connections . . ." Breaking off, her voice changing so that I could tell she was quoting something, though I didn't recognize it: " 'We see this world with the five senses, but if we had another sense, we would see in it something more.' "

Words like an incantation in the darkness: a kind of mystery, a kind of power. Felt myself resisting their pull.

"You think that's corny?"

"It isn't that. The phrasing is a little fuzzy."

"Yeah."

That audible smile again, making me feel like a stuffy professor. In fact the words moved me.

"Andy's a little fuzzy too, I guess. Doesn't really fit into the scientific picture."

"Well, there are several hypotheses . . ."

"Come on. Can't you just say what you think? You personally?"

A knack for making me feel like a pompous idiot. Felt my face getting hot, glad of the darkness but wondering how good a screen it was against this woman.

"I think what's commonly called a spirit control, in your case Andy, is a part of the medium's personality that's more susceptible to psychic influence than her normal conscious state. When she's in trance, it comes uppermost. The communications it offers are partly psychic perceptions, partly the projections and associations of her unconscious."

"Well, that's scientific, all right."

"You asked me what I thought."

"This psychic influence you mentioned. Is there a certified hypothesis for that too?"

"Several."

"And which do you favor?"

"Well, I was trained as a physicist. Once you've accepted certain concepts like the Principle of Complementarity—"

"Hold it, hold it." Laughing. "You've lost me already. I don't want a physics lecture. I guess I'm just trying to get you to talk about your own experience. Compare a few notes."

Cicadas silent now except for a solo somewhere in the dark vastness of the yard. Found myself listening to it: summer sound, summer night. No words would come. She spoke instead.

"Do you mind if I say something personal?"

"Go ahead."

"Look, I know it's none of my business. But I'm wondering why someone with a gift like yours should put herself in such a weird position. I mean, if you don't want anything to do with it, why aren't you still in physics, or raising a couple of kids in suburbia? You've chosen parapsychology as a profession, yet you stifle your own psychic potential as much as you can. That doesn't make sense to me. Why don't you at least train your gift so you can learn more about it?"

Completely dark now: neither vast nor close, the night enveloped us where we sat, holding us suspended without pressure. No moon yet, the only light an occasional sweep of headlights from a car passing on the hill. What she was saying was logical enough, yet I still couldn't answer, couldn't put into coherent sentences a lifetime's worth of fear, resentment, feelings of violation and helplessness, the overwhelming sense of being a freak. Seven years old, seeing my mother's face when I described the bad smell in a room where she'd had a private, vicious argument with my father the night before. Other people's thoughts thrusting into my mind like strange brutal hands touching me intimately. Emotions invisible to everyone else: the minister of our church with his frightening lust for little girls, which was as real to me as a block of stone while everyone said how wonderful he was with children. Finally beginning to sort things out in adolescence, learning to keep my mouth shut, close off my mind, protect myself at last. Starting to understand what was happening, but always the doubt underneath: am I crazy? Other moments when I knew I wasn't but wished I were, anything preferable to the truth. Then later, trying to make sense of it in terms of physics, juggling hidden variables and the state vector, ending up with one big question mark. Working with Jack, hearing him rave about the results of that first telepathy series, not needing telepathy to know he wanted to go to bed with me. And now this house, pressing from all sides, trying to find a way in . . .

I couldn't say any of it. Instead I shook my head, said something about the supper dishes, started to get up.

"Wait." Offhand, as if she were thinking about something else. But I felt a drag in my muscles as if the gravity on the porch had suddenly doubled. On some level I guess I wanted to hear what she had to say. No one ever understands. Jack and David are the worst, behaving exactly as if I could fly. It turns them on. A relief in some ways, this conversation.

"You know, you shouldn't be here. I feel like I should tell you that—like I should warn you. Because you people are sitting on dynamite, and you don't know what you're doing. Okay, I know you're mad now, but let me finish. Okay?

"I know you've worked out a way of screening out most of what goes on around you. All psychics do; they couldn't live otherwise. But you think that's going to do the trick here, and it won't. That stuff other people send out—that's nothing. It's ticker tape, leftovers, they don't even know they're doing it. This place is a different story. It's concentrated. There's a lot here. And it wants out. You can't keep blocking it forever. It's too much—sooner or later you're going to slip, and then . . .

"If you'd been trained, you could channel it, let it through a little at a time, on your terms. But you don't know how. You don't have control. And not having control in a situation like this could mean . . ."

Gesturing as if she were at a loss for words. The moon had risen enough so that I could see her hand, the fingers flung out to express—what? Immensity.

"Big trouble. Not just for you. For everybody in the house."

More than anything it made me mad. Partly because she was right: the house is more than I can handle. But mostly her attitude, as if David and I were total amateurs. Wanted to put her down.

"Look, it's nice of you to be concerned. But—"

"Look at me."

A beat of silence, just one, and then I felt her hand on my arm. I looked. Why? Not a question of reasons. Partly defiance, I know; beyond that I can't explain it. I looked: that's all. Nothing for a moment, just a gathering-in of everything around us; beside me only her outline visible, her eyes in darkness. I didn't like her touching me but couldn't pull away without losing face. Contest of wills. Little by little her hand on my wrist seeming to slow my pulse, then my breathing, until long spaces passed between one breath and the next. Between breaths I'm not sure where I was. Struggling to keep my awareness of the porch, hard boards beneath me and the smell of roses above: the more I tried to orient myself the more I seemed to drift. Couldn't concentrate. Like trying to walk a straight line when you're drunk. Then—I don't know how it happened. All the safe barriers were down; our minds joined in total knowing. No hiding from her what I felt, my shock and fury and humiliation, no disguising any of it. That terrible intimacy, feeling her completely—calm, indulgent, enjoying her power. I felt as if I were suffocating, drowning; tried to focus myself, push her away. Then the sound of the front door opening behind us, a lifeline, something to catch hold of, an external reference point, distracting her too. Self settling on me again, existing and solid, wrapping me like a blanket around a half-drowned child. Alone in my head. David standing there in the door, saying something—

"Sally? Supper's ready."

His voice bridging past and present: for an instant she wavered in between, then settled. She was sitting in the parlor without lights. Night had fallen.

"What are you doing in the dark?" David was saying.

"I guess I fell asleep," she said.

⋙ 27 ⋘

THE LIGHT was playing games with them.

Or at least it seemed that way. Their attempts to observe it had a definite element of farce. If they waited for it in one room, it appeared in another. The night they chose the sitting room, it chose the Thistle Room. The next night, when they tried the Thistle Room, it moved to the sitting room. When they tried strategy (Sally in the Thistle Room, David in the sitting room), it failed to appear at all.

"Look," Sally said at last. "This is dumb. By jumping around like this we're playing havoc with our probability of ever encountering the thing. Let's pick a room and stick to it. Sooner or later we're bound to get results."

In the meantime Colin had come up with a picture of Joshua Gilfoy as a young man. It was a portrait drawing in pen and ink, bearing the scrawled inscription *Rev. Joshua Gilfoy, 1867* and below it the name *Babcock.*

"You're a genius, Colin. Where'd you find it?"

"You'll realize I really am a genius when I tell you." For Colin, he was almost smug. "I know the library doesn't have much of a Gilfoy archive, but we do have mountains of stuff from other families contemporary with the heyday of the Gilfoys. I knew Joshua was a young man of consequence, and young men of consequence—"

"Always have their portraits done," David finished.

"Well, it was a good chance. We happen to have a lot of drawings from the Babcock family, who have been local artists by tradition through several generations."

226

"We have a Miss Babcock listed as living here in the house in the early 1930s," Sally said. "The man at the post office said she was an artist."

"Yes, that would be Iris. She had a certain vogue— may even have done that painting in your dining room. They were society painters, with a certain amount of flair and a lot of connections. This drawing must be by her father, Raskin Babcock. He was one of the more talented ones; it's probably an excellent likeness."

David was examining the drawing. "Fresh out of theological seminary, and ready to save souls. Look at those eyes."

They found the portrait of the young man they called Julian and put the two side by side on the parlor table. The resemblance was strong enough to make the differences all the more pronounced. Part of the contrast, Sally thought, was in the medium employed: the pen's quick incisive lines against the lit shadows of the photograph. But it was more than that. The face in the drawing had a restless eagerness that stopped just short of the fanatic; it showed, as David had said, especially in the eyes, which had been rendered with a splendid dark smolder. What showed as well, in the jaw, the forehead, even the back-brushed hair, was power. The other face looked formless at first in comparison. But behind the young blurred features there was the same strength, like rock, still rough where the other was chiseled and polished.

"What a pair," David was saying. "Can't you just see them? And Ginny in the middle."

She glanced at Colin, but he was looking at the pictures, or seemed to be. Colin, what are we doing to you? But she couldn't say that, and so she said, "What do you want to do about lunch?"

That night (it was Sunday) would be the beginning of their new policy regarding the light. They would wait for it to come to them. They chose the sitting room.

There wasn't much for them to do in the way of preparation. The capacitance meters had already been readjusted to allow for the increase in electricity that would be caused by their presence in the room. The other equipment had been checked over a dozen times. In addition to the Polaroid on its tripod in the corner, David had a movie camera. Their remaining equipment consisted of a pitcher of water and two glasses: the sitting room, with its windows closed against bugs, would be hot even at night.

Sunday afternoon dragged. They tried to sleep in preparation for the night's vigil, and David finally succeeded in drifting off. Sally lay facing the window, watching the fitful movements of the curtain and the leaves beyond. It was hot. She lay there sweating; now and again the breeze reached her like a faint cool sigh. The house was quiet, rooms rising on rooms, spaces where the light came silently, shadows high up under the eaves. In the house it was still, and out in the yard, and all up and down the hill along the hedges and picket fences and under the linden trees: the stillness of a summer afternoon that does not measure itself in minutes or hours, only in the wandering thoughts and waking dreams of those who wait for it to pass. David's breathing became part of the stillness. The curtain moved; the breeze touched her; she slept.

Night comes to an old house in a certain way. They know each other far too well for pretense, and so it must be a kind of game they play together, a ritual of seduction too beloved to relinquish. Over all the surfaces, flat and curved, angular and sinuous, broad and narrow, the shadows pursue the light—everywhere gray touching gold, the slanting rays lingering a long time before they yield. Any reflecting object, the brass foot of a lamp or the rim of a glass, becomes an outpost of the light, a bright sail in a spreading dark sea. But at last the shadows are in sole possession. Slowly they deepen while the whites turn blue and all the colors mingle into purple and brown and black, rich as the plumage of a night bird's wing. In the library the last gleam fades from the clock pendulum; across the hall in the parlor the curtains have lost their whiteness and retain texture only, a fretting and gathering of the darkness, shifting with each tremor of the air. Indeed it is all textures and soft sounds now in the house: the cool hardness of walls, the wide floorboards that creak a little as the wood cools, a faint scratching somewhere that begins and stops and begins again—could there

be mice? The library clock starts its chiming and the whole
house seems to poise itself and listen, counting the strokes
until the last one fades and the silence stretches unbroken. Outside, dusk hides the sharp gables and settles
down on the yard, the shaggy grass and darker line of the
hedge, trees spread enormously against the lilac sky. The
twilight smells of summer grass and roses. The house
seems to ride at anchor in a calm sea.

It was night when they woke up. A dog was barking
somewhere. Sally reached across David to turn on the
lamp by the bed; its yellow circle spilled over them. He
put a hand up to his eyes.

"What time is it?"

"Quarter to ten."

Rubbing his eyes. "I'm starving."

They made sandwiches and ate them in the kitchen.
David propped up the portraits of Joshua and Julian
Gilfoy on the counter and stood looking at them, a
ham sandwich in one hand and a cup of coffee in the
other.

"Imagine. You're twenty, twenty-one, the family rebel.
You come home from college—didn't Colin say he was
kicked out?—and find you've got a stepmother only a
few years older than you are. My God, of course he fell
in love with her. What else could he do?"

About eleven o'clock they went up to the sitting room.
So far the light had never appeared before midnight, but
they wanted to get settled and ready. With both windows
and the door closed it was stuffy in the room, but at least
the smell of insecticide had vanished. "Which goes under
the heading of small favors," David said. He was very
cheerful, she noticed; to a certain extent he took pleasure
in the routine for its own sake, the hours of waiting and
forced inactivity that would be translated in their report
as "successive nights of close observation." They sat and
talked quietly in the dark, sipping cold water; they had
decided to bring the coffeepot along but they were both
too hot to want any. From time to time David got up and
moved cautiously around the room, pausing at fireplace
or window or door for a minute or two, then taking his
seat again. Sally sat holding herself taut against the atmosphere of the room, remembering how easily it had un-

dermined her before. There was a sound—she tensed and then sat back again: David had picked up the water pitcher to pour himself a glass. She could see fairly well; the moon was up. Toward the floor things tended to disappear in shadow, but David's head and shoulders opposite her (he took a different seat every time he sat down) were framed in the pale light from the window. She could almost see him smile.

"Did I scare you?"

"Shut up."

It was hot. She turned to look at the luminous dial of the clock they had brought in, incongruous beside the old-fashioned lamp. 12:30. Strange how difficult it was to put colors back into things in the mind's eye, when the darkness had drained them all. The sofa she was sitting on was rusty brown. David's chair—blue? The lamp on the table, its glass globes moonlight-rounded, was painted with roses. The rug—but she couldn't remember what color the rug was. The pattern of the curtains had some gold in it somewhere—but she didn't believe a word of it: the grays and blacks were too real. David had stood up and was walking around the room again. She poured herself some water.

12:55. "We should have brought a Braille poker deck." David stretched; she saw his arms go up, shadowy, over his head. "God, it's hot."

"You could have been a used car salesman."

"Air-conditioned showrooms. Don't tempt me."

1:20. He had been standing at the window a full five minutes, coming back finally to sit down next to her on the sofa. It creaked; then she heard him yawn. She was too tense to be sleepy, too aware of the full air just beyond its skin of dark and heat and stillness. He rested his head against the sofa back.

"Don't fall asleep," she said, and he didn't answer. Had he gone off so quickly? She glanced at the clock again. 1:30. "Hey," she said. "Do you want coffee?"

"Shh," he said, and she was quiet, hearing nothing. Around them the house was silent, the room silent, curtains hanging motionless. His elbow was touching hers and she wondered why he didn't move it; he could not abide that sort of accidental contact—he said it made him itch. She drew hers away instead and he moved suddenly in the darkness, touching her face, taking it between his hands. It startled her. She could not see his eyes; it was too dark and then he was too close. His hands moved to her shoulders; he was kissing her, her face and then her mouth and she tried to speak. David, she tried to say, but it came out only a protesting murmur. What on earth was he doing—here, now? It was crazy. When she tried to pull away he wouldn't let her go. It was crazy but suddenly it didn't matter and she found herself holding him, reaching up to touch his hair, feeling the hard skull under its tangle of curls. In the darkness of a strange place the sense of touch, violently intensified, was all they had. His hands went down her back and then up inside her shirt and she started to shiver in spite of the heat, wanting him and almost afraid of this driving urgency that dismissed every sane, rational thought, everything but the rush of her own blood. He pushed her down on her back. She was too near the end of the sofa; her head hit the wooden arm and for an instant the room swam with colors, bright and painful. In the darkness behind the colors his hands jerked impatiently at her clothes. She felt him touch her breasts, the flickers of sensation sharp but somehow far away, fire on the surface of deep water; and then the colors faded and there was only the dark, layer on layer of dark filled with the touch of mouths and hands as they searched and found each other again and again. Then he was on her, in her. Sally gasped and closed her eyes.

It was a moment before she realized that with her eyes closed the room was no longer dark. She could see the half-open window clearly, leaves outside printed black against a copper sky. From downstairs there was a smell of bread baking; outside, some children called to one another in a game. It was very clear, like an overlay of translucent color superimposed on the obscure striving of their joined bodies. Against the unknown tranquil sky their coupling seemed futile, poignant, a gesture of foolish courage. She caught her breath; his face was hidden against her and she drew a handful of his hair through her fingers, straight dark hair indescribably soft—

She opened her eyes suddenly. The room was dark. Dark—yes, but the light was there, in the corner. She screamed then; David clutched at her. "Damn you!" she screamed. "Damn you!" Her hand, groping wildly, hit something on the table beside the sofa, knocking it to the floor. It struck; it burst. David collapsed on top of her.

➸➸➸ 28 ➸➸➸

HE INSISTED over and over again, late the next morning when they sat in the kitchen drinking coffee, that he had been aware of nothing out of the ordinary until she had screamed. They were trying to discuss it rationally, something that had been impossible last night, when she had been admittedly hysterical, and David in a kind of stupor that had frightened her more than anything else. Now the screen door stood open to the backyard, letting sunlight spill across the floor. In one of the trees two jays were having a noisy argument. They took to the air suddenly, two blurs of blue against the sun-dusted leaves, and Sally watched them out of sight, hearing David say, "I know it was an idiotic thing to do, but I swear I couldn't help it."

He was trying hard to sound chagrined. Her coffee was cold and she took the pot to refill her cup, seeing with disbelief as she poured that her hands were still shaking: the coffee came out in a wavy stream like a reading on an oscilloscope. She put the pot down quickly, but he hadn't noticed; he wasn't looking at her. Sipping her coffee, she held the warm cup in both hands. That straight dark hair—she had drawn it through her fingers. Was she crazy, then? And his face. If his face had not been hidden, whose face would it have been? She had told him about it as steadily as she could: all the details. About closing her eyes, about seeing the room lit by sunset, about the sounds and smells. The straight dark hair. She did not look at him while she talked. When she finished there was silence.

"That's wild." He leaned back in his chair; she heard it creak. "That's absolutely incredible."

She looked at him now: he was running his hand over

233

his own light-colored curls. "Incredible," he repeated softly.

"Don't," she said, without meaning to.

He looked at her in surprise. "Don't what?"

"I don't know."

"Sally." He swung round in his chair to face her. "You can see what happened, can't you?"

She stared at him and he reached out and took her hands in his.

"Think psychometry," he said. "Julian and Ginny must have made love on that sofa. You were perceiving that and some of the details got mixed in with what was really happening. That's all."

"That damn light, David."

His hands tightened, but he smiled a little. "I hope you didn't scare it away for good. It may not be used to pitchers of water flying around."

"It was like being spied on," she said.

"Sal."

"I'm just telling you how I felt."

"I know."

His smile was rueful; she made herself smile back. She knew she was being absurd. The light was not sentient. It had been on its nightly rounds—that was all. Pointless to read anything else into the incident, except, except . . . David released her hands and got up to clear the table. She watched his back as he piled dishes in the sink, emptied coffee grounds into a paper bag. There was a question she had been avoiding since last night, nor would she ask it now.

What possessed you?

If it was a pun, it was a macabre one. But why had he chosen that moment, that place? And what was it he had said a few minutes ago? *I swear I couldn't help it.* She knew from her own experience how powerful the room's atmosphere was; Rosanna had felt it too. But they were both psychic. Could it have affected David as well? He had turned and was looking at her.

"You okay?"

She nodded. No: she couldn't ask.

It was sunny out, and not as hot as it had been. She decided to do some work in the garden. Mrs. Hopkins, out among her flowers next door, waved and called a compliment—the yard looked wonderful. Sally, looking up, saw that it was true: the linden trees stood guard over a place of shadowy and sunlit green. The pansies she had planted too late were beginning to come up anyway, a faint mist of purple and yellow along the latticework under the porch, and some roses had bloomed too, pink and white, the old-fashioned kind with a spray of delicate tendrils in the center. Their fragrance hung over her as she worked pulling weeds. David came out the back door and dumped something in the garbage—a musical clatter: the remains of the water pitcher. Sally, seeing their neighbor's enormous gardening hat turn curiously toward the noise, smiled her first real smile of the morning—Mrs. Hopkins was imagining either an orgy or a violent quarrel, or both. But nothing anywhere near the truth.

The noontime sun was hot on her back. But there were plenty of weeds, and in spite of the heat it was pleasant to be able to reduce her life for the moment to a war against dandelions. She worked, without admitting it to herself, in a corner of the yard that allowed her to turn her back on both the house and the sundial, its base tangled in ivy.

About an hour later David put his head out the back door and yelled something. She turned, straightening.

"What? Ow." Her neck was stiff.

"I said, the guys I called last week about checking the stairs are coming. They just called. And one of the lights on the monitor panel has burned out; I've got to go to Buck's and see if they have something we can use as a replacement. Can you sort of listen for the door?"

"Okay," she said. He waved and disappeared. She went back to work, had progressed another few feet before she realized that she would not be able to hear anyone at the door from where she was. She got to her feet, rubbing her neck, and turned to look at the house. The white clapboards were shadowed with leaves; the windows reflected leaves; on the porch roof the nest of climbing roses stirred and was still. She took a breath and went toward it, out of the warm slanting afternoon light into the lindens' shade.

David had left the back door open. She caught the screen and eased it shut behind her, although there was no reason not to let it slam. The house was unexpectedly cool after the sun. She filled a glass of water at the sink, drank half of it, and put it down.

Quiet. The quiet reached out and touched her with the setting of the glass upon the counter—the quiet and the filtering light that seemed to come from everywhere and nowhere, surrounding her where she stood. She went out into the front hall and stopped there, looking up and around her slowly, feeling herself at the bottom of a well of stillness and brightness. All around her were rooms empty and yet not empty, saturated with presence and memory, waiting for her. She walked into the library, hearing her footsteps the only sound, and stood there motionless for a moment; gradually the open door of the little room drew her. She went and looked in at the narrow space with its slant-top desk and spindle-back chair, on the wall a woman's black paper silhouette curling beneath its glass. The room drew her in. For an instant she examined the feeling and was separate from it; then it was hers and part of her and she went inside and sat down at the desk and opened it, sensing as she did so that her movements were following a pattern worn in time, an action repeated so often over the years that it had left its mark in the air of the house like water licking a furrow in rock. The pigeonholes and tiny drawers, brass-handled, confronted her. She put her elbows on the desk and rested her face in her hands.

The hush closed around her then, made of floating light and the dark behind her hands. As she sat without moving it took her in, gathered her in until she was a part of it, waiting too. The pattern held her. Elbows on the desk's surface, face resting in her hands. Hard seat of the chair under her, door standing ajar. She was not conscious of the moment, if there was one, when the humming luminous silence broke itself up into sounds. But she heard footsteps on the floor above, a door closing somewhere—out in the front hall a voice asking a question with a rising inflection, and an answering murmur—the gentle *chink, chink* of a pipe knocked out against the hearth on the other side of the wall. And someone sweeping the floor, moving little by little across the library floor; she could hear the broom's short busy strokes. She did not move. She did not know if she could. It was not a question of that, but only of the house opening itself to her, waking live around her, as if it had been waiting. If she moved . . . If she did not move . . .

Footsteps were descending the stairs now, slowly, hesitantly; she could imagine a hand caressing the banister, stopping at the bottom. The broom was silent now, and the voices; she heard the steps enter the library and come toward the door of the room where she sat waiting, a strange calm upon her—heard them stop and hesitate and then slowly come forward again—

Knocking. There was knocking, but it was wrong: invading, intruding, bursting the globe of soundless light in which she was suspended: a loud careless knocking at the front door; and she started up, shaken, to find the radiance gone and the afternoon sun showing dust on the window pane. The men were here about the stairs.

Their names were Ernie and James. She thought they must be brothers, both of them brown-haired and loosely put together. Ernie, who wore glasses, was taller. He seemed to be the one in charge, doing most of the talking, directing operations. He carried a ladder up the stairs, a screwdriver and a pair of pliers clinking together in the baggy back pocket of his jeans, and stopped at the top to examine the monitor panel with its loudspeaker and rows of lights.

"Got the place bugged, huh?" He smiled benevolently down at her. Uncertain how much David had told him, she only nodded. He set up the ladder and climbed it, attaching a plumb line to the ceiling at the head of the stairs, feeding it out smoothly until the bob hung a few inches, swinging slightly, above the ground floor where she stood. She watched in silence, still trying to get her bearings. Since their arrival the house had closed itself off, withdrawn as if that space of time—how long had it lasted?—had never been. Had she imagined it, then? But she knew she hadn't.

"Want to give me a reading on the floor down there, James?"

The other young man checked the floor at the foot of the stairs with his level, then moved back to the point where the plumb bob hung and took another reading there.

"Looks good, Ern."

"How's the line look?"

"Good."

Sally, sighting over his shoulder, saw that they were trying to determine if the steps were actually parallel to the floor. But if the floor itself was not level . . . She bent and looked at the bubble. It was.

"They sure enough knew how to build in those days," James said. The voice made her jump; he was standing right behind her. She nodded. *In those days.* If she could credit what had just happened to her, those days were still present here in the house, all the past as live and actual as this moment in which she stood nodding her head. And yet there was nothing that could be documented, registered, measured, objectified in any way. At most, her experience might go under the heading Subjective Data—there to join all nameless fears, restless nights, things half seen and half heard, the abundant fabrications of the human brain. How much of it was inside her own head? If she were to tell David, he would insist on including it in their report on the house. She wouldn't tell him.

He came home just as the men were finishing up. James had checked each individual step with the level; Ernie had made half a dozen incomprehensible chalk marks on the side of the staircase before rubbing them all out. They lit cigarettes and sat on the bottom step to report to David.

"You're in pretty good shape," Ernie said, replacing his battered pack of Camels in his shirt pocket. "Your floors are level, which is more than I can say for the other two jobs we did today. You got two steps, the third and fourth from the top, that're warped on the tread so there's about a ten-degree downward tilt to them. We can easily sand those down for you, or build them up— you could do it yourself. The only other thing that's a little out of the ordinary is how steep the stairs are. You got a pretty stiff angle here, and each one of the steps is high on the riser and shallow on the tread. We're talking about a couple of inches both ways. Now, you said several people had fallen. Most folks are used to, say, a seven-inch riser and a ten-inch tread. Here you're talking about a nine-inch riser and a tread of barely eight inches. That's enough to throw somebody off balance if they're used to a standard step, and they're in a hurry, not watching what they're doing."

David was rubbing his head. "Well, thanks. That's what we needed to know. If you could fix those two steps, sand them down or something, I think—should we get it done, Sally?"

"I don't see why not," she said.

"Yeah, okay. If you could do that . . ."

It took them another half hour to sand down the two steps with an electric sander, sweep up the sawdust and apply a coat of stain to the wood. When they had gone David stood at the bottom of the stairs looking up, hands on hips. Sally watched him, saying nothing. At last he turned to her.

"Okay, it could be those two steps. Or it could be the—what was it?—nine-inch riser and the eight-inch whatever."

"Tread."

"Tread. Or it could be . . ." He held his arms out and let them fall to his sides. "It's so damned inconclusive. Like everything else in this goddamn house. Like that computer report of Jack's: even I can see a statistic doesn't mean anything once you've hung five million conditions on it. Number of steps, location of steps, weather conditions, time of day, age of people using the steps—isn't there one simple statistic for how many people fall downstairs in their homes every year? Doesn't that sound like something a government agency would be devoted to?" He broke off, exasperated. "What are you laughing at?"

"I'm not laughing."

"You're smiling."

Sally tried to rearrange her face.

➜➜ 29 ⬅⬅

BY THE END of the week she felt less like smiling. In four nights the light had not reappeared at all, and however low the probability that her breaking the water pitcher had frightened it off, still she felt obscurely at fault. She was sure David blamed her and it wasn't fair; he was at least as responsible as she was for the whole fiasco. She only wished he would accuse her so that she could say so. But he was treating her to his smoothest social manner; there was no handhold on that surface. Even her usual clear sense of him was numb, and she had no idea what he was thinking. Was he wondering about his impulse to make love to her in the sitting room? Even if he was, the impulse itself seemed to have disappeared. He hadn't touched her since. She was angry at herself for wanting him to; as a result she was sleeping badly and by Friday morning her temper was beginning to show it.

The telephone had rung three times since breakfast; David had answered it and found only silence at the other end each time. "Probably kids," he said. Then he had gone off to the attic, leaving her to make work in the kitchen; ordinarily she would have gone with him, but just now the aura of his courteous indifference was more than she could take. She took out the garbage, swept the kitchen floor and the back step, and was contemplating the grimy stove top in resignation when the phone rang again. The sound focused all her small frustrations. She went toward the phone, snatched the receiver from its cradle. "Who is this?"

A moment's silence was followed by a woman's voice, unfamiliar.

"Mrs. Curtiss? My name is Rose Pindar. I really must talk to you."

Five minutes later, when she climbed the attic stairs to find David engrossed in a pile of old newspapers, she was still too bemused by Mrs. Pindar's call to realize what effect it would have on him. But she had barely begun to tell him when he jumped up, scattering his newspapers, and came over to her where she stood on the top step. His whole face was alight.

"She's willing to talk? God, I can't believe it. It's what we've been praying for!"

She hadn't, she thought, been aware of praying for it; but as he took hold of her shoulders and squeezed them, smiling down at her with genuine warmth, she felt a kind of dazed gratitude to Mrs. Pindar that might have passed for thanksgiving.

There were conditions. Mrs. Pindar had been adamant about two things: she must talk to Sally alone, and she would not come to the house. She would meet Sally in her car at the bottom of Lilac Street: the car was gray. David seemed only momentarily disappointed about being excluded from the interview.

"She must have a reason for wanting to talk to you alone. And it's got to be something to do with Julian."

"Something every woman should know?" Sally said. Her sense of humor was returning—sensation creeping into a frozen limb. All tension between them had miraculously vanished; she felt lightheaded. "I'd better hurry; she said fifteen minutes."

"Don't forget to ask her about the light—oh, and the floor plan! If you could get her to mark one—"

"David, I really doubt—"

"Okay, okay. But take one, just in case. And remember . . ."

She finally got out the door. Mrs. Pindar had said she would park at the bottom of the hill. David saw her off from the front porch. When she turned at the gate to wave, she saw him make the thumbs-up sign, a tall figure on the shabby white porch framed by green leaves. Then she was on the sidewalk, starting down the hill, still too dizzy from her restoration to his good graces to concentrate in a more than cursory way on the interview ahead.

*   *   *

The car was waiting at the bottom of the hill, parked just off Tanglewood in the quiet shade of Lilac Street. Mercedes was one of a few makes she could recognize on sight, and her first thought was that she was glad she had changed her shorts for a skirt. Possibly she should have changed her T-shirt and sandals as well, and taken her hair out of its everlasting summer braid, but she supposed Mrs. Pindar was prepared to consider her, a woman scientist, as a creature on the fringes of decency in any case. The skirt had been David's idea, as camouflage for the handbag (she almost never carried one, and it felt awkward) in which the cassette recorder was concealed.

It was impossible, as she approached, to see the occupant of the car behind the pattern of light and shade reflected by the windshield. The windows were closed and the motor was running; she had a moment's humorous half panic about kidnappers before she bent to look in the window opposite the driver's side and saw Mrs. Pindar sitting there, looking exactly as Sally had imagined her: patrician face, hair the same smooth silver as the car, and—of course—gloves. The woman turned her head and their eyes met. Sally opened the car door. A wave of cool air engulfed her: the air conditioning was on.

"Mrs. Pindar?"

"Mrs. Curtiss? Please get in."

Sally eased onto the luxurious upholstery and closed the door. The hot summer's day outside became a silent film in a cool movie house, projected yellow and flickering on the windshield, discreet hum of the engine imitating a projector's whir. A car drove slowly past them; children streamed out of a yard across the street and moved soundlessly up the hill. Sally pulled her eyes away from the scene and looked at the woman in the driver's seat. There was time to notice the fabric of her dress— expensive and Japanese-looking, impossibly subtle hues of lavender and gray—and the soft gray gloves. Mrs. Pindar, after their initial exchange, appeared absorbed in the silent panorama beyond the windshield; she sat in profile, beaky nose above delicate chin. Sally was acutely aware of the tape recorder in her bag, its tiny reels in motion.

"On the phone you said there were reasons why I shouldn't be living in the Gilfoy house." She kept her voice mild, almost diffident. "I'm wondering if you can tell me what they are."

She saw the gloved hands tighten on the steering wheel, then loosen and slide caressingly along its curve, as if their owner was willing them to relax. When Mrs. Pindar spoke her tone was measured.

"Believe me, Mrs. Curtiss, I am not in the habit of making a nuisance of myself to total strangers. I am trying to help you."

How would David handle this? "I understand that," Sally said. "Please don't think I don't appreciate your concern. It's just that—if you could be a little more specific?" She was watching the hands and they remained still. But in Mrs. Pindar's face a movement caught her eye: a momentary crumpling of control, as if a taut piece of fabric had suddenly sagged. The words this time, when they came, were very quiet.

"There's something in that house."

"I know," Sally said. They looked at each other and she saw the other woman's eyes fill with tears. She was startled, then dismayed. She had spoken without thinking, out of her own unsettling experiences in the house, for an instant forgetting everything but the fact that here was someone who had shared them. Now she was disgusted with herself. Psychical researchers were supposed to maintain absolute objectivity, to be noncommittal, not to hint or encourage or confirm, and that trained part of her wished she could erase the tape, erase the whole moment from existence and begin again. Another part, more instinctive, noted the tears and knew that, unprofessional as it was, her response had made a bond between them, and Mrs. Pindar might trust her now. The fact that the tape recorder in her bag was betraying that trust as fast as its reels could turn bothered her only briefly. Mrs. Pindar's statement would keep her in David's good graces, and she would have done far worse to stay there. She said as gently as she could, "If you could just tell me what happened."

The other woman was looking straight ahead again. Sally waited in a silence that seemed to intensify in the sounds of the idling motor and the whispering flow of cool air from the dashboard vents. She was undergoing a small crisis of her own during this pause, playing a scenario for herself of what would happen if Mrs. Pindar decided, at this stage, not to talk. David would assume she had mismanaged the whole business—bungled it out of some pedantic insistence on staying totally detached, following the strict letter of the law of psychical research. And it was true that he would have played it closer to the acceptable line (or what she considered the acceptable line), maybe even crossed it, as he had done with Miss Ellen Flagg, putting words in her mouth about Julian and Joshua's quarrel. But that was an old issue. What concerned her now was her own process: all her principles draining away as she sat waiting for Mrs. Pindar to speak. Before this moment she would have said, and believed, that she would accept Mrs. Pindar's refusal to talk rather than compromise her own practice of the scrupulously careful research techniques she had been taught. Yet sitting there she was closer than she had imagined possible to manipulating the other woman into telling her story. A hint, no more, of something that had happened in the last few weeks—the touch she had felt at the sundial, or the afternoon she had heard the sound of footsteps—she knew it would work, and she would do it if it would spare her from going back to David empty-handed.

"There was just a feeling at first," Mrs. Pindar said. Her voice was faint, drifting at the end of the sentence. Sally took a breath of deep relief. "A feeling that . . . there was someone else in the house. That I wasn't alone."

"You were living there by yourself?" Sally said. She shifted the handbag slightly on her lap.

"Yes. It was during the war—1944." The date seemed to steady her. "My mother and aunt were planning to move in with me as soon as they sold my aunt's house in Masonville. They thought I shouldn't be alone . . . I had just received news of my husband's death. He was killed in the Italian invasion."

A pause, which grew. To Sally the process felt like trying to get a fire going with damp wood. You waited helplessly, after adding each bit of kindling, to see if it would catch or put the whole thing out. Cautiously she tried another twig. "This feeling—when did it begin?"

"I had it all along. In the daytime too, not just at night. As if I could look up at any moment and see someone standing there in the door. Sometimes I thought I heard sounds, like someone moving around in another part of the house. I told myself it was nerves—I'd just lost my husband, after all. So I went to see Dr. Bristowe and he gave me something, some kind of sleeping tonic, but I never used it. I couldn't. I didn't want to be asleep if he came."

"He?"

"It," the other woman said quickly. "Whatever it was."

"You said he."

"I didn't mean to."

"But you did," Sally said. "Why? What made you think of it as 'he'?"

Mrs. Pindar looked away; there was another long pause. Finally she said "I started to think it might be Jeff. My husband."

Sally drew breath. "I see."

"Do you? Can you imagine what it was like, being alone there and feeling this . . . presence all the time, just out of sight? When I would close the curtains at night I would feel him there in the room behind me, as if he were standing there smiling, waiting for me to turn around." She laughed unsteadily. "I didn't mind it, you know. I liked it. It made me feel . . . less alone."

Sally found herself nodding, remembering the quiet radiance sifting through the empty rooms, the house around her filled with it. Mrs. Pindar was talking now as if she could not stop.

"One night I stayed up late, reading, upstairs—in that sitting room with the white marble fireplace. I made a fire and it was very pleasant. I must have fallen asleep. When I woke up the room was so warm that I felt a little groggy, but I was sure I had heard a dog bark. I didn't get up right away—I just lay here. But all at once I had the feeling that Jeff was there, outside the door, that he was in trouble and he needed me. I knew it was crazy, but finally I couldn't resist it any longer."

"You opened the door?"

"Yes. I suppose I was still half asleep at that point.

There was no one there. But it was freezing cold in the hall, and I could still feel him, as if he were near by, and in trouble. I went down the hall to that big corner bedroom, the one over the kitchen. I was trying to find him, I thought I could help him, do something—" Her eyes brimmed with tears again and she stopped, her throat working. Sally, moved, wanted to touch her but didn't quite dare.

"And you couldn't? You couldn't find him?"

"Oh, I found him." The words jerked out one by one. "He was there. I saw him. Standing across the room. He—he must have looked that way when he was killed. His face was covered with blood."

"You *saw* him? Mrs. Pindar—"

"I saw him. It was only for a second. Then I ran. I couldn't help it. It frightened me so much, seeing him there, and the blood—I ran away from him." The tears had spilled over and were running down her face. "I don't even know how I got out of the house. The next thing I remember is running down the street. There was nowhere I could go, no one I could tell. I spent the night in the car. The next day I made arrangements to move out." She reached for her handbag on the seat beside her, groped in it and pulled out a handkerchief. "I never went back. But Mr. Gilfoy keeps on renting that house. People keep moving in. And Jeff—"

"Wait," Sally said. "Mrs. Pindar, please. Listen. That wasn't your husband you saw. It wasn't Jeff."

The hand with the handkerchief stopped in midair. "What are you talking about?"

"We have evidence of a young man, a member of the Gilfoy family, who died falling down the stairs in the house. The accident is connected in some way with the room where you saw—"

"Jeff," the other woman said. "I saw Jeff."

"You saw a man with blood on his face—"

"I know what I saw!" Mrs. Pindar laughed, a high harsh sound. "Do you think I don't know my own husband? Don't tell me what I saw. I was there!"

"Mrs. Pindar. We have reports of disturbances in the house going back to 1941, three years before your husband was killed. Don't you see, it couldn't have been—" The look on the other woman's face stopped her rush of explanation and she repeated quietly, "It couldn't have been." But she could see the words weren't welcome. It wasn't comfort, but a strange kind of bereavement she had caused; and now she could only watch with a helpless shrinking as Mrs. Pindar rested her forehead against the steering wheel and wept, the handkerchief forgotten in her hand.

Whether it was sensitivity or cowardice she didn't know, but she did not dare try to penetrate that grief. She found the handle and got the car door open: already she had become accustomed to the cool air inside, and the summer heat at her back was a shock.

"Mrs. Pindar—I'm sorry." There was no acknowledgment; had she really expected any? Clutching her handbag she climbed out onto the sidewalk. Mrs. Pindar did not move. "I'm sorry," Sally said again, and closed the car door softly on the stricken figure inside. Then she fled up the hill.

David set the tape to rewind, whistled softly, and said, "So that's what goes on in March."

Sally, sitting on the parlor rug, glanced up at him. His eyes were bright. "Apparitions," he said.

She shook her head. "I'm not sure I buy the apparition."

"Why not?"

"It's too classic. She was in such ragged emotional shape over her husband's death that the whole thing could be pure fantasy. She saw what she expected to see."

David considered it. "Well, but if you don't think she saw anything, why bother telling her it was Julian and not her husband?"

Sally grimaced. "I don't know. I guess because it seemed like the simplest way of making her understand it's not her husband who's haunting this house. She's convinced she saw it. But it doesn't mean—"

"She correlates on a lot of points." He counted them off on his fingers. "The room, for instance. The cold. The dog barking." Finishing off the hand: "And Julian was a young man. And we know from the newspaper account that he did in fact die of a head wound."

She was frowning. "But she admitted she'd just waked up. And it may have felt cold in the hall because she'd been in a room with a fire. And a young man with a bloody face—it's so general. Her husband was young too, and he was killed in combat. Okay, it's not impossible that she really saw an apparition, but it's unlikely. It's so easy to see how it could have been anything—a shadow or her own reflection in the window pane. She's obsessed by the idea that she failed her husband in his moment of need. Maybe they were having problems before he went overseas. For some reason she needed to punish herself—still does. She was devastated when I said we'd had reports of haunting phenomena predating her tenancy. Really devastated. She needs to believe her husband is here."

"Then why warn us away? Maybe we could help him where she failed."

"That's just what she doesn't want," Sally said. "She doesn't want anyone else in on it. I think she's jealous."

"Oh, come on."

"I do. Remember that anonymous note we got, warning us to get out? I think it was from her. And the Abbeys got one, and so did the Sterlings. She doesn't want people here. She's on her own private trip as far as the haunting is concerned."

"The note. Of course! *The house is bad* . . . Her own personal haunting, and she doesn't want to share it. You know, I can almost see her point—if her husband really were the one haunting the place." He got up and started to pace the room. "So you think her whole story is explicable in terms of hysteria?"

Sally rested her chin on her knees. "I don't know what I think."

It was not an entirely honest answer. She knew that on hearing Mrs. Pindar's story she had felt it to be true. From her own experiences with the house it was difficult to doubt it. But to admit this to David would call for a confession she was not willing to make. She was not ready—not yet, she told herself—to tell him about the things that had happened to her here. As for the apparition, she had gone from an initial intuitive belief to a healthy skepticism: she believed what she had told David, that Mrs. Pindar's vision was more likely a product of psychological stress than a genuine apparition of Julian or anyone else. That it had been genuine was, of course, a possibility. She recognized that, and she knew also that her reluctance to give any real weight to such a possibility was, more than anything, a reaction to David's enthusiasm for it. If he was convinced of the chance of encountering an apparition, there would be no getting him away from the house until he did—and she, for one, had no intention of staying here past the end of the summer, when their lease was up. True, for the past four days the house had been quiet, but it wasn't a comforting kind of quiet. She had an increasing sense of playing with fire, skating on thin ice. Neither image seemed to fit the roomy old house filled with summer shadows, but the feeling was there.

⇉ 30 ⇇

"I WAS JUST going to call you," Colin said the next morning when they walked into the library.

"What's up?"

"Well—" He had to break off; Mary Jo Carruthers was waiting to renew *Gone With the Wind*. When she had gone he settled his glasses and looked at Sally, then David. "What I was going to say is, I've done a little checking about the dogs."

"Dogs?" David looked blank.

"The ones Sally saw—the black retriever and the white shepherd."

"Oh, yeah. And?"

"Well, Thomas Stroud over on Linden has a black Labrador. But it's kept chained up."

"And the shepherd?"

"There are several in town, but none of them are white."

David looked at Sally. "And you're sure the dog was white?"

She nodded. "What about strays?"

"None have been reported. My source for all this information is Rachel Wilcox, the local vet. I've known her ever since she was a muddy little girl rescuing grass snakes from lawn mowers. She came in this morning and I thought I'd ask her."

"Colin," David said, "you're wonderful. Magnificent, in fact. Can we pay her a visit?"

"I think she's still here." Colin pushed his glasses down on his nose and peered over them. "There she is. The dark-haired woman, over by the window."

Rachel Wilcox, meeting them, radiated the quiet self-assurance that seems to come with an ability to handle animals. She had what David's father called "a jaw," but in spite of that her face was very pleasant. She shook hands with Sally, then with David.

"Yes, I'd say I know all the dogs in the area," she said in answer to David's question. "Well, some kid may have gotten a puppy in the last week or so that hasn't had its shots yet, but other than that . . ."

"And there are no white shepherds," David said. "What about, say, a light tan?"

The vet was shaking her head. "People around here don't go much for exotic dogs. All the shepherds in town are very prominently sable-marked, the standard kind. Easy to keep clean. Mr. Robinson says you've seen this dog more than once?"

Both men looked at Sally and she said self-consciously, "Several times."

"Well, I was going to say maybe it belonged to someone passing through, but it doesn't sound like it. People are pretty quick to call me about strays . . . On the other hand, it may be from one of the neighboring towns, Masonville or Helmingham."

"But why come all that distance just to run around in our backyard?" David said.

"Your backyard may be a secondary attraction. If there were a female nearby—"

"Beanie's the only dog on the block," Sally said. "And he's a he."

"Or else—" the vet said, and stopped.

"Or else?" David said.

"Well . . ." she hesitated again and then smiled, as if to make it clear that she was joking. "Mr. Robinson says you're renting the old Gilfoy house. Maybe the dog you're seeing is a ghost."

There was a longish pause. Then David laughed. "Well, actually that's what we're trying to find out."

Rachel Wilcox said, "I thought it might be. Rumor has it you're psychic investigators."

"Rumor has us cold."

"Have you considered trying an experiment?" The vet had dropped her joking pose. "I mean getting a dog and putting it out in the yard the next time you see your mystery dog?"

David said slowly, "You know, that's not a bad idea."

"I'm afraid I don't understand," Colin said. "As usual."

"Animals appear to have a sixth sense, or whatever you want to call it, that most people lack," Rachel Wilcox said. "If the white dog was—well, supernatural—another dog's reaction to it would be very different than if it were real."

"Rachel," Colin said. "I didn't know you knew all about psychical research."

"I don't. I know all about animals."

"What would the real dog's reaction be if the white dog was a ghost?"

"Terrified. Whining, groveling, probably hiding under the nearest bed."

"It's a great idea," David said. "Remember my telling you about the Morton ghost, Colin? The Mortons had a friendly dog that happened to approach the ghost during one of its appearances. As soon as the dog got close enough to realize its mistake, it turned tail and ran off howling. It's really the perfect experiment—we'll have to do it!"

Sally glanced at him. "Where are you planning to get a dog?"

"I don't know. Can't we rent one or something?"

"Come on, David."

"We can't? Well, somebody must have a dog. Jack has a dog. Of course we'd have to drive all the way down and get it—Colin!"

"Yes?" Colin said.

"What about Locky? It's his big chance to be written up in a scientific journal."

"David," Sally said.

He turned toward her sharply. "What? I'm not asking him to sacrifice Locky to science. I just want to borrow him for a few days."

"You heard what Dr. Wilcox said. If he's confronted with something paranormal it will terrify him."

"For Christ's sake," David said.

Rachel Wilcox chuckled suddenly. "If that dog isn't a ghost Locky will chase it halfway to Boston. He's made a battleground out of my waiting room more than once."

"Well, Colin?" David said. Sally looked away.

"Well," Colin said. Sally could feel him looking at her, but she did not turn. "Well, why not? I don't see how it could really hurt him."

It was arranged that he would bring Locky over later. Rachel Wilcox wished them luck; they all said goodbye. A boy with glasses and long hair came up to the desk with an armload of books, and Colin reached for the stamp pad.

"I gather," David said as they went down the library steps together, "you think this is a big mistake."

"It's a little late to be discussing that now, isn't it?"

"Sally."

She didn't look at him.

"I don't see what the big deal is," he said.

They came to the end of the walk and turned down the sidewalk to the corner.

"Colin's a friend," she said. "And I hate the way we're using him."

"Using—!" David exploded. "We're borrowing the god-damn dog for a couple of days! For Pete's sake."

"All *right*," Sally said.

"Well, how else have we used him? You mean to talk to Christine and the Flaggs? He loved every minute of it. The poor guy never had his nose out of a book until we got here—"

"Never mind, David."

"Don't talk to me like that," he said, and she stopped suddenly and faced him there on the sidewalk.

"What are you starting a fight for?" she said. "You've got what you want; now I have to pretend I think it's wonderful—is that it?" They were standing under a tree and she had a glimpse of his startled face, patterned by leaf shadows, before she turned and walked away.

*   *   *

It was hot, too hot for fast walking, especially uphill; she was sweating by the time she reached the front gate and stopped there, seeing the house tree-shaded in the midday sun that shimmered around the edges of things. She looked back down the hill. No sign of David; he hadn't tried to catch up with her. She wished he had. Meanwhile there was the house, roses on the porch showing pink among the deep green shadows of the lindens, the gabled roof thrusting its points up into the sunlight. She went down the walk and the cool under the trees touched her damp skin with a chill. The weathered wood of the porch steps was stained with rose petals that had been crushed underfoot.

Inside, it was quiet. She had shut the front door behind her and started up the stairs before she recognized the quality of that silence. She had met it before, that afternoon in the little room when she had heard the sounds—and now she stopped where she was, hand on the banister. "Oh, no," she said half aloud. "Oh, no you don't."

Was it listening? Light and stillness rose around her as she stood there; below her in the front hall the floorboards mirrored radiance like a shining pool. She stood scarcely breathing; then with an effort she tore herself free from it and ran the rest of the way upstairs.

But here it was just the same. To either side the corridor stretched away in shadow, lit at intervals by the noiseless sunlight that spilled from open doors—and for a moment, so quickly past that she hardly noticed it, she could not remember where she was. She stood without moving for perhaps ten seconds, and in that space she heard, quite clearly, a sound. It could have been a sigh, the kind made by a sleeper who turns restlessly in dreams. She felt a prickling at the back of her neck: it had been so distinct and yet she could not have said from what direction it came, as if it had been all around her. She waited, listening, a few seconds more, but it did not come again. The intensity of hushed light surrounded her unbroken. Abruptly she started down the hall, unwilling to stand passively waiting but aware that she was trespassing, asking for trouble. Hadn't Rosanna warned her? There was a loose feeling in her knees that she tried to ignore.

No haunted house ever hurt anyone. She reminded herself of that fact. The narrow strip of carpet in the hall had once showed an oriental design, reds and blues now frayed and faded, almost erased by the footsteps that had been muffled over the years as hers were muffled now. The door to Joshua's room stood ajar, revealing emptiness inside. She felt a faint chill in the air, but the center of light and silence that seemed to draw her like a magnet was not here. The door to the sitting room was closed. She went toward it and opened it without giving herself time to think, stopping in the doorway. The room was undisturbed except for the light that was itself a presence. She let her eyes wander over the fireplace, windows, chairs and low sofa, table with its rose-patterned lamp . . . Her knees, which had steadied, loosened again. On the table, beside the lamp, was the music box.

The music box. Her first panic was followed almost immediately by the common-sense realization that David must have put it there. It belonged downstairs, of course, in the parlor, on the vibration-sensitive platform he had built for it, but for some reason he had brought it up here and forgotten to put it back. She went into the room and bent over it, seeing the light dance on the ribboned grain of the wood. The silence closed around her as she stood examining the box and she straightened slowly, looking around her, taking it in her hand, hesitating only a moment before opening the lid.

The mechanism started jerkily, dropping the first few notes into the air and then, as if catching its stride, unwinding the old tune in a smooth skein of sound. Sally stood transfixed, the box in her hands, tree outside the window shedding a trembling halo of light on the sill, the melody emptying into the stillness without filling it; and abruptly she felt someone behind her, someone whose breath ruffled the fine hairs at her temple. She was not afraid. No. But she felt changed, transformed—felt a depth of something precious in her, compassionate, mysterious, yielding, a light surrounding a darkness. She bent her head. Warm breath stirred her hair again: he was very close. "Julian," she said, and then fear seized her—not of him but of herself, trembling inside with light and dark, so deep she feared the plunge as a child fears a dive into deep water; and as playmates' voices taunt the child, so the warm breath on her skin taunted her now. She trembled on the edge. But even the trembling was sweet, and the burning that was fear and more than that, making her dizzy so that she need not dive, need not jump but must simply fall, without willing it, into the depths, unless . . . Her hand moved quickly, from a place beyond her control, closing the box with a snap. The music stopped. She lifted her head with an effort and looked around: she was alone.

When she heard David come in downstairs she went to meet him. He glanced up, a little wary, as she came down the stairs; she remembered, cloudily, that there had been some sort of scene between them.

"Hi," he said.

"David—"

"Yes?"

"Why did you move the music box?"

He looked at her carefully without answering. Then he said, "What?"

"The music box. You put it upstairs in the sitting room."

He pushed his hand through his hair; he was sweating, she noticed. It was hot outside. "Sally. I did what?"

"Well," she said, "it's up there, and I didn't put it there."

He wiped the sweat off his upper lip, not taking his eyes off her. "Neither did I."

"Are you sure?"

"Of course I'm sure. Why the hell would I move it?"

"I'm asking *you.*"

"But I didn't," he said.

Sally sat down suddenly on the bottom step. "Great. Now we're getting apport phenomena."

He stood looking at her. Then: "It's up there now?"

She nodded, felt him go past her, the leg of his jeans brushing her shoulder, up the stairs three at a time. After a few minutes she followed. He was sitting on the arm of the sofa in the sitting room, pinching his upper lip and looking at the music box.

"I'll be damned," he said softly when she came in.

"Are you sure you didn't bring it up here?"

"For Christ's sake," David said.

"Then it moved by itself. That's apport."

"Looks that way." He went on pinching his lip, then looked up at her with a lopsided grin. "Remember when we thought it was going to be a peaceful summer?"

⫸ *31* ⫷

SHE SPENT the evening reading. Her knowledge of psychometry, or object reading as it is more often called in psychical research, was slight: it was a subject that had never particularly interested her. There had been some experiments at the lab, but she had been acquainted with them only in a general way. She knew that the idea was to try to "read" an object's history by handling it. But she had never studied the phenomenon in detail until now, when—unless she was simply losing her mind—it seemed to be happening to her.

In "psychometry," or object reading . . . the subject, by touching or looking at an object, can obtain information which apparently refers to events associated with it or with the life of some person who has previously touched it . . . She looked up frowning from the page; across the parlor in the bay window her reflection looked up too. There are ghosts—and ghosts. Looking down she made herself finish the sentence: *. . . the important thing being that there is a spatial relation, either direct or through some object, between the subject and the personality from whose life the events are reported.*

How can a thing, an unconscious configuration of atoms and empty space, carry with it a collection of past moments like fossils embedded in a rock? Was she now, this moment, leaving some imprint of herself, Sally Curtiss, at (glancing at the mantel clock) 9:22 on a Saturday night in July, on this room, this chair, this book? She turned pages, letting her eyes drift over words.

In 1939 an eminent parapsychologist had suggested that images might become fixed in a setting in which they could later be perceived by a person with the necessary sensitivity. Images: visual, aural, tactile. But how? Even if the physical structure of an object is altered in some way by its experience, how can the change encode anything so specific as a single moment in time, a certain shadow on a wall? The book offered no suggestions on this point; she shut it and stared at the cover without seeing. Supposing it happened—however it happened—what then? The result was that she felt warm breath on her face, or heard a sound of sweeping, or saw leaves etched black against a sunset sky. Sensory hallucinations, all of them, triggered by images mysteriously locked into the physical structure of some object and just as mysteriously released by her—what was the phrase?—"necessary sensitivity."

In spite of its fuzziness the hypothesis was comforting. It offered an explanation for those disturbingly insubstantial moments that seemed as much a product of her own brain as of the haunting. And it supported the idea that those moments were simply echoes of finished events, not the active attempts of a disembodied spirit trying, in its fragmented way, to communicate with her. David, she knew, favored the case for conscious haunting. She shook her head and across the room there was movement; she turned quickly to see, again, her own reflection in the bay.

Idiot. Her hands tightened on the book in her lap as if on the body of scientific thought. *An image fixed in a physical setting.* Music box, sundial, sitting room sofa, each with its images, the whole house an echo chamber for the past. Did that really explain what was going on here? For the music box it was a neat fit, for the sitting room sofa probably, for the sundial maybe. All three objects had presumably been handled or touched by Julian and, according to the theory, must retain some imprint of him. The sight of the two dogs, the household sounds she had heard on her afternoon alone—these were not so neat, but their connection could be postulated. But what about the voice that had called her to Joshua's room during Rosanna's sitting there? And what about the trance in which she had seen the churchyard shaded by elms? Was there a qualitative difference in those latter two incidents—the stamp of consciousness? Unless they had been only chance juxtapositions, echoes performing a random match, they seemed uncannily like responses to the situation at hand.

The hypothesis was loose, sloppy; the feel of it was wrong. Yet she wanted to believe it. It was safer and more manageable than the idea of the haunting as a conscious process involving actions and reactions, hers and David's and Julian's. She moved restlessly, shifting her weight in the chair; the book slipped from her lap and fell to the rug. She let it lie there.

She had felt him behind her, his breath on her skin.

She pushed the memory away as Locky came trotting in, tags jingling, coming to sniff at the book on the floor. Colin had brought the terrier over after supper and left him, and since then he had been with David—wherever David was. He had been keeping out of her way, his usual method of dealing with a disagreement. And she had to admit it worked. She needed him too much to sustain any kind of active anger against him, and he needed whatever was in this house, needed to match himself against the inexplicable. Her hands caught each other in a sudden clasp that hurt. Beside her chair the dog turned in circles and lay down on the rug, dropping its nose to its paws.

Not the buzzer, but the barking, woke them.

Coming from the foot of the bed in the middle of the night it was deafening, more than enough to bring them both bolt upright out of a sound sleep. David grabbed her arm.

"What in almighty hell—"

"It's Locky," she said, realizing. "He's barking at the buzzer. Listen."

David swore, and was gone. She heard the click of claws on the floor as Locky followed him out into the hall, then the silencing of the buzzer and David's vehement whisper: "Shut up!" She took the flashlight and went out into the hall. Locky had stopped barking, but he stood glaring at the blinking red light on the monitor panel and growling. Sally felt a tremor somewhere inside, threatening to become laughter. David was examining the panel.

"Thistle Room. Let's go."

She switched on the flashlight and they started down

the hall, taking the route past the master bedroom and the sitting room, beam of light picking out the faded wallpaper, threadbare runner underfoot, and now and again the bustling shadow of the dog accompanying them.

"Shouldn't we have locked him up someplace?" David said.

"Oh, he'll be all right."

The door of the Thistle Room creaked in the best haunted-house fashion. Sally switched the flashlight off. Inside it was quiet, faintly moonlit. She noticed at once the fragrance of roses from the porch roof outside the window.

"Well?" David said softly, and waited a moment longer, and then reached for the light switch. She caught his arm.

"Wait—"

He froze.

"Look."

It was almost touching him, hovering just at his left shoulder. He turned slowly, letting her hands guide him. "Oh boy," she heard him say under his breath.

It was smaller than they had thought from the photograph, more the size of a plum than a tennis ball, and it hung without moving in the dark air. It was brighter at the center than at the edges, no color and all colors, a constant weaving of flickering shades. Sally found herself marveling. It was so real, so obviously and plainly there, that she felt less uncanniness than a profound curiosity. What *was* it? They stood watching it for more than a minute before it began to move, floating across the room toward the window, then hesitating, sinking toward the floor, stopping almost level with the sill. Locky, whom they had forgotten, gave a short gruff bark and ran toward it, stopping just short. In the dim light from the window his furry head was silhouetted, cocked to one side in puzzlement. The light was perhaps six inches from his nose. Slowly his tail began to wag. Sally felt the tremor again somewhere under her ribs, a fluttering sensation rising to her throat. She glanced at David: he was watching the light, rapt. The laughter overpowered her then, in warm engulfing waves; she buried her face helplessly in her hands, trying to stifle it. David was saying, "What's the matter?" and she couldn't answer, could only point to the dog sniffing the light with his muzzle eagerly lifted, stubby tail wagging. It was the end, she thought; David would never forgive her this badly timed irreverence; if the light disappeared now it would be her fault forever. But she couldn't stop laughing—couldn't stop the giddy weakness in her bones. David looked at her and then at the dog. "For God's sake," he said quietly. Then he started laughing too; they leaned together in the dark, shaking with it, soft explosive sounds escaping them while the light hovered without moving in the air, inexplicable but serene.

⫸ 32 ⫷

IF NOTHING ELSE, the light's latest appearance freed her of all possible blame for its previous boycott. This was Sally's last thought before falling asleep. They had watched it for nearly an hour, and during that time they had determined that it was unaffected by any variation in their behavior. They had filmed it, talked out loud, walked around the room, turned the electric light on and off, and David, in an overflow of scientific zeal, had even put his hand through the shimmering circle without effect. When it finally disappeared around three A.M., they had reset their equipment and gone back to bed.

Thinking about it the next morning, while she was pulling weeds in the backyard, she realized that the relief she felt was more than simply a matter of being absolved from blame. It was, she supposed, what a desperately lost hiker might feel on encountering a familiar landmark. Spirit lights were so common in the history of paranormal phenomena that they could by now be considered classic; more, they could be seen, filmed, documented. They were fey and inexplicable, but they were undoubtedly there. And that quality was disturbingly rare in the Gilfoy haunting, where most of what happened seemed almost to have been designed to meet some high standard of inconclusiveness: an open music box might or might not have been shut; people fell down stairs that were found to be awkwardly constructed; a pair of dogs appeared, possibly strays, possibly not.

She straightened and leaned back on her hands, the hot grass prickling her palms. Even with her back to the house she could feel it behind her, center and focus of all her uneasiness; and now she shifted on the grass to face it, seeing the weathered white walls, the gables half hidden in the treetops, all in a wash of late morning sun and shadow that imposed its own pattern on everything else. A bumblebee buzzed close to her face, wanting for reasons of its own to light on her cheek; she waved it away and watched it go, furry, clumsy, its wings catching the light. This haunting bothered her. Whatever the explanation for it, psychometry or any other, she was beginning to wish the case was over. She didn't feel in control.

And David? What was it he had said the morning after he had made love to her in the sitting room? *I swear I couldn't help it.* Any more than she could help feeling the nonexistent hand that had touched her arm, over there by the sundial, or seeing two dogs playing in the yard at dusk. She was susceptible, and maybe David too; and that was bad. Their objectivity was crucial to their investigation of the house. Lose it, and the whole thing could spiral into a chaos of self-fulfilling prophecies. For herself she thought she knew the risks; she had, after all, spent most of her life under a barrage of extrasensory impressions, and she knew enough to question them even when she could not keep them out. But David's psychic aptitude had never measured anything above average (a fact that had always comforted her as much as it pained him), and she had counted on him to resist whatever tricks and traps the house might have to offer. If he could not . . .

You people are sitting on dynamite.

Rosanna had warned her. Sally stared at the house without seeing it, green eyes light and bleak as a lake iced over in winter. A breeze pushed the smell of hot grass against her face.

The screen door opened and David called, "Think it's okay to let the dog out?"

She glanced around the yard. "I don't see why not."

He opened the door wider and Locky trotted out, black and white against the green, beginning to investigate the fence between their yard and Mrs. Hopkins's. David joined her on the grass; together they watched the dog nosing among the tangle of vines along the fence.

David yawned once, then again, and lay back, eyes closed, a half smile on his face. He was in a good mood, pleased by their successful observation of the light, frustrations of the past week momentarily forgotten. Sally watched him. From up the hill the sound of an organ reached her raggedly; voices began to sing. With a start she realized it was Sunday. The hymn was familiar; she remembered singing it as a child.

> "Jerusalem the golden
> With milk and honey blest . . ."

The voices rose and fell dutifully on the surface of the summer morning, dragging a little behind the organ; she pictured the congregation inside the small white church with its clear pointed windows, the green graveyard outside. Beside her David opened his eyes and saw her looking at him. "I love you," he said.

For an instant it was all that existed: the words, the singing in the distance, the clear circle of sky overhead with its mosaic of leaves, green against bright blue. She had to swallow before she could answer. "I love you too," she said. His eyes had closed again. He lay there in the grass with one arm outstretched. The bumblebee had returned and was buzzing around his hair; she waved it away. Up the hill the churchgoers' voices strove toward the cadence, more enthusiastic than tuneful.

> "I know not, O I know not
> What joys await us there,
> What radiancy of beauty,
> What bliss beyond compare."

"I always thought that business about animals having a psychic sense was an old wives' tale," Colin said.

He had come to visit Locky and stayed to supper; they sat, as usual, in the kitchen. David had made an enormous bowl of chili which he set on the table with a flourish.

"Sally won't admit this, Colin, but I'll tell you a secret. She married me for this chili. About the animals, though—

you ought to know by now that parapsychology has a lot invested in old wives' tales. There's plenty of precedent for using various animals as psychic barometers." He ladled the thick chili with its dark red beans onto Colin's plate, handed it to him, and began to fill Sally's. "My favorite is an experiment done in a haunted house in Kentucky. The experimenter brought in a dog, a cat, a rat, and a rattlesnake and took each one into the allegedly haunted room to watch their reaction." He was serving himself now. "The dog snarled and backed out of the room and absolutely refused to go back in. The cat jumped out of its owner's arms and spat at a chair in one corner of the room. The rattlesnake took up a strike position focusing on the same chair."

"And the rat?"

"No reaction at all."

Colin shivered. "Somehow that's worse."

"It is, isn't it? God, this chili is good. I amaze myself. You know"—David gestured with his spoon—"even plants have gotten into the act. There've been experiments using electrodes and stuff that seem to show how sensitive they are to the thoughts and moods of the people around them. A green thumb means they're reading you as positive. If you're feeling negative or destructive, it can have a bad effect on their growth rate—even kill them. Except weeds, of course. They don't seem to care."

Colin, however, was not interested in plants. "Rachel Wilcox called me this morning," he said. "She checked with the vet in Masonville about white shepherds. He says no."

"Ah."

"They didn't show up last night?"

"They?" David said.

"The dogs," Sally said. "No." To Colin it was, she realized, the crux, the center of everything else: all the daily vigilance of cameras and tape recorders, data gathered and sorted, theories and dead ends—everything, in short, that she and David perceived as making up this investigation of theirs sank away and left for Colin, like shells on the sand at low tide, one or two simplicities: his dog's missed presence and the distance-lit figure of a dead woman who had captured his young imagination.

There would be no making him see, even if she had
wanted to, that David considered Locky's part a whimsical detail, something to be mentioned in a footnote if
at all. So by means of misunderstandings we manage to
live.

She held out her plate. "More chili, please."

David glanced at Colin. "What did I tell you?"

⋙ 33 ⋘

THE NEXT DAY marked the beginning of the end.

It started uneventfully enough: a sunny morning at the beginning of August. In the heat they slept late and came down yawning to their coffee. Outside, the green yard had lost its early freshness and taken on a heavy, settled-in look; all over town it was the same, trees drooping over the sidewalks with their summer's weight of leaves. After breakfast David went up to the attic to continue his self-imposed task of sorting through the Gilfoy family papers. Sally made herself another cup of coffee, washed the dishes, and decided to clean their bedroom.

Which needed it. The unmade bed, dirty clothes on the floor, half cup of coffee (how many days old?) on the dresser were doubly disgraceful in the bright sunlight streaming in. She started with the bed. Tucking in sheets, plumping pillows, smoothing wrinkles from the light summer blanket, she drew up the white tufted bedspread last and, seeing it needed washing, pulled it off to toss into the pile on the floor. Next was the jumble of books and papers on the table—David's notes on the case, her transcriptions of the tapes from the sittings with Rosanna, reference books, issues of the Psychical Research Society quarterly, all chaotically commingled. A photocopy of Stephen Foster's "I Dream of Jeanie," another of the hymn "Lead, Kindly Light." Former tenant Nicholas Abbey's note confirming the freezing cold in the master bedroom. And, underneath the note, the photograph of the young man they had decided was Julian Gilfoy.

The face no longer surprised her. By now she had abandoned, however reluctantly, her first image of Julian as the handsome, arrogant, dissolute son—seducing his stepmother, falling drunk to his death. Gradually a different impression had grown: of a boy rather than a man, a blunt gentleness. There was nothing particularly handsome about the face in the photograph, just a soft pseudo-belligerence like a strong young animal's: an unremarkable face, its potential still latent, the mouth and eyes still half bewildered by the strength in the shoulders and jaw. He had lived here in the house, stood perhaps on the same boards where she stood now, touched the same surfaces, watched the same patterns of light and shadow on the walls. He had been alive as she was now, warm hands, warm breath. That straight dark hair was soft as a child's— she knew that. Didn't she? You couldn't prove any of it, not the portrait's identity or the night on the sitting room sofa, but looking down at the young face she saw it trembling in her hand. *The science of things that cannot possibly happen, but do.* Her knees were weak, remembering.

There were footsteps in the hall, and David said, "Sal?" She dropped the picture facedown on the desk and turned toward him as he entered the room.

"Hi."

"That twenty-five-foot extension cord, the one I bought at Buck's—do you know where it is?"

"I think it's still in Joshua's room," she said. "Didn't you use it for Rosanna's sitting in there?"

"Oh, yeah. Yeah, you're right." He pushed a hand through his hair. "It's hot as blazes up there. I found a fan, but the outlet is way the hell the other end of the room. With that cord I can get the fan close enough to the window to get a little air in—if it still works, that is; it looks like it came over on the *Mayflower* at the latest."

"I'm pretty sure I saw it in Joshua's room," she said, overcome all at once by the oddest sense that he mustn't know she had been looking at Julian's portrait, wanting him out of the room. Only when he had left did she turn back to the table and pick up the photograph again. In retrospect she needed some sort of reason for this behavior, and she told herself that it was a simple wish not to encourage his obsession with Julian as a personality, an individual, anything more than a collection of emotional fragments inhabiting the house like the echo of a long-silent voice. Her eyes rested on the young unformed face for a moment; then abruptly she opened the table drawer, dropped the photograph into it and slid it quickly closed.

That afternoon there were errands to run: grocery store, drugstore, laundromat. Because of the apparent instance of apport phenomena in which the music box had been moved from parlor to sitting room, they decided to activate the monitoring system while they were out of the house. That posed the problem of what to do with Locky, and in the end it seemed simplest to take him along with them.

At least in theory. In practice he was unbelievably strong for a small dog, and possessed of self-will in inverse proportion to his size. They left him tied outside Saunders' while they went in for groceries; five minutes later Sally, choosing ripe tomatoes for a salad, found him trailing his leash at her feet, having evidently untied David's knot with little trouble. She took him back outside, not without a noisy confrontation with Leonie Saunders's yellow cat, which knocked over a pyramid of soup cans in its spitting retreat. The thunder of falling cans died away to the sound of Leonie's voice, unvaried from its customary flatness, saying, "Damn you, Sassafras." David, somewhere between guilt, chivalry, and foresight, bought an extra pound of coffee.

Locky was unchastened. There was another incident, this time with a collie, leaving the laundromat, and a final one outside their own front gate with the Campbell dog, Beanie, cut short when Mrs. Hopkins, watering hydrangeas on her front lawn, obligingly turned the hose on Beanie. They entered the house at last, exhausted, to be greeted by the monitoring system, which announced them obligingly as soon as they opened the front door. David dropped the leash and ran up the stairs to shut off the buzzer; Locky barked and chased him. Sally dumped the groceries on the floor and went after the dog, trying to catch him before the dangling leash caught on something and strangled him. In the midst of the barking stumbling confusion David managed to silence the buzzer and stood looking down at Sally, who sat halfway up the stairs holding the dog's collar while Locky wagged his tail and tried to lick her face. David shook his head.

"You know, I don't think I trust him to be properly

respectful of a ghost even if he sees one. Those phantom pups might be in for one hell of a shock."

Perhaps they knew as much, for they did not appear that evening. As dusk fell David drummed his fingers softly on the windowsill in the kitchen, where they stood watching. Behind them in the unlit room Locky scratched imaginary fleas. When he stopped the silence descended, broken only by the sound of the cicadas. One by one lightning bugs began to flicker among the darkening banks of leaves; David fiddled with the cameras on their tripods: the 35-millimeter loaded with infrared and the 16-millimeter movie camera with high-speed black and white. Sally watched the sundial's marble base; it was always the last thing to fade. At last David abandoned the cameras and leaned on the sill beside her, chin in his hands. Darkness fell undisturbed.

For supper they made sandwiches and took them into the parlor, where it was cooler. Even there the warm blackness just outside the windows made itself felt in the room, stirring the filmy curtains in the bay and punctuating the silence, as they sat reading, with crickets piping. It might have been the crickets, or maybe the flickering of one of the lamps, that made it impossible for Sally to concentrate on her article on newly postulated quarks; in any case she surrendered at last to an increasing restlessness and stood up from her chair.

"I'm going to take a bath."

David's head moved in what might have been acknowledgment; she envied his concentration. The dog, curled at his feet, looked up as she crossed the room but did not follow her.

The bathtub was one of the house's hidden treasures, sybaritically long and deep, resting on no fewer than six elegant clawed feet. She usually took a shower in the spartan tin closet in the opposite corner, obviously a later addition, and the bath, in contrast, was almost shockingly pleasant. She lay soaking in the warm water for a long time, hair pinned up on her head, listening to the sound of her own breath magnified by the porcelain cavern and feeling the intimate movements of the water against her skin with every slight shift of position. At first she made a conscious effort to follow her thoughts, but the jumble of images in her head didn't really deserve the name and she lay at last simply watching the room's reflection quiver and settle on the water's surface, the dim outline of her naked body beneath. The gold-white circle of the ceiling light, floating near her feet, had lulled her almost to a doze when the bathroom door suddenly opened.

Only a few inches: but she saw it move, felt the gust of air from the hall—chilly in comparison with the air inside the bathroom. For one moment, during which the water in the tub seemed suddenly cooler than was comfortable, she didn't move. She said, "David?" There was no answer. A moment more, a heartbeat; then she sat up, water splashing, and jumped out of the tub to snatch a towel and wrap it around her. If he was playing games . . .

There was no one in the hall. And the door was old, of course, and warped with years of damp, and she probably hadn't closed it properly in the first place. She did so now. But she had no desire to get back in the tub; the water was cold and so was she, and she pulled the plug and let it drain while she dried herself quickly, eyes on the door. David's bathrobe hung on a hook on the back; she put it on and tied the cord tightly before going back down the hall to their bedroom.

There, everything was as she had left it—room yellow-lit by the lamp on the table by the open window, the bed with its old-fashioned carved headboard, one drawer pulled half out of the dresser, lamplight gilding its edge. She sat at the table and took her hair down, brushing it until it hung smooth down her back. She was restless again, little currents running along her nerves. She set the brush down; as if of their own accord her fingers found the handle of the table drawer and pulled it open and took out the photograph that lay inside. She was looking at it almost before she realized how it had come into her hand, looking at the young face with its straight dark hair while from the open window the summer night flowed over her, darkness cradled in the hanging leaves, breeze swelling like a sigh. *Sighing like the night wind and sobbing like the rain, wailing for the lost one* . . . The words came as if carried on the soft rush of wind outside. The air smelled of summer on the wane. She put the picture down on the table but the eyes still seemed to meet hers, young and uncertain behind their surface belligerence. *Wailing for the lost one*—the dark hair she had drawn through her fingers, fine as the fringe on her mother's old silk scarf, the weight of his body—she closed her eyes against the memory and felt it move in her.

When she opened them again the room seemed to box her in, stiflingly close, and she got up and went to the door, standing to listen a moment, then back to the window. Out in the yard she thought she could make out the base of the sundial, a glimmer in the darkness; and for an instant it seemed as if another shape stood beside it, a shadow among shadows. She leaned forward, heart jumping; the night air touched her face. Listened: the crickets sang, that was all. Even the leaves were still. As she stood there it took hold of her like a drug, the silence and beckoning darkness, and she went to the door and had her hand on the knob before she caught herself. There was nothing out there—nothing. But the room, when she faced it again, was unbearable: airless and prim, and the breeze came again, night-sigh stirring her hair. At its touch a half shudder went through her. She needed to do something, something a little crazy, to release the frustration that was knotted like a fist inside her. The darkness was enough. She would go down.

The stairs creaked once as she descended; otherwise the house was quiet. A spill of light from the parlor. She edged around it and went quickly down the hall to the kitchen: there it was dark, tap dripping in the sink. Only a turn of the doorknob now. The screen latch clicked, and she was free.

In the dark the backyard was unfamiliar territory, night sky thick with summer constellations. She hesitated on the back step for a minute. This sudden immersion in the darkness outdoors had startled her into some awareness that her actions were not perfectly rational. The house at her back was a known quantity: she clung to it. Then, looking up, she saw the moon just rising over the tops of the trees, and something across the yard reflecting its light with a dim gleam—the sundial. She went toward it, the grass silky under her feet, feeling her heart beat under the thin robe.

The face of the dial was warm. She ran her hands lightly over the smooth metal. In the moonlight the broken pointer cast the slightest of shadows toward the words across the bottom of the dial.

I count only sunny hours.

This hour, then, was uncounted, a refuge out of time. The breeze rose, bringing an unexpected fragrance of lilac blossoms, and the next moment he was there, grasping her waist from behind, the light touch jolting through her from head to foot. His hands came up and covered her breasts; she turned in his arms and they kissed open-mouthed, standing by the sundial. She lost all awareness of everything but his mouth and body against her own, everything but her frantic need to be taken, to escape in this moment from all petty daily frustrations, all questions and considerations and constraints, all waiting and planning and taking care. Her robe had come open and she felt through his clothes the heat of him against her naked skin as he tangled one hand in her hair and bent her head back until she saw, over his shoulder, a cluster of dark linden leaves silhouetted, each in perfect heart-shape, against the lit windows of the house. And like an image juxtaposed over it, similar but not quite matching, she remembered the leaf they had found pressed in a book—golden, heart-shaped, brittle with age, put there long ago—and suddenly all desire evaporated and she was afraid. How could she be smelling lilacs when they had not bloomed since June?

"David, wait," she said. "Wait." He was rough; he was hurting her; she wanted him to stop. All at once the whole thing frightened her—their meeting like this, the smell of lilacs, the leaf shape like a motif linking past and present. But he did not stop; his hands were incredibly strong, and she tried to twist free and failed and tried again with the strength of panic and this time succeeded. The bones of her wrists ached where he had held them. He took a step toward her and in the moonlight she saw his eyes half closed, face covered with sweat.

"David!"

He stopped and stood motionless; then he put a hand up to his face and wiped the sweat out of his eyes and looked at her. "For Christ's sake, Sally."

He sounded furious, but he sounded like David. She pulled the robe closed and found her hands shaking too badly to tie it. "I'm going in," she said.

*   *   *

It took a long time for her hands to stop shaking. She had to try twice before she succeeded in putting her hair into a loose braid. When he came and stood in the door she didn't look at him. Finally he said, "Can I come in?"

She turned and looked at him then, their eyes meeting across a space of lamplight. He came into the room and stood by the dresser, touching things on top, needlessly rearranging. Then: "Mind telling me what's going on?"

Sally looked at him and he rubbed his head.

"Am I missing something? I haven't gotten that kind of reaction since I tried to kiss Becky Bramucci on the first date."

He was trying too hard and they both heard it. He came close to her and touched her shoulder and then the back of her neck. She felt herself start shaking again. "What's the matter with you?" he said.

"What were you doing out there?" she said. "Did you follow me?"

"No," he said. "I was already there. I saw you come out."

She faced him, their eyes inches apart. "What were you doing out there?" He started to shrug and she caught hold of his arm. "Well?"

He looked down at her hand and then at her face. "Christ," he said. "I wanted some fresh air. What's the matter with you?"

"David. Ginny and Julian used to meet at night by that sundial."

There was a pause; then he said, "For Pete's sake, Sally."

"Do you think I'm kidding?"

"No. You might be right. But so what?"

"I don't think we ought to stay here," she said.

It took a minute before he understood what she was saying, and even then she could tell he didn't believe she meant it. She let go of his arm and went to sit on the edge of the bed; he remained standing by the window. "Wait a minute," he was saying. "Wait a minute. I've missed something somewhere. Could we start over?"

He was leaning against the edge of the table, Julian's photograph lying unnoticed behind him. She saw it and felt nothing but an immense tiredness. "There are a few things I haven't told you," she said. She wondered where to begin. He was looking at her, his face unreadable.

"It's all entirely subjective," she said. "Nothing evidential." Even to herself she sounded defensive. David said nothing; she made herself go on. "There've been some instances of aural hallucination, always when I've been alone in the house. And a couple of other—I'm not sure what to call them. But what I'm getting at—"

"Hold it," he said. "We'll get to what you're getting at in a minute. First I'd like a few details, if you don't mind." He sat on the table and folded his arms, looking at her. She stared back. He didn't have to be so lofty, so righteous—didn't have to enjoy worming every detail out of her, fulfilling some self-image of the great scientist probing for the truth. But she had gotten herself into this, and it would be worth it if only she could make him understand.

"There really isn't all that much," she said. "There was one afternoon when I was here by myself. I heard sounds. Footsteps, voices, someone sweeping the floor."

"Where were you?" he said.

"In the little room."

"And then?"

"Nothing. That was all."

"The sounds just stopped?"

She tried to remember. "No. There was an interruption of some kind—you must have come home or something. No, I remember. It was the day the men came to look at the stairs."

"The sounds stopped when they came in?"

"Well," she said, "I stopped hearing them."

"Go on."

She took a breath. "Then—the afternoon I found the music box upstairs, when it was supposed to be in the parlor?"

She stopped and he said, "Well?"

"I opened it, I don't remember why. When it started to play I felt as if J—, as if someone were there in the room with me."

He was leaning forward, excited now. "That could be a psychometric thing, a reenactment—some real moment in the past."

"I guess so. I got scared, shut the box."

"And Julian?"

"I don't know. If it was Julian. Anyway, shutting the box seemed to"—she gestured futilely—"make it stop."

"Okay. What else?"

"Well, when I was cleaning the sundial. Somebody grabbed my arm."

"Grabbed your arm? Julian?"

"I don't know," she said. "There was nobody there. It scared the bejesus out of me."

He was grinning. "I bet it did. Sally, why didn't you tell me all this? It's fantastic. It's great!"

"It isn't great," she said. "Don't you see what's happening—what happened tonight? It's as if we're locking into some kind of pattern, starting to act out what they did." When he didn't answer she said, "Look on the table behind you."

He twisted around and saw the picture of Julian, picking it up and then glancing at her quizzically.

"I found it this morning when I was cleaning up," she said. "I put it in the drawer because I didn't want you to find it. Tonight I got it out again. Then I had this crazy idea of going outside. David, those aren't my feelings. But I'm willing to bet they were Ginny's, fitted so neatly into mine that I'm not sure anymore where she leaves off and I begin. Now do you see why I'm asking you why you went outside?"

He was silent, thinking it over. Finally he said, "Granting psychometry, which I think we can safely do, it's possible to explain all of this simply by expanding the theory a little. It's not a question anymore of you handling an object, but of the object—the house—handling you. Containing you within it. There's a constant feedback going on between you and it."

"That's the point I'm trying to make," she said. "It isn't just me. It's affecting you too."

"I don't think so. At least I'm not aware of it."

She stared at him: he looked so reasonable and sounded so stubborn. "If you're not aware of it, then you can't possibly control it. And being out of control in a situation like this can be dangerous." The words mocked her— hadn't Rosanna said the same thing to her when they had talked on the porch, weeks ago? "You know that as well as I do," she said.

He was running one finger along the edge of the photograph in his hand. "If I'm not aware of it, that could also mean it isn't happening."

"David—" She stopped and tried to think, but it was impossible. She went on. "It wasn't you tonight, out there—it just wasn't. And it wasn't you that night in the sitting room, on the sofa. If you can't tell, I can."

He looked up slowly; his eyes meeting hers were opaque. "For Pete's sake," he said. "I know I'm not the world's greatest lover, but that doesn't mean we have to regard all activity in that area as paranormal, does it?" It sounded light, but she knew it wasn't: that was David.

"You know that isn't what I mean."

"Well, damn it, Sally. You're saying it was Julian who made love to you and not me."

"I am not. I'm talking about this house as a sending agent and you as a receiving one, whether you're aware of it or not. You said yourself, that time, that you couldn't help it."

"Then it was Julian's impulse and my body? Great. Now you're talking about possession."

"Stop it, David. Just stop it."

She pressed both hands to her temples and then put her face in them, hearing him say, "Why can't you give me a little credit? I wanted to make love to you and I did. Is that such an unreasonable hypothesis?"

She looked up at him. An unreasonable hypothesis? They had never discussed it, and now was not the time—the bewilderment and awkwardness and frustration, the silence afterward too deep for talking. You were supposed to talk about it; all the books said so, and the magazines, and the talk-show guest experts. Lying in the dark, staring at nothing, listening to each other's breathing, afraid to ask, "Are you asleep?" Sometimes their hands had met by common impulse in the space between them—but they had not talked. It was the woman who was supposed to persist in discussing it; the books said that too. But she could not, she was incapable of forcing such an issue—afraid of blundering in, destroying what they had, of alienating him forever. At bottom she was afraid that it was some lack in herself, that what he loved was not her but the psychic gift that fascinated him so.

"Look," he was saying, "I know I'm a bummer with

sex, most of the time. But the fact is that there have been occasions when I've managed. That night was one of them. Tonight would have been another. And I dare say there will be others."

"Will there?" She had not meant it as a challenge, but his chin jerked up: now he was angry.

"That's a hell of a dare."

"I didn't mean it like that."

"The hell you didn't. I'm sick of what you didn't mean." He slid off the desk and moved toward the bed where she sat. "Okay, if you want to get laid, fine—that's what you're going to get. By me, personally, all by myself. Without any help."

She was angry too, now, and afraid—not of him but of having gone too far, said too much. Still the anger was uppermost, and when he touched her she shook off his hand and said, "Don't bother."

This time when he grabbed her it hurt. He forced her down on her back across the bed and bent over her; she turned her face to the side, closing her eyes involuntarily, not knowing what she felt, anger or pain or hope. He leaned over her for what seemed an interminable time, his breath on her face—but nothing happened, and at last he made a choking sound, not quite a sob, and released her and turned away.

⋙ 34 ⋘

"Is THERE any more coffee?"

David picked up the pot and shook it. "A little. Want it?"

"Okay."

The coffee scarcely covered the bottom of her cup.

"I can make some more," he said.

"No, I don't really want any. Thanks anyway."

The chair creaked as he sat back. There in the kitchen the tap dripped and the refrigerator hummed, while outside the jays argued and somewhere, a few houses away, someone cut grass with a power mower. She sat seeing the bruise on her wrist where he had grabbed it last night, hearing the sounds like a fragile barrier holding back a silence so immense that at any moment it might burst through and crush them.

David pushed back his chair.

"I'm going up to the attic. There're a couple more boxes I want to look through."

She nodded, not trusting her voice. When he had gone, his steps fading up the stairs, the silence was again something she could bear, a dull pressure under her ribs. It was not guilt she felt, not resentment. It was not a question of being right or wrong. It was just that they had gone too far; and now they went quietly, carefully, as if a sudden movement or a wrong word would bring the whole structure down on their heads. The fragility was what frightened her: had they been so close to collapse all this time and never known it? She had thought herself hardheaded about their marriage, coolly rational in deciding they could transcend its lacks and compromises. But last night it had seemed simply the sum of its parts, good and bad—more bad than good.

We're more than that. Aren't we?

But there the hollowness began, and in that void the thinking process was snuffed like a candle in a vacuum. There were flowers in a chipped pitcher on the table, pink roses; she saw them without seeing. Something nudged her knee—Locky, his eyes the color of old pennies, glinting with reflected light. She reached down, smoothed back the furry brows.

"How can you see anything through all that hair?"

The dog wagged its tail. Sally sighed and got up; she had been sitting long enough. There were the breakfast dishes, and the top of the stove needed cleaning—anything to keep her hands busy. While she worked her mind went over the facts, trying as best it could to separate them from the whole emotional tangle, looking for a moment's objective breathing space.

What was going on? David called it psychometry on an expanded scale. What had he said last night? *A question of the house handling you . . . a constant feedback going on.* There were times when the barrier between past and present seemed so fluid that she could, if she had the courage, pass through it—a kind of Alice-through-the-looking-glass. But it wasn't just her. It was happening to him too. On some level they were both collaborating with Julian, or with the house, to reproduce some pattern, some sequence of events bent on repeating itself, for whatever reason, with whatever elements were at hand. There was something present here to which people were susceptible—more or less so according to their individual personalities—and with which they had all interacted in one way or another: herself, David, Mrs. Pindar, the Abbeys, Christine Frey, even Mrs. Gardner who could not bring herself to talk about it, even Miranda Sterling who prided herself on her skepticism. An odd impulse, a disturbing dream, a sudden fit of weeping, a sensation of being not quite alone—most of the time forgotten, not worth remembering or reporting. She thought back now over the past weeks, recalling incidents so seemingly insignificant that she hadn't questioned them at the time. The mind has a genius for inventing reasons after the fact. How many times had she found herself on her way to the little room, when there was nothing she wanted there, nothing she needed—just finding herself at the door as if she had been shunted down some invisible groove worn in the very air? It sounded farfetched, even crazy; yet standing over the stove with a damp sponge in her hand she sensed the house around her like a living presence, sunlit and full. Something cold touched her leg. She jumped, dropped the sponge—it was Locky, putting his cold nose to her face when she bent to pick up the sponge, her heart pounding, feeling like an idiot.

"Scram, buster."

He danced between her and the back door, wanting to go out; she opened the screen and he ran to scatter half a dozen birds into the air. Sally threw the sponge into the sink.

Last night's supper dishes were still in the parlor and she went to fetch them. The room had grown too familiar for her to see it anymore when she entered; there was only an impression of the white-curtained bay collecting the indirect morning light like a bowl, leaving the rest of the room in bright shadow. The plates and glasses were on the rug in front of the fireplace—reminders that only last night she and David had been sitting there, irrevocable things still unsaid. She pushed the thought away. The journal he had been reading lay facedown on a chair; she picked it up and looked down at the words.

The brain, evolving as an organ whose purpose is to promote biological survival, has out of necessity reduced reality to a simplified version dominated by the five senses. But beyond this practical model is a world infinitely greater in scope and complexity, made up of memories, perceptions and images both personal and collective. The level of consciousness on which we operate from day to day is only a small cross-section of the whole. In altered states such as those induced by drugs, dreaming, or psychosis, the brain's primary function may be suspended, allowing brief excursions beyond the limits of personal consciousness. In such circumstances the boundaries of individual existence fade and the ownership of experience becomes ambiguous.

A breath of air lifted the page; she caught it and held it flat. *The boundaries of individual existence fade and the ownership of experience becomes ambiguous.* Like a dream in which shapes shift and change, pieces break away and rearrange themselves in outlandish ways that make a kind of sense. Whose experience were they having in this house: their own or Julian's? Or was it some precarious mingling of the two?

She read the passage again. *In altered states such as those induced by drugs, dreaming, or psychosis*—but they were awake, she and David; they weren't on drugs, and if they were crazy it seemed to be a madness that regularly afflicted inhabitants of the house. Was the house itself then like a drug or a dream, creating its own reality inside its walls? And the two of them a part of that dream-reality, subject to its laws? She glanced up: outside the window the green summer leaves danced and then were still with a stillness that seemed to settle like a bell of soundless light over the house and all it contained. Sally held her breath, then slowly let it out. Last night's plates and glasses were there on the floor; the clock on the mantel ticked a steady forward pace. She saw pencil marks in the margin next to the passage she had been reading. Was David wondering, as she was? She couldn't get a sense of him anymore; he was opaque to her, as if he had somehow closed himself off. As if he were hiding something. But what?

As usual, there were too many questions without answers; she collected the dishes and took them back to the kitchen. Locky was making a ruckus in the backyard, barking at something she couldn't see. When she opened the screen door and called him he ignored her. What was he barking at? The back of her neck prickled; he was uncomfortably near the sundial.

"Locky!"

This time he looked at her before resuming his frenzied barking. She let the screen bang behind her and started across the yard toward him. It seemed crazy, sun and blue sky overhead, to find her legs less than steady. A breeze skimmed shadows over the grass. She had almost reached the frantic dog when suddenly the ivy at the base of the sundial erupted; a gray kitten, fur stiff with indignation, shot out and streaked toward the lilac bushes that bordered the back of the yard. Locky gave chase. Sally followed, after the instant required to readjust her universe; pushing her way through the thickgrowing lilacs she was in time to see the kitten deliver a farewell hiss and disappear over the board fence that divided their backyard from the one behind. Locky gazed at the fence, tongue hanging out, while Sally cautiously examined the weeds she was standing in, trying to determine if they were poison ivy.

She decided they weren't. The dog was looking comically at her, plainly expecting a reprimand she hadn't the heart to give him, and she laughed, but there was no accompanying relief, no lifting of the tension that held her. Intellectually she knew the situation was ridiculous. You're an idiot, a child, seeing spooks behind every door, she tried to think, as she had earlier when he had startled her in the kitchen. Still the response—stung pride or common sense—wouldn't come. She picked her way out of the jungle of lilac bushes, glancing up at the house as she emerged.

A face was watching her from the attic window.

The sight of it, white and strangely malformed, flickering behind the leaves reflected in the glass, came like a blow, all the stronger for the joyous sunlight flooding over everything. She felt tricked in that instant; then almost at once some memory trace cut in and she realized it was David, the lower half of his face covered by a white dust mask. He was up there going through the papers; what was more natural than for him to hear the commotion and look out to see what was going on? But he looked so bizarre, a disembodied, nearly featureless face on the other side of the window, distant as if he were looking down at something on a microscope slide. If he noticed that she had seen him, he gave no sign. She lowered her eyes and started back to the house.

He came down for a sandwich about one o'clock. As at breakfast, his presence brought a kind of constriction to her breathing, as if there were not quite enough oxygen in the room. The worst thing was that he didn't seem to mind meeting her eyes. Of course they had quarreled before, and over the most idiotic things—lost keys, or his phobia about asking for directions. Once he had accused her of always having to be in the right; it was over a brand of olive oil, she remembered. In retrospect the incidents seemed lyrical, romantic. Now, he had left the lid off the peanut butter and she replaced it, screwing the lid tight as if she could seal off unwanted thoughts.

He went back up to the attic as soon as he had eaten. He was searching, she knew, for evidence to support what they had pieced together about the possible cause of the haunting. A diary, a letter—some positive proof of the affair between Ginny and Julian, the quarrel between Julian and his father. He wanted to link it all up: the music box, Rosanna's trance phrase "the lost one," the words to the song, the quarrel, the accident, the haunting —he wanted a neat sequence of mystery, clues, solution, each piece tagged and pigeonholed. And although she couldn't approve of what he was doing, still she envied him any absorbing task on this particular afternoon, when she found herself starting half a dozen meaningless little jobs and giving them up out of sheer depression. The light changed with agonizing slowness. She played with Locky, repaired a broken catch on one of the kitchen cabinets, looked with great thoroughness at a gardening catalog she had picked up at Buck's. For the first time in her life she wished she could knit. He had slept in the Thistle Room last night. Would tonight be the same?

It was almost dusk when she went to the foot of the attic stairs and stood there for a few minutes before climbing them at last. David had turned on the bare bulb that lit the place and on the floor she saw the dispossessed contents of various boxes: a pair of opera glasses, a straw basket, a glass doorknob, what looked like the broken pieces of a child's rocking chair. He looked up from the bundle of papers he was examining, his face less hostile than indifferent.

"Do you want to see if the dogs show up tonight?" she said. "It's almost time. Or do you want to just forget it?"

"Hell." He looked down at the papers in his hand, then out the window. "No, we might as well do it—finish out the week. Then we can write it off under bright ideas and give Colin his dog back."

They went down to the kitchen. The equipment was already set up, needing only one or two adjustments.

Sally called Locky; he came down the hall from the parlor and she glanced at David. "All set?"

"Go ahead."

It was not really much different from working with any other stranger. She switched off the kitchen light and joined him at the window. In the twilight his profile was just visible—the impatient set of his lips. She was glad Colin couldn't see it. Outside in the yard everything was still and they were silent as well, watching the shadows thicken under the trees. There were a few moments when the white roses on their spindly branches seemed to glow against the dusk. Next door, beyond the honeysuckle hedge, Mrs. Hopkins's back porch light was on, a yellow circle in the deepening blue. The lightning bugs were beginning: one, then another. She thought she saw a movement near the sundial—but no, there was nothing. The cicadas started their chorus. The dogs weren't coming. Maybe they had never come, or maybe they had been strays, or pets belonging to someone passing through—in any case, they weren't coming. Colin could have his dog back; this part, at least, would be over. She moved her shoulders restlessly. Then she saw them.

They were there, circling the sundial without a sound—a black Labrador and a white dog like a wolf. "David," she said, and simultaneously she heard the movie camera begin to whir.

"I see them," he said. "Move, I'm going to let Locky out."

She stepped back and he brushed past her in the dark kitchen; the screen squeaked. She kept her eyes on the dogs. The black one was chasing the white; then gracefully, invisibly, like a clever step in a dance, the roles were reversed and the white dog was pursuing. She had to squint to keep them in sight; by now it was almost completely dark outside.

"Did he go out?" she said. There wasn't a sound from the yard.

"He went out. Can you still see them? I can't."

She strained, then shook her head. Then, realizing he couldn't see her: "No. But you did see them?"

"Yeah."

They waited. Sally moved uneasily. "What's going on out there?"

"He's not making any fuss. Think he's too scared even to run?"

"I don't know," she said. "But I think we ought to find out."

"We'll need the flashlight," he said. "It's damn dark out there."

The flashlight was upstairs: she ran up and got it. When she got back to the kitchen David had turned off the camera and was out on the back step, whistling tentatively into the darkness. She switched the flashlight on and played it over the yard, expecting any moment to pick out Locky crouched trembling under a bush, eyes reflecting the stark beam of the light. Frightened half to death, and what had it proved?

"Where the hell is he?" David said. She moved the light slowly back and forth over the yard. "He's got to be here somewhere."

He whistled loudly. "Locky—here, boy—"

There was nothing.

"You call him."

"Locky!" Her throat was dry. "Come on, boy!"

They waited. David swore softly. "Let's go take a look."

They made a circuit of the backyard together, whistling, coaxing, swinging the light.

"He must have run into the front yard," Sally said at last.

"He could still hear us calling. Oh, well, let's take a look." They went along the side of the house to the front yard. The gate was closed; their calls brought no response. Sally felt herself starting to panic.

"What the hell could have happened to him?" She raised her voice. "Locky! Those damn dogs—they might have—"

"Jake and Jesse wouldn't hurt a fly," David said.

She felt the words like a physical impact: the bottom dropping out of everything. "What?" she said. "What did you say?" He was standing beside her and she swung the flashlight beam up, seeing for an instant his eyes light and empty. Then he blinked and covered them with his hand.

"Get that thing out of my face, will you?"

She jerked her wrist; the circle of light skittered against

the house behind him. She was having trouble catching her breath. "You called them by name," she said. "You called those dogs by name."

There was a pause before he said, "So what?"

"Well, how do you know their names?"

"What do you mean?" he said. "Colin told me."

Sally held her voice level. "Colin doesn't know their names, David. He didn't even know they existed until Miss Ellen mentioned them."

"Then I must have heard the names from her."

"I don't think so," she said. "We can check the tape."

He was silent for a second; then his hand touched her shoulder in the dark. "Hell, Sally, I don't know. They must be the names of some dogs I knew some time. I don't know." The hand squeezed gently. "Don't start all that up again. Let's find Locky, okay?"

She gave in; what else could she do? The worst thing was the knowledge that she was responding not to his logic (which was no logic at all) but to his touch and the warmth in his voice.

They searched for over an hour. The vacant lot east of the house, overgrown and partly wooded, was a nightmare; in the darkness every bush and hummock and tree stump took on the likeness of a small dog crouched in terror. They knocked their shins on fallen branches, stepped in soggy places, disentangled themselves from endless vines—all Sally's morning fears about poison ivy came back in force, and there were also unwelcome thoughts about snakes. She stifled them. David almost stepped on some animal that might have been a rabbit but was certainly—they told each other several times— not Locky. In the flashlight beam the lush green of the tangled growth was obscurely menacing. They called until they were both hoarse, and finally they gave up. Emerging onto the sidewalk they encountered a pair of small dark shapes standing close together.

"Who's that?" David shone the flashlight. "Oh, hi, Bobby. Matt."

The kids were big-eyed. "Was that you, Mr. Curtiss? Was that you in there yelling?"

"Yup. Lost our dog. You guys haven't seen him, have you? Little black and white dog?"

"No, sir." The boys moved off, whispering together, one voice rising: "You did too think it was the tramp!"

David went over to Mrs. Hopkins's house to ask if she had seen anything. Sally stayed behind, sitting on the front steps, hearing the sound of their voices beyond the hedge and trying not to think. When David returned he sounded relieved, almost cheerful.

"Mrs. Hopkins has a lot more sense than we have. She thinks he must have headed for home." He was coming down the front walk toward her as he spoke; she rose shakily from the steps and his arm came around her.

"And if he didn't?" she said.

"We'll have to call Colin in any case, sweetheart."

"I know. I know."

They went inside and he picked up the telephone to call Colin's house. She stood watching; their eyes met and held and she thought that the breach between them had been miraculously healed. Bad as losing the dog might be, they were in it together, and she could not prevent a guilty awareness that the weight in her chest had vanished. David put the phone down.

"No answer. He must still be at the library."

He was. David twisted the wire, hunching his shoulders. "Colin? Hi . . . Well, as a matter of fact, not so good. What? Oh, they showed up all right—but now we can't find Locky . . . Well, we don't know, exactly. We let him out, he didn't bark or anything, and now we can't find him. We think he must have gotten scared and run. He's probably on his way to your place . . . Yeah, well, that'd be a good idea." He listened again. The phone wire, wrapped around his hand, was beginning to leave marks. "Right. Okay. We'll be waiting." He hung up and looked at Sally. "He's on his way home now. He'll call us."

She sat down on the stairs, all at once too tired to stand, and he touched her shoulder. "The dog'll be okay, Sal. He'll find his way home."

"How did Colin take it?"

"He didn't seem too worried. Thinks Locky will show up."

"I hope he's right," she said. David leaned on the newel post, examining the worn-out toe of one sneaker. The house rose around them, silent.

It seemed forever before the phone rang again. David jerked the receiver out of its cradle on the first ring. "Colin? Yeah . . . What? Oh, well, that makes sense. You're right . . . Well, call tomorrow morning then, or sooner if he shows up. Sorry to put you through this. We both are . . . Yeah, okay. Good night."

He hung up the phone and there was silence. They looked at each other; then Sally lowered her eyes. Far beneath her concern over Locky and her relief about David a small nagging memory reasserted itself. *Jake and Jesse.*

The buzzer went off at 1:10. It seemed to her that she had just closed her eyes, and she sat up immediately. David didn't stir; she had to shake him. Finally he woke up enough to stumble out of bed and follow her out into the hall where the light on the panel blipped on and off. Sitting room.

"Never a dull moment around here." David rubbed his eyes, yawned, finished buttoning his pants. "Let's see what's up."

It was the light. They both saw it as soon as they opened the sitting room door—hovering a few inches above the sill of the window. Again Sally felt the slow unfolding of wonderment she had felt before—what *was* it? She had a sudden fleeting impression of a candle placed in a window. *Lead, kindly light, amid the encircling gloom.* David had gone to stand in front of it, hands on hips, looking down.

"Look how it's right in the window. Remember Christine said she thought she saw a light in the Thistle Room window once when she was coming home? Wonder if you can really see it from outside." He glanced out the window, then back at the light. "Wait here, okay? I'm going to check it out."

"I'll come with you," she said—too quickly, because he stopped and looked at her.

"Are you scared?"

"No," she said, and his warm hand reached out and closed on her cold one. "Liar," he said, and pulled her against him.

"I don't want you disappearing in the dark too," she said against his shoulder. He made a derisive noise but

his arms stayed around her. She closed her eyes, counting his heartbeats.

"Hey," he said.

"What?"

"It's gone."

"Gone?" She opened her eyes. He was right.

He released her and went over to the window where
the light had been, as if expecting to find some trace of it
remaining. But there was nothing, and nothing for them
to do but reset the equipment and go back to bed. There
they lay in the dark, neither of them sleeping. Sally
wanted him to touch her—just hold her, comfort her, the
way he had in the sitting room. The feeling wouldn't go
away. She moved finally, pressing against him; there was
one awful moment while he just lay there. Then his arm
came around her. "Don't worry, sweetheart," he said.

But she had been kidding herself, it seemed, about
only needing comfort, and lying there against him was
making it worse. She wanted him. After last night he
would think she was crazy. And she was beginning to
wonder herself. She kissed his cheek and made herself
move away, back to her own side of the bed. Did he
wonder why? After a moment he said, "I hope to hell
that film turns out."

The film, of course. "And Locky turns up," she said.

"He will." The sheets rustled as he changed position.
"Those mutts *must* have been apparitions to scare him
that bad."

Jake and Jesse?

But she didn't say it: the closeness between them was
too fragile, too precious, too recently won. "We ought to
get some sleep," she said.

☞ 35 ☜

WHEN SHE WOKE AGAIN there was gray light outside the window. He was propped up against the pillows in a sitting position. "Hi," he said.

"Did you sleep?"

"Woke up a few minutes ago. Know what? I'm starving." She yawned. "What time is it?"

"Ten past five."

"We might as well get up," she said. "I'm hungry too."

She took a shower while he made breakfast. By the time she had finished, the sky outside the bathroom window had gone from gray to white, against which the trees bulked black and unstirring. Back in the bedroom she stopped, half dressed, to scrutinize the yard below, but there was no movement, no sign of disturbance. Over in its corner the sundial's face was dark. *I count only sunny hours.* She finished dressing and went downstairs.

David was scrambling eggs, frying bacon, making coffee: everything perfectly orchestrated. She went out onto the back step and stood looking around the yard, the stone cool under her bare feet. After a moment she felt him behind her.

"We were dumb, trampling around out here looking for him. There might have been tracks or something."

"Tracks?" What was he planning to do—import a Boy Scout troop? "Come on, David. How could we think of something like that—then?"

"You're right. I think the bacon's ready."

The sun came up while they ate, wrapping the trees in

pale gold gauze. Sally kept looking out the window. David touched her arm. "Cut it out."

"I keep thinking he's out there," she said.

"He's probably been home since some ungodly hour this morning."

"Colin would have called us."

"I doubt it. He's too polite."

"Do you really think—"

"I don't know," he said. "Aren't you going to eat your eggs?"

She picked up her fork. "Is it too early to call him?"

"It's a quarter to six. He's probably asleep. Better wait till seven at least. Listen . . ." He patted the packet of movie film that lay on the window sill. "I want to send this to Jack by courier. He can have it developed at the lab. I'm not taking any chances with this baby."

"Where are you planning to get a courier?" she said.

His eyes went to the clock. "If I start now I can be in Boston by nine, drop this off, and be back by early afternoon." She said nothing and he looked at her. "Sal?"

She smiled crookedly. "I don't much want to face Colin by myself."

"Especially when it's my fault for borrowing the dog in the first place?"

"I didn't say that."

"It's true, though. Look, do you want to take this stuff to Boston while I stay here? Because it's got to get to Jack, and fast. If Locky hasn't come back, there may be something on this film that gives us a clue why not."

"You go ahead. I'll stay." She couldn't help seeing Colin's face.

"You'll be okay?"

She nodded.

At this hour the VW was the only car on the street. She stood at the gate and watched it go down the hill and turn left—heard the horn beep as it disappeared from sight. Then she turned back to the house. In the hazy morning sunlight the white frame walls looked fragile, insubstantial, like mist rising among the trees. As she climbed the porch steps even the fragrance of the roses overhead was no more than a suggestion, like a once vivid memory slowly fading.

The kitchen clock said 6:20. She went quickly up the stairs and got her sneakers, not stopping to put them on. The house seemed quiet, but no point in pushing her luck; she went out and sat on the back step, leaving the kitchen door ajar so she could hear the phone. One of the laces was knotted and she worked at it. The early morning peace lay undisturbed over everything: a bird called, a leaf cartwheeled across the sunlit grass. She put her shoes on and walked over to the bushes surrounding the sundial. In spite of what she had said to David, it was true that there could be tracks—but whose? If the dogs were apparitions they were hardly likely to leave tracks; one of Tyrrell's natural laws of apparitions was that they left no physical traces behind them; every first-year parapsychology student knew that. But Locky's? She surveyed the damp grass for a moment, then shrugged. She wouldn't know what to look for, even if, as David had pointed out, they hadn't already destroyed any sign that might have existed.

There was movement beyond the fence they shared with Mrs. Hopkins. Then the familiar gardening hat appeared, and the equally familiar watering can. "Good morning, dear; you're up early. Did you find the dog?"

"I'm afraid not," Sally said. "Not yet, anyway."

"Oh, he'll turn up—don't you worry. I had a cat once, jumped out of the car on the way to my sister's, fifteen miles from home. I tell you, I never expected to see her again, but one night a week later I heard something scratching at the back door and she walked in, cool as you please. She died last year, but my big orange cat, Taffy Joe I call him, he's from her first litter—"

The phone inside rang shrilly once, twice.

"Excuse me," Sally said. "The phone—"

"At this hour!" said Mrs. Hopkins.

It was David. "Hi. I stopped for gas and thought I'd check in. Did Colin call?"

"No," she said. "I guess I'll call him now. It's almost seven."

"Are you okay? What are you doing?"

"Mrs. Hopkins and I are having a girl-gab."

"God," said David, and hung up.

She cleaned up the kitchen before she called Colin. He answered on the first ring.

"Colin. Did I wake you?"

"Hello, Sally. No, I've been up for a while."

"Any sign of him?" she said, knowing the answer before he spoke.

"Not yet."

"Oh, Lord," she said.

"Someone must have seen him and taken him in, otherwise I'm sure he'd be here by now. I was going to start asking around . . ."

"I'll help you."

"Oh, you don't have to do that. I'll just—"

"For God's sake," she said. "What time can we decently start?"

"Well," he said. "Certainly not before eight. Tell you what—I've got to put a note up at the library saying it won't be open till noon or so. Why don't I stop by your house afterward? We can start from there."

"I'll be waiting."

She waited out by the front gate. The sun was already hot, but there was a breeze and the morning still held its early freshness. Behind her in the shade of the lindens the house would stay cool for a long time yet, the rooms standing quiet, faint patterns of sunlight spreading on the walls. If she had been asked to explain her unwillingness to stay inside alone, the question would have irritated and embarrassed her: her reasons were based not on the considered findings of the delicate and costly electronic instruments that monitored every room, but on something that would have caused not so much as a flicker of one of the sensitive needles. She was, quite simply, afraid. In the past she had read her colleagues' reports on houses where undefined shapes seemed to appear, rooms where dogs threw back their heads and howled. She had been present herself at investigations during which stones fell from the ceiling and empty chairs propelled themselves across the floor. She had observed mediums in trance speaking with what claimed to be the voices of disembodied souls, had talked with people who considered themselves possessed by demonic spirits. She had been intrigued, startled, amused, baffled—never afraid. But now, standing in the sun by the latticed gate, looking back over her shoulder at the house with its shady porch and white curtains hanging in the windows, she would not have ventured inside the luminous stillness for anything on earth.

Colin was coming up the hill. She opened the gate and went to meet him.

"You look exhausted. Did you sleep?"

"Some. You look tired too."

"We got up early. David's already gone to Boston to mail last night's film to our lab."

Colin showed interest. "You did get pictures, then?"

"Well, we hope so. We'll see."

They started with Lilac Street, Sally taking one side and Colin the other, knocking on doors and asking if anyone had seen a black and white terrier, about so big—? People were still eating breakfast at this hour. They came to the door with napkins or cups of coffee in their hands, listening with what seemed to Sally to be miraculous patience while she explained that she had lost her dog. Sometimes they turned and shouted to other people in the house, and the doorway would fill with faces, young and old, eyes fixed on her.

"How long's he been gone? Since last night? No, haven't seen him . . ."

"Little dog, huh? About how big?"

"Maybe he's got a lady friend. Sometimes our dog doesn't come home for a week."

"Did you look down by the interstate? Those cars come along there so fast . . ."

"Sorry, haven't seen him . . ."

"Hope you get him back . . ."

North of Lilac and running parallel was Flicker Street, the houses smaller and closer together. One woman's face lit up at Sally's question.

"Dog? No, I haven't seen a dog, but you didn't lose a little gray kitten, by any chance? We found her the other day and she's just the cutest thing in the world. I'd love to keep her but I'm sure someone's just frantic to have her back—"

"Thanks anyway." Sally turned away.

"I'm sorry, that doesn't help you much, does it?" The woman followed her down the steps of the house. "If I do see your dog I'll surely let you know."

At the end of the block Colin was waiting for her.

"Two people have suggested the interstate to me," he said.

"And one to me." She hesitated, then: "I can go and look—"

He interrupted her. "It doesn't make sense, Sally. It's almost a mile from here, and in the opposite direction from my house. He wouldn't run that way." He pulled his watch out of his pocket. "My sign at the library says I'll be back at noon. Let's look between here and my house."

The streets became a progression of doors, elegant or no-nonsense or shabby, painted black or red or white or green, paned with glass, brass-knockered or, in one case, exhibiting the family name ("The Turnbulls") in wrought-iron script. The faces looking out of all of them were identical in their expression of polite concern.

"Sorry, Miss, haven't seen him . . ."

"A black and white dog? I'm afraid not."

"No, can't say as I have . . ."

"Had a stray cat in here last week, but a dog, no."

Nearer Colin's house people knew Locky. They came out of their houses and looked up and down the street as if expecting him to appear.

"Not Mr. Robinson's little dog? Oh, no. I know he thinks the world of that dog."

Trees shed their dusty shade in smaller, denser patches as the morning wore on. A hot grass smell hung over everything; sound seemed suspended in the heat. Now and again a birdcall floated down, meandering like a feather caught in a warm current of air. Sally knocked, rang doorbells, repeated words that had ceased to have any meaning.

"Haven't seen that dog for almost a week, now that you mention it. When'd you say he disappeared?"

One elderly woman, hands white with flour, smiled tenderly at her. "Well, aren't you sweet to help Mr. Robinson look for him! Are you his granddaughter?"

"Just a friend."

They met on the corner, Colin shaking his head. "It's almost noon. I've got to get to work."

"Colin, I—"

"Don't worry, Sally. I'm sure he'll show up."

"I'll walk you over," she said.

On the way they could find nothing to talk about. Several people were waiting on the steps of the library, and Colin fumbled for his key.

"David and I can go out in the car as soon as he gets back," Sally said. "We can cover more ground that way."

"He'll show up," Colin said.

"Of course he will."

He stood beside her while people went inside. They were both reluctant to part without saying something more, yet there seemed to be nothing that had not already been said a number of times. In the bright sun he looked suddenly old to her, impossibly frail, but she made herself smile and touch his shoulder.

"We'll stop by later."

It was just twelve: too early, she thought, for David to be back from Boston yet. If she took a roundabout way home, along Main Street and up Linden, she could look around for Locky and probably pass time enough not to return to an empty house. Empty? It wasn't quite the word. But if there was a better one, she didn't want to use it.

Fatigue or the heat or the fruitless morning made Main Street, usually pleasant, seem hostile, its black sharp shadows of noon as harsh as those in a lunar landscape. Heat poured up from the sidewalk. A car went by, going too fast, and she winced. She had seen a dog run over once, as a child. The recollection came back now—the dull impact, the yelp cut off. She thrust the thought away. Colin was right, of course, someone had seen Locky and taken him in. Suppose the telephone had been ringing all morning? He had not been home, nor at the library either. Maybe even now it was ringing at the library; now he was picking up the receiver . . . Main Street trembled with the heat.

She saw the pickup truck belonging to the Flaggs parked

outside of Buck's. She had seen it several times since their visit to Miss Ellen, always outside Buck's, the back filled always with the half dozen towhaired children who sat without moving or talking. Now, on impulse, she crossed the street toward it. The children watched her approach. Their uncanny stillness would have unnerved her at any other time, but just now she was too preoccupied, her mind racing. It was Ellen Flagg who had told them about Julian's dogs. Jake and Jesse. If Miss Ellen knew the dogs' names—if Miss Ellen could remember . . . The small sharp voice sounded in her head, saying, *He had a pair of dogs, Julian did . . .* The dogs' names. Jake and Jesse. David's voice saying the words. *Jake and Jesse.*

Marcus Flagg came out of the store just as she reached the truck. He glanced at her briefly, then looked again. She thought he recognized her.

"Mr. Flagg?"

He was carrying a chain saw; he opened the door of the truck cab and dumped it on the front seat. The children, who had not perceptibly moved, were still looking at her. For a moment it seemed as if Flagg would get into the truck and drive away without answering her; then he turned and faced her. He said nothing. Sally hesitated and then blurted, "I have to talk to her—your aunt."

"She don't have anything more to say."

"I have to ask her something. Just one question. It's important."

His mouth moved as if he might be going to spit, but instead he said, "You can go sit by her grave if you want. I reckon even the devil can't stop her if she wants to talk."

Sally felt her throat constrict. "When did she die?"

"Two weeks ago."

"I'm sorry."

The blue eyes regarded her unblinkingly. He made a slight movement with his head; it might have been acknowledgment or merely a gesture of impatience. Then he climbed into the truck and started it up. As it pulled away she saw the children's heads swing around to face her.

So much for that. Jake and Jesse . . . She took the turn up Linden automatically. Common dogs' names, it was true. But why not Rover and Fido? Why Jake and Jesse— why anything at all? It simply didn't make sense for him to call them by name unless that was how he thought of them, so that it slipped out naturally . . . That look on his face, almost as if he were in trance. Jake and Jesse. Miss Ellen could have told her. But Miss Ellen was dead. She tore a branch off a bush she was passing, stripped the leaves off and threw the stem away, frustration rising inside her. Atmosphere was one thing, a subtle elusive influence, rising and sinking down again, impossible to isolate and say, *There.* To say that the atmosphere of the house was affecting David was to talk about psychological currents too delicate even to define with any degree of accuracy, let alone measure with any instrument. But information was something else. Information was made up of facts. If David was obtaining facts from living in the house, then that meant transfer of information. And transfer of information, without the use of normal sensory channels, meant telepathy. Between David and Julian; or between David and the residue of memory collected there in the house like dust over the years—it didn't matter which. The dogs' names would prove it, if she knew them. But she didn't, and Miss Ellen was dead.

Linden Street went steeply uphill, meeting the top of Lilac Street just at the church where Julian was buried. She hadn't been searching for Locky: halfway up the street she realized it guiltily, stopping to look back down the hill as if he might be there and she had walked right past him. But behind her the wide shady street was empty.

Two children pulling a toy wagon shook their heads solemnly when she asked them; a man parking his car considered and then shook his. Worried as she was about Locky, she couldn't keep her mind on him. Jake and Jesse . . . Was it possible they were mentioned somewhere among the personal papers in the attic—that David had seen the names in passing and retained them subconsciously? The church rose ahead of her at the top of the hill, dazzling white in the noon sun, the churchyard beside it green under its canopy of sycamores. She

turned onto Lilac Street and started down the hill, seeing
the Volkswagen parked out front long before she reached
the house. He was home, then. Should she confront him,
tell him what she thought? As a hypothesis it made
sense—a lot more, anyway, than the idea that he was
receiving information paranormally from the house. They
could go through the papers together. First they had to
find Locky, of course; that was this afternoon. But tonight . . .

The house was waiting for her.

Stillness enveloped her as soon as she closed the front
door, stillness and the now familiar radiance that filled
the entrance hall as if the walls themselves held the light
of the past like a reservoir, one moment after another
leading to this one in which she stood with her back
against the door, taking quick shallow breaths.

It was all here.

She forced herself to breathe more slowly, to take the
time to control her fear. It was simply a matter of resisting, sealing the chambers of her mind against everything
that was here, refusing the offerings of light and silence
that had led her, those other times, into something peril-
ously close to collaboration with the house. She could not
afford that now: David was here somewhere, more susceptible at this point than she was. For his sake as well as
her own she must resist. And then the music reached her,
faint and infinitely beloved over lifetimes beyond her
own, sweet with a borrowed poignancy that she could
taste without understanding why.

*I dream of Jeanie with the day-dawn smile, radiant in
gladness* . . . Even this rush of images she must deny,
these cherishing arcs and cradles of sound, smell of roses
on the wide porch in summer twilight, light hurrying
footsteps, all the colors muted and tender—she pushed
herself away from the front door and went toward the
parlor. The doors were closed; she opened them. David
sat in one of the flimsy chairs with his legs stretched
out in front of him, the music box in his lap. The lid
was open; from where she stood she could see the
gleam of the midday sun on the metal cylinder as it
turned. The melody surrounded him like the light. It
seemed a long time before he looked up and saw her: his

eyes rested on her a moment without focusing and then cleared.

"Oh—hi."

"What are you doing?" she said. It amazed her that her voice should sound so normal.

"Waiting for you." He followed her gaze to the box, hesitated and then closed the lid. The melody, abruptly truncated, hung for a moment in the air. Sally left the doorway and sat on the edge of a chair.

"We have to talk," she said.

He got up to replace the music box on the mantelpiece and sat down again. "Did Locky show up yet?" he said.

"No."

"Damn," he said.

"David, please listen to me." Something in her voice this time: he looked at her, crossed his arms.

"I'm listening."

About Jake and Jesse . . . But that was only a detail, the tip of the iceberg. Misgivings filled her: how could he have been sitting here like this, in the midst of that uncanny light and silence—sitting here with the music box as if he were helping the house set a trap for her? Or was he being used, bent as she was into some pattern more persistent than time itself? She lifted her hands, let them fall. "This whole thing has gone beyond the bounds of an investigation," she said. "We aren't in control here."

He uncrossed his arms with an impatient movement. "Sally, we've talked about this already."

"And got nowhere," she said.

"There's nowhere to get. You're under some sort of psychometric pressure from the house—perfectly normal under the circumstances. It doesn't mean we've lost control."

"Why were you playing the music box just now?" she said.

"For Christ's sake," he said.

"Well, why?"

"It intrigues me. I like the tune. I was killing time. How many reasons do you want?"

"The point I'm trying to make," Sally said carefully, "is that I'm starting to find myself doing things unconsciously, or at least unintentionally. I can usually make up reasons for them, but the reasons are after the fact."

"Well, mine are before the fact."

"How can you be so sure?" Their eyes met; hers flinched away first. Aside from the Jake and Jesse business, there was only the change in his sexual behavior to put him under suspicion. She was afraid to bring that up again and he knew it. She stared down at her hands, despising herself. David changed his tactics with a suddenness that disoriented her.

"If Julian's trying to control us, it must be for a purpose."

"A purpose?" she said.

"He must want something from us."

"David, you're assuming—"

"I'm not assuming. It's a hypothesis. If you don't like it, prove it's wrong."

"How?" she said flatly.

"Let's ask him."

He was serious. He sat looking across at her, his face intent, hands gripping his knees.

Sally said, "You mean a sitting? Ask Rosanna to come back?"

"I called Rosanna. No answer."

"Then—"

"We don't need Rosanna," he said. "We have you."

On some level she supposed she had been expecting this, so that the shock of it was at least brief, like the impact a small animal makes under the wheels of a car on a dark road. She shook her head slowly.

"No."

"Sally—"

"No! David, are you crazy? I'm not a trance medium. I don't know the first thing about it. I'd sooner try to fly a 747—it would make just about as much sense!"

"You're overreacting." He sounded very patient. "What could happen? I'll be right there—"

"You were right there the time we couldn't get Rosanna out of trance, too."

"Come on," he said. "She came out of it eventually."

"Eventually, yes. After we practically burned the house down."

"Sally."

"No."

He shrugged, got to his feet; discussion closed. "Okay. It was a suggestion. I'm perfectly willing to go on exactly as we've been doing. You're the one who's complaining about the way things are."

At some point she had started shaking and now she found she couldn't stop. He noticed it too. "Hey," he said. He came over to her chair, put his hands on her shoulders. She resisted the urge to shrug them off.

"I promised Colin we'd take the car and look for Locky this afternoon," she said. David released her.

"Okay."

≫≫ 36 ≪≪

AROUND SIX they stopped at the library. There were still two hours of daylight left in the summer sky, but most people were at home, sitting down to supper, and they had the street to themselves. The slam of the car door seemed muffled in this peace between afternoon and evening; trees stretched long shadows over the empty benches in the square. The low rays of the sun filtering through the maple above them showed it in startling depth: green, chambered, filled with stirrings of movement and fragmented gleams of light. David stood looking up at it, then shook himself.

"Let's get this over with."

Colin glanced up as they came in: Sally knew, from the tired movement of his head, that he had been doing it all day. They walked over to his desk. She let David do the talking: borrowing the dog had been his idea. The reading room was empty, chairs standing askew at the tables, a few books that needed to be shelved. On Colin's desk the pile of open reference works was impressive, but in front of him was a single sheet of paper unspoiled except for a string of words which must represent, she thought, his entire day's work. *By the end of the eighteen-eighties* . . .

"No luck yet," David was saying. "I've called in his description to the newspapers with circulation in this area—ditto the radio stations. And we've posted notices in Saunders' and Buck's and the post office . . ."

Colin said, "That's very nice of you—"

"Nice? I can't tell you how rotten I feel."

"Please, David. You couldn't have known this would happen. And I'm sure he'll show up soon."

305

David shifted his weight. "Sure he will. Anyway—will you come to supper?"

But the evening didn't have much in common with other pleasant ones. During one of a dozen silences over supper Sally noticed Locky's water dish, which neither of them had thought to remove. She let it stay—to make a point of putting it away now would only complete the atmosphere of a wake—but it added to her discomfort. Colin left early. David saw him to the front gate and then returned to the kitchen where Sally was staring out the window into the backyard.

"Jesus," he said. "Colin's really down."

Sally shrugged; night bugs buzzed in the yard. "Do you blame him?"

"Blame him? Hell, if he's thinking half the things about me I'm thinking about myself . . ." He opened the screen door and peered into the night. "That mutt's got to be somewhere." He let the screen swing shut and turned back to face her. "Sal."

"What?"

"What do you think's really happened to him?" He sounded anxious.

"I think he must have run like hell—enough to get himself disoriented."

"But why hasn't he shown up by now?"

"It's only been twenty-four hours. He may show up tomorrow or the next day or next week; he'll have been God knows where, he'll be filthy and starving, or—" She stopped, thinking, watching the darkness beyond the window.

"Or what?"

He was standing right behind her; she hadn't realized he had moved. It startled her a little. "Or he may get hit by a car or something. He may have been already."

He was quiet. Then he said, "I wonder if it's that simple."

"Meaning what?"

"Well—I don't know."

Sally turned away from the window. "Meaning he waltzed after Julian's dogs into the next dimension—do I follow you?"

"I'm afraid you do." He grinned weakly. "Sounds pretty goofy, huh?"

"Farfetched," Sally said. "I've never heard such a thing postulated."

"How about the Bermuda Triangle?"

She straightened the chairs around the kitchen table. "This isn't Bermuda."

They were on their way to the parlor when the phone rang. David made a dash for it. "Bingo, that's my ad—somebody's found him!"

But it was Jack Pennybacker, long distance from the lab.

"Jack! Did you get the film?" He motioned to Sally; they shared the receiver and she heard Jack's voice.

"Just screened it. That's why I'm calling."

"Well?"

"Well, what's all this with dogs? You two starting a kennel club up there?"

David grabbed her arm hard; she winced. "No kidding—they came out?"

"Well, the developing boys said they pushed the film and it's still pretty dark, but you can definitely see dogs."

"How many?"

"I counted three."

David let out a whoop, deafening Sally and evidently Jack as well, because there was a pause before he said, "And we got another film from you earlier, with a spirit light in it. What's going on up there, anyway?"

David laughed. "Oh, a little of this, a little of that."

"Did you ever get hold of a medium?"

"Yeah, one of the ones you suggested. Rosanna. She was terrific, but she couldn't stay long. Anyhow, we don't need her now. We're getting quite a bit of action on our own."

This time the pause was long enough for Sally to notice the pattern of static on the line. Finally Jack said, "Listen, I have to be in Boston over the weekend. Why don't I drive out, bring the films—we can screen them, you can tell me more about what's going on—how's that sound? Maybe you could even put me up overnight."

"Fine," David said. "Great. Of course we can't guarantee you any excitement, but the odds aren't bad. When do you think you'll get here?"

"Probably Sunday afternoon. I'll let you know."

"Don't forget the film."

He hung up the phone and they went into the parlor. She crossed the room to close the curtains in the bay window and heard David say, behind her, "Jack's really dying to get in on the action."

She met her own eyes in the window pane, then jerked the curtains together. "Or else he's wondering if we've cracked, and wants to see for himself."

"That's a possibility, I guess." He was beside her suddenly. "Don't you want him to come?"

Sally straightened a chair, not meeting his eyes. "Sure I do."

On the mantel the clock ticked audibly; her glance, drawn toward it, encountered the music box and flicked away. The lit lamps seemed, rather than dispensing light, to suck it in; beyond the bright solid globes the shadows were left untouched. David's chair groaned as he stretched his legs out.

"You know, I can't help thinking . . . it might have been better if nothing had shown up on that film of the dogs."

"Meaning?"

"Well, you know. If we saw them, and the camera saw them—maybe they were real."

"Maybe they were," Sally said.

"Then where in hell is Locky?"

She looked at him and he made a defensive gesture. "Oh, I know. He got scared—ran—got hit by a car—whatever. But what about when I first let him out? Why didn't he bark?"

She shrugged. "Maybe he's not as aggressive as Colin and Dr. Wilcox seem to think. Or maybe—" she stopped, considering.

"Go on."

"I'm just thinking. Maybe he didn't feel the need to defend this particular territory; maybe he wasn't here long enough to consider it his turf. Or maybe the dogs were females."

They weren't. She saw his mouth open to say it, saw him swallow the words. But where did his certainty come from? *Jake and Jesse.* The clock filled the pause skillfully with its ticking; then he rubbed his head. "Damn dog. If he's really gone for good, I guess we ought to get Colin another one."

"David, for God's sake."

"What?" he said. Then her tone penetrated. "Christ, don't start making like I've ruined his life again. You act like he's made of glass."

"He lent us the dog because he trusted us," she said, the words tight.

"Bullshit. He lent us the dog because he's sweet on you." He defused the words by yawning enormously, stood up from his chair and went out the door, moving his shoulders as though they were stiff. She heard him go down the hall to the kitchen and remained sitting where she was, speechless. Of course she knew that Colin idealized her in a way, much the same way he had idealized Ginny; she even remembered him telling her so. *She was like you.* Less an actual resemblance than an abstract one, the two of them linked by the house, herself like an echo from long ago. She could be aware of it without needing to examine it, pick it apart; and it surprised her a little that David should even have noticed. But it seemed he had, and had chosen this moment to throw it in her face. After all, if Colin had not been "sweet" on her, he would not have lent them the dog: if the dog had not been lent, it would not have been lost. Her fault—of course. She might have been angry if it hadn't been so ridiculous; as it was, her sense of the absurd battled with her sense of injustice and neither got the upper hand. David's voice came down the hall from the kitchen, casual as if nothing provocative had been said.

"If Jack's coming I guess we'd better get some beer."

A quiet night. She lay awake, listening for the buzzer, unable to sleep although she was tired. Beside her the rhythm of David's breathing formed a background for her thoughts, and that seemed appropriate: they were about him.

She was trying, as best she could in the darkness without her notebook or a calendar, to sort out the events of the last couple of weeks—to recall the occasions on which his behavior had struck her as uncharacteristic in one way or another. Putting the facts together was a shock. She could only suppose that she had desperately wanted not to see what now seemed more than obvious: that the house was influencing David in some elusive but definite way.

Wasn't it? The clarity came in flashes, dissolving in between to a mist of doubts and suspicions. He had seemed . . . she had felt . . . it was all subjective and none of it was provable, so that her careful list of disturbing instances could just as well be an inventory of her own mental and emotional disintegration. She went back to the beginning for the dozenth time. Nearly two weeks ago he had made love to her on the sitting room sofa while they were waiting for the spirit light to appear. Even leaving their past sexual history out of the question, still at the very least his timing was bizarre. They were in the middle of an experiment; and like all parapsychologists they had received enough sneers at the scientific legitimacy of their profession to make them more conscientious about its methodical aspects than many experimenters in the more accepted branches of science. In other words David's behavior was as unlikely as if he had initiated lovemaking in the midst of bubbling beakers in a chemistry lab. Unless—and she remembered her own hallucination at the time: the sunset sky, the children's voices in the distance—unless the echo of some past event had overridden his conscious intention.

She turned on her side, facing the window. How far did his susceptibility extend? There was the afternoon she had found the music box upstairs in the sitting room. He had denied moving it, but should she believe him? There were moments—when they had met the other night by the sundial, for instance, and then last night when he had said the dogs' names—when he seemed very near trance. Was it possible that in such a state he had moved the box without knowing it, put it in the room where it belonged? He seemed so little aware of what was happening, so open to an influence from which he felt himself immune.

From her own experience, especially the other night

when she had been unable to stop herself from going down to the sundial, she knew how insidious was that mingling of outside emotions and impulses with her own. The house did not push. It shaped and molded so gently that the pressure was all but imperceptible. According to David, he had gone out to the sundial entirely by his own wish, had spoken the dogs' names by chance or because they were something out of his own past experience, had played the music box alone in the house this afternoon of his own volition. And what reason did he have to think differently? He wasn't psychic. The experiments in which he had participated at the lab as either agent or percipient had never shown results attributable to anything but chance. He had never had to wonder, as she had, just whose thoughts he was thinking. Why should he start now?

That was the question. She turned again, restlessly, saw his shadowy face on the pillow. How was the house able to get through to him? What factors existed here to make him sensitive, when he had never before showed the slightest—

Not having control in a situation like this could mean big trouble.

Not just for you.

For everybody.

The words came like an impatient interruption from someone who had been listening to her dither long enough. Rosanna, sitting on the porch in the darkness, warning her. Sally turned on her back and stared at the ceiling. What was it the medium had said? That the psychic residue here in the house was too powerful, too concentrated to block. That if she were a trained medium she could channel it through herself, monitor and control it. But she was not a trained medium, and now it was more than she could handle. As a child she had tried to stop the water spurting from a garden hose, putting her hand over the cold metal spout and feeling, with a shock, the power of the water forcing its way out. Then, as now, she had been trying to protect herself: playing in the yard, her brother had turned the hose on her for a joke. The stream of water, hitting her palm, had sprayed out wildly through her fingers, soaking the two of them and everything around them.

Big trouble.
Not just for you.
For everybody.

She raised herself on one elbow and looked at David's sleeping face. She had thought he was safe, shielded from what was here; now it seemed that he was vulnerable, and she had put him in danger. Yet his face in sleep was as peaceful as a child's.

The next morning it was raining: not a downpour, just a light steady drizzle that was audible in all their silences over breakfast.

"I guess we ought to take another look around for Locky," David said without enthusiasm.

She glanced at him. "Where were you planning to look?"

"I thought we should take the car and drive along the interstate a couple of miles in each direction—just in case. Do you think it's pointless?"

"No. No, it's a good idea."

The sound of the rain rose softly to the surface again in the pause that followed. Sally was thinking. Last night she had come to the conclusion that the only possible way to convince David of what was happening was to show him clear factual evidence that he was being psychically influenced by the house. The dogs' names were her best chance. If she could find out what they were—there must be a way—and if they proved to be the names he had used, she would have the evidence she needed. Unless, of course, they were mentioned in the papers in the attic. In that case it made more sense to assume that he had seen and noted them subconsciously. She needed to search through the papers for any possible reference, and she wanted to do it without telling him what she was doing. If he were to go out by himself in the car, it would make the perfect opportunity. But how could she explain wanting to stay in the house by herself? He knew perfectly well how she felt. He would want an explanation—might even refuse to leave her here alone without one. And she didn't want to explain, didn't want to confront him until she was certain her suspicions were true.

He was looking at his watch. "It's past nine. We should get going." He left the table; she heard him open the closet door in the front hall. She got up and piled the breakfast dishes in the sink, ran water over them, still trying to think of an excuse to stay behind. David came back and tossed a jacket at her. "Come on."

Almost as if he wanted to get her out of the house. She shrugged the jacket on and followed him down the hall and out the front door, feeling the opportunity slip away and unable to think of a way to salvage it. Rain pattered down on them as they left the shelter of the lindens and opened the front gate. In the car she pulled the jacket more closely around her; the air seemed chilly. She watched as he turned the key and started the engine, then switched on the windshield wipers. The rubber blades squeaked against the glass. Beyond his profile she saw the bulk of the house in the trees, rain showing white against the dark green leaves. He let out the clutch and she said suddenly, "Would you mind going by yourself? I want to see how Colin's doing. You could drop me at the library."

It was the best she could think of, and the glance he gave her was odd enough to let her know it had been pretty poor. Then she remembered his remark the night before, about Colin being sweet on her.

"By all means," he said. She ignored his tone. Another car was coming up the hill and he had to look away from her, pay attention to his driving. Then the other car was past (the driver a solemn woman in a sou'wester) and with it the moment.

Nothing was said during the drive to Main Street. David switched on the radio, got static, switched it off. The wind was beginning to rise by the time they pulled up in front of the library; behind the shaking maple branches the yellow-lit windows had a welcoming look in the gray morning. Sally jumped out and got a gust of rain in her face. David was leaning toward the open door, saying something.

"What?"

"I said, do you want me to pick you up here on my way back?"

"Fine," she said. A vague notion of logistics came to her. "How long do you think you'll be?"

"Not much more than an hour—hour and a half at the most."

"Good luck," she said. She started up the library steps, puddled with rain and bedraggled leaves. At the door she stopped and looked back: the car was out of sight. An hour and a half at the most. She turned back toward the sidewalk and started to run.

⋙ 37 ⋘

As ALWAYS, the act of opening the front gate was the signal for a tightening of her defenses before she trusted herself to the house waiting under the trees. She was soaked with her run from the library. The stones of the front walk were slippery underfoot; overhead the heavy linden leaves spilled rain on her wet hair. The front door, swollen with damp, resisted her and then suddenly yielded, swinging open with a cool gust of air like an indrawn breath. With its closing behind her the sound of rain sank to a murmur and she stood there in the gray-lit front hall. The rain was the only sound, a soft rushing all around; together with the neutral color of the light it gave her a sense of being suspended in nothingness. She drew breath and started up the stairs, unable to resist the impulse to go on tiptoe. At the top she turned right, wanting to avoid Joshua's room and the sitting room. Linen closet, bathroom, Tonto's Room—she went by them quickly without stopping. There wasn't much time.

In the attic the rain was magnified into a dull rumbling. The fan-shaped windows showed her a view of dripping treetops against a sodden sky. David had made a work area for himself against the far wall; she switched on the bulb that hung from one of the eaves overhead and began to examine the papers he had arranged into piles over the surface of several boxes. It looked as if there were two categories, business and personal, and the personal was what she wanted to look at. Under the harsh light she knelt and started on the task.

Letters, newspaper clippings, a pocket-sized New Testament, a chart of bird migration in the United States. And not only papers; there was also a baby's bib embroidered with rabbits and an envelope of film negatives. Rain blew against the windows in sudden gusts; the panes rattled. She became acutely aware of how little time there was, picked up one pile and began to leaf through it quickly. Some things she could dismiss at a glance: three seashells sketched on a scrap of paper, a picture of an owl carefully clipped from a newspaper—it was amazing what people saved, and what David had considered noteworthy. She finished that pile and chose another, going through it as rapidly as she could, skimming letters and news clippings for any names they might contain, reading too quickly to receive anything more than a cloudy, pastel-tinted impression of an earlier and gentler epoch. Mrs. Lowrie had sung *"Voi che sapete"* at one of Mrs. Bristowe's musical evenings . . . A plaque was to be dedicated in memory of the Howard children . . . In the matter of his son's future Mr. Welles wished to consult Reverend Gilfoy . . . "It is freezing here in the mornings and gets very hot in the afternoons" . . . "So that pretty well takes care of next Monday" . . . "There were fireworks in town, but we could not see them from where we were" . . . "We had some music last evening and I thought of you" . . .

The dusty touch of the old papers clung to her hands. It was strange, now that she thought about it: all the hours David had spent up here, steeping himself in the past, poring over these trivial fragments that were somehow eloquent in their meagerness. But she didn't have much time, and haste made her clumsy: she tore an envelope addressed in a lacy hand to Mrs. Joshua Gilfoy. The letter came free. She unfolded it and read: *I can't tell you how much it comforted me to have you come and sit with me on Friday. And I wanted to report what happened after you left. You probably didn't notice that the light from the window was shining on your hair. But soon after you had gone Teddy came in to me and stood a while by my bed and finally said, Mother, was that an angel? I can hear you laughing as you read this. But I thought about saying yes.*

Somewhere in the house below her there was a sound. Wasn't there? She did not move except to lift her head, straining to hear. Nothing now, but she had heard something—a door closing, or a footstep echoing on a stair. Carefully she put the letter down on top of the other papers and crouched there listening. There was nothing. She reached again for the letter and simultaneously heard the protesting screech of a window flung open on the floor below, the noise stripping every nerve.

She sat back on her heels. The papers could wait. Replacing the pile with hands that shook ever so slightly she told herself that it was not a question of courage but of good sense. The house was using her to come alive and she could not fight it. She could only retreat. Whatever curiosity, scientific or personal, she might satisfy by cooperating with it was more than quenched by the memory of Rosanna's warning—the motion of her hand, fingers outflung, expressing a power immense beyond language.

Go.

Get out.

Now.

Down the attic steps slowly, hesitating on the bottom one with her hand on the door to the hall. The sounds had stopped. For perhaps half a minute she stood listening, hearing nothing but her own heartbeat. She was too well trained to run. On some level, standing there, she was grateful for the hours of study and fieldwork that had made her, if not comfortable, at least familiar with the kind of event that apparently violates the basic laws of everyday reality. She had seen dishes fly untouched from shelves, watched dice fall in predicted patterns as obedient as circus seals. She had never actually seen an apparition, although she had talked to people who believed they had, and there were even times (she recalled them all with painful clarity in this moment) when she had expressed a wish to see one. Now, standing at the foot of the attic steps and bracing herself to open the door to the hall, she did not lose control. But she was aware that her pulse was hammering and her knees shaky, and she had a deep clear knowledge that she did not want to see an apparition, now or ever. She did not want to experience any of it—sounds, sensations, the house's whole repertoire of phenomena.

Just go.

Now.

She pushed the door open and stepped through it and

saw then, unmistakably, a man's tall shadowy figure framed in the muted light at the far end of the corridor. Her head started to spin. It was Julian, she saw him; then the next instant it was David, as startled as she was, stopping short, then coming forward quickly.

"What the hell, Sally? I thought you were at the library!"

To her disgust she found that she couldn't speak. She looked at him, shaking her head, seeing again the instant in which he was Julian, then David—

"What are you doing here?" he was saying.

Suddenly her voice was there; she could feel it, and the words: "I couldn't face Colin." His face uncertain, not quite believing her, and she said, "What are *you* doing here?"

The pause opened between them, widening as they watched. Another second and it would be too wide to bridge.

"I forgot my driver's license," David said.

She looked at him.

"I figured since I was going to be out on the interstate, I'd better have it along. The state cops are so—you know." Gesturing.

"Yes," she said. "I know."

"I heard something in the attic—I thought—well, Jesus, Sal. You gave me a scare."

"And you me."

David laughed: too loudly, or it might have been the silence. She realized that the rain had stopped.

"This is classic, isn't it?" he said. "The two of us sneaking around . . ."

"Classic," she said.

"What were you doing in the attic, anyway?"

She had been waiting for that question; the answer was ready. "I went up to see if the roof was leaking."

"Good girl," he said, and she wondered if the praise was for her conscientiousness or for the readiness of the lie.

"What time is it?" she said.

"Almost ten. Let's give this interstate thing another shot."

She closed the attic door behind her and at the same instant the door of the Thistle Room, a little way down the hall, swung inward. They exchanged a look.

"Cross draft," David said. But together they went to the door and looked inside. The room was empty, rainy morning sky outside the window. She stood in the doorway while David went in, watching as he moved around the room, small space of patterned wallpaper, old-fashioned furniture: bed, dresser, rocking chair. The chair, she was grateful to see, was motionless. He stopped by the window; in the dull-lit floor his reflection seemed to descend limitlessly beneath him. "What's this?" he said, and she looked. On the white-painted sill some loose rose petals had been arranged in three neat rows: as they watched, a breeze moved the curtain and pushed them into a jumbled pile. It had all happened so gently, so quickly and unexpectedly, that Sally found herself doubting what she had seen. David scooped up the petals in one hand and held them out to her. Beneath lifted brows he was smiling.

That night, while he was taking a shower, she managed to go through the rest of the papers he had set aside. When she had finished she was fairly certain that no reference to the dogs was contained among them: the process had been too hurried for her to be absolutely sure, but under the circumstances it was the best she could do. The business papers remained. But a glance told her that those piles were mostly ledger books and receipts, and in any case the sound of the shower shutting off sent her back downstairs to the parlor, trying to keep her steps quiet on the stairs. She was too deep in the situation for its irony to strike her more than obliquely: that in this house the chance of encountering her own husband should make her jumpy as a cat. Again it struck her as odd that he should have spent so much time up in the attic—an enormous amount in proportion to the actual task of sorting the papers. There must have been hours when he had simply sat doing nothing.

Nothing? She remembered the afternoon she had been alone in the house, when it had come alive around her. If that could happen to her, why not to David? The thought sent a spreading chill through her. She had already come to terms with the possibility that he might no longer be psychically immune to the house, but the idea of him up in the attic day after day, actively collaborating with it, was too much. Was she being paranoid? He had always wanted a genuine psychic experience; she knew how eagerly he would welcome such a thing, and how little prepared for it he actually was. An image from the Tarot came to her: the young Fool, head high and a rose in one hand, blithely stepping out over a sheer cliff. A moment's utter panic clutched her before the scientific self kicked in again. This was all hypothesis. If she wanted to check it, all she had to do was ask. But she didn't know if she was ready for the answer.

Picking up the new issue of the *Psychical Research Journal* she turned the pages, listening for sounds upstairs. There he came out of the bathroom, went into their bedroom; she heard him moving around. Now he was coming downstairs. She looked down at the magazine.

He came in with his head wrapped in a towel; she glanced up. Their eyes met; they smiled.

"Good issue?"

"Not very."

David sat down on the rug by her chair and began drying his hair. After a moment he twisted around and put his head in her lap; the unexpected gesture touched her and she began, a little awkwardly, to rub his head with the towel. They did not talk. His eyes were closed. Sally was struggling with a volatile brew of emotions—mistrust of him and his rapport with the house, guilt about sneaking around behind his back; the warm weight of his head against her thigh added sexual tension to the mixture and completed her misery. She had a dizzying urge to talk, confess all her doubts, fears, hypotheses reasonable and otherwise. But how could she, when he wouldn't listen, when he had come back to the house that morning for God only knew what reason? She couldn't fathom him anymore, and it scared her. Against the white towel his wet curling hair looked as dark as Julian's. He yawned. Across the hall in the library the grandfather clock began to strike and the clear brass tones seemed to go straight through her, each mellow circle of sound renewed at the moment of fading, each trembling with the burden of those preceding it until the last softened into a mere vibration of the air and she felt the tears rise and spill over like a continuation of the sequence. She wiped them away but more came. David had opened his eyes and was looking at her.

"Sally, what's wrong?"

She blinked the tears back. He got to his knees, leaving the towel in her lap, and put his arm around her. "What is it?"

"I can't stand it here," she said. "I can't stand it. David, we can't stay here."

His arm tightened. "But we can't just quit, sweetheart. Not now. Jack's coming on Sunday."

"After Sunday, then." She knew better than to expect him to relinquish the chance of showing Jack his prize, his big fish. "After Sunday let's go."

"Sal," he said.

"Please."

"Do you hate it that much?"

"It isn't that." A shudder went through her.

"I don't understand you," he said. "Look at what we've got here. It's a chance, a perfect chance, to really learn something, and you want to throw it away."

"I'm scared," she said softly. His other arm closed the circle, drawing her close.

"There's no reason to be scared."

"How do you know?"

"I just know."

How? But she didn't say it; she didn't want to know. Not now, when he was holding her, when this was all that mattered. She pressed her face down into the hollow of his shoulder, letting her body accept the closeness it craved, shutting her mind to thoughts and questions. After a minute he reached past her and turned out the lamp and pulled her down on the rug beside him.

If indeed there exist places where the boundary between two realities becomes fluid: if in these places past, present, and future exist as a seamless web and distinctions such as those of subject and object are obliterated—if such places exist and this is one of them, how then distinguish in the darkness of an old house one human embrace from another? The darkness is out of time. Every touch and whispered word has been given and spoken not once but always, returning on itself in shimmering echoes within the compass of some room where the web of now-time crosses and recrosses, weaving together all that is and has been in a pattern beyond understanding. Names and faces shift and blur, mingling in the way of dreams. Identity slips away. We are you, her, him, us, and the echoes answer themselves, reverberations in infinity.

➤➤➤ 38 ◄◄◄

THE WHITE DOG was in the lead, ears pricked and tail waving, clearly visible against the dark clump of bushes. The black one followed a few paces behind, its motion more perceptible than its actual shape. A moment later they both disappeared behind the bushes.

"Damn," David said. "We should have put the camera in one of the upstairs windows. Damn."

"Here they come again," Jack Pennybacker said.

The black dog was in front now: Sally could distinguish its blunt muzzle. She stared at the flickering square of light on the wall. The film was grainy and very dark. "There's Locky," David said. A blurred shape had appeared at the edge of the frame. They watched as it seemed to move toward the center. The projector whirred. David squirmed in his chair.

"I can't see a goddamn thing."

Jack clicked something on the projector; the film froze on a single frame. "Look, here's your little dog, right?" His finger dipped into the cone of light, an enormous shadow indicating a small blur about a third of the way across the frame. "Right?"

"Yeah."

"And here's the white dog . . ."

"Yeah—"

"That's the sundial," Sally said.

"The what?" Jack's face, half light, half dark in the spill of light from the projector, turned toward her.

"There's a marble sundial in the middle of those bushes."

They all looked at the whitish patch near the middle of the frame.

"Then where's the white dog?"

"Can we run it back a little?" David said. Jack clicked something; the film came to life and the Locky-blur retreated to the left. He clicked again and the film stopped.

"There's Locky."

"Okay. Now is *that* the white dog?"

David looked at Sally.

"Yes," she said.

"Where's the black one?"

David said, "I think I'm going blind."

Sally leaned forward. "I don't see the black dog."

"How about this thing here?"

She narrowed her eyes, then shook her head. "Maybe."

"Let's just run it all the way through," David said. "Maybe this is one of those movies with a terrific ending."

Jack set the film in motion again. The blur that was Locky moved toward the center. There were other blurs, whitish against the mottled flickering gray.

"It moved," Jack said. "That thing you said was a sundial moved."

David said, "I can't see a goddamn thing."

Sally said, "Where's Locky?"

Jack ran the film back. "Is that him?"

"I can't tell."

They looked at one another in the dark, shrugging. "It'll never make Cannes," David said. "Let's see the other one."

The film of the light was a disappointment. To Sally it looked smaller and not so bright as she remembered it; at moments she lost sight of it altogether. A fuzzy blob dancing along the bottom edge of the frame intrigued them until they identified it as the top of Locky's head. The film ended abruptly in a dazzle of scratched endfootage. No one said anything. David switched on a lamp: the library appeared around them. Jack started the film rewinding and leaned back, clasping his hands behind his head, looking at David, then at Sally.

"Interesting," he said.

David stumbled over an empty beer bottle beside his chair; it rolled hollowly. He bent to pick it up and said, "Sally saw the dogs before Miss Ellen told us about them. She just assumed they belonged to a neighbor. But the local vet says no."

Jack was lighting his pipe. "Did you check with the previous tenants to find out if they'd ever seen any such dogs?"

"Yes," Sally said. "They hadn't. But several of them have reported the sound of a dog barking, under circumstances that may have been paranormal."

"So your apparitional dogs are audible as well as visible?" Jack said.

She frowned. "Well, they've always been perfectly silent when I've seen them. So it's hard to tell. And by the way, I didn't mention seeing them until after Miss Ellen told us about them. So it's not evidential."

A cloud of smoke rose from Jack's pipe; his eyes followed it to the ceiling and descended slowly to rest on her. "I trust you. Unofficially, of course."

David had been collecting the empty beer bottles; now he set them on the table next to the projector. The film had finished rewinding and he shut the projector off. "Look, Jack. How could those mutts be paranormal and show up on photographic film?"

Pipestem between his teeth, Jack opened both hands. "You're asking me? You've seen the experiments with Ted Serios. How does he do it? Apparently he's able to project his own mental images onto photographic film—"

"But this wasn't a mental image. It was visual. An apparition."

"Who's to say an apparition isn't mental as well as visual?" Jack said. "Call the apparition of the dogs a collaboration between agent and percipient—the house and you. Now suppose the camera picks up your perception of the apparition, the way it does with Serios. Of course it would have to be very powerfully projected—" He broke off, glanced at Sally, then began examining the bowl of his pipe. David looked at her. She shifted in her chair.

"Look, you two. I'm not Ted Serios."

No one said anything. Finally David said, "But what happened to Colin's damn dog?"

"There you've got me," Jack said. "How long has it been?"

"Getting close to a week."

"He may show up yet. The others haven't been back, I take it?"

David looked embarrassed. "We haven't really been watching."

"Hm," Jack said. "Hm." Smoke rose from his pipe.

Sally said, "If you're thinking the next time the dogs show up there'll be three of them, I'm going to sign you up to write scripts for late-night television."

"I'm not thinking anything," Jack said. He smiled at her through clouds of pipe smoke, his thin face with its short beard and balding head like a genial apparition itself. "Oh, I almost forgot." He took a paper out of his jacket pocket, unfolded it and fanned the smoke away. Sally saw a typed paragraph. "Here's your tramp."

"No kidding—you found him?" David almost knocked over the neat row of empty beer bottles in his eagerness to grab the paper. "Nice work, Jack . . ." His voice trailed off as he started to read.

"Well?" Sally said.

"Okay, wait a second. Okay. Male Caucasian, age approximately fifty, reddish hair and beard, eyes hazel, five-ten, a hundred and forty pounds. Name unknown. Cause of death, broken neck. Found in the early morning hours of February eighth, 1953—that postdates pindar, Murray and Sterling—at the foot of a tree in the backyard. Apparently fell while trying to climb the tree. Neighbors heard a dog barking and called police. No identification on the body and he fitted no description of any missing person."

Sally hummed the opening bars of the *Twilight Zone* theme and then said, "Do tramps commonly carry ID?"

They ignored her. "What struck me," Jack said, "was the bit about the dog barking. And the fact that the guy was trying to climb a tree."

David looked at him, then at the paper in his hand. "My God, you mean Julian's dogs might have chased him—"

"Well, it just seems like an interesting connection," Jack said. Sally could see that he was trying to appear scientifically detached, but she knew he was as bad as David. Going through the house that afternoon they had been like a couple of kids, both talking at once, trading theories like so many baseball cards. Myers, Tyrrell, Johnson, Schmeidler, Bozzano—field theory, infestation, collective hallucination, aetheric memory: to them it was the ultimate Sherlock Holmes mystery, a challenge to which they brought their wits and all the latest tricks and gadgets of the scientific trade. To her, lagging behind as they went room by room, the glib enthusiasm echoing back through the sunny, dusty air was like an abrasive dragged across her nerves. She tried to take some reassurance from the discussion of theories and experiments and technical monographs; she was, after all, a scientist—an enlightened being, a creature of intellect. Knowledge equals power. But deeper down, some other more primitive self, less educated but wiser perhaps, flinched in the face of all that the theories failed to encompass. She felt it mainly as a wavering of actual physical equilibrium, a shifting of accepted boundaries—as if her muscles were more sensitive to the atmosphere of the house than was possible for her mind. The light slanting through windows and open doors was buoyant and serene, the voices ahead of her trusted and familiar. Then why this sense of walking a fragile bridge over an abyss? Surely science had the situation under control. She called up the maxim of her student days: *Nothing in life is to be feared; it is only to be understood.* But the part of her that understood best was filled with misgiving.

They put Jack in the master bedroom, but the night proved uneventful. Twice David woke her, leaning over to pick up his watch and look at it, throwing himself back on the pillow with a sigh. It was hard on him and she could be sorry—almost. But what did he expect? Hauntings were notoriously temperamental—or perverse if you wanted to go that far. They happened when and where they were most unwanted, couldn't be produced or reproduced in a laboratory setting, were as touchy as chess wizards. And Jack knew that. But it didn't stop David from wanting to show off his prize.

The next morning while he was making breakfast she found Jack out on the front porch filling his pipe.

"You smoke too much."

"I know," Jack said. He was squinting out toward the street, across the yard flecked with gold and green toward the white pickets dazzling in the sun. "This is a nice little town. Unspoiled, I think they call it. Reminds me of the idyllic childhood I never had."

Sally leaned on the porch railing, breathing the faint cool fragrance of roses overhead. "How'd you sleep?"

"Like a baby."

"David was counting on some action," she said. "He's very disappointed."

Jack grunted. "When he's been in this business as long as I have he'll get used to it."

A car went down the hill, the sound of the motor fading into the morning distance. Jays squawked in the trees.

"I miss you," Jack said. "I've been thinking about you a lot."

It took her by surprise, but he had always been able to do that. She didn't look at him. They had been lovers briefly, four years earlier during her first stint at the lab, and since she had broken it off he had never shown a hint of anything more than friendliness. The whole thing had been understandable enough: her confrontation with telepathy had shaken her faith in the omnipotence of science and in herself—she had needed steadying and Jack had given it to her. But he had a wife and kids; she had despised herself for continuing the affair after their first more or less accidental encounter, and it had ended in a few months, before David had come to work at the lab. She had never told David, and she did not think he knew about it. Through the open door the smell of frying bacon, mingling with the roses, reached her.

"I wouldn't have said anything," Jack said, "but you seem pretty unhappy. I thought maybe . . ." He lit his pipe and puffed, letting the sentence drift with the smoke.

"It's not exactly a picnic here," Sally said. "There's a lot of pressure."

"From the house?"

She looked at him then, sharply. "Yes. From the house."

"Don't get me wrong. I'm very fond of Dave."

"Good," she said. They stood at the railing looking at each other. At last Jack laughed.

"Okay, okay. Don't give me an inch—I didn't expect you to. I know you."

He left soon after breakfast. She and David saw him to the gate, said their goodbyes, watched the car down the hill. When David went back to the house she lingered behind, wondering if she had been stupid, if she had thrown away her chance. She could have confided in Jack, told him the whole situation here; he would have listened, at the very least offered a new perspective. But she could not expose David to him like that, not when things were as complicated as they were, not when he said *I know you* in that smug way, with its biblical implications, as if he were reminding her. And she didn't need reminding.

Bright sunlight danced at the edge of the trees; beyond the shimmering curtain of leaves the house was almost invisible in the shade. It was hot standing at the gate— running a hand through her hair she felt the top of her head giving off heat like an oven.

"Morning, ma'am."

She turned, recognized the blue-shirted postman on the sidewalk.

"Hi."

"Going to be another hot one today." He held out the mail, some scientific journal folded in half and rubber-banded. Sally took it.

"Thanks."

He glanced back once as he moved off, saw her still watching him, raised his hand in a sheepish wave. He knew about the house, wondered about David and her— the whole town probably did.

Hey, mister. Do I look like I've seen a ghost?

David was upstairs in their bedroom; coming in the front door she could hear him bumping around. She climbed the stairs and found him making the bed. He plumped pillows, pulled up the spread, smoothing out the last of the wrinkles and glancing up at her.

"Did you see Jack's face? He was dying of envy. If there'd been any action at all last night we couldn't have gotten him out of here with a crowbar." He turned toward the dresser and began rummaging in a drawer. Sally sat on the bed, watching his bent back, twirling the rubber band on the magazine around one finger. Natural that he should need to square his disappointment over the house's failure to perform for Jack. But she wasn't sure what kind of rejoinder he wanted, and so she made none. He didn't seem to notice. He found what he was looking for in the drawer—it turned out to be a belt—and buckled it on. "Christ, I wonder how long it's been since he was out in the field. Must be boring as hell running those Ganzfeld series day in and day out. No wonder the poor guy gets popeyed at the idea of a little excitement."

"I'm sure he could arrange for more time in the field if he wanted to," she said, and caught herself. Defending David to Jack, Jack to David. Whose side am I on? The rubber band, twisted beyond endurance, snapped all at once, stinging her hand, and she looked down. There was a letter tucked in the fold of the magazine. The handwriting, shaky letters on a long white envelope, was one she recognized immediately. It was Samuel Gilfoy's.

"The point is," David began; then he saw the letter and stopped. "Who's that from?"

"Mr. Gilfoy." She picked it up. "Addressed to you."

He was already reaching for it; she couldn't decipher his face. She handed it over, watching while he tore it open and skimmed it.

"What's he want?"

David shrugged a little. "He's asking if we want to extend our lease."

"May I see?"

His hesitation was something she chose to ignore. He handed her the letter and she read:

Dear Mr. Curtiss, In answer to your inquiry about extending the lease on the Lilac Street house, I am perfectly willing to do so. Your suggestion of a lease of one year, open to renewal, is satisfactory to me and I am having one drawn up as you requested. You should receive it shortly. I am glad to learn that the house suits you. Yours sincerely, Saml. Gilfoy.

She kept on looking at the letter far longer than was necessary for her to memorize every word, because she did not want to look at David. When she did so at last, he met her eyes without flinching.

"When were you planning to tell me about this?" she said.

He shrugged again. "As soon as I knew something positive."

"But it wasn't worth discussing with me beforehand?"

He sat down on the end of the bed, facing her. "Look, I know you don't like the idea. But how can we stop now? August thirty-first our lease is up. That's less than three weeks away. Can you honestly say that in three weeks you'll be able to walk out, lock the door, and say 'That's that'?"

"I could do it tomorrow," she said. "Nothing would make me happier."

David plucked at the bedspread. "I don't understand you, Sally. This is the chance of a lifetime—a house that's really haunted and available for as long as we want it. Any psychical researcher in the world would give his right arm for an opportunity like this."

"Then let them." The air between them jumped suddenly with her intensity. "Let somebody else come in here and read capacitance meters till their eyes fall out. But not us, David. Not you and me."

"And let somebody else get all the credit?" He looked as horrified as if she had asked him to burn the house to the ground. "Is that what you want?"

"I want," Sally said, "to wake up in the morning knowing exactly who I am. And exactly who you are."

"Don't start that again."

"I'm not starting anything. I'm telling you how I feel—not that you seem to care. I've told you before how I feel about this house, and what do you do? You write to Mr. Gilfoy and say we're having such a wonderful time we'd like to stay for a year."

"That isn't what I said." His tone was patient. She picked up the letter.

" 'I am glad to learn that the house suits you.' "

"Look," David said. "I told him things were going well from an experimental point of view. I thought they were. I think they are. Doesn't that matter to you?"

She met his eyes. "I've told you what matters to me."

After a moment he looked down, then back at her,

fingers tapping his knee. "Okay. I'll make a deal with you."

"A deal?"

"Yes. The main reason I wanted to extend the lease was to give things time to develop. But I think we can hurry them along—if you'll cooperate."

Sitting on the white sun-patterned bedspread with the birds outside the window racketing in the summer trees, Sally felt cold. "What do you mean?"

"A sitting to contact Julian."

She was too chilled to be angry. "No, David. I told you. No."

"Okay." He started to get up and she panicked.

"Wait a minute. What if I said yes?"

"I told you. It would speed things up. We probably won't need to extend the lease."

"All right," she said. The panic had crystallized into icy clarity. "That's your half of the deal. Now listen to mine. We leave the day after the sitting. No matter what happens—whether we contact Julian or not—we leave. We leave this house."

It startled him. "But suppose we contact him, and—"

She grimaced. "You can say goodbye to him."

His whole body went taut; he leaned toward her. "Then you'll do it? You'll do a sitting?"

"I didn't say that. Would you agree to those terms?"

He took a breath, then: "Yes." They stared at each other for an instant; she was aware of his racing excitement, her own cold stillness.

"Let me think about it," she said.

And she did think about it. In order to reject the deal outright, she would have had to possess the hope of an alternative solution, and she did not. She had already, on the previous Friday, taken an hour out from grocery shopping to sit in the pay phone booth at Kimball's, calling one source after another in an effort to discover the names of Julian's dogs.

It had been a series of blind alleys. The older of the two kennels in the surrounding area had been in business only sixteen years; they were understandably appalled when she admitted to looking for a record of a sale that had taken place around the year 1900. A call to the

Boston Public Library (now that she needed Colin most, she was shy of using him) directed her to the American Kennel Club, but there too the bottom fell out of her search. White, it seemed, was a disqualifying color for the German shepherd breed; such a dog would not have been accepted for registration. And while black was one of the acceptable colors for a Labrador retriever, the Labrador had not been officially recognized as a breed until 1903 in England, and some years later in the United States. A last-resort call to the County Health Department put her in bleak possession of the information that dogs had not required licensing in the county until 1947.

As her chance of confirming the dogs' names dwindled to nothing, so did her hope of proving to David that he was susceptible to the house. She had to admit that it was a long shot in any case: a trivial tidbit of information that was, nonetheless, one of the few pieces of potential proof in this maddeningly subjective case. Jake and Jesse—what else was there? A feeling here, a hallucination there, doubts and questions overshadowing all else. Even if she had been able to find positive proof that David had paranormally acquired the knowledge of the dogs' names, did he even need such proof? It was within the scope of the possible that he was aware of the house's influence on him, that he was collaborating with it in some more or less conscious way. And that was what she was up against.

Until now she had refused even to consider the notion of a sitting with herself as the medium. She had been present at a number of sittings in the course of her career in parapsychology, but always as an observer, watching with detachment and a measure of distaste. Among her colleagues she was more skeptical than most about the quality of the paranormal information obtained through mediums, whom she regarded, in general, as irresponsible and slightly unbalanced. Now, added to that mistrust, there was the disturbing memory of her interaction with Rosanna, whose personality and professionalism had made her less easy to dismiss. She had felt not only challenged but bested by Rosanna, and it had shaken her. Now she had to push beyond all that: try and weigh the possible drawbacks and advantages of a sitting as unemotionally as she could.

First of all there was her inexperience. She had never been trained as a medium. Certainly she had seen professional mediums at work, but that experience would help her no more than an afternoon spent watching a unicyclist help someone astride the single wheel for the first time. She had never developed her own psychic gifts; in fact, she had consistently stifled them except for her telepathy work at the lab. Who knew if she could rely on them in a crucial situation? And then there was David. It was fairly clear that a sitting would be limited to the two of them. If Rosanna was out, that left Colin, and she refused to subject him to such a situation. That meant she had to trust David, and she didn't think she did.

The next point, her fear of the house and what was in it, her sense that time and identity were skewed here in some elusive but menacing way, could not be considered rationally. She left it, and went on to the final question of what would be accomplished by a sitting. Even if she got up the nerve to go into trance, even if they managed somehow, through beginner's luck, to contact Julian, what then? The idea that he wanted something from them—that there was a question they could answer or a request they could fulfill—was simply David's sense of melodrama working overtime. More probably things would go in circles, the way they had during the first sitting with Rosanna: he was lost, he wanted to go home. And there was no answer to that. To think they could offer him some recognition, some comfort, wasn't feasible. What they were confronting was more than likely an echo, a pattern, nothing that could hear them or understand. And if it wasn't? Then she didn't know. And she didn't want to.

As usual when she wanted to retreat from David, she spent the afternoon working in the yard. It was not something that had interested her at all until this summer; the process of planting and weeding and pruning had always seemed tedious, a waste of time for anyone with better things to do. But she found a deep satisfaction in the way summer, under her bumbling auspices, had transformed the yard from its initial barrenness into a green place. The roses around the sundial had become respectable enough to merit the attention of some kind of bug, and she had gotten a box of white powdered poison from Buck's guaranteeing the death of a long list of creatures. She dusted the bushes with it now. The roses were her triumph; every flower won from the sparse-leaved stems seemed like a miracle. They would bloom through November if the snow held off that long; then in the spring there would be first the crocuses and forsythia, then daffodils along the fence, irises by the porch steps, and everywhere the lilacs, best loved of all, their aching fragrance warming the still-cool air, and the linden leaves unfolding heart-shaped on the black branches of the trees . . .

The wind blew, a cool breath from the trees touching her where she stood in the hot sun, holding the box of poison in an unsteady hand. They were all around her, bright and fragrant, the ghosts of flowers long dead, as she stood looking around the yard. Then she hardened herself and the banks of color shimmered and faded. A whispering of innumerable leaves came to her. In the shade of the trees the rising white walls of the house seemed to waver as if they too would disappear.

"Sally?"

She spun around. It was Colin, coming along the side of the house, the sun glinting off his glasses. She went to meet him.

"I knocked at the front door, but there was no answer. I thought you might be out here." He was carrying an envelope, which he held out to her. "I came across this. I didn't know if you were still collecting Gilfoy trivia, but I thought you might be interested."

She set the box of poison down on the grass and took the envelope. "I was going to call you," she said. "Have you—heard anything?"

"Not yet." There was a pause, then he gestured at the envelope. "Aren't you going to look at it?"

She opened the envelope and took out its contents: a photocopy of a page from a book, several paragraphs marked in red. She glanced at the first couple of sentences and felt her heart close in on itself, then looked up at him, at his expectant face.

"Go ahead, read it. It mentions Reverend Gilfoy."

But she knew that already: she had recognized the first

sentence. It was the diary excerpt he had found for her, weeks ago, when she had first started to research the Gilfoys at the library. He looked so pleased with himself that she lowered her eyes to the page, hoping her face didn't show what she felt. And in fact she did read it, or try to, here and there a phrase penetrating her distraction. *Every Sunday, of course, we went to church, wearing our very best clothes. Papa always wore his beaver hat . . .*

How could he have forgotten? She kept wanting to shake him, say bluntly, "You gave me this already. Don't you remember?" Colin who was so sharp, who never missed a beat. Of course anyone could forget; it had been weeks, and so much had happened since—but she felt betrayed by this lapse that showed his frailty so clearly, made her see him all at once as an old man, someone to be humored and protected. No longer an equal, the friend she needed. *And Louisa once confessed to me that when she said her prayers she always imagined God as looking like Reverend Gilfoy . . . He was not quite perfect, however, for he was completely tone-deaf, and used to roar out the hymns in a monotone.* It had been Colin who had remembered that fact, who had pointed out how unlikely it was that the music box had been a gift from Joshua Gilfoy to his wife. *I heard that he had remarried, a woman much younger than he . . .*

"This is wonderful, Colin." The gentleness she reserved for young children, animals, and old people: how naturally it came. "Come on inside; I'll make some tea. David must be up in the attic or he would have heard you knocking."

In the kitchen he sat at the table while she put water on to boil. Turning away from the stove she caught him looking out the window the way she herself had looked a hundred times since last Tuesday, as if Locky would suddenly, miraculously, be there, sniffing around the hedges, cocking his head at some unfamiliar sound—as if force of wish and will could conjure him up. If only it could. Borrowing the dog had been such a stupid whim, unnecessary and inconclusive. She crossed the room and sat down at the table across from him, heart aching for him, her resentment gone. After a moment he shifted his eyes from the window to her face and smiled a little, and she put her hand on his where it lay, old and freckled and veined, on the table; and that was how David found them.

He appeared in the doorway quietly; the movement, more than any sound, was what caught her attention. She looked up.

"Hope I'm not interrupting anything," he said. The words had an edge; she saw by the startled motion of Colin's head that he had heard it too. She squeezed his hand before withdrawing hers, then got up and went to the cupboard for mugs.

"We're having tea. Want some?"

"Sure." But he kept his belligerent stance in the doorway. She met his glance over her shoulder; he glowered back at her. It was so unlike David, whose polite indifference usually increased in proportion to his anger, that she remained motionless for a second, staring at him, thinking, What did I do?

He lent us the dog because he's sweet on you.

Hope I'm not interrupting anything.

She looked away, making her hands move, taking down mugs from the shelf, setting them on the table. Was he honestly jealous? Of Colin? It didn't seem possible—might even have been funny, but his behavior was so strange. It was making Colin uncomfortable, and her as well. He crossed the room and sat down at the table. Sally found three teabags in the cabinet and put one in each cup; the water had started to boil and she took it off the stove and poured it. There wasn't enough for three cups.

"Two's company," David said. The obvious sneer got under her skin; she started to answer him angrily and found the kettle being taken out of her hand.

"I'll put some more water on," Colin said.

"Thanks."

He filled the kettle and set it on the stove while they watched, doing a creditable job of lighting the burner, for someone unfamiliar with the temperamental Jezebel. Sally complimented him on it as he sat down and he smiled.

"All those old iron monsters are alike. I grew up with one."

"I nearly burned my eyebrows off the first twenty times," she said.

"It just takes practice."

"If you live long enough," she said, thinking that this conversation must be how it felt to be an acrobat: this launching of self into space, hoping and trusting to be caught by someone whose frail human strength was no greater than your own—the effort, the strain, the emptiness of David's silence below. There was no net; they would fall forever.

At last conversation failed. They sat without speaking, the two cups of tea unclaimed on the table. David's hostility seemed to flatten the air itself. Sally, only guessing at the reason, felt as if she had slipped into some nightmare, not so much terrible as absurd. He couldn't seriously be jealous of Colin. That was too ridiculous. But of course she could hardly say so in front of Colin, whose uneasiness was obvious as he sat tracing the edge of the table with one finger, utterly bewildered by David's unspoken displeasure. He clearly felt, as she did, obscurely guilty for no reason at all, as if they must be at fault in order to merit this kind of treatment. In the silence a sound became audible: the faucet dripping, musical and insouciant, into a pan of water in the sink.

Plip. Plip.

At last David shoved back his chair and got up from the table, went to the sink and wrenched the tap handle. Sally bit her lip. Silence descended again—then another drop fell.

Plip.

David swore and jerked the handle again.

"It probably needs a new washer," she said, because she had to say something, had to camouflage the barely controlled violence of his behavior. He grunted, possibly in response, and strained at the handle, the tendons standing out in his neck.

Plip.

Sally looked away; then there was a sudden gush of water as he slammed the tap open and let it run full blast, splashing and clattering among the things in the sink.

Under cover of the noise Colin got to his feet. "I really have to be going," he said.

He hadn't touched his tea. Sally stood too, trying to catch his eye, but he was too uncomfortable to look at her. David twisted the tap handle hard to the closed position once more; in the ensuing hush she prayed and her prayers were answered. No more drops fell. David turned and looked at them.

"Going already, Colin?" He seemed himself again; victory over the tap had miraculously cleared his mood. "You just got here."

"I really have to get back."

On the stove, the water in the kettle was boiling. Sally turned the burner off and they walked Colin out to the front porch, stopping on the top step.

"Thanks for coming by," Sally said. She made an effort to meet his eyes again, but he was looking out toward the street. David, standing behind her, put his hands on her waist and slid them up over her ribs, stopping just short of her breasts. When she stiffened, his grip grew tighter.

"Take care, Colin." It was David at his most charming, his most friendly, and this she didn't trust either. "We'll see you soon. Call us right away if—well, you know. If you hear anything."

Colin made his promises, started up the walk. Sally, wanting him out of earshot before she confronted David, stood still; but David, anticipating her, let his hands drop and turned back into the house. She followed him inside, shutting the door behind her.

"David."

Starting up the stairs he turned. "What?"

"Just what were you trying to prove?"

"Prove?" he said. "Can't I even touch you without a reason? Sorry. I guess you'd rather hold hands with him."

This was the moment, of course, to slap his face, but he was too far away, and more than that something warned her, some intuition that this was not David but the house working through him. She looked straight at him. "That's not funny," she said. "And you really hurt his feelings."

The sudden flushing of his face made the lightness of his eyes very noticeable. "Why the hell are you always worrying about him? He's an old man, dammit! Just an old man! What about me?"

In the crying out of the young voice she thought she heard what she was listening for: the echoing jealousy, trapped in the very walls of the house—Julian's jealousy of his father over the woman they shared. His outburst had brought him three steps closer to her and she could see him sweating.

"It's you I'm worried about," she said. Her voice shook.

He stared at her for a long moment, then rubbed the back of his neck as if it were stiff. "Oh, Christ," he said. "I can't even lose my temper, can I? Let's forget it, okay? I'm sorry. Let's just forget it."

⋙ 39 ⋘

AT SUPPER she ate with her head down, watching her plate. She wished he would talk, but he was silent, getting up to heat water for coffee when they were finished, then sitting down again. She looked at him at last. He sat leaning back in his chair, unsmiling, his gaze going past her.

Do I know this man?

The lines of his face were familiar. She knew the particular smell of him, the shape of his hands. But he sat across from her like a stranger in a restaurant, some slight acquaintance with whom she found herself now awkwardly alone. She looked down, heard the coffee water start to boil, heard him say, "Are you mad at me?"

Sally glanced up again: he hadn't moved. He was still leaning back, one arm over the back of the chair. Their eyes just missed meeting. "Why should I be mad at you?"

He raised his eyebrows. "Beats me." Changing position then, leaning forward to put his elbows on the kitchen table. The movement brought him closer and she could see the faint lines on his forehead and around his eyes as he said, "Maybe for being a son of a bitch?"

The metamorphosis from strange to familiar was as sudden as if he had put aside a mask. Her own relief frightened her. She got up and poured two mugs of instant coffee and brought them back to the table and sat down again.

"Maybe," she said.

He touched the back of her wrist. "Don't you see my point at all, Sal? I just hate the idea of leaving this thing half finished."

"I don't know what you mean by finished," she said.

"I don't either." He reached for his coffee, looking at

341

her. "But I know we're right in the middle of something. Don't you want to see it through?"

"I don't think I can," she said.

He moved in his chair. "You mean you don't want to."

"It isn't a question of wanting. This place is wearing me down; every day it's a little harder to keep my head clear. I can't go on indefinitely." This was oversimplifying, but she could not afford to let him realize how much of her fear was for him.

"But—"

"David, I just can't."

She drank her coffee: it was tasteless. He sat looking at her.

"What about the sitting?" he said.

"I can't do that either."

"You said—"

"I said I'd think about it. I did. It's a crazy idea."

"Look," David said. "The whole damn science is crazy, if you get right down to it. We're not in the banking business, for Pete's sake. You knew that when you got into it. Now we're here, we're right in the middle of something, and you want to quit because it's crazy. That's terrific. That's just great." He took a swallow of coffee and scowled at the mug. "This stuff tastes awful."

Sally said, "I'm sorry. I know I'm letting you down. I didn't realize it would be like this. I just can't take it." She heard her own voice, the edges beginning to fray. "I can't stay here."

There was silence, enough for the crickets to start up again in the backyard. David turned his coffee mug slowly on the table: once around, then again, and glanced up at her finally, saying quietly, without emphasis, "Well, you'll have to go without me. Because I can't leave."

To her the moment seemed to stretch interminably behind and before them: the hot kitchen with the two of them facing each other across the wooden table, summer night black beyond the screen, the house hanging above them beam by beam and room by room. They sat suspended as if in the glare of an unexpected illumination that bared more than either of them had wanted to see. She blamed herself for not realizing what she was asking, for forcing him to make a choice he would rather not have made, dragging into the light something that had been decently obscure until now. But now it was out: the house mattered more than she did—this structure of wood and plaster and the unseen world knit into its atoms by some process no one could guess or understand. In all her considering it had never once occurred to her that he would refuse to go if she insisted on it. Now he sat there across the table hollow-eyed, looking past her at the wall, and she found unexpectedly that none of it mattered anymore—his feelings or hers, whether they went or stayed or the floor opened beneath them and they dropped into nothingness. The moment seemed to have existed always, this instant of knowing her exact value to him, in spite of her refusal to see it. Its center was emptiness. And because she could not face that, not yet, she fell back on the fact that he wanted her to do the sitting, that he could not do it without her; that as long as he needed her for something connected with his obsession, at least she mattered that much. "All right," she said. "Okay. We'll do the sitting. When?"

He stirred as if waking from sleep, dragging his eyes away from the wall to rest on her. He had been somewhere far away; she watched while he returned to his face. "Really?" he said. "You mean it?"

"Yes," she said, and he leaned forward, gripping his mug so that the muscles stood out in his arms.

"Why not tonight?" he said.

His degree of readiness surprised her. She had assumed that, to a certain extent at least, she was calling his bluff. But he had evidently been thinking about this for a long time, planning it down to the last detail. He explained while she listened.

"The obvious place is Joshua's room. It's been the center of the most spectacular haunting activity, and we got our best results in there with Rosanna's sitting." He was intent on his idea, the invisible shape that kept him from seeing her more than peripherally, if at all; but even if he had been watching closely he would not have seen her flinch. The recollection of Rosanna's sitting—Rosanna with blood and tears on her face, the screams wrenching out of her—this scarcely touched her now. Most of her feelings seemed to have been sealed off by some automatic device like the valve that closes watertight compartments in a damaged submarine.

"What instrumentation are you going to use?" she said.

"Just the tape recorder and the self-recording thermometer to pick up any significant temperature drops. Other than that—" He stopped and she said, "Well?"

"Well, my idea was to have some psychically charged objects present as well. The music box, for instance. And the pictures of Julian and Joshua."

It reminded her of descriptions she had read of medieval spirit summonings: the magicians with their ceremonial circles, triangles and secret seals drawn on virgin parchment with the blood of a black cock. At least the sundial was too heavy to be lugged inside and up the stairs. "You mean as bait?" she said.

He shrugged a little, refusing to take offense. "Well, it can't hurt."

The room, when they went upstairs to look at it, had a bare inhospitable look, like any unoccupied room at night when the lights are suddenly switched on and the comfortable darkness is forced to retreat beyond the windows. It seemed stuffy; for once she didn't notice the chill. Other than the desk and the big four-poster bed there were only the two chairs left over from the sitting with Rosanna. David crossed to the window and opened it; night sounds came in, and a faint breeze.

"That's better."

Sally stood just inside the door, feeling nothing but a cold weightlessness around which her hot skin was wrapped like a garment that would not warm her. She couldn't say that she was afraid; fear didn't seem relevant. She felt only indifference, a detachment beyond which she was vaguely aware of David moving around, setting up the equipment, replacing the bulb in the desk lamp. He went out of the room and came back with the music box; she watched without comment as he put it on the desk and then produced the two pictures, drawing and photograph, of the Gilfoys, father and son. To label his behavior unscientific did not occur to her at that moment; she had gone beyond such considerations into a state that was already curiously close to trance. Small sounds came to her: the scrape of a chair leg on the floor, the hum of the tape recorder, the faint scratching of the self-recording thermometer keeping tally on its revolving drum. Outside the window the chattering of the cicadas reached its peak and sank gradually away. David was looking at her.

"Ready?"

She went forward slowly and sat down in the chair he indicated. He closed the door and turned off the overhead light, leaving only the lamp on the desk lit. Then he took the chair opposite her, tape recorder on the floor beside him. For a moment they sat there; without speaking he started the tape. She watched it begin to wind. Too late now to say anything: it had begun. And what could they have said in any case? It had begun. The burden of action had been lifted from her; she had only to give herself up, to let it happen. She waited, feeling nothing, thinking that the joke would be on them both if she failed to go into trance—if the house rejected her now, after all. As the seconds went by it began to look as if that might happen. She began to feel the pressure of performance, to understand what real mediums went through on the occasions when they did not slip quickly and easily into trance. The thought even crossed her mind that she could fake it—tell David whatever he wanted to hear, whatever would convince him to leave. With that thought came the first impulse back toward hope, toward survival. But just at that instant she felt the house.

In a way it was a relief to let the barriers go down one by one, surrender to the pressure to which she had become so accustomed that she could gauge its strength only now, as she stopped fighting it. There was a moment of sheer panic when she felt the sensation of the house pouring into her as uncontrollably as water over the lip of a too full vessel: first drop, then trickle, then flood. But by then there was no stopping it. The fullness was more than she could have imagined—she wondered how she had been able to resist so long. Bewilderingly full, a maze of echoes and images in which she felt herself at last a part of all that was here, the lighted seasons of the past like webs of clear color laid one upon the next, a bending and refracting that took her down and down. At first she was stunned and dizzied by the fragments moving through what had once been the boundaries of her self—at first she caught at each one, only to lose it in a swirl of others, dazzling showers that drenched her and were gone.

And yet not gone. It was all here.

There seemed to be no order to the vivid swarming; then little by little she began to sense the shape of the house rising behind it, a shadow-geometry against which she could orient herself. But self there was none, at least in the old sense of limits, separations. She was the house— and more, so much more that she drew back from it, gathering only what she could understand. A faint sound like many distant voices, lights and murmurs and shadow-shapes in which some single thing came clear for an instant before fading back into the whole, another taking its place. White boards patterned with the clear green shadows of leaves, mirrors reflecting the stillness of summer afternoons, the smooth gold disc of the clock pendulum beating like a pulse behind its glass: each thing itself and more than itself, echoes at infinite points in time touching others at infinite points in space so that it was impossible to separate them, herself among them, a confluence in which none was complete without all. This was the pressure she had felt since coming to the house—the pressure of its substance to flow through and not around her.

Slowly she found that there was no need to separate things in order to see them clearly. It was only by taking them as a whole that she could recognize in each part its image, oblique but not unfamiliar, from the world she knew. The whole was a pattern that shifted constantly while remaining always the same. It was impossible. There was no saying, in words, how it was done: and yet watching she grasped it somewhere at the very root of consciousness. She stood at the edge of the sea.

Julian

She had forgotten David. He was part of the pattern too, the recurring figure of a young man, restless core of energy turning this way and that, incessantly searching. Now his voice came from a great distance. She found she could perceive her own body too, in a clumsy, cloudy way as if she had had too much to drink.

There was something in her hands. No need to seek its identity in the conventional way, through shape or texture: she knew at once that she held the music box.

Other hands held it too, hers cupped within them like the petals of a flower; she felt the pressure of those other hands on hers. The box spilled light like a lantern, a bright flickering in which she seemed to see a little way into the shaping of the patterns that dominated the house. Fragments moved into the compass of the light and then were gone. The sharp fresh smell of an early spring morning. Someone sitting on a bed and rocking in the kind of grief that cannot be still. A sound of singing voices, running footsteps. The touch of warm breath on skin, silence, the movement of shadows on a wall, resolving at last to the slow golden journey of late afternoon light down a lace curtain. Forever it seemed to journey. The curtain stirred; the light pierced it in pinpoints, as if it were sewn with diamonds.

Julian

Again the voice calling from far away, small but persistent, filling the curtain like a wind. It ballooned inward toward her: for one horrifying instant she saw a tracery of blood-red veins on the fabric as if it were a living membrane stretched to bursting. Then it sank back; the veins disappeared. But now ragged holes showed in places; blackness came through them.

Julian

Can you hear me

The assault took her without warning. All at once she was seized, hurled into the darkness beyond the ragged curtain, buffeted by a violence beyond all meaning, a storm of black wind howling around her. She tried to fight back but it was no use—she did not know how. The onslaught was too sudden and too brutal; images rained on her like blows, black against the darkness: they forced her resistance, entered and possessed her—an incoherent soundless screaming, a struggle without form, using her mind to find its shape.

She saw fire. It leaped against the blackness of a grate. Out of the fire a dog lunged, flame-eyed and jaws agape, straight at her. She cried out but could not hear herself over the dog's frenzied barking, and then—

And then there was silence. Darkness. Nothingness. Only the shock and fear that gripped her, held her, until at the center of the void a flicker of light appeared. Grew brighter. Fire leaped against the blackness of a grate.

The fire was a face, the face a hand, the hand a dog's head. A pandemonium of barking broke out: flame-eyed, jaws agape, the dog lunged.

Within its jaws there was only darkness, an uncreated negative place in which she was suspended, lost and afraid, for an immeasurable period. Then a glimmer against the darkness, like a candle's friendly flame.

lead kindly light

But the flame grew higher and hotter until it became a fire. In the black vise that held her she struggled to break the sequence and could not. Fire leaped against the black grate, now fire no longer but a burning face, twisting and growing, smoke pouring from the mouth and eyes. The smoke became a hand, then the head of a barking dog—a cry broke through her, not her own but the voice of mindless terror and despair funneling up and out. She fought to hold herself apart from it, from the images breaking over her. Somewhere outside her there was a tiny absurd voice.

Julian, what is it

Tell me

like a child shouting at a storm. For this was not Julian or anything that deserved a human name—only a senseless fragment repeating itself in futile monotony like a jammed gear. And she lacked the power either to disrupt it or to wrench herself free: all she could do was crouch apart in one corner of her mind while the thing screamed its frenzy from her throat. The fire leaped, the dark jaws opened; and each time, in the black nothingness beyond, she felt her grip on her own sanity slip a little more. All fear of lightlessness, of isolation and loss waited there, each encounter leaving her diminished, less equipped to face the next.

Sally

The voice this time like a hand outstretched to pull her back, out of this nightmare world into his solid one. She caught it: voice, name—struggled to hold, felt the desperate power of her possessor rise boiling and foaming as if, deprived of its outlet, it would explode. The strength of it paralyzed her even while she held fast to the sound of David's voice. Then suddenly she was free.

❊ 40 ❊

FOR AN ENDLESS SPACE she clawed at the threshold of consciousness, suspended between dimensions, stretched to a vaporous shadow at the very fringe of existence. In this place there were black winds that could blow such shadows to shreds in an instant; and against them only the idea of the sensory world like the thin bright sliver of light beneath the door of a lit room. But self and senses gradually closed around her; gradually she began to understand that something was wrong. The room was dark and savagely cold.

"David?" she said, and winced; her throat was raw.

There was no answer.

She felt a sensation inside her like an animal struggling inside a sack—childhood terrors of the dark, unseen hands reaching for her—"David," she said again, and the silence came back to her.

Where

Freezing air welled up from the boards of the floor beneath her. She caught her breath, hurting her throat again, fully conscious now and understanding that it was real, all of it, the dark, the cold—

David

Where

Inside her the fear moved again in its fragile sack of reason. She fumbled for the lamp on the desk—couldn't find it—found it, shaking fingers searching for the switch.

Not afraid

just cold

cold makes you shiver

Finding the switch: click. Nothing. Click. Click. Nothing.

"Damn you," she said, hearing her voice fray like a

349

thread about to snap and finding she could not stop, trying the lamp again and again click clickclickclickclick like the frantic scrabbling of claws as reason gave way and let out the terrified childself that knew nothing of science or logic. The darkness around her was thick with presence. Everything blurred together: she was on her feet, running against something in the dark and hearing it fall, hitting her hip on something, hands flailing for the door and finding nothing, only emptiness and then, just as she thought her heartbeat would choke her, one hand striking the open doorframe.

David

Call him

Call his name

But she could not. Her throat closed when she tried, as in a nightmare where screams turn to whispers. She clung to the doorframe, immobilized by the sense of presence in the house that pressed down on her like a weight, beginning to drive her deeper into herself, into some dark cave where even consciousness was only a feeble stirring. All her training, all her knowledge meant nothing now. It was as if the mindless terror-state that had found and used her in trance had burst through her into the external world, filling the house as it had filled her, surrounding her now in the shape of wall and floor and ceiling, the dark and the brutal cold. She turned suddenly, instinctively, and looked into the room behind her.

Fire leaped now in the blackness of the grate, reflected in the windows across the room. And in the flickering light she saw him. The left side of his face was covered in blood, the soft dark hair matted with it. As she watched, his hands moved weakly, like a newborn's, toward his head and then away. She backed into the hall, her throat tight with the cry caught in it; then broke and ran for the stairs, but somehow he was ahead of her, stumbling down the hall, hands groping as if he were blind. She could see him in some strange fashion both vague and clear, as if her reality and his were twisted together in a pattern that did not quite mesh: superimposed on the dark corridor of the present were the glowing gas fixtures of the past, the light wavering and uneven; and by their illumination she followed the staggering figure as it lurched from one side of the hall to the other toward the stairs. Ahead was the monitor panel, unlit, and she saw him stumble through it as if it were made of smoke, although which of them had actual substance at that moment she was incapable of judging. And there were the stairs, descending into black-ness. He hesitated at the top. She cried out then, and for one impossible instant she thought he had heard her: his head turned blindly toward her and she saw his bewildered face for a second before he fell.

There was no sound. As she ran forward and started down the stairs the darkness closed around her again, complete, so that she had to feel her way, one hand on the smooth banister, one step and then the next, bending her shaking knees by an effort of will. Down and down, with the black void settling on her like a weight, heavier with every step and the steps going on and on, and in the darkness she knew that there were too many of them and that she had gone beyond the house, much too far, that the weight pressing on her now was the weight of the earth itself, of the grave. Then she felt the newel post at the end of the banister and knew she had reached the bottom. She took one more step and nearly fell over him where he lay.

For what seemed like a long time her heart simply stopped beating. In the interim she knelt and rolled him over (he had been lying on his face and there was blood on the floor, a spreading puddle) and bent over him and laid her head against his chest. When she heard his heart beating, hers began too, abruptly, like a slacker called to order.

"David," she said. It came out a whisper. Now she could make out his face, pale, and the dark blood stream-ing down the left side, more blood than she had ever seen in her life. She tried to find the wound and could not and the blood seeped through her fingers, burning them, the only warmth in the world. Crouching there she seemed to feel the house moving, swinging like a pendu-lum between past and present, the pattern bending them inexorably to its shape. Out of the darkness a hollow boom of sound suddenly shook the floor beneath them, reverberating in her bones, coming again and then again and again in a rising tempo like a frantic heartbeat, and she winced each time it came, hearing herself start to whimper like an animal, hearing her voice say, "David" again, grabbing his shoulders and shaking him.

There was no response. Then his eyes opened and he was looking at her.

"Lost," he said. The voice was unfamiliar. The eyes, not David's, looked into hers. Her head spun; she thought she would faint.

"Lost," the voice said, and the hands clutched at hers, the fingers icy. She pulled free and tried to get up and found her legs wouldn't hold her.

"Oh God," she said, "oh God," catching and holding him against her, feeling the violence of trembling that shook him. For those few moments she could not have said with any certainty who they were or where in time, only that she held him at the center of a spinning vortex. Then she realized that the storm of noise around them had stopped, and that he was no longer trembling. When she looked into his face the eyes were closed.

She fumbled for a pulse, a heartbeat, could find neither—stumbled up and dragged him across the floor to the front door, flinging it open, seeing the dark bulk of trees against the starred night sky. He was a dead weight in her arms. She managed to pull him across the porch and down the front steps and then her knees gave way and she collapsed on the walk, his head and shoulders in her lap. One of his sneakers had come off somewhere. She looked from the vulnerable bare foot up at the house: the dark glint of windows, sharp gables enormous against the sky. The roses on the porch roof were the color of ashes.

He moved against her then and she looked down at him. In the blood-streaked face his lips moved, formed words.

"Sally? What . . . happened?"

⫸ 41 ⫷

IT WAS, Dr. Bristowe said, probably nothing more than a mild concussion in spite of all the blood. He sent Sally to the bathroom to wash it off her hands while he took X rays; then, while the films were developing, he put five stitches in the surprisingly small cut on the left side of David's forehead and forced Sally to drink a cup of hot tea, which she did not want but which finally stopped her hands from shaking. A buzzer sounded. The doctor went into the darkroom and came out with the X rays, four of them, still dripping. He clipped them to a long lightbox on the wall and touched a switch: the box flickered into life, illuminating the cloudy images. The skulls grinned as if conscious of being on display. The doctor, a big white-haired man in a cotton plaid shirt, examined them in silence. Sally divided her attention between the X rays and the doctor's face (intent and peaceful like some large grazing animal's); David, on the examining table, raised himself slowly to a sitting position and winced at the pull of the new sutures against his skin. From the doctor's living room on the other side of the examining-room door came the murmur of a television set.

For Sally the mundane details—duct tape patching a rip in the upholstery of her chair, canned laughter from the TV set, the white T-shirt showing at the doctor's neck—were what she clung to for comfort, placing each small thing between herself and that moment in the dark house when she had held David's body in her arms, their linked figures like a fulcrum for two realities met in perilous balance. The theories of modern physics were one thing, this night another. Her hands had started shaking again and she pressed them together, seeing the bloodstains on the front of her shirt as she looked down.

"No harm done to the inside, far as I can see." The doctor gave the X rays a last glance and clicked the lightbox off. "That cut'll smart a bit when the local wears off. Take aspirin if you need to. Stitches ought to be ready to come out in a week or so. You folks say you're renting the Gilfoy house?"

She was fairly sure they hadn't said, but it must be common knowledge. They had merely said that there had been a power failure, that David had fallen in the dark. His one bare foot had not been mentioned. Dr. Bristowe was looking at her and she nodded.

"Old house," he said. He picked up her wrist and held it, glancing at his watch. He had already taken David's pulse, tested his reflexes, looked into his eyes with a bright little light. Now the big warm fingers on her wrist made her uneasy, as if he could read some version of what had happened in the hurrying of her blood.

"I'm not the patient," she said, trying to smile, and the doctor smiled back, eyes sharp blue under white brows.

"Never said you were." Another glance at his watch and he let go of her wrist, turning back to David. "If you feel sick, call me right away. Otherwise call me in the morning, let me know how you feel. All right?"

"Fine. And thanks a lot." David slid off the examining table, steadied himself. Sally took his arm. The doctor looked at them.

"Ought to have Sam carpet those stairs for you."

He saw them out, joined by his wife, who got up from watching her TV show to walk with them to the front door. There were more thanks and good nights; David and Sally went down the front walk to their car. If they had happened to look back they would have seen, across the dark lawn, the doctor's figure standing on the lit porch looking after them, motionless as if lost in thought.

Sally drove. It was not far and they did not talk. The headlights cut a double swath in the summer night, down dark streets that were deserted although it was not yet midnight. When she pulled up in front of the house and turned the engine off she sat without moving. David started to open the door on his side and she said, "Wait."

The seat squeaked as he turned. "What is it?"

"We have to talk, David."

"Can't we do it inside?"

"In *there*?" she said.

He leaned back in the seat and let his breath out slowly. She heard everything in that long exhalation: he was starting to stiffen from the fall, the anesthetic from the stitches was wearing off, he was thinking that these first aches and twinges were only the beginning. More than that, there was a feeling that powerful hands had wrung his mind out, wrung it dry. He only wanted to sleep. She was tired too, and lightheaded, but it was a light in which a great many things seemed clear. Sitting next to him, she knew it was an unequal battle and was glad of it. She wanted to win.

"We made a deal," she said.

"Sally—"

"A deal. Are you going back on it? Whatever's in that house, David—do you want it to destroy us? Because that's what it's going to do."

He started shaking his head while she was talking, went on shaking it even after she had stopped, a movement like the rocking of a disturbed child. "He doesn't want to hurt us," he said.

"Quit making a screenplay out of it! I'm talking about survival. You could have been killed tonight!" Her voice, hoarse, hurt her ears as much as her throat. She swallowed and closed her eyes.

Finally David said, "Look, I know what you're thinking. But you can't possibly despise me as much as I do myself."

She opened her eyes and looked at him; he sat with his head bent. "What are you talking about?" she said.

"I left you. I got scared and ran."

She stared at him, for a moment hearing only the bleak sound of his voice, and then the words themselves. The words themselves. *I left you. I got scared and ran.* A laugh came like a spasm of nausea; she felt tears burning the back of her eyes and recognized the beginnings of hysteria. She fought it down. "That wasn't you," she said.

"No? Who was it, then?"

"Oh, God," she said. She rested her forehead on the

steering wheel and closed her eyes again. "Don't you understand? Listen to me. That isn't Julian in there. It isn't a person. It's like a—I don't know, something mechanical. Once it starts, it just goes. And if you happen to get in its way, you go with it." She was silent, remembering the nightmare images assaulting her. "It doesn't mean anything," she said, lifting her head, looking at him. "Are you listening?"

"Do you remember your trance?" If it wasn't an answer, at least it sounded more like the old David, the beginnings of curiosity.

"It didn't make any sense," she said. "It was just a sequence of images like a film loop. Repeating itself over and over."

"Images? Like what?"

"A fire." The memory tightened inside her. "Then a face, I think, or maybe a hand." She decided not to mention the apparition of Julian until she had had a chance to think about it. "And something about a dog."

"A dog? One of Julian's?"

"I don't know. I guess it could have been. It was barking— attacking. Oh, it's like telling a dream: as soon as I say it, I know it isn't right. But the emotion—it's like some crazy *thing* let loose, out of control. That's what you felt. That's why you ran."

David sighed. "I ran because I was goddamn scared. The barking started up, and then the lights went out, and you started screaming—"

"That was *it* screaming, not me. It was using me when it wanted to scream, the way it used you when it wanted to run. It's some kind of terror-state, David—something Julian must have felt, but isolated, completely cut off from everything else. It's pure terror, cycling in a closed circuit. We got in its path. Do you really think it's coincidence that you fell down those stairs?"

He said, "I fell down the stairs because it was dark and I was running. I appreciate what you're trying to do, but Sally—oh hell. There's no point in talking about it." He opened the car door suddenly and she grabbed at him.

"What are you doing?"

"I'm going in."

"You're—"

They struggled ineffectually for control of the door

handle; Sally gave up abruptly and tried to start the car instead. The engine turned over once and then died as David jerked the key out of the ignition. She grabbed at his arm, missed—he was halfway out of the car when she lunged across the seat and caught hold of his belt. He grunted, swore, lost his balance and fell back into the car, the back of his head narrowly missing the door-frame. They went on grappling for a moment, arguing in short breathless bursts.

"We made a deal—"

"—Let go, goddamn it—"

"—You said—"

He stopped all at once and put his hands up to his face. There was no sound but their breathing and the crickets outside in the summer night. Then he said, "Christ, my head hurts." Sally said nothing, only tightened her grip on his belt.

"Sal, be realistic. We have to go back in there some-time. We have to sleep."

"Not in that house."

"Then where? You want to spend the night in the car?"

"We can go to a motel," she said. "There's one in Masonville."

David said, "Look, we're both covered with blood. I've only got one shoe. And besides, I just threw the car keys into the hedge."

There was silence.

"You can ask Mrs. Hopkins to let you spend the night," he said. "Tell her we had a fight."

"So you can go in there and do what? Carry out more scientific investigations? Are you crazy, David? I'm not saying that whatever is in that house—call it Julian if you want to—is conscious. I'm not saying it's out to get us. But it's dangerous. And if you get in its way you're asking for trouble."

"Look," he said. "We went about this all wrong. I'll admit I was expecting tonight to be more or less like the sitting we had with Rosanna in Joshua's room. I thought I could get through to Julian. I wasn't prepared for what happened, and I panicked. That was my fault. If we'd discussed all the possibilities thoroughly beforehand, knowing what we know about the house, we could probably have predicted—"

"That you'd end up dead? I doubt it."

"I'm not dead," he said tiredly.

"You could have been. Easily. Just like that. Like Julian. Do you know your heart stopped just before I got you out of there? *Your heart stopped.* You came that close."

She thought she had impressed him. Then he said, as if he hadn't even heard her, "If I'd thought about what to expect—"

"What to expect? Did you think it was going to be a tea party? The dance of the blessed spirits?"

There was a pause, and he said, "I don't know."

His face was in profile to her, dark against the darkness outside. The painful honesty in his voice made her ashamed of her sarcasm. She said, "I don't think you see how dangerous it is for you. Because you don't understand what's happening, or you won't. I'm telling you there's a pattern in that house, a sequence that keeps repeating, and it's stronger than we are, and it's destructive. Julian ran out of that room in terror, and so did you. And he fell, and so did you. And he was killed. It isn't something you can help, or change, or fix."

"Okay." He touched his head, winced and let his hand drop. "You think it's hopeless. You think we ought to just pack up and leave, like all the others."

"You know what I think."

"And all the work we've put into it? And the evidence we're getting?" She was silent and he said, "And Julian?"

"What about him?"

"Maybe we could find a way to break the sequence. He's stuck in it. Lost. The lost one. If we could just help him find his way—"

"How?" she said flatly. "Shock therapy? Half a teaspoon of baking soda in a glass of water? He's not a soul in torment, David! Whatever is in that house doesn't have a mind. It's just a series of unpleasant events that make life difficult for people who are trying to live there." She pushed away the thought of those eyes looking at her out of David's eyes, the cold hands grasping hers as if she were their only hope. She wasn't certain that what she was saying was true. But she knew she wanted nothing more to do with the house.

"You don't believe that," David said.

"Stop it," she said. "Stop picking on me."

"Couldn't we just try?"

"Try *what*?"

"To break the sequence. To help him: let him go. All right—get rid of the unpleasant events, make the house habitable again. A place where people can live."

"Look," she said. "If you want to ask Jack to find somebody to sprinkle a little holy water on the doorstep, it's fine with me. He knows all kinds of people. Maybe it'll work, maybe not. Just as long as we stay out of it—especially you." He said nothing and she said, "Does your head hurt?"

"Yes."

"We ought to try and get some sleep."

"Where?"

Their eyes met as best they could in the darkness of the car and she said, "Here."

She slept the dead sleep of exhaustion, not waking when he left the car. When she opened her eyes to gray light, neck aching and a bad taste in her mouth, she was alone. Outside the car, the hedge, not yet greened by the sun, showed monochrome and there was no sign of life from the house among the trees. She got stiffly out of the car. The slam of the door seemed loud in the dawn stillness, the day around her chill and stale as ashes from a dead fire. For several minutes she stood at the gate looking down toward the house, shivering a little in the cool air. At last she turned; and slowly, then faster, started walking down the hill.

⋙ 42 ⋘

"IT'S INSANE," Sally said. "It's utter madness. We've completely lost our objectivity."

"It certainly sounds like David has."

"We both have."

The window was open: laughter floated up from the street below, where a group of nuns waited to cross. Boston, and a window looking out over the Common. Trees tossed their leaves in the late morning light.

"Why don't you just leave?"

"He won't."

"You asked him?"

"Yes."

"And he said no?"

"He wants to stay."

A pause. Then: "Leave him."

Sally turned. The previous night showed in her face; her eyes and mouth had a bruised look that added years. "I can't," she said.

"You already have. Just don't go back."

Sally turned to the window again. Rosanna came forward and stood beside her looking out over the Common. "There's nothing else you can do," she said.

"Just walk out?" Sally said.

Rosanna made an impatient gesture. "Whatever hold that house has on him, it isn't something you'll find in one of those scientific quarterlies of yours. I don't particularly enjoy saying I told you so, but you two have started something you can't finish. You've got to cut your losses."

"I can't just write him off as a loss," Sally said. Her voice was shaking and she stopped to control it. "You told me what would happen and I didn't listen. What's happened is my fault. I can't walk out on him."

"Jesus," Rosanna said. "Jesus." She shook her head, still looking out at the trees, then turned to Sally. "You're exhausted, baby. You don't need to be making any decisions, the head you're in." Moving back into the room, toward the kitchen. "I'm going to make coffee. Sit down."

Sally stayed by the window a little longer, listening to the sounds from the kitchen, and then went and sat down on the couch. It was a small apartment, the walls exposed brick, one filled with shelves of books and records, pottery, a glossy stereo system. An African mask hung over the fireplace, grotesque and beautiful. She closed her eyes for what seemed only a second, opened them to the smell of fresh coffee. Rosanna handed her the cup, watched while she took a sip, then moved away. "When was the last time you had something to eat?"

"I'm not hungry." The coffee buzzed in her brain. She felt Rosanna behind her; the medium's hands touched her shoulders, beginning to knead the stiff muscles.

"Jesus, you're tight." Strong gentle fingers working the knots out of her neck and back, bringing a return of warmth and sensation. An involuntary sound of pleasure escaped her. As the tension drained away she could feel her resolve slipping too. Why not relax, let herself be taken care of for a little while, surrender to the comfort that was here? She took a quick gulp of coffee, burning her mouth, leaning forward to put the cup down, the movement pulling her free from Rosanna's hands.

"Please help me," she said. She kept her eyes on the cup in front of her. The low table was made of some exotic wood, black stripes on a golden background, like a tiger's pelt. There was silence.

"Well, there's something you can try," Rosanna said at last. "If your scientific principles will let you."

"What?" Sally said. Now she turned; now their eyes met. The medium's were bleak, bottomless.

"Exorcism," she said.

It was late in the afternoon, and the university cafeteria was all but deserted; the few occupied tables drifted like islands in the sea of impersonal space. By one set of double doors an elderly professor sat by himself with a newspaper; toward the center three female students were engaged in earnest discussion. The inevitable lovers were over by the stacked trays and utensil bins, their profiles blurred against the bright red and yellow plastic condiment dispensers behind them. Against the opposite wall, a stark windowless stretch of brick, another couple sat opposite each other. They were not lovers; even the most casual observer could have seen that. They had been there for over two hours, the woman doing most of the talking, the man asking a brief question at intervals. They were drinking the cafeteria's horrible coffee. Every so often she pushed her hair away from her face with a gesture that said she was completely unaware of her appearance, and she did so now, as she stopped talking at last. The man, who wore black-rimmed glasses and a three-piece suit, had scarcely looked away from her since she had begun.

"What I want to know is," she said, "am I crazy?"

He picked up his coffee cup, looked into it thoughtfully, drank. When he had put it down he said, "What am I supposed to tell you, Sally? Do you want a simple yes or no?"

"Can you give me one?"

"I'm not a shrink, for God's sake. I'm a psych professor. Ask me something I can look up in the book."

"Alec, please help me."

"I will. I will. Take it easy."

Sally pushed her hair back again and looked out across the deserted cafeteria. She had known Alec in college, and since then they had kept up a relationship that incorporated, in a friendly way, the antagonism between psychology and psychical research. She recognized that in coming to him for help she was inviting a skeptical point of view. But after her conversation with Rosanna she thought a little skepticism might be comforting.

"Of course you realize," he said, "that as a psychologist I have to consider everything you've told me the purest fantasy."

She glanced toward him, then shifted in her chair to face him again. "Can you explain it, then?"

"Every single incident. Every word."

"Really, Alec?"

"Really."

What else did she expect? She felt a surge of some emotion—relief or regret, she wasn't sure which. He leaned back in his chair and began to count off points on his fingers in a way his students would have recognized.

"First. You and David went to the house with the idea already in your minds that it was haunted. That made you sitting ducks for this medium woman; you said yourself nothing happened until she got there. Second, once she supplied the proper mumbo-jumbo, the three of you just fed into one another emotionally—and fantasy flourishes in that kind of atmosphere. Look at the Salem witch hunts." She smiled faintly as he went on. "Third, it's not the ghost, but David's *belief* in the ghost that's affecting his personality and making him behave in a way that you see as a dangerous pattern imposed by the ghost. Questions?"

She was thinking. "Well, to start from the beginning: what about Rosanna's hits—the things she said in trance that later checked out as fact?"

"What things? You mean what she said about the ghost? Look, Sally, let's get something straight. *There is no ghost.* Okay? Listen. This medium of yours comes along and gives you a standard séance spook—a young man calling himself 'the lost one.' You and David then hunt around until you find a family member who fits the profile. You investigate his life and gradually become obsessed with it to a degree that begins to affect your behavior. You created this ghost yourselves. Don't you see that?"

"No, I don't." She felt her face flush. "It didn't happen like that. First, we didn't hunt around for someone to fit the profile. Julian's grave *was* lost. And it had that weird epitaph, about being far from home. And the phrase 'the lost one'—it comes from the music box song. Rosanna couldn't have known about Julian's connection with the box. We didn't find out ourselves until after she'd left."

He pulled off his glasses and polished them with a paper napkin. "The grave was lost. Okay. Headstones fall over in graveyards all the time—with or without weird epitaphs. Did you check to see how many others had fallen over?"

She had been leaning forward; now she sat back. "No."

"Well. You parapsychology people love to select your data."

A low blow. Sally gave him an exasperated look, but he only shrugged, replaced his glasses and settled them on his nose. "As for the music box, you talk about Julian's connection with it. But you created that connection. You have no basis for believing that he gave his stepmother the box. More than likely it was given to her by her husband, Joshua. Same initials, right? But you people decided they were Julian's. Why? Because Joshua wasn't a young man when he died. He didn't fit the profile."

"Look, we did assume they were Joshua's initials, at first. But then Colin pointed out that Joshua was tone-deaf, and the phrase about the lost one—" she stopped, biting her lip.

"Recursion, pure and simple. Your hypothesis becomes your proof. You'd never convict anyone in a court of law on that kind of evidence."

She had heard how feeble it sounded even as she was saying it. Frustration silenced her for a moment. Then she tried again. "Well, where the hell, in your view, did Rosanna get that phrase in the very first sitting? There was only one music box in the house, and it plays that song. And the song has that phrase in it. And Rosanna didn't know about the box."

"But you did. And David did. You must have given her some kind of subliminal clue—"

"Oh, subliminal clue my foot. Even if that were possible, which it isn't with something that specific, we couldn't have done it. Neither one of us knew the words to the song at that point."

"You recognized the tune, didn't you? It's a well-known song. More than likely you heard the words at one time or another and retained them on a subliminal level."

Sally lifted her hands and let them fall. "Alec, that's such a cop-out. You might as well say telepathy, or spirits, or UFO's. Why should my subliminal level start working overtime all of a sudden? It's not normally so busy."

"We could argue that, on the basis of your so-called

psychic talents. But for right now I'll just say you've been in an exceptionally high-key emotional climate."

There was a pause. Sally thought that there was no point in losing her temper. She had come to him for precisely this viewpoint. He was trying to help her, in his way, and he was her last hope. She said carefully, "Alec. I know you find this hard to believe. But David and I have had scientific training. You know I was trained as a physicist. He's done graduate work in anthropology. We don't get all fluttery and hysterical at the idea of investigating an unknown."

"Well, what about that medium? Those people are unstable as hell—walking dynamite, every one of them. You were already frustrated when you brought her there— desperate for something to happen. She picked up on that; the two of you responded, and off you went."

"You say 'those people.' If there's no such thing as psychic, what makes her different from anyone else?"

"Multiple personality. Hyperemotionalism. Repressed sexual hysteria."

"Come on, Alec."

"I'm just telling you. A lot of mediums are notably promiscuous. I was reading somewhere that Houdini used to get propositioned regularly in his medium-debunking business. What was this medium's—"

He stopped and she said, "What?"

"Well—what was her relationship with David like?"

Sally stared at him for a minute and then looked away. "Well, not sexual."

"Not overtly. I don't mean they were having an affair. But—"

"Look, I told you—"

"Okay, okay. But even latently these things can give off a hell of a charge."

She looked into her coffee cup, then back at him.

"More questions?" he said.

"The dogs. The stairs. The apparition of Julian. No, never mind all that, I know what you'll say. What about the lights?"

"You're the physicist. You tell me. There must be half a dozen theoretical explanations for phenomena of that kind. Whatever physical condition or set of conditions is causing those lights to appear is the only thing in this whole business, I'd say, that deserves investigation. I mean, look at the facts. You saw a weird light. But what else has actually, indisputably happened since you've been living in the house? You lost a dog and David fell down the stairs. All the music boxes and gravestones and hallucinations of young men with head wounds in the world don't make it add up to anything more than that. And the fact that—"

Sally had not been listening, and now she interrupted him. "You mean you're ascribing the change in David's sexual behavior to some kind of repressed thing for Rosanna?"

He shifted his glasses on his nose. "Possibly. Although there's a likelier cause."

"What?"

"Isn't it obvious? Your ghost was quite a lady's man from what you've been telling me, and one with Oedipal leanings—it doesn't take a Freudian analyst to see that. His father's wife may not have been his biological mother, but she was close enough. Now, David's sexual problems very possibly have an Oedipal root. What could be simpler for him than to imagine himself possessed by this very potent young man? It lets him out of the guilt and in on the fun."

"But he doesn't believe he was possessed by Julian. I told you—he got furious when I suggested it."

"Use your head. From the little you've said, I gather David has refused to confront his problem by getting therapy or in any other straightforward way. He can't deal with it. By accident he stumbles into a situation that magically deals with it for him—no fuss, no bother. He can perform like a normal man; it's a miracle cure. Do you really think he wants to hear complaints—especially from you?"

She was staring at nothing, and when she spoke it was scarcely audible. "But last night, in that godforsaken house, when he fell and I turned him over and he looked at me—Alec, *that wasn't David.*"

He leaned back in his chair and exhaled audibly. "I can make you a list of reasons why your subconscious would be only too happy to have David become someone else. If you want me to."

The words knocked all the fight out of her. She couldn't

move, could only close her eyes. "Don't bother," she said. She heard his chair scrape the tile floor as he shifted, then heard herself say, "But his jealousy of Colin, it came from nowhere, out of the blue. And it was so—crazy."

"Jealousy is an innate response. Take two males of any species—"

"Colin is an old man!" she said. "And so was Joshua Gilfoy."

"I know." When she looked at him he shrugged. "But again, you're overlooking the obvious. When exactly did this jealousy begin?"

"I don't remember exactly. But—"

"But it was after you borrowed the dog, right? After you lost it?"

She nodded.

"Isn't it perfectly natural that David, who is feeling guilty over losing Colin's dog, should want to avoid him? The sight of Colin reminds David that he has done Colin an injury. Now the resourceful subconscious comes up with a handy way to avoid seeing Colin, and that is to become angry with him, quarrel with him. What David has always perceived as a harmless, whimsical closeness between you and Colin suddenly becomes a threat. He thinks he is jealous and in fact he *is* jealous—because Colin, as the injured party, is collecting all your sympathy while David, as the perpetrator, is out in the cold."

She looked away from him, thinking, feeling the pull of the pat logic and resisting it. She said, "But David and I have been married more than a year. We've established patterns. Now something's disrupted them. If it isn't the house, what is it?"

He leaned across the table, took hold of her shoulder and shook it gently. "Sally, for a bright girl you're asking a lot of dumb questions. Do you really think you and David achieved some kind of stability in that amount of time? From what you've told me, I'd say your marriage was heading for a crisis centering on sexual frustration. Throw in some anger, some guilt, some feelings of worthlessness. David wouldn't help himself and he wouldn't let you help him, and the two of you put all your energies into ignoring the problem. That only works for just so long." He released her shoulder and sat back, glancing at his watch; she knew he had a class to teach. "The situation in the house happened to provide a kind of solution—and it's just proof of what I'm saying that David was so quick to take advantage of it. The house may have precipitated your crisis, but it didn't cause it. If you hadn't gone there you'd still have had to face those issues sooner or later, believe me."

She was almost convinced. Questions rose in her mind, almost surfaced, then sank away as she answered them herself. She looked at him finally. "Then all the differences I've noticed in him—"

"Are due to the problems you brought with you and his own expectations about the house. And yours."

She was quiet. So was he. After a minute or two she said, "All right. What do I do?"

"Get him out of there."

"I've tried. I've *tried*."

"Call the little men in the white coats."

"That's not funny."

"It wasn't meant to be. Listen, Sally. What you've described to me is a deteriorating mental condition. People are sensitive to atmosphere—all people, some more than others. Put them in a crazy situation and they start acting crazy. Put them in a normal situation and they act normal again. What matters is getting David out of that house, not how you do it. I can get a couple of guys, we can drive out tomorrow and bring him back."

"He wouldn't come," she said.

"Why do you think I suggested a couple of guys? We won't give him a choice."

She was shaking her head. "No, Alec. No. He'd hate me."

"Maybe for a few days."

"No. You don't understand."

"Sally."

"No."

He sat looking at her for a minute, then glanced at his watch and pushed his chair back. "I'm late for a class. You know how to get in touch with me. You asked me to help you: that's the best I can do." He leaned across the table and kissed her cheek. "Let me know," he said.

A bench under a tree in the Common. She sat watching the changing figures that went past her, an old man in an overcoat even in the August heat, kids with radios, women with strollers, businessmen with their ties blowing. The radios and the shouting of children's voices made a criss-cross pattern on the air. Across the path on a stretch of green lawn a paper cup and a crumpled candy wrapper were having a confrontation in the fitful breeze.

The paper cup was the aggressor. It rolled toward the motionless wrapper, then took a sudden spin away as the wrapper twitched. Not sleeping, after all. It chased the cup a little way, then stopped. Both were motionless, considering. The stillness stretched: a test of nerves. The cup began to rock tauntingly from side to side. The wrapper refused to be baited. Now the cup tried a new tactic, a slow pivoting roll that brought its open end around to face the stolid wrapper, which quivered but did not give ground. Cup began to inch forward—wrapper took a quick tumble back. Cup rolled off to the left, then to the right, a rhythmic zigzag bringing it closer with each pass. Wrapper appeared mesmerized, frozen, waiting. The open mouth approached: an inch away it stopped. Savoring the anticipation? The leaves of the trees hung down; even the cries of children playing seemed to die on the air. Sally's eyes felt dry and stretched as if she had not blinked in a long time. Then the branches overhead rose in a swell of wind; the children shouted and the radios played; with a great leap the cup sailed into the air and away.

⋙ 43 ⋘

THE TELEPHONE WAS RINGING. After the third ring she began to count. Four. She had never noticed, on the receiving end, how long a pause there was between rings.

Five. Only a slight concussion, Dr. Bristowe had said. But head wounds were dangerous. She should have been there to look for suspicious signs. Drowsiness. Nausea.

Six. The thinking process congealed into a cold hard lump inside her.

Halfway through the seventh ring his voice said, "Hello?"

"David." It came out sounding strange; she realized she had been holding her breath.

"Sally. Where are you?"

"I'm in Boston," she said.

There was a pause, and then he said, "Are you coming back?"

She looked around her at Alec's apartment. He had given her the keys after failing to talk her into coming home to a family dinner at his house in Winchester. The apartment was small and shabby and in a bad neighborhood; Alec hung on to it as a remnant from his student days. On one wall was a poster, an enormous blow-up of a white rat facing into the camera. The moist pink nose was the size of her fist. "I don't know," she said. She wished he hadn't put it like that, wished he had said, "When are you coming back?" or "What the hell are you doing in Boston?" Then they could have proceeded by slow steps, her series of uncertainties leading them little by little toward the real issue. Now instead they seemed to have taken a sudden jump, irrevocable, beyond which was nothing. She looked away from the rat's nose. David said, "Sally?"

"I'm here."

"I know there's absolutely no reason for you to trust me. But there's something I have to tell you. The house is clean."

"What?" she said, not understanding.

"He's gone."

"Gone?"

"Yes. The sitting must have done something, released some kind of energy or something."

"But how do you know?" she said. "How—"

"You can feel it. Or not feel it, that is. He just isn't here anymore."

"Did you . . . do anything?"

"You mean draw a magic circle and say, *Get thee hence, spirit*? No. It must have been the sitting."

She sat holding the phone, not knowing what she felt. "But David—"

"Listen." He was excited. "A hell of a lot of energy got released last night during the sitting. Know why the lights went out? I checked the fuse box. Every fuse in the place was blown. Not only that, the inkwell in the library got thrown clear through the window. Shattered the glass. I found the inkwell in the hedge. It was quite a pitch"— she heard papers rattle—"twenty-eight feet, four and five-eighths inches."

Sally started to laugh from sheer relief: he sounded so like himself. "The *inkwell*?"

"You know, the brass one we found in the attic. It's shaped like a dog." A pause, as if he heard the meaning of the words for the first time in speaking them; and she felt the silence echo inside her, a kind of space before knowing. Then David said, on a long expelled breath, "What is it with dogs in this place?"

She said slowly, "There was a dog in the trance."

"And those mutts in the yard. And the barking we've been hearing all along—the previous tenants heard it too. And the Abbeys' dog going crazy. And now this action with the inkwell—" She heard a thud: he had hit something, probably the wall, with his fist. "What does it mean?"

"Why does it have to mean anything?" Dog lunging, eyes like fire, jaws wide. She shifted her grip on the phone. "Are you sure it's over?" she said.

"It's got to mean something. It's like a motif, some kind of symbol that just needs interpreting. Sally, it's some kind of key to the whole business. Tell me again about your trance."

"It was just a sequence," she said. "A fire burning, and somehow turning into a dog. And the dog attacking."

She could all but hear him thinking after she had stopped talking. There was static on the line where none had been before. Then he said, "It's got to add up. A dog attacking, and the inkwell breaking the window. There's got to be some sort of symbolic relationship—the dog, the violence. Listen. Is it possible that one of Julian's dogs could have gone crazy and attacked him during the quarrel with Joshua?"

"Wouldn't it have been more likely to attack Joshua?" she said.

"Okay, so the dog attacks Joshua. And the attack gets encoded into the trauma that causes the haunting. Because it was violent and frightening and—"

"That doesn't make sense," Sally said.

"Why not?"

"Well, it just doesn't. If your dog attacked someone you might be shocked, or upset. But it wouldn't be that kind of raw terror."

He was quiet, thinking: static on the line again. Then at last: "Look, the inkwell fell off the table the night we had the sitting with Rosanna in Joshua's room. Remember? We didn't know if it was just coincidence. But last night it happened again—to an even greater degree. There's a connection between the sittings and the inkwell."

"So?" she said.

"So maybe the inkwell doesn't stand for the dog. Maybe the dog stands for the inkwell."

"But we know the dogs existed," she said. "Miss Ellen told us—"

"Not those dogs. I think they're red herrings. I'm talking now," David said, "purely about the dog in the trance. Who did the inkwell belong to?"

She couldn't see what he was getting at. "How should I know?"

"Come on, Sal."

"You want me to say Joshua."

"Who else? And that was Joshua's room where we held the sitting, and presumably Joshua's desk in that room. Now wouldn't it make sense for Joshua to keep his inkwell on his desk, where he did his paperwork?"

"Get to the point," she said.

"Okay. Joshua summons Julian to his room. There's a confrontation. He learns the truth about Julian and Ginny. He goes into a rage, hits Julian with the nearest heavy object to hand—the inkwell. In essence, the dog attacks."

"But—"

"It's solid brass," David said.

"But Julian died falling down the stairs," she said.

"Did he? Maybe he did. But would he have fallen if he hadn't already been injured?"

Dog leaping red-eyed—brass reflecting the firelight? The telephone receiver was slippery; she switched hands and wiped the free one on her jeans. Those eyes opening, looking into hers. The unfamiliar voice, the cold hands . . . "Well, that's all theoretical," she said.

"Yeah."

The short word bothered her. He didn't need her support. He was too sure.

"And another thing," he said.

"What?"

"Let's talk about blood. If Julian's injury happened on the stairs, why is there blood associated with Joshua's room? Rosanna got a nosebleed during her trance in there. And the apparition Mrs. Pindar saw, the one she thought was her dead husband? It was a man, the face bloody. Remember? And it was in Joshua's room. Not on the stairs."

A man, the face bloody. "I saw it too," she said.

"You *what*?"

"I saw him. When I came out of trance. It was dark, but when I got out into the hall I looked back into the room, and there was a fire in the fireplace. And he was there. One side of his face was covered with blood." There was total silence on the other end of the line and she said, "David?"

"You really saw him?"

"Well, I thought I did. It could have been—"

"What happened then?" David was not interested in what it could have been.

"Well, he was in front of me. Staggering down the hall. When he got to the head of the stairs, he fell. I went down. And there you were."

As if two conflicting realities had at last found a point where they could meet and mesh. Vertigo rose in her and she forced it down and heard him saying " . . . explains the haunting, the lost one, the ruckus in Joshua's room, the cold. Every time we contacted him in there he was in some kind of shock state. The images in your trance didn't deal with the fall, they dealt with the dog. With the attack. You said the idea of a dog attacking didn't fit with the kind of terror involved. But suppose your father tried to kill you? Suppose you knew you were dying?"

Shuddering body in her arms at the foot of the dark stairs. She shook herself free of the memory. "We can't just assume that's what happened. How could Joshua try to kill his own son?"

"Why not? He got Flagg killed, didn't he? Flagg took Rebecca away from him. And Julian took Ginny. He must have seen history repeating itself. What difference would it make, right at that moment, that Julian was his son?"

His certainty was like a steamroller. She took a long breath and let it out. "Okay, maybe. But David—it's not evidential. You can't prove any of it."

After a moment he said mildly, "I know that. But what it means is that somehow, in our bumbling way, we've released him. However it happened, he's at peace now. You can come home."

After she had hung up the phone she sat for a long while without moving. She felt a profound emptiness and at the same time a heaviness that made the slightest movement seem beyond her resources. It was more than last night's insanity and today's dead ends, more than her promise to David just now that she would catch tomorrow's bus back to Skipton. It was more than the simple desire for clean clothes and sleep. She was tired in every nerve and muscle of body and mind, drained from the events of the summer as if from a punishing dream that had released her only now, tonight.

He's gone.

David had his story now: beginning and ending, hero and villain, mystery and solution. The fact that he was incapable of proving a word of it mattered to him very little. It satisfied some deeper need, the urge to wield the hand of the magus, restore the boundaries between life and death. Or some such thing. The giant rat face in the poster confronted her, pink nose questing. For what?

She lay back on the bed, hands behind her head, staring at the ceiling where the lamp cast a circular glow that diminished outward into shadow. No way of knowing if David's reconstruction was accurate or a grotesque misreading of the few facts they possessed. And it made no difference. Right now only one thought could penetrate the depths of her tiredness.

He's gone. The sitting must have done something, released some kind of energy.

In theory, at least, it was possible. A dissipating of whatever quirk of physics caused the phenomenon known as haunting. What was Myers's phrase? *Mere dreamfancies of the dead.* Possible that the intangible substance of personality had lingered on in the house, dreaming the past to life within its walls, half waking now and then in a recurring nightmare of terror and loss. Possible that last night, in one such moment, she had met and comforted the spirit of the dead boy and sent it on its long-delayed journey. Equally possible that she and David were enacting a neurotic drama of their own design, painfully obvious to everyone but themselves.

The day's voices still echoed. Alec's: *It's not the ghost, but David's belief in the ghost that's affecting his behavior.* Rosanna's, as if in answer: *Whatever hold that house has on him, it isn't something you'll find in one of those scientific quarterlies of yours.* Two conflicting viewpoints, and herself skittering between them.

What was the truth? After all, she had lived through it; she ought to have some inkling. But she was confused.

Alec's perspective had shaken her: she had not realized they had jumped to so many conclusions, overlooked so many possibilities. *Headstones fall over in graveyards all the time . . . Did you check to see how many others had fallen over? . . . What has actually, indisputably happened since you've been living in the house? You lost a dog and David fell down the stairs.* They had been careless; they had been much too subjective—the picture was disconcerting. Had they really used the house as a metaphor for their own problems? *Not the ghost, but David's belief in the ghost . . . What could be simpler for him than to imagine himself possessed by this very potent young man?* Alec hadn't subjected her part in all this to the same hard-nosed scrutiny he had David's, but she had a sense, telepathic or otherwise, of what he could have said if he had chosen to. That she had some kind of investment in David's impotence—that what frightened her was not the idea of his possession by Julian but David himself, sexually capable, no longer owing her a constant tacit apology. It made her flinch mentally, then brought a hot rush of denial. *That isn't true!* But the idea refused to fade entirely, a faint persistent stain that she couldn't now *unsee.*

She moved restlessly on the bed. *What if Alec's wrong? What if in spite of everything, all our mistakes and our lack of objectivity, we still managed to unravel what really happened: the cause of the haunting?* The trance images flickered in her head—the fire, the dog's open jaws, the shadowy stumbling figure she had followed down the hall, then lost in the darkness of the stairs, only to find David there at the bottom. As if the two had coalesced into the trembling body she held in her arms, not knowing whom she comforted. Her mind veered away from the memory only to strike up against a dozen others. The face in the photograph, its youth masking strength like the velvet on a deer's new antlers. Soft dark hair she had drawn through her fingers. *Wailing for the lost one that comes not again.* The music box with its carved initials. *J.G. isn't Joshua. It's Julian.* Colin's voice: *Sally, Reverend Gilfoy was not a music lover.* David's: *He's an old man, dammit! Just an old man. What about me?* Sitting alone in the empty house, box open on his lap, listening to the rusty clockwork melody. That violent embrace beside the sundial, heart-shaped leaf lighting a window between past and present. Alec saying, *I can make you a list of reasons why your subconscious would be only too happy to have David become someone else.* And Rosanna: *Well, there's something you can try, if your scientific principles will let you.*

Exorcism—

She got off the bed abruptly, went into the bathroom and switched on the light. Brownish stains on the walls marked some occasion when the ceiling had leaked badly. She washed her hands and splashed cold water on her face, looking at herself in the dingy mirror over the basin. The sight of her shirt, stained with last night's blood, made her grimace; on impulse she stripped it off and threw it in the basin, scrubbing it under the running water until the stains were gone. Tiredness overwhelmed her then; she hung the shirt to dry in the shower stall, turned off the light and went back into the other room, unconsciously crossing her arms over her breasts against a nonexistent chill. In fact, the room was stifling, but half naked she felt much too vulnerable, and she pulled the faded Indian bedspread over her when she lay down again.

Exorcism.

He's gone.

Could she believe David? Did he believe it himself? Alec would say that what David believed was all that mattered—that if David believed Julian was gone, then he was gone. Okay, he's gone. Then what? Then the haunting's over. An end to the terror state that centered on the master bedroom, the cold and the pounding noises that sent tenants packing. An end to night visits from the light Susan Abbey had christened Tinkerbell. To the sound of an unknown dog barking, the too frequent accidents on the stairs. An end to the pair of dogs performing their ritual chase in the garden at dusk. An end to the bright buoyant stillness filtering through the empty rooms, bringing back quiet sounds of occupancy, and to countless other impulses, dreams, desires, infinitesimal warpings of thought and action, the parallel world that cast its gentle shadow over the house. In a way she could be sorry, if it were truly over and all danger past, that their investigation was finished, that they had learned so little and now it was too late. She could even afford to be sentimental—at least she did not know how else to characterize a feeling that in putting an end to the haunting they had exorcised something tranquil and beautiful from the house along with the terror, leaving an empty shell. White walls among the trees, climbing roses softly blowing. *I dream of Jeanie with the day-dawn smile, radiant in gladness . . .*

Well, it was over. And whatever the truth, whether it had been a genuine haunting or a Freudian extravaganza, she could wake up in the morning knowing, as she had told David, exactly who she was and who he was. That was what mattered most to her. She didn't want to think about what mattered to him. But the sitting had been his idea, and he could take the consequences.

She reached for the lamp and turned it out, lying there in darkness in the unfamiliar room, feeling fatigue press her into the mattress. Her brain wouldn't turn off. Was it simple physics, some undiscovered set of equations, that had made the house what it was, trapped the past there like a live firefly in a jar? *He's gone. The sitting must have done something, released some kind of energy.* But where had it gone? She knew her thermodynamics: energy can be neither created nor destroyed, only changed. If the sitting had released energy, then somewhere that energy still existed—radically altered in form, maybe, but still there.

She overslept, missed the noon bus and spent the afternoon at the movies, a Fred Astaire classic that left her feeling as if she were recently off the boat from Mars. At the bus station, too, she found herself surrounded by people whose worries clearly did not include possession by spirits of the dead. *People are sensitive to atmosphere. Put them in a crazy situation and they start acting crazy. Put them in a normal situation and they act normal again.* She was still hearing Alec's voice, although Rosanna's had fallen silent.

The five o'clock bus got her into town late in the day, set her down outside the post office in a wash of sunset

light that flooded the length of Main Street, stretching all
the shadows to extravagant proportions. She was the only
one off at the Skipton stop, descending the air-conditioned
steps into sidewalk heat that lapped at her knees. At the
level of her face the air was cooler and she breathed it in.
For a moment she thought she could smell lilacs. But that
was impossible: the last lilacs had been dead and gone for
two months.

She had Main Street to herself. The stores had closed
for the night—Kimball's red and white awning neatly
cranked up, the wide doors of Buck's closed and locked,
post office blinds pulled. Across the square Colin might
be keeping late summer hours at the library; briefly she
wondered if Locky had shown up and knew, without
knowing how, that he hadn't. Kermie's was open, a drift
of jukebox music from the door. She set off down Main
toward Tanglewood, letting her hands swing.

The light carried her like a dazzling tide. She walked
without effort, scarcely feeling her legs under her, inside
her head a golden buzzing like the busy movement of
countless light particles. The theatrical sunset covered
everything indiscriminately: houses, cars, a fence with
morning glory growing along it, a roller skate abandoned
at the edge of a lawn, a torn sheet of newspaper in the
gutter, linking it all into a connected whole. She felt, as
she had in trance, the obscure presence of pattern, of
significance. Then she turned the corner onto Tanglewood,
out of the direct path of the setting sun, and suddenly it
was easier to think, to chastise herself for fuzzy-minded-
ness—to wonder instead if there was food in the house
for supper, and whether David had found the car keys
. . . The thought of seeing him filled her with conflicting
feelings. That moment the other night at the kitchen
table, when he had chosen the house over her, had
seemed like the nadir of their relationship; her awak-
ening the next morning, alone in the car, had seemed like
the end. Even while she told Rosanna she couldn't leave
him, she had been wondering if she had not already done
so. Now she felt as if they had been given another chance.
Her emotions, bounced from despair back to hope again,
were beyond her control. Nervous, eager, wary—on top of
it all, she found herself wanting him, vividly and explic-
itly, a combination of fantasy and muscle memory pass-

ing over her in a wave, leaving her shaken. She took a breath and let it out: oriented herself again in the external world. Across the street a screen door banged; a voice called, invisible behind a hedge.

As she came to Lilac Street and turned up the hill, a group of kids, on their way down, passed her in a rush—five or six of them, heading along Tanglewood at a run. With the diminishing sound of their steps on the pavement a profound stillness settled on the street and she noticed that it was evening, violet haze above the treetops meeting the flushed sky overhead. In the bushes bordering the sidewalk a single cricket began to pipe and then subsided. The sun was behind the hill now; ahead of her the street, deep in shadow, rose toward the sky. Again the fragrance of lilacs—elusive, impossible—touched her.

Reaching the gate at last she paused and stood looking toward the house. The windows were dark and the lindens softened the outline of the walls; she noticed that the grass needed cutting. Not a light showing anywhere—had he gone out? The car was there, parked in the street. Suppose he hadn't been able to find the keys, suppose he had walked to Saunders' to buy groceries—but Saunders' was closed by now. It worried her. Last night on the phone he had said he was fine, but head wounds could be tricky. She stopped those thoughts with an effort. Probably he was in the kitchen making supper, forgetting that he hadn't left a light in the front of the house to welcome her.

The gate was open. She went in and automatically closed it after her, hesitating with one hand still on it—unnerved, in spite of her logic, by the pale, silent shape in the trees. Had it really changed? It looked the same: wide porch, steep gables, clapboards needing a coat of paint. She took a step, then another, trying to sense the place. Where was the pressure she had felt from the beginning, the very first day? Cautiously she relaxed her guard, ready to raise it again in an instant. But there was nothing here to guard against. *He's gone.* The house had lost its brooding aspect; instead it seemed to float on the darkening grass, light as a ship emptied of its cargo, walls white in the dusk. The weight of accumulated moments, all the fullness she had felt in trance, had vanished. But where? *Energy can be neither created nor destroyed, only changed.* As she reached the porch steps a light came on inside; the front door opened and David stood there, his face in shadow, lamplight shimmering behind him. She could smell the roses above her on the porch roof, and behind them, unmistakable now, the fragrance of lilacs.

Energy can be neither created nor destroyed

Then he stepped back; he was smiling, he was all right, and she felt a quick rush of relief. It was only when she followed him inside, when he shut the door and came close to her, that her doubts returned.

"David?" she said.

only changed

But he stopped her questioning with a kiss.

ACKNOWLEDGMENTS

Researching this novel was possibly the pleasantest part of writing it, and I would like to acknowledge the following sources: *Apparitions and Haunted Houses,* by Sir Ernest Bennett; *Lectures in Psychical Research,* by C. D. Broad; *Ritual Magic,* by E. M. Butler; *The Facts of Psychic Science,* by A. C. Holms; *Towards a General Theory of the Paranormal,* by Lawrence LeShan; *Psychic Exploration,* by Edgar D. Mitchell (edited by John White); *Perspectives in Psychical Research,* by W. G. Roll; and *The Grey World,* by Evelyn Underhill.

I would like to give special credit to Michael Grosso for his excellent article "The Survival of Personality in a Mind-Dependent World" *(Journal of the American Society for Psychical Research,* October 1979), part of which is paraphrased on page 261.

Buy them at your local

bookstore or use coupon

on next page for ordering.